DEAD OF WINTER
KNIFE'S EDGE, ALASKA
BOOK ONE

REBECCA ZANETTI

Copyright © 2025 by Rebecca Zanetti

All rights reserved.

No part of this book may be reproduced in any form or by any electronic or mechanical means, including information storage and retrieval systems, without written permission from the author, except for the use of brief quotations in a book review.

To the Mah Jong Girls—Each of you will have your own place in this series, though thankfully, your real-life adventures are far less murderous. (I hope).

First to Gail English, our mom and the queen of Mah Jong tiles—this one's for you. Thank you for your endless patience as we stumbled through learning the rules, and for proving that the real treasure isn't the win but the laughter around the table.

You're more than just the heart of our game nights—you're the heart of our family. The grandkids hit the jackpot having you as their Gaga, and we all hit the jackpot having you in our lives. Your love, humor, and fierce spirit have shaped us all.

This one's for you—with love, admiration, and a silent prayer that I'll one day master the game as well as you.

CHAPTER ONE

A brutal sun cut across the icy Alaskan landscape with a defiant glare, brightening instead of warming the frozen runway outside. Mountains rose all around, their jagged peaks rocky through the barren snow, an invitation from Mother Nature to challenge her and lose.

FBI Special Agent Ophelia Spilazi rubbed her arms through her leather jacket, safely ensconced in the warming hut. The silent, empty, lonely warming hut that truly didn't provide warmth. A wooden bench ran alongside one wall, the only furniture in the rickety structure. Icicles hung from the eaves outside, several long enough to touch the ground, while the meager sun warmed them, making the ice sparkle like diamonds.

The sheer isolation of the area was both intriguing and ominous.

A low hum pierced the thundering silence outside, and her breath quickened in natural response. She craned her neck to see out the frozen, crud-covered window to the unreal blue sky, her shoulders tensing even more as a dot of a plane dipped over the nearest mountain and dropped fast to land.

She blinked.

The small plane hit hard, bounced several times, and skidded back and forth before lurching to a drunken halt to the right of the so-called runway.

The plane shuddered and the engine silenced, the machine looking miniature against the wild mountains that served as a backdrop. Her stomach lurched. She wanted to take another Valium, but she had to at least appear professional to these nomads who chose to live in the middle of absolutely nowhere.

The pilot jumped out, and she stopped breathing at her first sight of him. Wavy black hair framed a hard-cut face, scruff covered his rugged jaw, and aviator glasses shielded his eyes. His ancestry was difficult to gauge, but his features were native and strong. Possibly some Inuit or Indigenous American heritage. He had to be well over six feet tall, muscular and oddly graceful—even with a slight limp.

She zeroed in on his left leg. He favored it slightly but didn't allow it to shorten his stride.

Interesting.

He wore a heavy leather jacket, jeans, and dark boots, his shielded gaze having a punch of power, even through the dingy window.

She swallowed, grateful that sunglasses hid her eyes, which had to be wide and full of doubt after witnessing that excruciating landing on the ice. The man approaching her wasn't anything close to the old, grizzly, and bearded pilot who'd brought her from Anchorage, the one who had said—repeatedly—that she was nuts to keep going west with a late but devastating winter coming. She'd imagined someone similar picking her up today.

This guy was beyond imagination.

He pulled open the door and paused, instant heat rippling from him. "Special Agent Spilazi?" That voice. A slow, deep roll that contrasted with the stark beauty around them.

"Call me Ophelia." She held out a hand, still feeling off-balance. She was tall for a woman, very, but he towered over her.

His dark eyebrows rose, and he shook with her after a brief pause that almost went on too long. His hand was warm, big, and gentle, the shake to the point. "Your title suits you better."

Electricity zipped along her wrist from the contact. It took her a moment to digest his comment and then hide her surprise, again glad she wore the sunglasses to protect her eyes and expression. Nobody in DC would've been so forward upon meeting her.

"You don't know me," she countered.

His grunt was neither assent nor denial. He released her and grabbed the two overlarge suitcases, hefting them easily, turning back toward the waiting plane.

Her mouth opened and closed. She scrambled to follow him into the frigid air. "Do you need me to take one of those?" Both had been over the weight limit on her commercial flights and a pain to lug through the Anchorage airport.

"No." His stride didn't shorten.

Well, all right. If he wanted to put out his back, it was fine by her. Although, he didn't seem to be struggling much. In the slightest. The guy looked to be in great shape, no doubt about it. He opened the plane's cargo door and roughly plunked the suitcases inside, partially turning. "Backpack here or up with you?"

She'd forgotten her pack and couldn't help the sigh that escaped when she shrugged it off to hand over. The meager case files she held had been heavier than expected after a long trek. While she didn't like having her gun out of reach, she wouldn't need it in the air. Shooting her pilot would be a disaster. "Back here is fine."

He secured the pack with the luggage and gestured around the other side of the plane.

She faltered and then preceded him, carefully picking her

way across the ice in her new boots. Once on the other side, she waited for him to open the door to the co-pilot's seat. Her knees trembled.

Only one eyebrow went up this time. "Afraid to fly?" He leaned against the side of the craft, his stance casual in the freezing cold as if he had all day for a conversation.

The guy didn't like complete sentences, did he? She nodded. Before he could launch into the usual lecture, she held up a hand. "I understand flying is safer than driving, and there are all sorts of measures to keep airplanes accident-free. I also know you could land this on any flat surface and get us to safety." None of that mattered when anxiety rose.

"Honey, I could barely land this thing here with plenty of room. If anything goes wrong, we're dead." He pushed the sunglasses up on his head, revealing eyes greener than the sharpest emerald.

A vise gripped her throat, an invisible one, and she breathed deeply to calm herself. "You're not a pilot?"

He lifted one powerful shoulder in a tough-guy shrug. "Not really."

Her spine straightened on its own. "You don't have a pilot's license?"

His flash of a grin was as charming as it was unexpected. "Nope."

Her shoulders snapped back. If he said one more word, her body would be at full attention whether she liked it or not. "Then what the hell are you doing flying that thing?"

"We got notice in Knife's Edge that you were out here. Somebody had to come get you. I was the only one sober enough." He rubbed the scruff across his angled jaw.

"Sober enough?" She backed a step away. The sparkle in his green eyes caught her. Was he messing with her?

He studied her face and then gave another grunt she couldn't decipher. "Listen, Agent."

"Ophelia," she protested, her stomach doing odd flip-flops that had nothing to do with her fear of flying.

"I'd like to keep your title in mind." He pulled the door open wider. "A hungover pilot is the least of your worries in an Alaskan winter. Another late but dangerous snowfall has about another day to arrive, and winds will make flying impossible. Darkness is gonna fall for months—for good, it'll seem. You want me to take you back to Anchorage right now. Trust me."

Trust him? Yeah, right. "I'm not getting into a plane with you." Being unwanted was nothing new to her, yet her chest chilled even more.

He might've winced, but the hard planes in the stone that made up his spectacular face barely moved. "I'm your only choice unless you want to wait for spring. I doubt you know how to hunt, so you'll starve in that little warming hut before you freeze. Well, probably."

She grabbed her temper with sheer will and shoved her glasses onto her head. "There must be another pilot and another plane coming at some point."

"No other plane and no other pilot. Probably for months." He looked up at the startling blue sky. "Winter is a month late, so it's gonna come in fast. Today."

She drew her phone free of her jacket and shook it. No service.

He chuckled. "Where would you put a cell tower around here?"

Good point. She slid the phone back into the warmth. "How intoxicated are you?"

"I'm fine. Also, the winds are better, and the runway's much bigger in Anchorage, so how about I take you there? Cell service actually works there all the time, and in Knife's Edge, it's spotty —to say the least. It's already December, and you don't want to miss the holidays with family, do you?"

Her temples began to ache. "I'm fine. Really. We should go."

"You should reconsider." His voice crashed beyond gruff to nearly raw. "Trust me. Knife's Edge during wintertime is no place for a city girl."

She'd stopped being a girl a long time ago. He'd come just to make her return to the city? Not once in her life had she backed down from a challenge. However, this one may result in her crashing into a mountain. Either way, she had to get into that tiny plane with him, so she'd continue on her mission, and it wasn't like she had anybody to worry about for the holidays. "This woman can handle it. Please take me—safely—to Knife's Edge."

His grunt failed to provide reassurance. "It's your mistake to make." He leaned in to tug a seat harness out of the way, bringing warmth and the scent of something new. Spicy, male, and undefinable. "Our window to fly is short, and the drinks are already lining up at the tavern. Gotta go. Now."

Could he get any grumpier? "You had better not get me killed," she murmured before she could stop herself.

He sighed. "Get in, Ophelia. The only thing to do with fear is to confront it. Every damn time."

The man sounded like he knew what he was talking about, although sometimes running from fear was the smartest thing to do. Obviously. She accepted his hand and climbed up, settling into the surprisingly comfortable leather seat.

Without waiting for an invitation, he leaned inside, grasped the chest harness, and pulled it over her head, securing it tightly with the buckle at her waist, his thick hair brushing her arm, and his hand millimeters from her breast.

She blinked, her body instantly warming.

He slowly lifted his head, his eyes mere inches from hers. She stopped breathing. Again. Their gazes met, and it was a moment. One of those inexplicable, real, human connections that's felt and not reasoned. She didn't try to find a word to say because there wasn't one. Awareness, the same one she shared, darkened his eyes.

The moment passed as quickly as it had landed. He stepped back and securely shut her door before striding around to climb into the pilot's seat, making the entire craft hitch and fill with that spicy winter scent. Silently, he handed over headphones, which she quickly donned, not liking the sense of being unbalanced.

"Whose plane is this?" She spoke into the microphone of the headset.

He fiddled with a bunch of levers. "A guy named Trapper Matt owned the plane and died three years ago at the age of a hundred. He left all of his belongings to the town of Knife's Edge, so I guess it's the town's. It'll be put in storage for the winter as soon as our late winter begins, which might be tomorrow."

Hopefully the town performed regular maintenance on the craft. "Who are you?"

"Brock Osprey. Temporary pilot today."

She stiffened. "Osprey?"

"Yep." The plane instantly started rolling down the ice, hitching and wobbling.

That last name was not a good coincidence, by any means. Her voice wavered, and she planted a hand against the door. "You're one of Hank Osprey's adopted kids." She only had Brock's name and the fact that he'd served as a Navy SEAL in her slim FBI file and hoped to have his military records soon.

"Yep."

Just wonderful. "Hank's murder is one of the cases I'm here to investigate." The most important one, and her main reason for heading to the small town. Another chill skittered down her spine. Why had she left the gun in the pack?

Brock yanked the levers back, and the craft lifted unsteadily into the air. A gust of wind hit them, pushing them sideways.

Dark clouds rolled in from the west, visible from their vantage point off the ground. "At the moment, an old death is the least of your worries." He yanked the stick, and the plane continued to bump through the air, climbing higher.

"Hank died about a year ago. That's not an old death."

Brock grunted. Again. "A year is an eon when you live in the middle of nowhere." A gust of wind shoved them to the side.

"Maybe, we, well, should we wait until the storm passes?" she whispered, even her lips trembling.

Another wind gust slashed them, and he tightened his hold on the stick. "The storm never passes, sweetheart. Not in Knife's Edge."

She started to ask more questions when a large facility to the east caught her attention. A massive antenna field, satellite dishes, and grids of transmitters spread out from a sprawling concrete building and covered at least fifty acres. "What in the world is that place?"

"That's the Electromagnetic Vibrational Experiment," he said, spelling out the letters with an almost casual tone. "We call it EVE. It began as a government project, but a private corporation took over years ago. They study the ionosphere."

She turned to him again, nodding to keep him talking.

He sighed but appeased her. "They only let the mail and supply plane that comes twice a month in the winter land on their runway—when it can get in. Sometimes it can take months with our weather. I'm surprised you haven't heard the conspiracy theories about that place that run the gamut between manipulating the weather to mind control experiments. It's all bunk. The facility just conducts research. So they say."

She shifted to look out the window. "Can we fly closer?"

"No. Restricted airspace, except for their own supply plane." He made another adjustment. The wind battered the small craft.

"Restricted airspace in the Alaskan wilderness? I do love a good puzzle." She had to figure out this one.

"That isn't a puzzle, and it's not what you're here to do," he said mildly.

Interesting. Was that a warning? She switched topics to throw him off-balance. "Who do you think murdered Hank Osprey? You must've cared about him, right?"

"Yes, and nobody murdered him. Nobody wanted Hank dead." Brock's tone remained calm, but tension showed in his firmer grip on the stick.

Oh, he definitely knew more than he let on. "Don't you want to know for sure? I will find out what happened." Whether Brock and his town liked it or not, she excelled at digging for the truth—and this marked her last chance to keep her job. She couldn't give up.

Brock gave one of those grunts she couldn't decipher. "That's your choice." His face might as well have been carved from the jagged rocks around them. "Hold on. We have to drop fast. It's going to be a rough landing."

CHAPTER TWO

Brock Osprey didn't have time to deal with many things in the world, and a pretty FBI agent—city girl, no less—with eyes as blue as a deep lake and an ass made for a man's hands topped the list. Hell. At the moment, she *was* the list. The woman smelled like fresh strawberries, and wasn't that a pisser? He loved strawberries.

He unceremoniously plunked Ophelia's luggage on Widow Flossy's weathered front porch before knocking heavily on the door. The wind whistled from the west, a foreboding chill that was coming fast, knocking against the cheerful Christmas lights already iced over on her eaves.

A shuffle came from inside, and then the door opened a crack, cloudy brown eyes looking way up from a tiny face. "Brock." She pulled the door open all the way, and her scrawny neck stretched as she craned to see beyond him. "I thought you planned to fly the FBI agent lady back to Anchorage."

A huff of breath, feminine and somehow a little sexy, came from behind him.

"Nope." He grabbed both suitcases again and strode inside, carefully wiping his boots on the interior Chirstmasy green welcome mat covering Flossy's polished wooden floor. A Christmas tree decorated in red and silver sparkled from the corner, and a row of Santas appeared to march across the fireplace mantle. "She in the blue room?"

"Oh, um, well now...No. Let's put her in the pink room." Flossy blinked behind thick glasses and reached out a gnarled hand. "Hello there. You must be freezing. Come inside, sweets."

Brock turned toward the polished curved staircase, ready to ditch the bags and get back to dealing with his family.

"Brock Osprey." Flossy released the woman and slapped him ineffectually on the arm. "Your manners are better than that. Much."

Ophelia snorted. Not so lightly, but still sexy.

Heat tinged Brock's ears. His manners were nowhere near better than this. "Sorry, ma'am," escaped him before he could stop the words. He partially turned. "Mrs. Floridian Veltinbelt, please meet Special Agent Ophelia Spilazi of the FBI."

"Call me Flossy," Flossy said, just as the agent said to call her Ophelia.

The women laughed at the same time, caught together in some weird, shared moment he'd only seen women bond over.

Instead of grumpily asking if he could now deliver the bags to the pink room, Brock forced a smile and reminded himself that he was an adult and should probably act like one. Plus, Flossy wouldn't hesitate to grab a wooden spoon and smack him on the ear, and he had enough brain issues. "May I help with the bags and deliver them to the pink room?" he asked, tongue in cheek.

Flossy smiled, approval dancing in her faded eyes. "Of course. You're so kind to help, Master Chief Osprey." She leaned to the side to better see the city girl. "He reached such a high rank and became a true hero in the Navy, you know."

Oh, for Pete's sake. He grabbed the handles of the bags with a little more force than necessary and stomped up the stairs to the third door on the left.

"He's still a mite cranky from his time in the service," Flossy explained, not so quietly, from the first level. "Anyhoo, welcome to my Bed and Breakfast. I have three guest rooms, but you're probably my only guest for the rest of the season. Are you sure you want to be here for winter? I have to tell—"

The rest was cut off as Brock entered the room. The sight of all the bright pink furnishings and white lace brightened his mood. It definitely didn't fit the taste of the city girl in her black leather jacket and stylish boots.

The voices came closer, and Flossy brushed by him, gesturing toward the antique milk glass lamp. "That was my mama's."

He turned just in time to see the agent's reaction to the room, then halted.

Genuine wonder widened the woman's eyes as she took in all the girly pink and lace. "Oh, Flossy, it's so beautiful." Her husky voice hushed, and an almost childlike delight brightened her angled features.

He gaped. Pure and simple, that unguarded moment slammed into his chest stronger than a punch he'd taken from a drunk Russian while on a mission years ago. He frowned, staring at her, trying to decipher what he'd missed when taking her measure earlier.

She didn't notice and instead headed right for the hand-crocheted doilies, perfectly arranged across the dresser. "Oh, these are lovely. Did you stitch them?"

"I did," Flossy said, standing even taller—hitting almost five feet. "You're so kind to notice."

"And the quilt." Ophelia rushed for the thick bedcover, running her hand over the colorful squares. "Did you create this?"

Flossy's papery cheeks turned the same color as the rest of the room. "Yes. I have a quilting group. There's not much to do around here in the winter, and we spend hours together creating—often sending our finished work off to shelters to warm others." She leaned in and pointed to a square with a perfectly shaped silver owl. "My husband, God rest his soul, was nicknamed Owl because he was so observant, so I insert an owl into every quilt I ever create."

"That's so sweet," Ophelia murmured, reverently looking at the perfect stitching of a brown bear in a square. "Also, I'm sorry for your loss."

"You're a kind one, Ophelia." Flossy patted her arm. "It's been about thirty years, but I do still miss the man. If I added you to a quilt, I'd create a lovely and graceful gazelle." She eyed the younger woman. "Are you sure you want to stay here for the winter? Once snow falls, there's no way out."

Ophelia straightened as if remembering her job. "Oh. Yes. I do."

Flossy clapped her small hands together. "Then you really must join the quilting club. I can teach you."

Brock steeled himself for the instant rejection, preparing to soothe Flossy's feelings.

Ophelia bit her lip. "That's kind, but I'm, well, not very good at that sort of thing. You know. Sewing, cooking, those types of skills." Her voice dropped, and truth to shit, she sounded genuinely regretful.

Why hadn't anybody taught her that stuff if she'd been interested? Brock bit his tongue. Yeah, she was sexy and hot and had legs long enough to wrap around his waist and hold tight. But this sweet side of her? It was too much. Too alluring and intriguing, and damn, he didn't need this crap on top of the massive pile already falling on him.

Flossy hopped. "Quilting just takes practice. I promise nobody will judge you, and like I said, there's not much more to do when the darkness falls during the winter. Just say you'll think about it."

"I will." Then the woman had the audacity to smile. Really smile. Kind and genuine and beautiful.

Brock grunted. Life already tortured him enough. He had to do something about this.

THE ROOM EXUDED A DELIGHTFUL CHARM. Sweet and inviting and all pink. Ophelia had wished for this kind of a bedroom while growing up in government-sanctioned apartment buildings. Well, without the very cranky and overlarge male taking up all the space in the doorway and grunting with what sounded like disapproval. He hovered near the tiny, elderly widow as if afraid Ophelia would somehow hurt the petite woman's feelings.

Okay. That was kind of sweet. Insulting but sweet.

His gaze caught hers—green and dark and intense. "You left your backpack in the truck." Without waiting for an answer, he turned on one massive boot and headed down the hallway.

Was she supposed to follow?

Flossy, dressed in a gray cardigan that reached below her knees and touched her tall slippers, turned to trail him. "Get your backpack. I'll rustle up some warm food. You must be starving after traveling all day." She walked down the quiet hallway toward the curved staircase, still talking. "I assume you traveled all day. It takes hours to get to Anchorage and then even more to reach Knife's Edge. You must be hungry."

Ophelia's stomach growled, and she followed the elderly woman down the stairs. "I'll, ah, just grab my pack and meet you in the kitchen." She assumed the room was beyond the formal living room with its floral sofa and matching chairs, and if Flossy cooked nearly as well as she quilted, then dinner would be phenomenal. It had been so long since Ophelia had eaten a good home-cooked meal that she nearly forgot the backpack and ran straight to the kitchen. However, a little decorum wouldn't hurt anything, and she needed to remember her job. She'd come to the small town to investigate most of its inhabitants, so she had to take it down a notch.

Clearing her throat, she opened the heavy oak door and stepped onto the rough front porch. Small snowflakes cascaded down as if in a dream, and she looked up, watching the snow fall from a darkened sky with clouds now covering the moon. Wow. Night had arrived quickly.

"Get used to the darkness."

She yelped and jumped to see Brock at the bottom step. The shadows swallowed him, leaving only the sizzling green of his eyes visible. He took a step toward her, looking dangerous for the first time. Like a predator in the night. "Maybe I like the dark." Her voice shook just enough to be noticeable.

His grunt, once again, told her nothing. A quick jerk of his head toward the B&B conveyed that he wanted her to go back inside, and a perverse part of her wanted to stand in place. Smack dab in the middle of his path.

So, she did.

He took the second step, leaving them eye to eye. Man, he was tall. Most guys would've asked what she was doing or requested she move.

Not Brock Osprey.

He stood there, his eyes glittering, and his wide shoulders catching snowflakes that instantly melted.

Her breath quickened, and she stared him down with her best FBI look—or she tried to, at least. No reaction came from Brock for long enough that her heartbeat began echoing between her ears.

Finally, he spoke. "Are you, for some odd reason, trying to challenge me, Agent Ophelia Spilazi?"

It certainly appeared so. She didn't really have an answer

that made sense, so she bit her tongue. What in the world was she doing facing down a mountain man in the snow for absolutely no reason other than he had gotten under her skin—without trying to do so? "I don't know how to decipher your grunts," she said, instead of going with the truth, whatever it might be.

His chin, rugged and strong, lifted just enough to be intimidating. "My last grunt meant for you to get your sweet ass back inside the warm house."

She gasped, and her hackles rose. "Oh, you did not."

"I did." More snowflakes landed on his five-o'clock shadow, mixing with the dark bristle. His nose was straight, his cheekbones high, and his skin smooth and bronze. "You're out of the city, Agent. You might want to take note of that fact and head back to safety at first light."

Did he want to tick her off? Something told her he wouldn't make the effort, so he was just being himself. "I'm here for the duration." Why did this man make her want to smack him? As a reasonable woman who had graduated at the top of her class, she could handle all sorts of personalities. Yet this guy, without even trying, was truly pissing her off. "I can't help but think you want me to leave. Why is that? Are you afraid I'll do my job and solve your guardian's murder?"

He took the next step, and his coat brushed hers. "No."

Prickles erupted along her skin when she had to tilt her head to keep his gaze, even though he stood a step below her. "If you're trying to intimidate me, it's not working." Good. Her voice had steadied.

His long eyelashes brushed his cheeks as he slowly, very slowly, blinked, the move oddly threatening. That strong jaw moved, but before he could speak, a phone buzzed in his pocket. Keeping her gaze, he handed over her backpack and withdrew the cell to press against his ear. "Osprey."

Cold swirled around her, and she shivered, her cheeks chilling.

The door opened behind her. "Oh, Ophelia. It's freezing out there. Get inside," Flossy said, fluttering across the porch and grasping her arm to tug.

Ophelia let the woman turn and lead her into the home, where warmth instantly slammed into her.

Heavy footsteps thunked as Brock followed. "All right. Thanks, Amos. I'll spread the word." He slipped the phone back into his pocket, more heat coming from him than the B&B interior.

Flossy peered around Ophelia. "That was Amos? How fortunate we still have cell service. Maybe it'll hold up better this year. Well? What did he say?"

Ophelia partially turned, acutely aware of the odd current running between the mountain man and her. What in the world? Perhaps all of the travel had exhausted her.

Brock kept a hand on the door. "Storm tonight with a clearing for maybe twenty-four hours." His gaze dropped to meet Ophelia's, no expression revealed in them. "So, if you want out of here, according to our one and only weather guru, your chance will be tomorrow afternoon. Otherwise, you might be here for months. Think about that, Agent."

He gave Flossy a nod and then stepped back, shutting the door.

Ophelia breathed out for the first time since meeting Brock Osprey. If he thought she could be easily frightened, he had another think coming straight for him. She turned, smiled at Flossy, and finally focused. "So. What can you tell me about the Osprey family?"

CHAPTER THREE

Morning brought more snow and a jacket piercing wind.
Keep going, just keep going, one foot in front of the other. The mantra ran through Ophelia's mind as she tucked her chin and fought the wind, taking step after step along the icy sidewalk. White swirled around her, thick and mysterious, the freezing cold coating her leather jacket and sinking through the material to her skin and bones. Darn, it was cold.

She'd slept better than she had in years, awakening to the delicious smell of bacon and eggs. Flossy had eaten with her, giving her town gossip without any bite. Nobody seemed to know or care about who'd shot Hank. It was odd, and Ophelia couldn't shake the feeling that, so far, the two people she'd interviewed had evaded the truth.

When she pushed Flossy, just a little bit, the elderly woman had started cleaning up and then insisted upon Ophelia wearing a thick blue knit hat with matching mittens over thermal hand liners, which proved surprisingly effective.

Her feet, on the other hand, were freaking freezing.

The B&B stood on the Main Street in town, only blocks

from the sheriff's office. It turned out that walking several blocks in a whiteout held more peril than she'd expected, and she rolled her eyes at herself. While the remote town failed to provide a car rental service, surely somebody had an old truck she could either rent or buy. She'd get on that after she found the sheriff's office.

Snow blew across the vacant street, slamming against her legs. She seemed to be the only person dumb enough to be out in the brutal blizzard. Slipping, she yelped and quickly regained her footing. This might've been a bad idea.

She slogged through the snow and past the Green Plate Restaurant, a wooden building with weathered green eaves, closed without explanation. Well, except for the snow blowing into her face. Probably a good reason.

A shadow caught her attention across the street and to the side of Bob's Bait and Outfitters, which stood dark and silent this morning. She blinked, twisting her head to see better. Nothing but snow and more snow. Great. Now she imagined shadowy threats. Even so, the skin at her nape prickled like somebody watched her.

She focused on not falling, trying to see through the billowing snow peripherally. On the other side of the road after Bob's, a long wooden building housing a row of offices—all closed this Thursday morning—took a beating from the weather. A human form appeared at the far end, big and dark. She blinked, and he disappeared.

Had she really seen someone? Or had the snowy air distorted her vision?

Headlights cut through the murk, and a truck slowed while coming her way.

Awareness, that of a woman by herself on the side of a road, any road, straightened Ophelia's spine. Her gun nestled reassuringly against her back, and she angled her right arm to retrieve the weapon if necessary.

The truck, covered in snow, stopped. The window slowly rolled down. "What the holy hell are you doing out in this storm?" Brock asked. In his deep voice, it came out more of a grunt than a snap, but anger lingered nonetheless.

She paused and then relaxed her shoulders. If he hadn't tried to push her out of the plane the night before, then he obviously didn't want her dead. Yet, anyway. "What are you doing out?"

"Coming to see you." Definitely a growl this time.

Warmth, unexpected and unwelcome, flowed like a fine wine through her veins. "Why?" Did that sound flirty? She might as well swing her hips and twirl her hair at the guy.

His sigh didn't come close to holding patience. "Get in the truck." He leaned over and shoved the passenger-side door open in the middle of the snowy street.

She faltered. The truck's interior looked nice and warm, and she wasn't sure how much farther she had to struggle in the storm to get to the station. But nobody told her what to do. She really wanted to get into the truck. "Ask nicer," she said, coughing out snow.

His eyes darkened. "Okay. Plant your fucking ass in the truck before I get out and haul you in here."

Her head snapped up. "That was *not* nicer." Both of her hands went to her hips. She could just shoot out his tire, but that'd create paperwork and possibly a psychiatric evaluation, and she didn't have time for that nonsense. "You are such a complete dick." Turning on her heel, she slipped, regained her balance, and charged back down the sidewalk.

Hence her surprise when he suddenly blocked her path. Holy crap, he'd moved fast from the truck, across the snow, and to the sidewalk. She was still waiting for clearance to obtain his military file, which now she feared might be heavily redacted. His years as a Navy SEAL probably provided a dangerous skill set.

She skidded to a stop and looked up. Today, he wore a thick

red-and-black flannel coat, jeans that outlined powerful legs, and yet another pissed-off expression. "What the heck?" she hissed.

To his credit, he knew better than to grab her. "The storm is getting worse. Get in the truck, and we'll argue where we won't freeze to death."

"No." Yeah, she wanted inside that truck, and staying in the storm felt stupid, but he'd ordered her, not so nicely, and a woman couldn't take that kind of crap. Plus, she worked as an FBI agent, for God's sake. At least, for now. "I need to get to the sheriff's office. Get out of my way, or I'll get you out of my way." She meant every word.

"You know how to fight?" Snow landed on his dark eyebrows and jaw scruff, warming and melting instantly.

"You bet your ass I do," she said, more than prepared to take him down.

He rubbed his jaw. "Huh. I'm Navy. You're FBI. Probably great training."

Now he sounded...interested? Seriously? "FBI beats Navy every day." All right. That probably wasn't true, and she hadn't exactly excelled in hand-to-hand, although she knew decent moves.

His lip quirked. "Not a chance, city girl. You trained in a nice gym with yoga mats. I trained in sand and blood. I'm eight inches taller and about a hundred pounds—at least—heavier than you."

"So you'll land harder," she countered. How could she be having this ridiculous conversation in the middle of a blizzard? "Are you freaking crazy?"

"Could be." He cocked his head to the side, his gaze warming. "How about we thumb wrestle for it?"

All right. He was touched in the head. Why were the sexy ones always nuts? "There is no way I'm taking my hand out of this glove." The wind whistled a harsh tune, slapping ice against her chin.

"That's the first smart thing you've said since you got here." He blinked snow out of his eyes. "How about this? It's been a while since I had to use manners, and I'm way too rusty. I'm sorry I swore at you, and I have the key to the sheriff's office. I'll open the building if you let me drive you there."

As an apology, it worked. He'd given her an out and sounded somewhat sorry, so she ran to the still-open door and jumped inside the glorious warmth, sighing with pleasure and not caring one whit that she dropped snow all over his seat as she shut the door.

He slipped onto the driver's seat and quickly flipped a U-turn, sliding across the ice.

"Tell me you're sober," she mumbled.

"Close enough," he said, settling back.

Heat blasted from the dash, and she sighed, her skin still stinging. "Why don't you like me?" The words shocked her as they came out of her mouth.

A flick of his wrist had the windshield wipers going faster. "It's not that I don't like you. I just don't want you here in town."

She blinked. Once and then again. "Excuse me?"

He sighed, the sound long-suffering. "Listen. We're about to get snowed in for months, and most folks go a little nuts the first time. You're a government agent. You're going to make a lot of enemies quickly, I'm responsible for you, and you're just too damn pretty to have to deal with every day."

Her mouth opened and then closed. There was so much to unpack in that sentence that she didn't know where to start. "Um. All right." He found her pretty? Her chest warmed. Wait a minute. "You are not responsible for me."

"Sure, I am. I brought you here. The choice belonged to me." He ducked to better see the white world outside.

Talk about some kind of backwoods rule. "You were the only

one sober enough to fly yesterday—the only one for miles. You had to come and get me." She stretched her legs out, pushing her feet closer to the blissful heat.

He lifted a shoulder, and snow fell onto the seat. "Yeah, but I could've taken you to Anchorage and kicked you out there. I made the choice to fly you here, and that makes you my problem in everyone else's eyes."

Problem? "I'm not anybody's problem," she muttered. This was insane. "Also, why would my solving a couple of cases tick people off? You'd think everyone would want these disappearances or homicides solved."

He shook his thick hair. "People live here because they like the solitude. They want to be left alone, and you're about to turn over a bunch of rocks that should remain in place."

Caution ticked down her spine. Was he warning her off? Again? Hadn't they dealt with that the night before? "Let's talk about Hank some more. Tell me about him."

Brock stiffened. "Nope."

She turned to study him. While she was nowhere near a behavioral analyst, she'd dealt with enough suspects to trust her instincts. "He raised you, right?" She waited until Brock nodded. "Tell me something about him. Anything."

"He didn't like the federal government."

She huffed. "The documents from the Knife's Edge investigation are flimsy, which concerned my boss, FBI Assistant Director Bill Burrington. Your guardian saved my boss's life during a combat situation decades ago, so Hank's death can't be a mystery. That's why I'm here. Supposedly, your Sheriff Blazerton has records and case files regarding several crimes for me to investigate, and I'm looking forward to meeting him."

Brock didn't twitch. "Your info is outdated."

She finally released her grip on the door. "What do you mean?"

"Sheriff Blazerton died in May. I heard he had a heart attack in the middle of church services. He was a good old boy, and we've missed him. Almost made it to ninety years old, which is impressive around here. Very."

"You've been without a sheriff for more than six months?" she gasped.

"Yep." The tone had an edge to it.

She stilled. Now what? Wait a second. "You said that you *heard*. Don't attend church?"

"Nope. But I left town beginning of May when the weather finally let us move again and just returned last week. Went on a walkabout to deal with shit. That's all I'm saying about it." His tone did not invite additional questions.

Fine. "At least you can tell me about your family."

"Long story short, since you're looking into us. We lived in a very small village even farther away from civilization. An avalanche took out the settlement, and only four of us kids survived because we were at a daycare, or maybe a relative's, outside of the outpost. The caregiver apparently had a heart attack during the avalanche, and we lived on our own for a few days, or so legend says. None of us remember anything about that time. A trapper named Hank found us, took us in, and that's the end of it."

"Hank Osprey." She clasped her hands in her lap. "So, he adopted all four of you."

"Yeah. Hank wasn't the most creative of sorts. He named us A, B, C, and, of course…D." Brock's tone carried both sadness and anger, with an edge that hinted at a warning.

She shook her head. "He named you A, B, C, and D?"

"Yep. A couple of us might be genetic brothers or cousins or whatever, and we do look alike. All with green eyes and Inuit features. Regardless, when Hank took us, we all became brothers. We lived off the grid and finally visited Knife's Edge, where the sheriff made Hank give us real names and do formal adoptions. We became Ace, Brock, Christian, and Damian. See? Simple explanation." Brock shrugged.

"How intriguing. What about birthdays? Do you celebrate those since you don't remember your childhood before that time?"

He grinned. "Yeah. One year, a traveling circus came this far out, and Hank sat us down with a fortune teller lady. She looked into a crystal ball that appeared more like a marble ball and gave us all birthdates based on horoscopes or something like that. I celebrate on April tenth because I guess I have the characteristics of an Aries, whatever the hell they may be."

Made sense. Aries held a strong sense of duty and loyalty, and those fit Brock perfectly. "I think Hank chose good names. Plus, Osprey is a strong surname, so you lucked out there."

"Also Hank's choice."

She frowned. "How so?"

"The guy grew up somewhere in the mountains and didn't have a last name until he wanted to join the Navy at seventeen and see some of the world outside of Alaska." Brock slowed the truck and parked on the street, probably next to the curb. The sheriff's station stood two stories, brick and dark. Heavy snow already hung off the eaves and had begun blocking the front door. "Hank saw an osprey flying high above on the way to the enlistment office, and there you go. It's a good damn thing he didn't see a pile of dog sh—poop."

"That's a fascinating story." She forced herself to open the door and step into the frigid air. Had the entire town closed down for the day? Seemed so.

The wind cut into her as if also wanting her gone. What had she been thinking, heading to the middle of nowhere to find peace? "Should've gone to a spa," she muttered, ducking her head and trudging up the three frozen steps to the wide, burgundy-colored metal door.

"Amen to that." Brock kicked snow out of the way and dug a key out of his pocket.

She partially turned toward him, trying to hide her shivers. "Don't you feel like you need to avenge your guardian? If you loved him like I think you did." Did she need to unravel family drama?

Brock paused with the key and looked down at her, his eyes a darker green than they had been the day before. "We take care of our own here. If somebody did shoot Hank, it happened by accident, plain and simple. Nobody wanted him gone. I know, deep in my heart, that nobody murdered Hank."

She swallowed. The mores of a small town, one isolated from the rest of the world, were probably skewed. "The truth matters," she whispered. They'd already gone over this. It seemed a night to think hadn't changed Brock's mind any. "How can you not want justice?"

His chin lifted a micro fraction. "Darlin'? If I needed justice, I'd get it myself." He turned and unlocked the door, shoving the dented metal open with one powerful shoulder.

She couldn't hide her shiver this time.

CHAPTER FOUR

Brock kicked several stacks of the local newspaper, published once a week, to the side of the entryway. Chilled air and dust wafted around, and he shut the door behind them. The lonely energy of silence in the long-vacant building—mostly vacant, anyway—hung as heavy as a wool blanket.

"Where is everybody?" Ophelia whispered.

"Not here." Dusty papers covered the long, wooden door placed over cement blocks that served as a reception desk. A metal folding chair, also stacked with papers, sat on the other side with a file cabinet and blown-up photograph of Knife's Edge Mountain mounted on the wooden wall. He grunted. The place was a disaster. Even the two chairs and table in the waiting area overflowed with stacked boxes and manila file folders.

Ophelia looked at the mess. "I don't understand."

"I'll turn up the heat." The place ran on the grid, and since the pipes obviously hadn't frozen and burst, the heat must be running at some level. He strode behind the desk to the hallway that led to the two back offices, conference room, and jail cells.

Finding the thermostat on the wall, he twisted the heat setting from forty degrees up to seventy. It wouldn't hurt to warm the place a bit, anyway.

Ophelia picked her way around boxes and cartons to his side, craning her neck to see down the hallway. "Care to explain why this place hasn't been visited in months?"

"No." He turned and thrust the key into her hand. "There's nobody about, but lock the door behind me." Well, almost nobody. But she wouldn't find the steps to the basement, so why worry about it? He'd given her the truth about Hank, that he had no clue who'd shot him, but the idea still sat like a rock in his gut. Besides. Her fresh strawberry scent drove him nuts, and he had enough to deal with right now.

She grasped his coat by the arm, and he halted. "There has to be somebody we can hire for sheriff." Puzzlement, as well as determination, glittered in her pretty eyes.

"Don't need one, but you can try to find one." In fact, that might be a good idea. When she released him, he moved toward the door. "Lock this. I'll be back in a couple of hours to drive you to Flossy's." Ophelia should be safe with the storm outside keeping everyone away, but it never hurt to be doubly careful. A lot of folks didn't like the idea of the federal government getting involved in local matters.

The wind fought him when he opened the door, and he quickly shut the heavy metal before jogging down the icy steps to his sturdy truck. The storm strengthened around him, but he'd already chained his tires, so he easily maneuvered down the snowy road, past the one hardware store, to turn along the river road and drive up the mountain.

The world was white with a hint of glacial blue. With Ophelia out of the vehicle, he turned off the heat. The snow grew thicker as he reached his brother's drive, noting it hadn't been shoveled in way too long. Soon they'd have to switch to snowmobiles to travel anywhere but the town's main drag. He tried to hold on to his temper, but after a morning dealing with the scent of strawberries, he failed to keep the heat from rising inside him.

He stopped the truck in front of the sturdy hand-cut log cabin, relaxing a mite at seeing smoke curling from the stone chimney. At least Ace managed to keep warm this time.

Ice encrusted the snow piled near the front door, and Brock looked around for a shovel. The fucking thing had to be buried somewhere in the bushes. Enough of this crap. He pounded on the door, his gloved fist not making enough sound, so he ripped it off and pounded harder, ignoring the ensuing pain.

"Go the hell away," came from inside.

Enough. He twisted the knob, unsurprised to find it unlocked. He had to use his shoulder to force it open, pushing gloves, boots, and various items of snow gear across the entryway and out of the way. "If that's wet, it'll ruin the wood," he muttered in a mantra Hank had issued at least a million times through the years, then slammed the door shut.

Expansive windows offered a snowy view of Knife's Edge Mountain outside. To the left of the windows, a log fell off another in the massive cast-iron wood-burning stove, knocking against the amber glass that obviously hadn't been cleaned in eons. His brother lay face down on the sofa directly across from the stove, his arm hanging off the side. His lower legs and feet extended over the end of the threadbare edge, several holes showing in his frayed socks.

An empty bottle of homemade rye—probably from Lefty's still—had rolled beneath the hand-carved coffee table. A couple of drops marred the wood, but they just matched the other stains.

"At least you're dressed," Brock grunted. Although who knew when the jeans and black flannel had been washed last?

A low snore came from somewhere in the cushions.

"First thing, we get you into a shower." Maybe that'd sober

him up. Brock reached for his brother's shoulder, gripped it tightly, and began to lift.

Ace instantly grabbed Brock's wrist, pivoted on the sofa, and yanked him toward the floor while twisting onto his back and throwing his now-free shoulder into Brock's gut as gravity took over.

Brock went down and hit the table, his cheekbone smashing a leg. He shoved it across the floor and ripped free of the hold. He shot both arms up to defend a punch, threw one, and connected with Ace's jaw. "Wake the fuck up, Ace." He rolled free and stood, settling his stance in case his brother charged.

Ace sat up, his light green eyes bloodshot and his dark brown hair sticking up in every direction. His beard was long enough that he looked like one of the mountain men who lived alone up in the peaks. He blinked. Once and again. "What are you doing here?" His voice, while always rough, now went beyond raw to the abrasive tone only excessive alcohol could create.

"That was a nice move." Brock relaxed his stance. His brother's time in the Navy hadn't gone to waste. Even half-asleep, he could fight. "My patience with you is about gone."

Ace snorted and prodded his jaw where Brock had hit him, his fingers tangling in the long beard. "Right. I heard you got back into town last week. Did you have a nice walkabout?"

"Yes." Brock left town in May, needing time to deal with Hank's death, his former career, and his future life. He'd explored the mountains of Alaska, often by himself, spending time on the ocean, rivers, and in forest land not touched by human beings. Finally, a week ago, he'd figured it was time to come home. "Thanks for asking. Rumor has it you're drinking your liver to death."

Ace snorted. "My liver is fine. How's your new job going? Getting to it after the nightmares finish with you?"

The breath Brock sucked in felt hot. The words, from Ace,

cut deep, and he had to clench his hand into a fist to keep from punching out again. "If you don't get into the shower, I'll take you."

Ace stiffened. "Think it'd be that easy?"

"No." Didn't mean it wouldn't happen. "Seriously. I'm done with this."

This time, Ace's snort held derision. For himself. "You're not the only one." He nodded toward a dead, frozen deer on the deck outside. "Last month, Christian dressed out and harvested a small part of a buck for me. Now, he leaves doe carcasses without dressing them. Next month, he'll probably drop a squirrel out there and stop trying to feed me."

Brock stilled. "You've seen Christian?"

"Nope. Of course not." Ace tugged on his stained shirt, muscles rippling. At least he hadn't gone soft. Yet.

Brock could only deal with one problem and one brother at a time. "Go take a shower. I'll rustle up something for breakfast." At Ace's lifted eyebrows, he shook his head. "No. I'm not working that deer for you. You're on your own."

Ace rolled his eyes and stood, wavering slightly. He looked around the cabin as if seeing it for the first time in days. "Huh." Then he turned and headed toward his bedroom with attached bath, calling over his shoulder, "I wouldn't mind a delivery from Lefty's, if you need to be helpful. Just so you know, I'm not taking a lecture from you, bro." Then he disappeared.

"I know," Brock muttered, moving into the adjacent kitchen, surprised to find fresh eggs and condiments in the fridge. Somebody was making deliveries. He'd have to tread lightly, despite the biting urge to punch his brother into knocking it off. Ace had never taken well to a lecture or a punch.

By the time Brock had finished scrambling eggs and heating deer sausage, Ace emerged from his room, dressed in clean jeans and a plain white T-shirt that pulled tight across still broad muscles. Ace's extra inch of height on his brothers, at six-foot-six, had always amused him, but Brock was broader than the rest of the brothers. Although Ace stood as solid as the mountains around them. Even with a liver swimming in moonshine. "You shaved. I'm honored." Brock slid the food onto two plates.

Ace pulled a chair away from the rough wooden table, his now-smooth jaw rugged, and a fairly new scar slashing across the left side down to his collarbone. "Thanks." He immediately dug into the eggs as if he hadn't eaten in days.

Brock took his seat, eating slower. "The wound healed nicely." Would Ace ever tell him about his last mission?

Ace lifted his head, his eyes a bit clearer. "Have yours?"

It was useless to pretend he didn't understand the question. "Well enough that I'm not drowning in moonshine. After we eat, I'll take you to Smitty's." The guy was the closest thing to a shrink they had, considering he'd worked as a bartender for most of his life before retiring.

Ace stabbed a sausage with his fork. "I'll lie on Smitty's couch the hour after you do, brother."

Heat climbed up Brock's neck. "Smitty doesn't have a couch."

"Not my point," Ace said calmly, finishing another sausage.

"Considering I've left my house and actually interacted with other human beings, maybe we should fix you first." Though there probably wasn't a fix, not a complete one, for any of them. "You do have a job. It's time you start doing it."

Ace finished his breakfast and sat back. "No. Winter's coming, and the plane will be grounded. I won't need to fly until next spring." He swallowed, his eyes sunken. "If then. Maybe not even then."

"You know the only way to beat a horse that's thrown you is to get back on it. You need to fly." He should've made Ace sober up and pick up the FBI lady. Right? Why didn't that sit well with him? "I'll go up with you in case you have problems." Or a panic attack and tear apart the entire plane.

"No," Ace said, crossing his arms.

What a stubborn dick. "You're gonna want to work with me on this. If Damian ever makes it home, he'll psychoanalyze you until you beg to pilot yourself away from him." Christian would take things into his own hands at some point, and only God knew what he'd do to help Ace.

Ace grunted. "I'm not afraid of him. Christian, either." Ace lifted his chin. "Are you?" The dare lumbered low and strong. The words they couldn't say with the questions they couldn't ask. "Brock?"

"No," he said, meaning it. "They're our brothers. No matter what." He leaned in, saying the few words he could. Maybe offering comfort? "So are you. Brothers and family, like Hank said."

Ace's nostrils flared. "Yeah. Like Hank said."

Brock cleared his throat. "The FBI agent wants to talk to all of us about Hank's death." He held up a hand to prevent Ace's explosion. "You only have to meet with her once, and you should do it today over an early dinner. The Green Plate should be open by five. Trust me. This woman won't stop until she interviews you."

"Woman?" Ace drawled, his eyes clearing.

Brock nodded.

"Is she pretty?"

How did he answer that? The agent was stunning. "If you like them tall, nosy, and stubborn," Brock muttered. "She smells like strawberries."

"Well, now, brother. You like them tall and stubborn, and aren't strawberries your favorite food?" Ace's lips twitched into a smile.

For a moment, a very brief moment, they were themselves again. But Ace's smile soon disappeared. Brock looked around the messy kitchen, ignoring the sense of loss. "I'll help you clean up." It had made sense for Ace to take over Hank's cabin since

Brock had already built his own, and Christian wouldn't ever live so close to town. Damian might return someday, but they'd figure that out later. Putting Damian and Ace in the same cabin held a certain appeal—for a bystander. Brock cleared his throat. "Hank would've hated the mess."

Ace stilled. "Hank would've hated a lot of things, Brock."

Brock inhaled sharply and then calmed himself. He couldn't go there. Just couldn't. "I'll start with the kitchen. You take the living room."

Ace shoved away from the table. "Whatever."

CHAPTER FIVE

Dust, oddly chilled, billowed up from the conference table when Ophelia dropped yet another box of case files onto the scarred surface. Sheriff Blazerton had been good at his job, and most of his organized files included rather cranky-sounding notations.

She flipped off the cardboard lid and dug through yet more records of trespassing, poaching, and some crime called *being a jackass*. There seemed to be an endless number of those type of files.

The heater clunked heavily, forcing warmth through the too-quiet office. While billowing snow smashed against the windows, the storm had forced the wind to take a break for a while. Silence surrounded her, eerie in its intensity. Setting the folders aside, the Hank Osprey case file caught her eye. Adrenaline warmed her blood, and her spine straightened. Finally.

She pulled the rickety chair back, wincing as it scraped loudly across the dirty floor. The sound grated in the quiet. Shivering, she sat and opened the manila file folder. Notes lined several pages, the script neat and factual, the print masculine and sure, the ink heavy on the page.

Cause of death was listed as shotgun spray to the torso that injured the heart, followed by drowning, based on the amount of liquid found in his lungs. So, somebody shot Hank in the chest and he fell back into the water, just filling his lungs enough to drown. The shot would've killed him anyway. In addition, he sustained lacerations on his head from some sort of blunt-force trauma, probably from falling into the rock-filled water.

She scanned the remaining pages, finding a map and diagram of the stream he'd fallen into but no pictures.

Why had no photographs been taken? All of Blazerton's other case files included photographs—especially of crime scenes. She sat back, pursing her lips. Had Blazerton neglected to document the scene? Or had the pictures somehow disappeared? She scanned the hallway outside the room. The office held two exterior doors, several windows, and no alarm. Anybody could've gained entrance to the building and stolen pictures.

She flipped up papers to reach a piece of yellow legal paper, which held more notes from the sheriff. Hank's four charges, Brock, Ace, Christian, and Damian, had all been in town at the time of his death. That, alone, was odd, especially since their career paths were so varied. All four men had gone into the Navy like Hank had, but they'd pursued different avenues once there. Ace became a fighter pilot, Brock a SEAL, Christian a special operative with innuendo of being a sniper, and Damian an intelligence officer of some sort.

Fascinating. Hopefully her request for their complete military records would be approved soon.

Unfortunately, the fact that the four warriors didn't want to discover who'd killed the guardian they supposedly loved put them all at the top of the suspect list. Period.

The interview notes appeared short and to the point. All

four men denied knowing anything about Hank's death, and none admitted to being around Crocker's Creek at that time. She got lost in the file, reading quickly.

It was the first case file where the sheriff hadn't made personal notes or given his opinion throughout. The last notation, scrawled in rough handwriting, declared the death to be accidental.

She swallowed and sat back, frowning at the file that created more questions than answers.

"Um, hello?" A male voice wound through the silence.

She jumped up, tipping the chair over and yanking her gun free. "Who's there?" Relaxing her arms, leading with her weapon, she swung into the hallway and aimed for the voice.

An older man wearing a bow tie, eyes wide, jumped and immediately launched himself back through a doorway that she'd assumed covered a closet. The door slammed shut, a lock sliding loudly into place.

Adrenaline flooded her, and she crept toward the door. "Come out with your hands visible," she barked in full agent style. No sound came from beyond the door. She lowered the weapon and took point where she could see if he twisted the knob. "This is the FBI. Come out. Now!"

A thunk sounded and then several more. Something hitting the door? She leaned in to hear better.

"No, no, no. No FBI. No, nuh-uh. No FBI." More thunking echoed. "Gun. Saw a gun. Was a gun. Barrel of a gun." Thunk. Thunk. Thunk.

The outside door opened, and she set her back to the wall, keeping the entire floor in sight.

"It's me, city girl," Brock called out, his footsteps heavy on the wooden floor.

She relaxed—marginally.

Brock came into view and froze, his gaze on her weapon. A

reddish-purple bruise on his cheek looked new. "What are you doing?" Before she could answer, his focus swung to the closed door. "Ah, shit." He moved between her and the door, placing his hand on the worn wood. "Amos? It's Brock. You're okay."

The thunking stopped. "Brock?" The sound came through muffled.

Brock leaned toward the door. "It's Brock Osprey, Amos."

"Gun. There was a gun. Big gun. Barrel of a gun," Amos said, his voice sounding softer as if he'd retreated away from the door. "You know I hate guns. Everybody should."

"Sorry. The pretty lady made a mistake," Brock said. "Put the gun away," he mouthed to her.

She blinked and then slid the weapon into the back of her waist.

Brock turned to the door. "Amos? There's a nice lady out here named Ophelia. She doesn't have the gun any longer. Would you like to meet her?"

"No." Very faint footsteps echoed and then disappeared.

Brock turned, his jaw hard, his eyes blazing. "What did you just do?"

She couldn't back up with the wall behind her. "Me? If somebody lived in that closet, you should've told me before leaving."

His nostrils flared. "True. I didn't think Amos would make an appearance. My bad."

His bad? She gritted her teeth. "I take it Amos lives in the closet?"

Brock moved away from the door. "He lives in the basement. Has his own entrance and heating system." He strode past her toward the conference room.

She followed, relaxing her jaw. "Amos the weather guy?" Brock had mentioned him last night.

"Yep. He's our weather guru." Brock looked over the pile of manila file folders.

Amos had been repeating himself and hitting his head on the door? "Is he, I mean, is he on the spectrum?" She walked around the table and retook her seat, her limbs heavy as the adrenaline receded.

Brock shrugged. "He's just Amos. You scared him, so you'll have to meet him another time. He's harmless, I promise." The sunglasses were perched on his head, and his eyes had turned an unreal green. He drew off his jacket and shook snow onto the floor. "Find what you needed?"

"Kind of," she admitted, gesturing toward the vacant folding chair across the table, ignoring the instant difference in the atmosphere around them. Brock Osprey had a presence, that was for sure. Masculine and tough. "What happened to your face?"

Brock touched the bruise. "I woke up a bear. Long story."

Fine. Whatever. She pushed a file out of the way. "I'll give Amos some time, and then I want an introduction. For now, I'm going to concentrate on two cases to start. Hank's and Tamara Randsom's, and then I'll move to the other missing person investigations the sheriff put together."

Sheriff Blazerton had created a file for the missing Tamara Randsom on May sixteenth, earlier that year, noting his suspicions that she wouldn't have left her kids behind with no contact—and that was the only information in the file. Ophelia called the local newspaper, and a nice reporter named Arthur informed her that the sheriff had died on May seventeenth by having a heart attack in the middle of church, and nobody could save him.

Ophelia wanted to continue the sheriff's work since he hadn't had time to pursue the investigation. She had already conducted a quick social media search and discovered pictures of Tamara with her children and with various town residents during parties or at outdoor events. Tamara's final post showed the kindergarten graduation day of her youngest child on May tenth. So she disappeared between May tenth and sixteenth. The woman looked to be around forty, with curly brown hair and sparkling brown eyes.

Further research showed a divorce decree between Tamara and Leo Randsom filed in Anchorage earlier in March. "Can you offer insight into either investigation?"

"Nope." Brock shrugged. "A hunter fucked up and shot Hank, and I'm sure it was an accident, so I don't want to know more than that."

Ophelia barely kept from shaking her head. "Hank? He died in December, which surely is outside of hunting season."

Brock snorted. "Season? Yeah, probably. But folks around here hunt for food and not sport, and if they need food in December, they hunt. That's a fact. So let it go."

Her job and her boss wouldn't allow her to let anything go. "Somebody shot Hank in the chest, and we have to find out who pulled that trigger. After sustaining the shotgun wound, he still had time to draw water into his lungs and drown before he could bleed to death." It made little sense that Brock didn't want to know, unless he covered for the person who did it.

He stared at her, no expression on his rugged face.

She didn't peg him as a murderer, but she'd learned long ago that people often wore different masks, so she had to start thinking of him as a suspect instead of an intriguing and badass mountain man who once served his country. Her gun remained at the back of her waist and would be her constant companion during her job here. "What about Tamara?"

"I left town in May after the weather cleared to explore Alaska and become accustomed to the fact that I'm no longer serving as a Navy SEAL—before Tammy disappeared. Didn't even know about it until I returned last week."

Ophelia studied his rugged face. "That's a long time to explore."

"Alaska's a big state."

True. Yet, she didn't like the timing. "You left right before she disappeared?"

His jaw firmed. "I left when the weather allowed me to do so. Seriously. I barely knew Tammy and had nothing to do with her disappearance. She and her husband Leo had divorced, and rumor has it even today that she might've just taken off and moved to a big city. How do you have jurisdiction as to her disappearance, anyway?"

Excellent question. "Tamara worked as a U.S. Geological Survey Scientist, a federal agency, under a grant to study Alaska's natural phenomena, most specifically glaciers and volcanic activity. That gives me jurisdiction." The sheriff had included the woman's grant information in his investigation. Ophelia decided not to mention that the grant period had expired the end of April, after Tamara had turned in her final documents, making a notation that she'd apply for a follow-up grant shortly. That had never occurred.

Brock shrugged and the scent of pine-filled snow wafted from him. Masculine and strong. "I forgot that Tammy worked as a scientist—obviously remotely. If a federal employee disappeared, why has it taken so long for the FBI to investigate?"

Ophelia shifted on her seat. "She held a grant and did not serve as an employee." So much for keeping the truth to herself. "All right. She completed the grant. But in looking through Sheriff Blazerton's files, I believe he suspected foul play, and I'm here to work." It was unfortunate the sheriff hadn't had more time to look into the case.

"So you don't have jurisdiction."

"I do if Tamara disappeared on federal land." True but a stretch. "Even if you didn't know her well, this is a small town with very few secrets, I'm sure. What have you heard?"

"Nothin'." Brock dropped onto the chair, and dust wafted up. "The Randsoms moved up here from the lower forty-eight about five years ago, probably to get away from all the people, just like the rest of us. They live miles upon miles outside of town, up by Silverhowl Peak, and are self-sufficient. After the divorce, Leo courted the youngest McDaniel daughter. I heard they married in July."

Ophelia reached for her notebook. "Wow. Very quickly. Name and age of the bride?"

"Loretta, and I have no clue as to her age. Late twenties, I'd guess. A good two decades younger than Leo." Brock sat back and crossed his arms, revealing cut muscles beneath his T-shirt.

Interesting. "I need to interview them."

Brock sighed. "Lots of folks move here because they don't like people, just so you know. Other people, I mean."

"Yeah, I caught that." She sat back, pretending nonchalance as she switched topics. "You and your brothers? Are you close?"

His chin lifted. "We're brothers."

That didn't seem like an answer—unless it actually counted as one. "Is there anything you wouldn't do for them?"

"Nope." His matter-of-fact tone held no defensiveness.

Okay. She had to tread lightly here. "Is there any reason one of your brothers would've wanted Hank dead?"

"Of course, not." His expression gave nothing away, but he stopped moving. Completely. His eye contact remained sure and solid on hers.

She was missing something, but she had no clue what. The thrill of the mystery, of the hunt, rippled through her. "Was Hank a good guardian?"

"The best." Brock tugged off his leather gloves and tossed them onto the scarred table. "Taught us to hunt and fight. How to survive this world no matter what it threw at us."

Sounded helpful but not all that warm. "Was there love? Comfort?" she asked.

Brock's upper lip quirked. "Not exactly. But there was a solid form at our backs, a wall of family, and that's better than any hug."

She needed their damn military records. Had they undergone psych evaluations? "So, your guardian taught you to hunt and kill, but he didn't teach you about emotion?"

A glint entered Brock's eyes. "I guess he figured we'd learn that from women when we got old enough."

Was that a challenge? "Have any of you been married?"

"No." Brock lifted a shoulder. "Well, not really. Damian had a short-lived marriage for a couple of months, but I think they annulled it, so that doesn't count, right?"

She perked up. "Damian was married? To whom?"

"Hell if I know. He just mentioned it one Christmas after we'd gotten into the Knob Creek whiskey, and that's all he said. Except her name was Stella. Great name, right?" Brock tapped a finger on his glove. He held up a hand when she started to ask more questions. "Honest. That's all I know about Stella, and Damian hasn't mentioned her since."

Well. There had to be records somewhere. "All four of you happened to be home, on leave, when Hank died."

Brock changed in front of her eyes—in a way she could never explain. His expression remained calm, his body still, and his gaze direct, but he...changed. "I don't think that's relevant."

"Sure, you do," she countered. "All four of you are suddenly home on leave, from different units in the Navy, at the same time? It's statistically impossible that's a coincidence."

His chin lifted. "You're right. I had just been honorably discharged, and my brothers came home for Christmas on leave and also for Hank's seventieth birthday. He died the day after he turned seventy, three days after Christmas."

Her skimpy case file hadn't revealed that fact. "You know, the sheriff's case file on this is as sparse as I've seen a file, especially Blazerton's. Is there any reason the sheriff would've wanted to hide the truth about Hank's death?"

"Nope."

"I need to speak with your brothers," she pushed.

He nodded. "We'll meet Ace in about thirty minutes at the diner for an early supper. You can question him all you want."

Good. "The little I gleaned from the notes the FBI assistant director gave to me showed that your discharge occurred last December, then Ace's in April, and Christian's just this recent October. I couldn't find anything on Damian."

Brock shrugged. "He's in intelligence, and that's all I know."

Wonderful. "You have no clue where he might be?"

"Nope."

Terrific. "How about Christian?"

Brock lifted a hand. "Couldn't tell you. He's around here somewhere living off the land and will show his face in his own time."

"That's odd."

"Is it?" Brock shrugged. "I guess."

Fine. She could pursue two cases at once. "I'll need to interview the Randsoms later today about Tamara's disappearance."

"Call her Tammy." Brock shook his head. "People who live outside of town don't want to be bothered."

She'd already figured that out. "Listen, Osprey. Alaska is part of the United States. Hank died on federal land, and I can make the argument that Tammy disappeared on federal land, or at least worked on a government project for EVE, which surely has government contracts, so the cases are federal if we want them. We do."

One of his dark eyebrows rose. "For a woman who wanted to fit in by using her first name and not her title, you sure fell back on the agency real quick."

Heat filtered into her cheeks that he'd figured her out so quickly. "The FBI appointed me as special investigator in these matters, so you might want to remember that I have the full force of the federal government behind me." Yeah, she sounded like a tight-ass.

His smile was slow and daunting. "Darlin', you're in the middle of nowhere. Even the federal government can't find you here. You might want to keep that in mind."

A lone, solitary chill clacked down her spine. Was that a threat?

CHAPTER SIX

Brock had just placed his hand on the diner's door when the hum of a snowmobile caught his attention. Ace came into view through the darkness, his headlights on and a black knit hat low on his forehead.

"No helmet?" Ophelia asked, pausing next to Brock.

It was a miracle his brother had bothered to come for dinner. "His hard head would dent any rock it might hit." He'd talk to Ace later about being a dumbass and not wearing a helmet. Hank had always made sure they had something on their heads.

Snow drifted gently down, covering them as Ace stopped the machine at the curb and stretched off, his gaze on the agent through the dark night and billowing snow. "I'm glad I shaved. Hello." He even took off his glove to shake her hand.

Brock barely kept from rolling his eyes. "Special Agent Ophelia Spilazi, please meet my brother, Ace."

They shook hands. "Call me Ophelia."

Was it Brock's imagination, or had her voice softened? A spurt of something he didn't like blared through him, and he grunted, yanking the door open. "Let's get inside where it's warm."

The smartass look Ace cut him might get Ace another bruise to match the one on his jaw from earlier. "After you, Sheriff."

Ophelia stumbled and then partially turned, her dark hair swishing and dropping snow onto the interior rubber mat. "Sheriff?"

"No," Brock said, pausing inside the doorway just as Ace chuckled, moving past them and the long, wooden counter that ran the length of the kitchen. Ace headed for a table in the back, next to a roaring stone fireplace. Christmas decorations showed on each table with bulbs and smiling Santas.

Ophelia's eyes darkened to a midnight blue, and a fine pink filled her pale cheeks. "Why did he call you—?"

"Hey, Sheriff." Gus leaned down on the other side of the window from the kitchen, his huge frame filling it. "Looks like you brought the FBI lady here. Thought you was gonna drop her butt in Anchorage." His grizzly gray eyebrows drew down.

"Knock it off, Gus." Janet, his wife, stood up from behind the counter, her hands full of straws. Gray liberally streaked her black hair, and her blue eyes sparkled. "Hi, hon. Welcome to Knife's Edge."

"Thank you," Ophelia said, her head tilting. "Did you call him the *sheriff?*"

Gus snorted. "The sheriff eats for free, as you know. You eating for free, Brock?"

"No," Brock growled, grasping Ophelia's elbow and propelling her past several empty tables.

Gus rolled deep black eyes and stood, revealing only his green flannel shirt. "Dumbass," he muttered, turning back to his grills and disappearing from sight.

Brock's ears heated as he pulled out a chair for Ophelia across from Ace, who'd already sat so he could watch the door.

The woman took her seat, looking around. "We're the only patrons."

Ace nodded. "It's only five, but it seems later because it's been dark for a couple of hours. The dinner rush, which means about five more people, won't come in 'til six or seven."

Ophelia brushed snow away from her dark hair, which looked like silk. The mass spread over her shoulders, and the smell of strawberries tickled Brock's nose. His phone buzzed from his pocket. He reached for it, already pissed off that somebody was calling him. Why did the cell service still work, damn it? "What?"

"Brock? It's Sylvie Yankovich. Wyatt went out earlier to ice fish, and he hasn't been back. He promised to return before nightfall, and it fell about two hours ago."

Brock nearly bit through his lip to keep from asking why the young newlywed bothered to call him. He sighed. "Sylvie, you know I'm not—"

"Please, Brock," Sylvie whispered. "I've heard the stories. All of them. What if—?"

"The stories aren't true. Don't believe in silly tales created to keep kids from venturing into the tundra." He tried to keep his voice as calm as possible, and as truthful, because who the hell really knew?

Sylvie sniffed. "I don't know what to do."

She should have refused to move to the middle of nowhere with her new husband at the age of nineteen. "Sylvie," he started.

"Forget it. I shouldn't have called you. I'll go look for him myself. It's not a big deal." Her voice trembled, and she cleared her throat.

Damn it all to hell. The young woman would never find her way home, and then he'd have to go searching for both of them. Why did people think they could move to the middle of nowhere and survive without any learned skills? "No. Stay inside where it's warm. I'll go look for him. Did he head for a crick or the river?"

"Um, he said Arctic Crick today. I tried his cell, and he's not answering." The kid sounded like she was about to cry even harder.

"I'm shocked you still have service at your place, but I'm sure Wyatt doesn't, if he's out fishing. So if he doesn't answer, no worries." Brock said. "Next time have him take a radio. For now, stay there in case he comes home. If so, call me." He clicked off and slid his phone back into place. If he held the sheriff job—which he did not—he'd make sure everyone moving to town took a wilderness survival course. Maybe several of them. "I've got to go."

Ophelia jolted, and Ace grinned.

"Shut up," Brock muttered to his brother.

"No problem, Sheriff." Ace flattened his broad hands on the table. "Take the snowmobile. I'll make sure your agent gets home tonight."

Yeah, Ace was gonna get punched again. Brock grunted and turned on his heel toward the door. Janet stopped him with a brown paper bag, no doubt containing a cheeseburger cooked just the way he liked it.

"Here you go, Sheriff. Can't have you out on an empty stomach." She handed him the food and turned back toward the kitchen before he could protest, her thick boots squeaking across the dented wooden floor.

Could this day get any worse? When he found Wyatt Yankovich, he planned to scare the stupid kid back to Anchorage. If he found him alive.

OPHELIA LEANED back in her chair, a million questions gathering in her mind.

The waitress bopped up while also pulling her thick hair up into a ponytail. She looked to be in her fifties or early sixties, with fine lines spreading out from her light blue eyes. "If it isn't Ace Osprey. It's about time you stopped drinking yourself to death all by yourself." She pressed a hand to her ample hip. "It's much better to drink with others, you know."

Ace nodded. "Yes, ma'am. Janet Luna, this is Ophelia Spilazi."

Finally, somebody who didn't introduce her with her full title. Ophelia smiled. "This is a nice place you have."

"Thank you." Janet smiled brighter than the neon pink sweatshirt she wore. "How'd you talk the sheriff into bringing you here? Thought he was dumping you in Anchorage."

Had the entire town talked about her? "I didn't give him much choice," Ophelia admitted.

Janet's lips pursed. "Huh. That's a new one for Brock." She tapped her fingers together. "Tonight, we have burgers, the beef kind, and spaghetti, also with beef meatballs. That's it."

Okay. Both sounded good, so she'd go with the safer choice. "I'll have a burger cooked medium," Ophelia said.

"Gus cooks it the way he wants." Janet turned her focus on Ace. "You?"

"Same," Ace said. "And a beer."

Ophelia straightened. "What kind of wine do you carry?" She could use a glass after the day she'd had, although she was starting to understand why Ace drank alone in his cabin.

"Red or white but no pink," Janet said, partially turning. "Gus?" she bellowed. "Two burgers with cheese and fries."

Ophelia barely kept her mouth from dropping open at the casual approach. "I'll take red. Thank you." This would be an adventure.

"No prob, Olly." Janet turned and loped toward the kitchen, her boots noisy in the vacant restaurant.

Ace chuckled. "You're here less than one day, and you

already have a nickname. Welcome to Knife's Edge." He sat back in his chair, studying her.

She returned the exploration. Ace Osprey's hair ran a shade or two lighter than Brock's, and his eyes appeared a smidge lighter green, but his jawline appeared to be the same. The men shared the same straight nose, high cheekbones, and broad shoulders, although Brock seemed thicker. They definitely sprang from the same genetic pool. "Your brother failed to mention he's the sheriff." Should she feel foolish or angry? Anger seemed to be winning, considering how hot her blood felt.

Ace shrugged. "The town voted him in six months ago after he took off for his walkabout. He keeps refusing. Didn't want to be on the ballot, but that's what happens when you don't attend the annual town meeting in June. You get elected sheriff."

She unzipped her jacket and slipped out of it, placing the leather material around her seat. The fire crackled and warmed the room nicely. "Let me get this straight. The town elected Brock to serve as the sheriff, but he doesn't want the job, and nobody cares."

"Yep." Ace grinned when Janet plunked a beer bottle down next to a generous pour of red wine. "Thanks."

Janet nodded and hustled off.

Had Brock told the truth about needing time alone? Made sense. But had he needed that time to deal with more than his discharge from the Navy? Did Hank's death weigh on him? If so, how and why? Ophelia sipped the wine, which exploded on her tongue and warmed down her throat. "This is delicious," she murmured, taking a bigger drink. What vintage had they secured here?

"You never know with Gus." Ace tipped back half the bottle before speaking again. "Returning to Brock. I honestly don't know if he's gonna win this one or if the town is. I mean, Brock's outnumbered by far, but truth be told, he's the most stubborn son of a bitch I've ever met. Begging your pardon, Agent."

"I've already noticed that myself." Ophelia shared a grin with Ace before returning to business, the good wine instantly mellowing her. "Who do you think shot Hank?"

"Ah. Getting right to it, are you?" Ace twirled the bottle on the table, his gaze catching the refracting light. "I have no idea who shot Hank. It happened around Christmastime, and I'm sure plenty of folks headed out hunting, so it could've been anybody who fired accidentally." He drew the bottle up and finished it.

Ophelia took another healthy drink of the wine. "That's the same story Brock gave me."

"Isn't a story. It's the truth." Ace looked up as Janet brought over another beer bottle and whisked the empty one away.

Ophelia shook her head. "Somebody shot Hank, yes. But the autopsy report shows water in his lungs, so he actually drowned. Whoever shot him could've possibly saved him after shooting him." Probably not, according to the report. He'd only lived long enough to fill his lungs, but she didn't have to tell Ace that.

Ace watched his bottle again. "You read the autopsy report. Interesting. I never saw it. Did Hank sustain any other injuries?"

"Like what?" she asked, the base of her neck tingling again.

"I don't know. Any type of animal scavengers? We have many around here."

What an odd question. "No. The autopsy report didn't include any such facts." Did relief filter across his face? The expression disappeared as fast as it had appeared.

He sighed. "Listen, Olly. Around here, a year ago might as well be a century. Hank's long buried, and so is your case. You're not going to find anything more."

So her new nickname might stick. She'd figure out how she felt about it later. This wasn't her first difficult case, and she always found more evidence. She swallowed, switching topics to keep him talking. "Tell me about your brothers."

Ace finally looked up, his light green gaze piercing. "Well, Brock is the sheriff and is responsible for you, which seems to have made him crankier than usual. That's saying something."

She ground her back teeth together. "You guys need to join this century. No man is responsible for me."

Ace grinned. "That's not a chauvinistic position. You could be male or female, young or ancient, human or horse. Brock brought you to town before the snow hit, and that makes you his problem if you turn into one. I really wouldn't turn into one if I were you. Brock seems easygoing, albeit stubborn, but he's not a guy you cross. Ever."

She set her wineglass down. "Is that a threat?"

"Of course not." Ace leaned back as Janet delivered two large platters holding burgers and an obscene amount of large-cut french fries. "That's just a fact."

Ophelia reached for a fry and paused when it burned her hand. "Where are Christian and Damian?"

"Dunno." Ace reached for his burger. "Christian is around here somewhere, but he really doesn't like people, so you probably won't meet him. Damian is in intelligence, and he gets word to us once in a while, but he can't say where he's stationed."

Well, then. "When you and Brock say that Christian is around here, what exactly does that mean?"

Ace paused in bringing a fry to his mouth. "The words are clear. Christian is usually in the mountains, so that means he is where he is."

She frowned. "Huh?"

Ace shrugged, obviously not willing to go into more detail. The Osprey brothers presented a solid wall she couldn't get past.

She'd have to start with Ace and Brock for now. She

munched on a fry, humming happily at the salty taste. That Gus sure could cook. "Let's start back at the beginning. Walk me through Hank's death. Who found him?" That salient fact hadn't been listed in the sheriff's report, either.

Ace took a large bite of his burger and chewed thoughtfully, studying her intently. After he'd swallowed, he placed the food back on his plate. "Haven't you already interviewed Brock?"

"Kind of, but we're just getting to that day." She ate another fry. "Why?"

"Brock found Hank's body. It's common knowledge. I figured you already knew that."

She jerked and barely kept from swearing. What the heck? Yet another fact Brock Osprey had kept from her.

What else was Brock hiding, and why wasn't that fact included in the sheriff's investigative file?

CHAPTER SEVEN

Brock's feet hurt, his ears burned, and his temper was so close to fraying that he should go bury his head in the snow and just avoid people. The darkness of Knife's Edge cloaked a gleeful danger, and just when he'd forgotten its power, a damn nineteen-year-old went and got himself missing with temperatures plummeting below zero, matching the current visibility. As in there was none.

Searching more tonight would lead to certain disaster. Hopefully Wyatt had found shelter.

Seeing Ace and Ophelia still at the diner, cozied around the table with Janet and Gus, drinking Gus's famous homemade spiked cider, didn't help Brock's mood any. The restaurant was obviously closed since it was nearly midnight, and didn't Ace seem to be having a good time?

Brock shoved open the door.

Ace took one look at his face before standing. "Ah, shit, Brock. You didn't find him?"

Brock shook his head, yanking off his gloves and letting the heat force more feeling into his hands. "Nope. Janet? Start the phone and radio tree."

Janet nodded, her face pale, and stood to walk toward the kitchen. "Monica has a new satellite phone and I'll call her first." She glanced at Ophelia. "She's my niece and is a lucky tall girl like you. I'll see if she has an extra pair of snow pants in case you go on the search tomorrow morning." Janet disappeared into the kitchen.

Gus also stood, his flannel dotted with grease and his deep eyes somber. "You want the blue flare or the red one?"

Brock wiped snow off the scruff on his jaw. He wasn't the sheriff, damn it. "Blue. The wind and snow make it impossible to see right now, and several areas of the crick haven't frozen over enough to walk on, so we'd just lose more people if we search tonight." He hated having to wait until dawn.

"I have the flares from the police station since it's, ah, been empty for a bit. I'll get a blue one." Gus turned and headed back into the kitchen and storage areas beyond the counter.

Ophelia stood, her intelligent eyes serious, and her skin enticingly smooth over her angled features. "What's happening?"

"Lost moron," Brock said shortly.

Gus exited the kitchen with the flare gun. "Got blue. If you fire one, I'll fire the second before dawn." He turned and bellowed over his shoulder. "Jan-Jan? Call Amos and find out what time dawn will fall."

"Already did." Janet's voice emerged muffled from the kitchen area. "He said dawn at eight-thirty a.m. and sunrise afterward at nine-forty."

Brock nodded. "Good enough."

Ace moved around the table, his gaze serious. "I could go out with you tonight."

Brock studied him and then shook his head. "The wind and snow are too heavy. No visibility at all. We wouldn't see the guy if he stood right in front of us." He accepted the flare gun from Gus. "I'll be back in a minute." Striding back outside, he struggled through the storm to the center of the street, pointed up, and fired the flare. It shot high through the snow and blasted out a bright blue the wind quickly swallowed. Hopefully Gus would have a better result in the morning.

Brock ducked his head against the chill and hustled back inside, handing the empty flare gun to Gus. "Thanks. I'll be here before dawn." He jerked his head toward Ace. "I'll take Ophelia to Flossy's and return for you on the snowmobile. I'd like to leave the truck in town."

Gus reached for car keys beneath the counter. "We'll drop Ace off on the way home. Brought the truck today."

"Thanks," Brock replied. "Ophelia? Let's get going."

Her eyes wide, she surprisingly didn't argue and instead plunked the knit cap onto her head and shoved on her mittens and jacket.

Ace turned. "Bye, Olly. See you tomorrow." He brushed by Brock. "Take your time. I'll help Janet get out provisions for tomorrow."

Was there a hint of prodding in his brother's tone? Brock ignored it and escorted Ophelia outside, grasping her elbow to lead her to the quiet machine. He should've grabbed a helmet on the way back. It was a good thing they only had to go a few blocks, just down Main Street. "You ever ride one of these?"

"No." Her chin jutted out a fraction.

"You'll be fine. Just hold on behind me, and we'll be there in a second." He straddled the seat and held out a hand to help her into place behind him.

She settled in, instantly grasping the sides of his jacket.

He started the engine, planted his feet on the warm slides, and pulled her arms all the way around his waist to clasp at his belly. The last thing he needed was her slipping sideways or off. She didn't fight him. Instead, she let him position her the way he wanted. Was she always this pliable? Something told him there was no way in hell.

The feeling of her behind him, her chest against his back, her thighs tight against his legs, propelled warmth through him stronger than a good shot of Lefty's whiskey. Even though the wind pelted sharp stabs of ice onto his face, he could swear he caught a hint of strawberries.

Then, just to make his life a living hell, she turned her head to the side, pressed her cheek against his shoulder blade, and sighed, her body relaxing and going soft against his.

Every nerve he had flared wide awake, his body taking over his brain with raw hunger. He tightened his grip on the handles and then opened the throttle, easing into the street and taking a wide U-turn. She held on tighter, and he felt her breasts against his back, even through her jacket and his.

Or maybe that was his imagination.

The sweet scent of strawberries wafted up, and he twisted the throttle, opening the engine and driving down the middle of the street, where berms would stay out of his way. He thought he'd experienced hell a couple of years previous in a desert with heat and pain, but this was worse. Cold and ominous with the forbidden smell of strawberries that he would never be able to taste. No matter how much his mouth watered, even in this blazing cold.

He drew abreast of Flossy's B&B, smoothly reached for Ophelia's arm, and gently tugged her out from behind him. "Have a nice night, Agent." His back was suddenly freezing, and the scent of snowmobile fuel made him want to cough.

She blinked snow from her pretty eyes and secured his jacket sleeve with two gloved fingers, the snow reaching the middle of her boots. "You have got to be kidding me." More snow landed across her dark hair, and standing in the storm, she looked like an avenging winter goddess.

Holy crap, his imagination was totally fucking with him. He had to get away from her. "Excuse me?"

She pulled on his arm. "You are coming inside and

explaining all of this to me. I've been patient with you so far, but if I have to pull the FBI card, I will."

FBI card? His temper, aligned with the urgency of the missing kid, uncoiled like a live wire. "Your card doesn't mean diddly out here, and you know it." Except it did. If she called in reinforcements, the town would be crawling with federal agents, and wouldn't that just piss everyone off? He'd be on everyone's shit list, considering he brought her here, and when a guy lived in the middle of nowhere, he had to work with his neighbors. Even if they wanted to bury him beneath an avalanche. "Tomorrow."

"Tonight." She pulled harder, her nose turning red from the cold.

He looked through the murk toward the other end of town. It'd be a suicide mission to go back out to search for Wyatt before the storm broke, or at least before natural light arrived, but he'd been considering it. With a curse that wasn't quite muffled, he swung off the Polaris and stood so suddenly she took an instinctive step back, slipping on the ice.

He caught her arm before she could go down, tugging her and fighting gravity. She skidded across the icy walk *toward* him this time, colliding with his body. She clutched his arms for balance, her jeans against his.

God, she really was going to kill him.

He warmed from his toes to his ears, the fire much hotter in certain parts of his body. She looked up, snow on her dark lashes, confusion in her sapphire eyes. Her lips, full and lush, parted.

Would she taste like strawberries? The thought tortured him, unbidden and unwanted.

Her gaze dropped to his mouth, and inevitability caught him. He leaned toward her, his head lowering, and the front porch lights snapped on, wide and bright.

Ophelia jumped. "Oh." Red infused her face. She released his arms and turned, carefully picking her way across the snowy walk and up the three stairs, pausing and partially turning at the top. Tension showed in the line of her shoulders. "I mean it, Brock. I have a right to know what's going on. Either you tell me now, or I'm calling DC."

He'd almost kissed her, and she'd almost let him, and now she issued orders safely from the snowy porch. He willed all arousal into the abyss and decided to go with temper instead. "Fine." He stomped up the steps.

Flossy opened the door and squinted out. "I just got off the phone with Delores. Many folks saw the blue flare, and the phone and radio tree is in full effect. Monica's new sat phone is very helpful." She opened the door wider, and heat spilled out. "Come inside. I have fresh scones and will make coffee, Sheriff."

His stomach growled, and he gestured the stubborn agent inside before him. They shed their wet outerwear in the front alcove, hanging up their coats and moving into the floral living room in stockinged feet.

Ophelia sat on the sofa, drawing one leg up under the other and tugging a pillow onto her lap. Her gaze sharpened. "What does a blue flare mean as opposed to a red?"

He dropped onto a dainty chair, his entire body beginning to ache for too many reasons, including healed combat injuries that didn't like the cold, as well as unfulfilled arousal. The agent had more on her mind than the town customs, but he'd play her game. "Blue means meet at first light for a search, red means come right now."

She leaned back, her gaze serious. "How many people would've seen the flare in that storm?"

He shrugged. "No way to know. For folks we can reach by phone or high frequency radio, the phone tree will get them. Others, those who saw the flare, will notify their nearest neighbors. It's what we've got, and it has worked for years."

"So, the whole town will show at first light to go searching?"

He nodded. "The town and anybody in outlying areas will come in—anybody who can, that is. We'll perform a standard grid search until we find him—if he doesn't make it home sometime between now and dawn."

She breathed out. "How old is Wyatt?"

"Nineteen. He and his new wife moved out here a year ago, saying they wanted to live the simple life they'd seen on some television show about living in the wild. Nice kids, pretty smart. But I searched all over that crick and didn't see hide nor hair of him." Frustration coated Brock's throat.

Ophelia pressed her lips together and exhaled. "In this weather, with these temps, what are his odds of survival?"

Brock dipped his head. "Not great and not horrible. If he found shelter from the storm, he's waiting it out. If he was injured and unable to find shelter, we'll have another funeral to plan for the spring when the ground isn't frozen—unless he wants a Viking burial, which is easier." Brock leaned forward and clasped his hands together between his relaxed legs. "We're not going there yet, though. We'll find him."

Flossy bustled in with a coffee set on a tray decorated with holiday elves and piled high with raspberry scones. "You kids serve yourselves. I'm helping in the kitchen with the phone and radio tree, and I'm trying to reach everyone who has a high frequency radio, which isn't that many people. We need more of those." She placed the tray on the polished table and stood, her housecoat brushing the spotless floor. "You're doing a good job as sheriff, Brock."

His nostrils flared on their own. "I'm not the sheriff, Floss. I'm just helping out." His voice roughened as he tried to keep from snapping at the elderly woman.

"Keep telling yourself that. Olly? Talk some sense into him, would you?" She turned, lifted her white and frilly housecoat, and trotted back into the kitchen.

He sighed. "Olly?"

Ophelia glanced toward the now-closed kitchen door. "Janet gave me the nickname at the diner a few hours ago, but I don't know how Flossy heard it."

"If it was hours ago, everyone has heard it by now." Especially with the phone and radio tree being employed. Olly. Interesting. It fit her in a cute and sweet kind of way. "I take it nobody has ever called you that?"

"Oh, no." She ducked her head and poured two mugs of coffee that smelled like licorice.

Was he reading into her tone, or did she sound, well...off about that? He accepted the coffee when she leaned toward him. "Thanks. Did you have any nicknames?"

She sipped delicately, her face thoughtful. "My mom wasn't big on nicknames, and she liked Ophelia for me. Thought it sounded classy and royal. Like a princess."

"You were a princess?" She didn't seem like the tiara and high heels type, but what did he know?

Her smile softened the harder angles of her face. "No. I was a tomboy through and through. Which was a good thing, really. We didn't exactly live in a castle."

Who did? When had he ever asked a woman so many personal questions? What was it about this one that had him turning into a guy who tried to connect? The last—the very last—thing that could happen with this FBI agent, this smart woman looking into Hank's death, was a connection. Brock took a deep drink of the smooth brew and let it warm his insides.

She glanced at the wild storm outside. "I feel weird just sitting here when there's a lost teenager out in that."

God, did he understand that feeling. "I know. But the safest course for everyone is to wait until the storm either dies down or until first light, or we'll end up with a lot more missing people. We can only hope that Wyatt reached shelter." He waited for her to get to the point she'd been mulling over since he'd picked her up. What was it?

She turned toward him again. "Ace said you found Hank's body the morning of his death. How about you explain why neither you nor the sheriff's case file revealed that fact?"

Ah, fuck Ace. He had to go and open his damn mouth.

CHAPTER EIGHT

Ophelia watched Brock's expression closely, noting no difference. Yeah. Well trained.

"Dunno about the sheriff's file except he determined that some idiot out hunting outside of season killed Hank. As for me, I didn't see it as relevant," Brock said smoothly.

Nice try. "You found Hank early in the morning, correct?"

"Yeah. I got hungry and decided to ride to town on my snowmobile to get breakfast." His eyes darkened and pain lurked in their deep depths. "Saw him in the creek, blood everywhere, his eyes open in death. Didn't see anybody else around."

"What then?" She tried to keep her own emotion at bay. His filled the room, pulsing with hurt.

He shrugged. "I drove into town to notify Sheriff Blazerton so he could head out to the scene. Then I called my brothers."

"So you never tried to find out who'd shot him?"

"Nope. Nobody wanted Hank dead." Brock's jaw looked like it turned to stone. "Blazerton agreed, and the file is closed. Done. Over."

Not even close. But his closed off expression promised he

had finished talking about Hank's death. For now, anyway. "Are there any other relevant facts you've left out?" she asked.

"Nope."

Fine. She'd wait to question him again. "Should we talk about the fact that you almost kissed me?" The moment had occurred, and they needed to deal with it. The problem? She couldn't say for certain that she hadn't wanted him to kiss her. Sure, she'd had a few drinks, but nobody she'd ever met compared to Brock Osprey. Something about him—tough, intriguing, and somehow sweet. Frankly, the guy probably knew how to kiss. But she worked for the FBI, sent to Knife's Edge on assignment, and at best, he counted as a witness in her case. At worst, he landed squarely on the suspect list. "Brock?"

"Yeah, Ophelia. I almost kissed you, and you almost kissed me back." He held up a hand to stop her from protesting. "We don't need to play games here. We almost made a mistake, and we both know it."

Well. She did know that, but come on. Her ego might be taking a bit of a beating, but at least they'd landed on the same page. If he could act casual, so could she. For now, she'd get a base measurement on him when he told the truth for the next time she questioned him. Her gut feeling whispered that he was no killer. But again, he was hot and sexy, so could she trust her gut? "Tell me about Knife's Edge."

If her switch of topic surprised him, he didn't let it show. "The town was named for Knife's Edge Mountain, which is to the north. The peaks form what looks like a blade's edge thickening to a handle. When the snow clears, I'll show you."

Made sense, and she warmed from the nice room and not from the fact that he just made plans for the future. Nope, not at all. "Why don't you want to work as the sheriff?"

"That's my business."

Ouch. But fair. Unless his reason had something to do with the fact that he didn't follow the law. Every question that popped into her head centered on Brock Osprey, and she had to realign her focus. "Who's Amos, and why does he live in the basement of the sheriff's station?"

"Amos is our resident genius who calls the weather. He's amazing, and that's where he wants to live, so that's where he lives." Brock leaned toward her and snatched a scone.

Perhaps the man shouldn't be on his own. "How old is Amos?"

"Heck if I know. He lived out toward the northern peaks with his aunt, who passed away a few years ago. The town took him in after that because that's what we do. Plus, we need him. He's great at his job, which you'll learn if you stick it out very long."

Was that a challenge? "Oh, I'm sticking it out until I solve my cases, Sheriff." Yeah, she'd baited him with the title, but he deserved it. Plus, from what she could see, he excelled at the job. Except he didn't want it.

She reached for a scone and savored its delicious flavor. After finishing it off, she eyed another, but it probably wasn't a good idea considering the probable calorie count. "Why did you get so tense when I asked about the EVE facility?" The intriguing place wouldn't leave her mind.

He smiled, the sight almost charming. "Is that a technique you learned at the FBI?"

"Yes." She sipped her coffee. "Though, frankly, it's how my mind works. I move between topics quickly. I didn't mean to throw you off." Not much, anyway. She cleared her throat. "Where did you learn your technique?" At his raised eyebrows, she cut him a look. "The changing of the topic technique combined with answering a question by asking one."

"By dating a prosecuting attorney back east." He shrugged, drinking from the thick mug.

Curiosity took Ophelia. As usual. "I take it you're not still dating. Why not?"

"I shipped out." He took another scone, apparently just fine with the sugar. "We both knew it would be temporary and casual, and I haven't seen her in years." He looked Ophelia over, his gaze lingering on her mouth. "We lack single women in Knife's Edge. You're going to be in great demand."

Amusement bubbled through her, even though she should probably be a mite irritated at the comment. "Is that an offer, Brock Osprey?" Her voice came out flirtier than intended, but she did enjoy the slight pinkening of his rugged cheekbones.

His grunt didn't reveal much. "Well, if it looks like you're dating someone, you will be left alone. Mostly."

Was he offering a fake-boyfriend scenario? "What is this? A Lifetime for ladies movie?" She took another strong pull on her coffee, humming as her body finally began to warm. "You're offering to be my pretend boyfriend to help me out?"

His upper lip quirked. "No. I'd want quid pro quo."

Her mouth opened, and she quickly snapped it shut. "Excuse me?"

He finished his drink and placed his cup on the matching saucer. "Listen. We're attracted to each other, and the nights get mighty cold in Alaska. I don't need complications, and neither do you. So, I'm all in if you want a relationship with me, a casual one, and I'll definitely provide cover for you. You're gonna need it."

She blinked, and her mind slowed briefly. Had he just offered sex? Man, he had. Yeah, he had a hot body, and those eyes could warm the coldest of hearts, but just how arrogant could one guy be? "I'm not sure, but I think you might be a complete jerk."

"You wouldn't be the first to say so." He stood, an intimidating presence in the ultra-feminine room. "But give my offer some thought."

She stood, unwilling to let him tower over her too much as her brain and temper kicked right back into gear. "I think, Sheriff, that you've underestimated me if you think I can't provide both my own cover and my own orgasms." What an ass.

He coughed out a surprised chuckle. "Damn, woman. I'd like to watch you do both." He strode across the room, stepped into his boots, and opened the door, partially turning. "David Laurence will most likely pick up Flossy in the plow truck tomorrow to head to Sam's Tavern. If you want to help out at the tavern's search headquarters, come with her. As for tonight, get some sleep and think about you and me." He left, shutting the door quietly behind him.

She swallowed several times, staring at the closed door. Her body flushed hot and then cold. She felt rightfully insulted and embarrassingly intrigued.

It took her several moments to realize that he'd never answered her question about the EVE facility.

THE BRUTAL SNOW storm nearly made him miss his turnoff. Visibility truly sucked.

By the time Brock drove the snowmobile down his driveway and pulled to a stop by his large metal shop, he wanted to slam his head into the nearest snowbank. What had he been thinking propositioning an FBI agent? He parked the machine and levered off, ducking to shove up the door, and ignoring the shadow to the side of the building. He drove the snowmobile inside and then returned, pulling down the heavy metal door. The wind whistled through the snow-covered trees, spreading flakes in every direction. "You coming inside?" he asked, kicking through the snow to the front door and not looking back, the freezing air stealing his breath.

Christian appeared at his side, long and lean, his boots thick and a black knit hat covered in snow protecting his head. "Yeah. When did you spot me?"

"Not sure I did." Brock twisted the doorknob and stepped inside the instant warmth as his brother followed. "Just felt you close."

"Huh." Christian tugged off the hat and partially turned, whistling softly.

A sleek animal, its coat white as the snow, bounded from behind the shop. He stopped at the doorway, shook wetness off, and then gracefully stepped inside.

Brock dropped to his haunches and waited for the animal to sit and grant permission, keeping his face clear just in case. When the animal waited, he ran both hands through the thick fur along his flanks. "Well. You're new." He leaned back, studying the animal as it studied him right back. All-white fur with one blue eye and one bluish-brown, the animal was probably around a year old. "Who is this?"

Christian kicked out of his boots and hung his jacket on the peg by the door. "I've been calling him Tikaani, although he might want another name. Will probably shorten it to Tika. Found him last month down at Sawyer's Crick with his leg caught in a trap. He's been hanging close since."

"A trap?" Irritation caught in Brock's throat, heating him. He lifted the animal's front left paw and then checked the others. "He healed well. What do you think? Husky and wolf?"

Christian nodded. "Best guess. Arctic wolf and Siberian Husky mix, and he's gonna be big. The paws are huge."

Beyond big. Tikaani served the little guy well. It meant wolf warrior. "So, puppy. Where did you come from?"

The animal, appearing bored, turned and loped over to the fireplace, where embers still glowed. He sneezed and flopped onto the rug, closing his eyes.

For a wild animal, he'd settled in quickly. Brock stood, studying the other wild animal in his life. "You hungry?"

"No." Christian loped as gracefully as the hybrid had and sat on one of the two patchwork sofas. "Ace is drinking too much."

He leaned back and plopped his thick socks on the sturdy coffee table, turning to stare at the dying embers. "It's time to get him to Smitty's."

"Look who's talking." Brock toed off his boots and removed his outerwear, instantly heading to stoke the fire and pile on a few more logs from the stack in the alcove by the fireplace. He was as careful and quiet as he could be, and the wolf-dog didn't twitch. "You smell like fabric softener, brother. Not my brand." While Christian often let himself in to use the laundry room, he obviously hadn't recently.

"You want to talk about spring-fresh scents?" Christian asked dryly, his gruff voice edged with humor.

"No." Brock moved to the stall bar near the floor-to-ceiling windows and poured himself three fingers of scotch. "You still not drinking?"

Christian cleared his throat. "I have enough demons."

Didn't they all? Brock took a deep breath and turned, sitting on the other sofa across from his brother. Christian's dual eyes, one black and one green, remained clear and veiled, as usual. Should they talk this out finally? If so, finding the words felt impossible. Brock took a generous drink of the single-barrel brew.

For once, Christian spoke first. "I saw the blue flare."

Brock swirled the caramel-colored liquid in his glass, watching the firelight catch its depths. "Wyatt Yankovich went fishing and didn't come home. The storm is worse, so we need to wait until daybreak."

"Missing ain't dead."

Brock studied his brother. "No. We both know that dead is dead."

Christian's expression didn't change. As they aged into their thirties, he looked more and more like Damian, with his angular face and high cheekbones, an intriguing fact given how opposite they seemed as brothers. Christian had tied his black hair at the nape, lacking even a hint of a highlight like Ace's hair, yet he and Ace shared the same jawline.

"You ever think about a DNA test just to see what exactly we are to each other?" Brock surprised himself by asking the question.

"God, no. The government doesn't get another shot at my DNA. We gave it up in the service, and I think they should destroy any samples after we get out." Christian scratched a bruise across his wrist. "Besides, we're brothers. That's all that really matters, right?" The question held weight.

Brock nodded. "Yeah. That's all."

"Is that why you won't be the sheriff?"

Brock paused with his drink halfway to his mouth. "No."

"Right." Christian dropped his feet to the floor. "You hear from Damian?"

Brock took another gulp before answering. "No, but Christmas is in a few weeks. He usually tries to call around that time if he can."

"It's time he came home. It's time we all did," Christian mused.

Brock's eyebrows lifted of their own accord. "You going to rejoin the land of the humans and stop being a nomad?" Even as a kid, Christian liked his solitude. Hank had to bribe him to join the local hockey team, where he excelled at defense, of course. "What's going on with you, C?"

"You have a week, Brock." Christian stood silently, and somehow, the pup heard him and stretched to his feet. Man, they moved in perfect sync with each other. How intriguing that they shared dual-colored eyes.

Brock stood. "A week for what?"

The wolf-dog looked from one to the other of them.

"To get Ace to Smitty for help." Christian strode to the doorway and pulled on his boots, the pup following him.

"Or what?" Brock asked, tipping back the rest of his scotch.

Christian shrugged into his jacket and turned to face him. While always muscled, he'd filled out even more in the last couple months while braving the elements or whatever the hell he'd been doing in the wilderness all by himself and now with his wolf. "Or I'm taking Ace to dry out where he has no choice, regardless of the consequences."

The two would probably kill each other.

Brock placed his glass down and then straightened. "Getting him help might mean talking about Hank's death. You ready to do that?"

Christian's expression slid away faster than an avalanche off Meyer's Peak. "Anytime, brother. Are you?"

Was he? Brock wasn't sure.

"That's what I thought. See you at daybreak." Christian slipped outside into the storm as if he belonged there. Maybe he did.

CHAPTER NINE

Terror slashed like knives through his veins as he ran through the snow-covered Alaskan forest, gasping for air. The claw marks on his face burned as if they'd scoured straight to the bone. Blood seeped from the wounds, hot at first, then cooling into icy trails. Tears leaked from his eyes, blurring his vision as he veered left in the sheer darkness, feet slipping out from under him in the heavy snow.

He hit the ground hard, tumbling and rolling until he came up covered in snow, a raw patch, barely visible in the night, of red marking where his face had hit the frozen earth. Pain flared in his arm—broken, useless—but he pushed through it. The wind shoved him forward, fierce and relentless, driving him deeper into the wilderness. Above him, clumps of snow fell from the trees, crashing down like warnings.

He groaned and blinked against the swirling snow. His brain screamed at him to stop, to lie down and give in. Just a few seconds of rest. But instinct, stronger than reason, shoved him forward. His boots punched through layers of snow, each step heavier than the last. The sound of his own ragged breathing filled the empty forest, but somewhere behind him—closer than before—a branch cracked. His pulse spiked. He wasn't alone.

This isn't happening. It couldn't be. Why the hell did he come to Alaska? He could've stayed in California, safe beneath the sun, where things like this didn't happen. But he'd wanted adventure—something different. Now, he would've sold his soul for warm sand beneath his feet.

Another snap echoed through the darkness. Panic licked up his spine as he stumbled again. The biting cold gnawed at his bones, but the fear was worse. The woods pressed in on him, silent witness to his desperation.

The trees thinned ahead, their outlines swallowed by the night. His heart pounded as he thought he caught a glimmer of movement in the shadows, but he refused to look back. There wasn't time. He forced himself to focus on his goal—the river.

His only chance was to dive in and let the current take him down to Knife's Edge, if he didn't freeze. Hypothermia was his last concern right now. He'd rather die in the river than on the unforgiving ground.

Pain coiled like a vise around his broken arm, sending sharp shocks of agony through his body until his vision blurred. The river wasn't close—not yet—but it had to be near. It had to be. The faint memory of rushing water tugged at his fraying mind, but the only sound pounding through his skull was his own hammering heartbeat. The fear of dying out here—alone, hunted—gnawed at the edges of his sanity like teeth sinking into flesh.

His foot snagged on something—a branch, a root, who the hell knew? He went down hard, his body skidding across the snow-crusted ground. The impact knocked the air from his lungs, and the sharp metallic taste of blood filled his mouth as he bit down to keep from screaming. Panic surged hot in his veins, but he swallowed it back.

Screaming meant giving away his location.

The cold seeped into his core. He tried to push himself up, but his arms trembled under the weight of exhaustion. The river had to be close—so close he could almost feel the icy spray. But was it real? Or just a cruel trick his mind played as his body shut down?

Finally, he forced himself to his feet and broke into a run, adrenaline fueling his strength.

The snap of another branch shattered the air behind him, louder this time. Closer this time.

Then a crash sounded behind him, loud and deliberate, something massive plowing through the forest. His tears spilled over, scalding the fresh cuts on his face. The bastard behind him wasn't just hunting—it wanted him to know death was coming.

He pushed harder, faster, willing his limbs to obey. But his legs were leaden now, each step slower than the last. His breath hitched with panic. The storm raged around him, beating at his body, battering him down—but the storm wasn't the worst thing out here. Not even close.

Through the wind's howl, he heard it—a new sound, low but steady: the click and gurgle of water against rocks. The river. Relief surged through him, stronger than the cold, stronger than the pain. If he could reach it, maybe, somehow, he could cross it. Maybe the current would sweep him away before his pursuer reached him.

He didn't have a plan beyond survival. He wanted to live.

Memories swamped him. His first crush in high school. His wedding day. The first day he'd learned how to ride a snowmobile. All of the special moments that came in between that he didn't spend enough time enjoying.

The sound of rushing water grew louder, just ahead through the trees. He could almost see the faint shimmer of the river through the dark. He sprinted toward it, arms pumping, lungs straining—

The blow hit him from behind like a pissed off linebacker.

He flew forward, airborne for a breathless second before he crashed face-first into the icy ground. The impact snapped his head back, his nose breaking with a sickening crunch. Pain exploded across his face, hot and sharp.

He slid forward, limbs splayed, body scraping against the frozen ground. Blood gushed from his nose, warm against the cold, spreading in a dark stain beneath his face.

His arm flailed out, desperate to reach the river. His fingertips skimmed the snow-covered ground, grasping, digging.

He didn't make it.

A crushing weight pinned him down. His ribs groaned under the pressure, barely able to expand as he sucked in short, ragged breaths. He tried to kick, to twist free, but his legs wouldn't move. The cold and pain had drained the last of his strength.

Above him, the storm screamed, but the world around him felt eerily still. His heart pounded, thudding slower now, fear curdling into something else—resignation.

No.

He wasn't ready. He hadn't come all this way just to die here, alone in the dark, with no one to even know how he'd fought.

The weight on his back shifted, and he felt hot breath against his neck. He clenched his fists, snow slipping between his fingers. The river was right there—so close it may as well have been miles away.

Please.

He didn't even know what he was pleading for anymore.

The last thing he heard wasn't the storm or the river. It was the low, guttural sound of something victorious. Something fucking evil.

And then there was nothing.

CHAPTER TEN

Ophelia's first time in a snowplow felt a little anticlimactic. Flossy sat between her and David Laurence, a handsome man who had to be in his late twenties with sparkling brown eyes and hair who whistled a soft tune as he shoved snow to the side of the road on the way to the bar. The headlights caught the snow still cascading down, and even though Flossy had assured Ophelia it was dawn, the outside remained pitch-dark.

David pulled over at the end of Main Street, next to a large wooden tavern with a sign in the window that read *Sam's Tavern*. Another road crossed Main Street and looked like it followed a wide river in each direction. "I'll leave you at Sam's and plow the river road as far as I can. Flossy, please tell Monica that I'll be back in about half an hour. Also, nice to meet you, Ophelia."

Ophelia opened her door, helping the elderly woman out. "Thanks, David." She assisted Flossy across a freshly shoveled walk, then through a round, wooden door into instant heat. Many people, all wearing snow gear, milled around drinking from thick mugs. A Christmas tree decorated in blue and gold took up an entire corner with paper-made decorations all around the bar, but raw tension spiraled through the place.

Flossy nodded grimly at a group of white-haired ladies setting out food on a pool table covered with wooden planks.

Ophelia looked around the tavern. A wooden hand-crafted bar ran along the north wall with bottles of alcohol behind it on a shelf, two pool tables took up space to the far right, and tables dotted everywhere else. A roaring fire burned in an actual brick fireplace in the center, viewable from both sides. Behind the bar, a slender woman with long black hair and deep black eyes bustled around, filling the mugs and offering what appeared to be a comforting pat or hug once in a while. She had pale skin and lovely native features. She had to be in her mid-twenties and stood several inches shorter than Ophelia's five-ten.

"Where's Sam?" Ophelia asked.

Flossy pulled her toward the bar. "Sam?"

"Yeah. Sam's Tavern. Where's Sam?" Ophelia wound through bodies to reach the bar, allowing Flossy to lead her.

"Oh." Flossy motioned the bartender over. "Amka Amaruq? This is Olly Spilazi."

Amka hurried over, plucked two mugs from beneath the counter, and set them in front of the women. "Hi, Olly. Leaded or unleaded?" She reached for pewter carafes near the bourbon.

"Leaded," Ophelia said, her nose twitching at the scent of the fresh coffee.

Amka poured from one carafe while reaching for the second one to pour Flossy's. The older woman must like decaf. "Sorry about the rough intro to town. We don't usually lose people until after January."

Flossy nodded.

Oh. She spoke with complete seriousness. Ophelia took a drink of the coffee and almost moaned at the smooth and delicious taste. "Any word on the young man?"

Amka shook her head, her eyes concerned as she turned to

refill the leaded carafe. "Nothing, but we keep warming cabins within a couple of miles of most known fishing holes. Hopefully, he headed to one if something happened. We have a lot of missing people, but we usually find them. Well, sometimes." She set down the carafe, her skin nearly translucent with the firelight warming the area. "Alaska is a dangerous place."

"So I understand," Ophelia murmured, taking another sip. "Do you work for Sam?"

Amka shook her head. "Nope. I own the bar."

"We own the bar." A brown-haired man dressed in a brown checked flannel shirt and dark jeans, sitting on a stool a little farther down the bar, held out his mug for more coffee. He smiled at Ophelia, his gaze running over her form and then back to her face—the only person in the place who seemed relaxed and not on edge about the missing Wyatt. "I'm Amka's fiancé, Jarod Teller. Nice to meet you, Agent."

If the guy claimed to be Amka's fiancé, he shouldn't be checking out Ophelia's boobs. Ophelia nodded, turning back to face Amka and dismissing Jarod. Maybe she'd read him wrong. "You purchased from Sam?"

Flossy snorted. "You really can't ignore any sort of mystery, can you?"

Heat filled Ophelia's cheeks. "No. Never could. Now, who the heck is Sam?"

Amka took pity on her, poured her more coffee, and finally spoke. "I bought the bar from a man named George, who purchased it from a lady named Lulu. As far as we know, a Sam never existed. But the name works, and it stuck, so there you go."

How odd. Or perhaps eccentric served as a better description. Ophelia took another drink as Amka headed back down the bar, refilling cups as she went.

Jarod cleared his throat. "So, Olly. You really think you can solve old murders?"

"Yes," she answered, not looking his way.

His stool scraped back. "I'm pretty free during the days if you need a guide around town," he offered.

"You could say that again," Flossy mumbled into her cup.

A woman hustled up, this one as tall as Ophelia. "Hey, Flossy. Did David head out to plow to the river road? I have a coffee thermos for him."

Flossy nodded. "Yes. Ophelia, this is Monica Luna, David's fiancée. Monica, please meet Special Agent Ophelia Spilazi."

Luna? "Related to Gus and Janet from the Green Plate restaurant?" Ophelia asked as Monica had a large radio in one hand and held out the other to shake.

"My aunt and uncle, and I work there as well," Monica said. "It's nice to meet you." She smiled, her blue eyes sparkling and her curly brown hair around her shoulders. "I'm in charge of the high-frequency radios this year." She glanced at Flossy. "We need to apply for another grant. We're definitely low." Someone called her name and she turned. "I'll set up the grid board as well. It was nice to meet you, Ophelia." She hurried away.

Amka leaned over the counter to peer down at Ophelia's feet. "You're going to need better boots than those for our winter here."

The front door opened, and Ophelia turned to see Brock entering with Ace, both in full snow gear. She instantly went hot and then started, surprised. When he caught her eye, he smiled. She smiled back, trying to appear casual and not like a dorky teenager. What in the world had gotten into her?

"He's like this generation's Humphrey Bogart, right?" Flossy whispered, her mouth partially covered by her mug.

Brock cleared his throat, and the din quieted in the tavern. "All right. Dawn is breaking, and we have three buildings open while we search. Sam's Tavern will serve as headquarters. Anybody searching have at least one partner who knows where you are at all times and then check in here with updates. The high frequency radios are by the door, and we only have enough for two people to share one. So know where your partner is at all times."

For a guy who didn't want to be in charge, he seemed like a natural.

He glanced at his wristwatch. "Miller boys? Where are you?"

Two young men, probably in their late teens, stepped forward from behind the food. Tall and lean with sandy blond hair, they both wore full snow gear. "Here, Sheriff," the slightly taller one said. At Brock's frown, he coughed. "I mean, Brock. Sorry."

Brock didn't address the title. "Give me the status of the warming huts."

The second kid set down his plate. "All warming huts along Samson's Crick, the bigger river, and the three finger tributaries are stocked and ready to go. The one closest to Jaordney's Creek, northwest of Pike Creek, crumbled to the ground before fall. Looked like porcupines got to it and ate most of the wood."

Brock nodded. "Good job, guys. Okay. We have food and drink here, while hot food and relaxation can be found at the diner as usual. Finally, Doc has the clinic open for anybody with injuries. There should be no instances of frostbite. Next to the radios is a box of hand and feet warmers. Take all you want. Let's go."

Groups started shuffling toward the door, their snow boots clomping.

Ophelia moved for Brock, surprised again when she had to keep looking up to meet his gaze. "I'd like to help search." Maybe she could get a feel for the land around them and talk to other searchers.

Brock grunted.

Two men, both grizzled and wide, moved from the bar. "I'll take you, Agent," said the first.

"I'm a better driver," said the second, smiling and revealing a missing front tooth.

Brock sighed. "No. If you're going with anybody, it's with me." He looked at her jacket. "You need snow gear. It's freezing out there."

While she didn't like the order, at least she knew he could drive a snowmobile. She swallowed.

Amka leaned over the bar. "I have an assortment in the back room, Olly. People leave stuff here every winter. I'm sure we can find something for you."

"I'll help," Jarod said.

Amka cut him a look and then gestured for Ophelia to follow her behind the bar and to a swinging door, grabbing a thermos on the way.

Ophelia paused. "I don't want to slow you down, Brock. I could stay here." It wasn't in her nature to stand by and do nothing, but she didn't have a snowmobile, and she didn't want to be a hindrance.

"You'll just cause issues here, and I don't have time for anything else right now, especially since I'm not the damn sheriff." His gaze softened slightly. Was he teasing her? "You won't slow me down, but I'll be out for quite a while. I'm fine having you ride behind me."

She really wanted to go. "Okay. I'll be right out." She dodged around the bar and pushed open the swinging door to find Amka digging through boxes in a large storage area that led to what appeared to be a back door. An adjacent window showed the day slightly brightening outside through billowing snow. Another doorway to the left led to a small bedroom with a bathroom beyond it. "You live here?"

Amka lifted bright pink snow pants out of a box and stood. "No, but if the weather gets bad, it's easier to stay here. Also, I sometimes have folks sleep it off." She winced and held out the pants. "They're definitely not your color, but they look long enough for your legs." She eyed Ophelia. "Your very long legs. You lucked out there."

"Ha." Ophelia accepted the pants and kicked off her boots to pull the snow pants over her jeans. "It didn't feel like it when I towered over every boy in the ninth grade."

Amka chuckled. "Probably not." She reached for a pair of brown boots with fur over the top. "These are mine. They should fit you. Size?"

"Eight." No way did they have the same sized feet.

Amka tossed them over. "These are eights because I like to wear three pairs of socks. You'll be fine with one pair, so long as you use the boot warmers after riding for a while. Make sure you crush them up before inserting them."

"Thanks." Movement crossed out back, through the window, and she straightened. "There's somebody—"

"I know." Amka grasped the thermos and unlocked the back door, pushing it open. A man came into view, caught sight of Ophelia, and stopped short of taking the thermos.

Ophelia set her stance, her right hand loose in case she needed to go for her gun. She knew danger when she saw it. The man stood well over six feet, with long black hair and a broad chest. The darkness obscured his features, but something about his eyes caught her attention, even in the dim light.

Amka sighed. "Christian Osprey, meet Olly Spilazi."

Oh. The mysterious third brother. Ophelia remained in place as Christian took a step closer. The light illuminated him, showing one green eye and one black. His features appeared similar to Brock's, but she couldn't pinpoint just one that was the same. A white wolf, or maybe a huge dog, stepped up to stand by his knee.

"Oh," Amka breathed, dropping to her haunches and reaching for the wolf-dog.

"No." Christian held out a large hand between the woman and the animal. "He's wild, Amka. Keep your face out of reach, just in case." His voice stayed low and rough, but his gaze remained soft as he held her arm and helped her up.

She patted the animal's head and handed over the thermos. "Coffee. Strong. Are you going on the search?"

He nodded, glancing at Ophelia and then at the fluorescent pink pants. Amusement tilted his full lips for a second before he turned back to Amka and accepted the coffee. "Thanks."

"You're supposed to have a partner," Amka said, pressing a hand to her hip.

"Got one." Christian jerked his head toward the now-standing animal.

Ophelia cleared her throat. "I'd like to interview you about the death of Hank Osprey, Christian. When will you be available?"

He took a step back. "Nice to meet you, Olly." Then he was gone. Fast and graceful.

Ophelia stilled. "He seems rather...blunt."

"That's Christian." Amka shut the door and grabbed a black jacket lined with light purple fur from another box. "This one will keep you warm." She tossed it over.

Ophelia caught the heavy coat, her gaze remaining on the closed door. "Do you have any idea what happened to Hank?"

"Nope. Just know that somebody probably accidentally shot him while hunting out of season."

Well. She'd heard that line before, now hadn't she? Had there been a meeting to get the story straight? Ophelia switched tactics. "Does Christian drop by for coffee often?"

Amka turned back around and shrugged. "He checks in once in a while and often brings fresh meat. He's not good around crowds or people. Yet."

Jarod pushing the door open and strutting into the room stopped Ophelia from asking additional questions. "The sheriff is ready to go, lady agent." He paused, looking at the wet floor by the door from Christian's snowy boots. "Don't tell me that freak came by again."

Amka rolled her eyes. "You should suit up if you're going out." She handed Ophelia a pair of bright green gloves and then headed back through the doorway with Jarod on her heels.

Ophelia followed, slipping into the down coat and zipping it up. At least it covered some of the obnoxious pink. Her boots clunked on the wooden floor, and she had to walk heel to toe to keep from tripping.

By the bar, Jarod leaned over and said something to Amka that appeared intense.

Ophelia began walking toward them and slipped, her feet flying out from under her.

CHAPTER ELEVEN

Brock caught Ophelia before she could hit the floor. "Don't move quickly in those snow boots until you get accustomed." He released her, his gaze narrowing at Jarod. "Is everything okay?"

"Yes. Of course." Jarod leaned back from Amka, his smile probably charming to some. "I'll stay here and help at the tavern."

Amka, all business, grabbed another thermos from beneath the bar. She filled the silver flask and handed it to Brock. "For you and Olly. Keep in contact."

"Yeah. Keep in contact." Jarod reached for a beer in the cooler and continued around the bar to head toward the food on the pool table.

The guy had always been a jackass, but it seemed he'd gotten worse. Yet another problem to deal with later. Brock motioned toward a massive whiteboard leaning against the far wall, stained black in many areas from years of use. He raised his voice for the crowd. "We've separated the search area into grids. If you haven't done so already, write your name in the grid you'll be searching before heading out."

He looked Ophelia over, reaching for a knit hat from his pocket. "It's orange, which seems to go with the rest of your ensemble." She wore a myriad of colors, from an obnoxious pink to green gloves to a dark jacket with purple fur, and somehow, she made it work, looking adorable instead of her normal sexy and edgy. He plunked the hat over her head and then pulled the coat hood over it, securing the ties at her throat.

"I look ridiculous," she murmured.

"So long as you're not freezing, it's good." His voice stayed gruff as he reminded himself that they didn't stand on the same side of pretty much anything. Except for the search today, and even that felt iffy. Her soft skin wouldn't take the wind well, and he didn't have a balaclava, much less an extra one. When was the last time he'd taken the time to care for a woman? This had to end. Even so, he couldn't help but ask, "Amka? You have any Vaseline?"

"Sure, Sheriff." Amka blanched. "I mean, Brock." She dug beneath the counter and stood, tossing over a small jar.

Ophelia frowned. "What are you doing?"

He dug a finger in and then reached for her cheekbone.

She took a step back. "Seriously. What?"

Why was he taking care of her skin? He didn't care about her soft and way-too-tempting face. "The wind is going to cause damage. This'll protect you." Grasping her arm with his free hand, he gently brushed the gel across her cheekbones and the top of her nose. Yep. Soft like a fine canvas.

He was becoming maudlin in his old age and needed to get away from this woman as soon as possible. Her eyes lightened to an enticing blue, softening as she held still for his ministrations, surprise still evident. For a tough FBI agent, she had a sweetness that hit him like a siren's call.

Closing the lid, he placed the jar on the bar and gestured Ophelia toward the doorway. "If your hands or feet get too cold, let me know. We'll use the warmers then."

The idea of warming her—in any way—shot a spiral of heat through him. He had to get a grip. Pausing, he looked back at the crowd, all gearing up for a rough day of searching. "Remember that we've had a late freeze. Most cricks, creeks, and rivers won't be frozen over, no matter how solid they look. Keep the sleds on solid ground. Same with feet." Sylvie had called him for help, so that put him in charge. No other reason, he tried to remind himself. He shoved the door open and stepped into the storm, which might calm soon. Hopefully.

"I spoke with your brother." Ophelia followed him into the snowstorm and instantly chilled his desire.

He had to keep her away from his family. "You talked to Ace again?"

"No. Christian. He came to the back door for coffee and wouldn't answer my questions."

Ha. Christian wouldn't answer anybody's questions. "You should probably avoid him. He won't help on the investigation, and he isn't good with people. Not at all."

"Is he dangerous?" She tugged her gloves farther up her hands.

Christian was definitely dangerous. "Not to you. He just isn't a big fan of new people, and he definitely won't want to talk about Hank or Hank's death. It hit him hard, and with everything else he's dealing with, he's not ready to handle it." Why was Brock still talking? He wasn't a talker. But whenever this woman asked him questions, he became a chatterbox. Still, he couldn't let the agent believe Christian posed a threat to law enforcement or women. He most certainly did not.

The snow had lightened, and flakes dropped onto her nose. "Are you sure I won't slow you down today?" The doubt in her voice came through softly but clearly.

"Don't be sweet, Olly." He couldn't deal with sweet, so he swung a leg over his hill climber. "This is a Ski-Doo. There's room for both of us, but you'll have to press close." God help him.

"Um, okay." She used his shoulder for balance and swung her leg over behind him, settling naturally into place as if she belonged there. Her long legs felt right against his.

He tried to concentrate. "The ride will be rougher than the one last night down the street to Flossy's. Hold on and try to match your movements to mine. If I lean left, do the same—but not much." He paused. "Forget that. Just plaster yourself to me and let me move you. We'll ride along the river for a few miles. It can get rocky." He held back a helmet for her before donning his own.

People filtered out, all heading to snowmobiles, side-by-sides, and four-wheelers to tackle their assigned grids and searches. He'd figure out later why he couldn't trust her safety to anybody else because any single man in that tavern would've willingly let her ride behind him.

Instead, her body plastered against his, and damn if the smell of strawberries, even through his helmet, didn't make his mouth water.

This ride would be hell.

ABOUT TWO HOURS into the ride, Ophelia had seen enough snow for a lifetime. The wind pierced her from behind, and she began to shiver, even with all the gear. Brock drove the snowmobile smoothly and efficiently with the two handles, watching the speedometer protected by a short windshield. He avoided rocks and tree branches sticking up from the icy ground while the river flowed next to them, often appearing iced over.

She had her hands clasped tightly at his waist and kept her thighs pushed against his, trying to gather even an iota of warmth. His broad back and tall shoulders blocked her view, so she turned her head and watched the river to the side, looking for any indication of the missing man. White and more white, interspersed with some green from trees and a little ice-blue when the river flowed smoother, were the only colors anywhere around.

Finally, Brock turned off to a barely there trail between snow-capped spruce trees. He slowed into a quiet alcove protected by mammoth boughs and then stopped, the silence sudden and absolute when he cut the engine.

She swallowed and released him, groaning at the ache in her arms. It had only been two hours, for goodness sake. The blood rushed through her ears, and the skin along her chin tingled from the chill, although the sun had finally begun to break through the clouds and sparkle off the snow. Her lower back and neck ached from the bouncing.

He pulled off his helmet, tucked his gloves in it, and reached back for her arm. "You okay to slide off?"

"Yes." She forced herself to swing one leg free and step into the snow, sinking down to mid-calf.

He partially turned, swung a leg over, and lifted the face shield from her helmet. Then he grasped her shoulders, his eyes a deep green and a shadow already starting to cover his rugged jaw. "I felt you shivering. How cold are you?" He took in her face, his expression serious and practical.

Her teeth chattered, but she shook her head. With the silence, it felt like they were the only two people in the entire world. The solitude threw her off-balance and created a sense of intimacy and trust that neither of them could afford right now. She lifted her chin. "I'm fine."

"Uh-huh." He looked closer and then glanced down the trail. "Most of the wind is coming from behind us, so I couldn't shield you from it. We could use the hand and feet warmers, but that won't help your core."

She couldn't let him regret bringing her. They needed to proceed as work colleagues, and she had to carry her own weight. "It isn't your job to shield me." An odd sensation filtered through her, and it took her a moment to recognize it as regret. Maybe she should start dating once she finished this job and headed back to a city. Anchorage must have available men, right? She tried to keep her expression placid, even as too many bizarre thoughts ran through her brain. The cold must be getting to her. "I'll be fine, Brock. Let's get going."

He tugged a radio out of his pocket and pressed the side button. "Ace? It's Brock. Status?"

It figured that Ace would be his partner for the buddy system. The radio crackled. "Ace here. Status good. I'm about three miles east of the river, heading in from that direction. I haven't seen anything, but I wasn't expecting to yet."

"You alone?" Brock asked quietly.

"I have a shadow with a large wolf-husky pup at his side," Ace said dryly. "He's on a Polaris and broke off a few times to climb hills, but he's keeping close."

Ophelia wiped snow out of her eye. "Christian?" she whispered. Did the guy stay away from even his brothers?

Brock nodded, pressing the button to speak. "The agent and I are leaving the river trail and heading along McDonnel Plough from the other direction. Check in again within a couple of hours." Brock slipped the radio back into place. "I have an idea. This trail is pretty smooth for the next thirty miles, and the snow will be thick enough through here that rocks and roots aren't a problem. Let's put you in front for a while."

In front? She frowned and looked at the sled. "Why?"

His too charming grin disappeared way too quickly. "You'll see." He held out a hand.

She swallowed and then took it, anticipation rippling through her. Even with the current somber search, it'd be fun to drive the powerful machine. "Well, okay." She gingerly lifted her leg, and when Brock moved back, she settled into place in front of him. Heat from his body, even through their heavy coats, slid her way, and she fought a grateful moan. Business. This was business. There could be nothing personal between them.

He pulled his gloves on and then reached for the helmet, no doubt putting it on with the face plate up. "Hands here." He took her hands and placed them on the grips. The very warm grips.

"Hey," she murmured.

"They're heated." He set his big boots on the runner behind hers and partially lifted her knee. "Put your feet up along the slide, as far as they'll go."

She did so, and instant warmth surrounded both feet. "Those are heated, too."

"The engine heats up by the top, so you'll stay warmer." His rough voice kept businesslike. "This is why you should always drive your own sled unless it's springtime. If you're sticking around, you'll need to learn how, so let's start now."

With his solid body behind her, the wind couldn't get to her, either. Not much, anyway. She settled in better, her butt brushing his thighs.

Was that a groan from him?

He started the engine and tapped her right hand, his voice roughening. "This is the throttle. Press it forward with your thumb to increase speed. Start by gently pressing it, and just keep it slow until you get the hang of it." He put her hand on the left grip and showed her a lever. "This is the brake. Use it anytime you want. Don't worry about the speedometer, and just watch the trail ahead. My hands are right outside yours, so if anything goes wrong, I'll handle it. Give it a go, Agent."

That was the third time he'd called her by her job title instead of her name. Did he wish to distance himself? If so, with his body wrapped around her, it would be more difficult than he hoped. Plus, she had an active case—or two—and nothing would shake her free until she had answers.

For now, she would drive this powerful machine with his powerful body shielding her. She shivered, though not from the cold this time. Yeah, she needed to learn to drive her own snowmobile.

That would be safer. Without question.

CHAPTER TWELVE

The woman had a penchant for speed, which made her all the more likable. After the first hour of riding, Brock relaxed his hold on the throttle, letting Ophelia take the lead. She had good instincts with the trail, finding the smoother areas and avoiding the thicker snow. She excelled naturally, and didn't that just rub him the wrong way?

He could easily see over her helmet, so he scouted the area on either side for any clue as to Wyatt's location. The fishing creek remained over several large hills, but the blizzard had been bad, so Wyatt could've easily wandered in the wrong direction. Unfortunately, the snow had piled up, so if he lay buried or had stumbled even just a few feet into the tree line, they could pass the man without seeing him.

The third hour in, the sun decided to give up the fight to another dark set of rolling clouds, casting shadows across the snowy landscape. If another storm came in, they'd have to turn back while they could.

He waited until he saw Cliff's Bend in the river before tapping Ophelia's hand.

She hesitated, caught his meaning, and let off the thumb

throttle until they'd stopped in the middle of the trail. Relaxing against him, she kicked her leg over to sit sideways and flipped her face shield up with a click. "Did you see something?"

"No." The sound of wind and frigid water hitting the rocks and ice competed with the crash of heavy clumps of snow falling from tree boughs. Warmth from the meager sun heated the chunks enough to break free of the trees, but the strengthening wind and chill would soon change that. "We need to traverse deep snow and climb that first hill to the right, so I'll have to drive. Do you need to, ah, take care of business while we're here?" He could kick a trail for her behind some trees.

She frowned and looked around. "There's an outhouse around here?"

"No." The shock of amusement that flashed through him made him press his lips together.

She blinked. "Oh." She wiggled on the seat, her gaze thoughtful. "Um, how long will the next stop be if I wait?"

He couldn't believe he found himself having this conversation with an FBI agent who totally wanted to screw up his life, but here he was, and thank goodness his brothers weren't around. Well, probably. He didn't sense Christian, so he most likely shadowed Ace to make sure he didn't drink during the search. "We have a series of hills to climb, and the terrain will be difficult, so this is the best place for quite a while."

She wrinkled her nose and looked around.

"Hold on." He jumped off and strode through the snow, kicking a decent path to a set of pine trees and around it, making a good-sized area. Then he returned to her. "Just follow the trail, and you'll be fine."

She shook her head. "Thanks, but I'm good. Really."

The cute city girl didn't want to freeze her butt in the snow. He shouldn't like that about her. In fact, he shouldn't be liking *anything*, yet he had the strangest urge to kiss her. Again. "You sure? We have a while to go, still."

Her frown darkened. "Fine." She pushed off the sled, wobbled a bit, and then stomped through his trail and around the trees.

He chuckled as quietly as he could and turned to slough through the snow closer to the river to relieve himself and give her some privacy. He'd been peeing in the snow since he learned to walk, but it probably seemed an odd experience for somebody from the city. Her boots and snow pants wouldn't make it easy on her, but offering to help didn't seem gentlemanly. Not that he was a gentleman. But, still.

She was a smart woman. Surely, she'd figure it out.

He waited a few minutes, watching the shocking blue of the melted glacier water flowing over rocks, and then headed back to the sled just as Ophelia emerged from the trees, her face a very pretty pink.

While he'd love to mess with her a little, they had to get moving. "Another storm is moving in, and our window for searching is short. We're going to head up that hill and over two more, then we'll be at one of the main fishing holes for Arctic Crick." He handed her the discarded helmet.

She turned to follow his gesture. "Um. There's no trail."

"We'll make one." Being gentle and reassuring didn't come naturally to him, and now wasn't a good time to learn those attributes. "You need to hold on and move when I do. If you can't, just hold on, and I'll move you." He tilted his head and eyed her long legs. "We've ridden for a while. Do you still have strength in your legs to grip tight?" Should he have forced her to stay behind?

She straightened. "Of course."

Concern licked through him. Nobody had found a sign of Wyatt yet, and time drew short. "All right. We're going fast, and I may need to stand. If I stand, you crouch, just holding on. Got it?"

"Sure." Her forced nonchalance belied her slight caution as she straddled the sled.

He reached into his pocket for warmers and cracked them, gently taking off her gloves to place them inside. "If your feet get too cold, let me know when we're at a good stopping point, and we'll insert more into your boots." He tapped down her face guard and settled his helmet into place, flipping his up. "If, for any reason, you panic, hold on tighter. Don't let go." That was the biggest risk for a second rider on a hill.

"Got it."

They'd see about that. He sat, ignited the engine, and turned the sled to aim between two naked-looking cottonwoods. "Hold on, Agent." Flipping his shield down, he squeezed the throttle and shot forward into the forest.

OPHELIA'S THIGHS ACHED, her neck tingled, and her hands had chilled, but hill climbing felt freaking amazing. Brock moved with the machine like they were one, and she just softened against him to move with him. They rode straight up powder-covered hills, down along gullies, and then back up another hill, all covered with heavy rocks and different species of fully-grown trees. These were nowhere near as large as the jagged mountain peaks that seemed to surround them on every side, but Brock had to half-lift several times, and she followed, holding his hips tightly.

They reached the top of another hill, rode along the ridge, and then he turned to descend. Below them, a wide valley spread out, bisected by yet another rushing river crusted with ice. This one ran thicker than several of the streams and creeks they'd skirted but not as wide as the main river that extended from town.

Her lungs compressed, making her breathe heavier. They

had definitely changed altitudes, and even the snowdrifts stood higher and icier. It had been winter up here for much longer than in town.

Brock wound the snowmobile between thick trees. Every time he ducked, she followed suit. Soon they rode close to the newest river, heading toward the west, and more snow, river, and trees. A loud howl somehow surrounded them. Wolf pack?

She swallowed and slid her arms closer around his torso, holding tightly.

He slowed, found a small gulley beneath some trees, and coasted to a stop.

She tugged up her visor. "We're here?"

He partially turned, lifting his shield. "We'll ride along the river and sweep left to follow Arctic Crick. I'll have to cross the river, so we'll get a little wet, but I'll try to find a shallow place."

She gulped and looked over at the water. "Why not go here? The ice covers it." The blanket looked solid.

He shook his head. "The sled is heavier than you think. It'll be another couple of weeks before we can cross the rivers safely around here. For now, just keep an eye out for anything that looks odd or out of place. We found a missing tourist once by spotting his fishing pole leaning against a tree. He lay half-submerged in the river, but it was summer, and he'd managed to keep his head above water, even with a broken leg. You ready?"

"Yes." Her entire body felt like it had been through a spaghetti strainer, but she held his waist again, already swiveling to look all around them. How could Wyatt have survived the night out here? It must have gotten to at least ten degrees or more below zero the night before. Perhaps she should look for some sort of shelter. That'd be branches over snow, right?

Brock drove along the river across rough ground, and the snowmobile bucked several times. Finally, he tapped her leg in warning before turning sharply and gunning the engine, rushing over river rocks and cracking ice in a narrower part of the river. Water dragged across her boots, and she tightened her hold with her legs, her breath catching in her throat.

Then they reached the other side. He drove away from the river, along a narrow stream, and wove around bare cottonwoods that looked lonely and cold in the wintery landscape.

She blinked against the constant white, trying to see anything out of the ordinary. Brock slowed the sled, driving as close to the stream as possible and scouting the tree line. The entire area appeared untouched by any human for centuries.

They drove for what seemed like forever, and the snow began falling heavier, the wind picking up as if in tune. The stream widened into a river that appeared fathomless beneath a crust of ice. Her eyelids started to get heavy, and her body settled against his.

She yawned in the helmet, stopping halfway at seeing a patch of black in the snow. Stiffening, she tapped his leg and pointed farther ahead.

He twisted his head and then lowered it, speeding up.

Her heart beat faster, and she stiffened as more black came into view, right near the rushing river. A black coat, lightly covered with snow. They reached a couple of feet away, and Brock cut the engine, jumping off before the sound dissipated. He shoved through snow up beyond his knees.

Ophelia pushed off the sled, sinking into the powder and following Brock's tracks.

He bent and wiped off what appeared to be jeans. It was a man, face down. Brock shoved more snow off the guy, and red mixed with the ice. A lot of frozen red. Blood? It had to be. Ophelia tugged off her helmet and set it on the crusty snow, leaning around Brock. Grunting, he grabbed the man's hips and flipped him over.

Ophelia caught sight of the guy's neck before Brock turned,

blocking her view. He pulled off his helmet and handed it to her. "Take these back to the sled."

She accepted his helmet out of instinct and then placed it by hers before pulling off her gloves to take her phone out of her pocket. "I know he's dead, Brock." The body definitely appeared frozen.

Brock swallowed, his darker skin pale, his green eyes blazing. "You don't need to see him."

The kindness of his move caught her before she touched his arm. "It's sweet, but I'm an FBI agent. This isn't my first body. Do you always protect women from bad things?"

His chin lifted. "Women? No, just you." He sighed. "I served with plenty of strong and impressive women in the service. Trust me when I say that you don't want to see this."

She paused, oddly touched. Just her? "I can do my job." With that, she strode around him, her phone ready to take pictures. Her instant gasp echoed through the trees. "What in the world?" A Caucasian male of about fifty years old lay face up, half his face clawed off. His neck hung from several tendons, and both eyes had been gouged out. Bile rose in her throat, and she swallowed it down. "Wh-what could have done this?" She took several pictures.

Brock remained silent.

"This isn't Wyatt," she whispered. The guy appeared to be in his fifties. Maybe sixties.

"I know," Brock said, reaching for his radio. "I don't know his identity."

Something caught her eye, and she reached down, brushing more snow off the jacket. *EVE* stood out, neatly embroidered across the right chest.

"Ah, crap," Brock muttered. "Give me a second." He walked back to the snowmobile, grabbing the helmets and gloves on his way.

She stood and took several more pictures before shoving the

phone into her pocket. While cell service didn't exist out here, the camera worked perfectly. "We should—"

A crack echoed before the snow billowed up next to her. Then another one.

"Shots fired!" Brock bellowed.

Awareness hit her the second before she ducked.

Brock leaped for her, but she fell back, her butt hitting ice. It cracked, and she fell through into the river, plummeting. Her jacket snagged on a rock, dragging her farther down.

Ice-cold glacier water swallowed her whole, covering her scream.

CHAPTER THIRTEEN

Brock dove for Ophelia, landing on his stomach and sliding across the icy ground. He reached the river just as she tried to shove up and then went down again, yelping and swallowing freezing water. If the current caught her and dragged her under the ice, he'd never get her. "Damn it." He rolled his legs around and went in feet first, plunging down and grabbing her. The freezing cold caught him, stealing his breath. He snagged her shoulder and yanked her toward the bank, but her jacket twisted on a branch trapped beneath a rock under an overhang of ice. The combined force twisted her around and pulled down.

He dove beneath the ice and ripped the coat apart, splitting the zipper as he held his breath. Something fell against his foot. Her gun?

He shoved the coat away and freed her, kicking off a rock, his foot sliding off. His radio dropped, smacking his ankle. Damn it.

Keeping his eyes closed, he propelled them up and broke the surface, his lungs screaming in pain. He struggled against the current and caught sight of an icy overhang. Wincing, he tried to grab it with his glove, curving his fingers beneath the sharp edge. Grunting and fighting the cold, he yanked his body out with one hand, keeping hold of Ophelia even when the ice gave away. He scooted out of the water, trying to stay low.

Wind chilled him, and snow blasted into his eyes. He twisted around, grabbed her shoulder, and forced her out and onto the ground, fighting the heaviness of his water-logged snow clothes.

She lay on her back, struggling, gasping, and coughing out water, her lips already turning blue.

"Stay down." He planted a hand on her wet torso and levered up to his knees, partially protected by a snowbank. His vision swam, but he drew his gun from the back of his waist. Hopefully, the weapon still worked. No movement showed through the snowy day, but somebody waited there. He aimed for a cottonwood and fired, hitting it dead center. The sound split the hush with an ominous threat.

Silence echoed back. His arm ached, and his hand shook, but he fired again, missing the tree but making his point. His vision blurred, and he blinked several times to focus.

A flashback tried to return him to the desert, to heat and pain, but he shoved it away for the moment. He'd deal with the past later.

Ophelia partially rolled to her side on the icy ground, coughing out more water, her body shuddering.

"Hold on, baby. Just a couple more minutes," he whispered, trying desperately to see movement in the trees. The wind threw snow at him, and his damaged left leg went numb. He had to get Ophelia out of the elements and into warmth, but the shooter remained present. Armed. Waiting and dangerous.

He lifted his arm and fired two more shots, and branches cracked loudly, crashing down.

Several seconds later, an engine ignited. It sounded like a

four-wheeler. Birds squawked from the forest interior, protesting the disturbance.

Everything in him wanted to hunt and pursue the shooter, but he didn't have enough time. He tucked his gun into his pocket and stood, lifting a shuddering Ophelia up with him.

Her face turned as white as wax, and her blue lips barely formed words. Her body sagged, her knees giving out, her arms flopping by her sides.

He shook her, leaning in. "You have to stay awake. Just stay awake." He'd lost his radio. They needed warmth, and they were at least thirty minutes away from shelter, through the icy storm. If he didn't get them somewhere safe, they'd both die. Hypothermia would take them. He dragged her to the sled and shoved her on, straddling the seat behind her, planting her hands on the heated grips, and pushing her feet up the runner. Water poured from their clothes, icing over almost instantly. Shit. This was bad.

She slumped against him, and he drove with one hand, wrapping his free arm around her waist and yanking her against his body. "Fucking stay awake," he yelled.

She jerked and then nodded, her icy hair sticking to his chin.

His limbs dragged with weight, and his feet felt like hot pokers slicing ice beneath his toes. He sped up, taking a turn too fast but managing to stay on the river trail. He drove past two more fishing holes and turned toward the jagged mountains to the west. Snow billowed around, hampering visibility, but he knew their location.

His arm started to go numb, and he shook it, still driving. They didn't have time to stop. There was no more time. Period.

Ophelia had gone quiet and unmoving, but he didn't have the energy to shake her. Hopefully the engine and hand heaters at least kept her conscious.

Finally, he drove out of another grove of spruce and spotted the warming hut built against mountain rocks, shielded by a rock cliff. He reached the front and cut the engine, hauling Ophelia with him like a sopping wet and frozen doll. He dragged her to the door and kicked it open and then closed, shutting the storm out. "Take off your clothes." He moved toward the fireplace where the Miller boys had already left logs stacked with kindling ready to light. God bless those kids. He dropped to his knees. His hands shook, and his arm felt like it weighed a hundred pounds, but he opened the box of long matches and struck one, instantly lighting the kindling.

The fire caught quickly, expertly structured.

Still on his knees, he forced his coat zipper down with freezing fingers and shoved the wet garment off. Much lighter, he stood, turning to face Ophelia, who hovered in front of the long bench that ran the length of the far wall. It was the only furniture in the room besides the several provision boxes piled against the adjacent wall.

Her hair hung in a frozen mass around her pale face, and she stared at the fire as if not seeing it. Ice coated her hair and sweater. She'd stopped shaking, which was a bad sign.

He reached her, unzipping her sweater. "Olly? You're in shock. Stay with me." He removed her frozen wool. Her badge hung from a chain around her neck, and he gingerly lifted it over her head to place by the jugs of frozen water. Then he unzipped the snow pants, dropping them and gently nudging her to sit on the bench.

She fell like a log, and ice cracked from her pants. He pulled off her boots and socks, bending to check her toes. He couldn't tell if she had frostbite or not. Lifting, he removed the rest of her clothing. Even her undergarments were wet, so they had to go.

She blinked, her gaze unfocused.

He flipped open the lids of the two nearest boxes and drew out sleeping bags and blankets, wishing he hadn't lost his radio.

He threw several heavy blankets onto the floor in front of

the fire and clumsily zipped two sleeping bags together before reaching for her and lifting her, nearly dropping them both from the effort. Murmuring something reassuring to her, he wasn't sure what, he zipped her into the bag, sitting her to face the fire and lean against the heavy bench. "Don't fall."

Move. Just move. A mantra he'd learned a long time ago. All he wanted to do was climb into the bag with her and fall asleep. He flipped open another bin lid, found a can of broth, and struggled to pull up the tab. Grunting, his fumbling fingers finally worked, and he dug for a small pot to dump the contents into.

"Keep breathing, Ophelia," he ordered, setting the pan right in front of the fire and tugging a cup out of the bin. He shuddered, and dizziness attacked him. He rode the waves until the room cleared so he could remove the rest of his wet clothing. His pants had been waterproof, unlike hers, so he kept his boxers on and then reached for the sleeping bags, partially lifting her up so he could climb in behind her.

He pulled the bags up to their necks and wrapped his arms around her chilly waist, partially lifting her to sit on his lap. Her thighs were even colder than her butt, and he bit back a wave of pain. She felt ice-cold against him, and considering his core temperature had dropped dangerously low, they faced disaster.

His fingers tingled, which was good, but his feet still ached. He winced, his lips cracking. "This is gonna hurt you more than me." He pinched her hip.

Her slow murmur didn't reassure him.

He pinched harder.

"Hey," she mumbled.

"There you are," he said, gripping the tender area again. "Stare at the fire and let it warm your face and dry your hair. Don't make me pinch you again."

She elbowed him in the gut, glancing off. "Stop it."

"Stay awake." He eyed the fire as it crackled. "You need to talk to me, Ophelia. We can't sleep until we warm up, so talk."

He brushed her wet hair out of his way, revealing her slender neck. A purple bruise was forming beneath her ear. "Talk."

"Sleep," she mumbled, starting to shiver again.

He pinched her.

"Brock," she snapped, still facing the fire. "Geez. Stop pinching."

Better. Her voice sounded clear. He rubbed her hip, which would no doubt have a bruise. "I need you to take inventory. How do your fingers and toes feel?"

"Like they've been frozen off," she muttered. She remained quiet for several moments, her breath shaky but steady.

"Pull your legs up, feet pressed together for warmth." He waited until she did so, wrapping around her from behind. "That's good. You'll warm faster." For a tall woman, she didn't take up much room in the bags. He reached around her, tipping the broth into the cup and bringing it toward them. He tested the metal. Warm but not too hot. "Take this and hold it."

She grumbled but pulled her arms free of the bags and reached for the cup, her soft hum of pleasure shooting through him to uncomfortable places.

"Good," he murmured. "Now, sip it slowly. The salt and warmth with the little bit of protein will get your blood moving to heat you up. Drink just a little bit for me." He kept a hand on hers since she shook so fiercely. "I'll help you." He let her take several sips before he relaxed. "Okay. You'll be all right."

She slipped her arms back into the bag, leaning against his bare chest, her body feeling fragile and soft. "Thank you."

"You're welcome." He wanted to close his eyes and rest, but now wasn't the time. They both had to be warmer before he could let his guard down to sleep, and there was no guarantee they'd found true safety. With her trusting him, defenseless and naked in the bag, every protective instinct he'd ever had surged through him, the responsibility heating him as nothing else could. "I'll keep you safe, Ophelia."

She murmured something, no doubt not truly understanding the vow he'd just made. While she might be an FBI agent and a strong woman, right now she was naked and vulnerable, and he'd always been a fighter and protector. Nothing would harm her on his watch, and the depth that vow reached in him caught him by surprise.

The gun sat next to him on the bench, just in case. The storm increased in strength outside, battering against the doorway. That could only help them right now.

"You drink some," she murmured.

He took the cup and drank a swallow, letting the broth heat him throughout. Her body remained cold against his, but her shivering had stopped.

Finally, she stiffened just a little, coming out of her stupor. "Am I naked?"

CHAPTER FOURTEEN

Ophelia stared at the fire, her body slowly warming. "Brock?"

"Yeah?" His breath brushed her hair, which was drying around her face. He gently pulled her right arm out of the sleeping bag and held her wrist in front of them, lit by the fire. "Wriggle your fingers."

She did so, and pricks of pain tingled up her arm.

He drew her hand up. "Again."

"You're bossy when naked," she mumbled, wriggling her fingers again. They still ached, but not as badly.

"You have no idea." He rubbed his calloused fingers over hers. "You're warming, and I don't see frostbite." He tucked her arm back in as gently as he'd taken it. "Next hand?"

She wiggled her hand, keeping it nicely inside the sleeping bag. "I'm good."

"Take your hand out, or I'll do it." His voice sounded calm, but that thread of steel ran through it.

At the moment, she wouldn't win a fight with a kitten, but she still could make a go of it.

"Please, Olly."

It was the darn *please* that did it. "Fine." Keeping her body covered and trying not to move against his hard body, she tugged her other hand from the warmth of the bag. Her body felt like gravity pulled at her from every direction. She wriggled her fingers, and he leaned to the side, his chin brushing her bare shoulder.

"Your fingers look okay."

Good. She slid her arm back into the bag, acutely aware of her bare butt on his groin. "Why did you get to keep your underwear?"

"My snow pants were waterproof." His breath brushed the nape of her neck.

Spirals of warmth circled in her abdomen. "So, you could've kept on your long johns?"

"Yep. But skin to skin is warmer." He palmed her biceps. "You're not gonna like this, but I need you to turn around so I can check your nose and ears."

Skin to skin and turn around? A sense of challenge and adventure rustled through her. "All right." She scooted toward the fire, rested on her knees, and then turned to face him, straddling his thighs but not pressing against him. A whole new kind of shiver wandered through her.

He held the top of the sleeping bags, keeping them up around their necks. His eyes gleamed a predatory green in the darkness. "Now wiggle your nose."

Here she was, naked and wrapped in a sleeping bag with the hot sheriff, and he wanted her to wiggle her nose? "Are you crazy?"

"No. Frostbite attacks fingers, toes, noses, and ears," he said, lifting his hand to rub a knuckle across her nose. "Hurt?"

Her breath caught in her throat, and she shook her head. Her body felt languid, and the warmth surrounding her was intoxicating. A tattoo covered his left pec above his heart, extending over his shoulder. A deadly Osprey with a sharp beak, wide wings, and wicked talons. Keeping his gaze, she tapped each finger against his chest, finding a knife scar to the left of his heart and free of the bird of prey. A deep one, blade in. "That had to hurt."

"Yeah."

"Wiggle your nose," she murmured. "How are your fingers, toes, and the rest?"

"Fine. I wasn't under the surface as long as you. Not even close." He ran his finger along the shell of her ear. "We got you out quickly, but the freezing cold ride to the hut took too much time, so we have to keep an eye on your health. Understand?"

She nodded, unable to do anything else. The moment felt too intimate.

"All right. We need to stay wrapped for a little while so I can't look at your feet. I'm going to reach around you and press against your toes." He checked out the shell of her other ear, and she shivered. He paused. "You okay?"

She gulped. "Yeah." Her voice was throaty, but she'd swallowed water, so that must explain it.

He reached around her, gently gripping the toes that were pressed against her butt. "Tingles or pain?"

"A little, but not too much." The wind whistled eerily outside as darkness dropped hard and fast. She shivered. "What time do you think it is?"

"Probably around three in the afternoon." He tucked the sleeping bag closer around her neck. As much heat came from him as from the fire behind her, and she didn't want to turn back around. He'd kept from looking inside the bag, anyway. Her thighs brushed his, and other parts of her warmed. There had to be mere centimeters between her breasts and his chest.

He winced and straightened out his left leg.

"You okay?" she asked.

"Yeah. Took a bullet in combat but sometimes the leg still aches a bit. No worries."

Snow scattered against the door.

She licked her chapped lips. The fire cracked, and she jumped. "Is my cell phone still in my pants?"

"No. Both your gun and phone fell in the river."

Just fantastic. She looked around the small hut. "What if the person who shot at us comes here?"

"My gun is right behind me, but we won't need it. The storm is bad enough that nobody can walk up to the hut, and I'll hear any snowmobile or four-wheeler long before it pulls up." He brushed hair away from her eyes. "You're safe. I won't let anything happen to you."

Her hand now flattened on his chest, and his heart beat steadily beneath her warm palm. "I think that's my line. FBI and all."

His grin was a quick flash of teeth that mesmerized her. "Didn't we agree that soldier tops agent?"

That image flashed through her brain fast and hard. While he probably hadn't meant the innuendo, her body didn't catch that fact. "I can deal with danger," she mumbled.

"You just can't let a man take care of you, now can you?"

Even the words made her uncomfortable. "I've never known one to stick around long enough to try." She wanted to ask more about the knife wound, but he probably didn't want to share stories from the service.

"No dad?" he asked.

"Nope. Took off when I was just six, and I don't remember him." But she remembered her mother, who'd done her best. "We were poor, and my mom drank too much, but she loved me." Her vulnerability felt overwhelming in her naked state. "She died of cirrhosis of the liver right before I turned twenty."

He shifted his bulk. "I'm sorry. No husband or fiancé in your world right now?"

"Now you ask that?" she whispered, oddly comfortable, considering she sat naked in a sleeping bag with a man twice her size—straddling him. His answering smile almost softened his face. "I've dated some, but work has always taken precedence." Truth be told, she'd never found a man as interesting as work. Until now. "What about you?"

It was impressive how he kept his gaze on her face and hadn't snuck a peek at her breasts. "I fell in love with my third-grade teacher, Mrs. Wimplevat, who baked the best snickerdoodles in the entire world. No other woman has ever come close." At her chuckle, he released the bag and settled back. "Okay. I've dated some and even had a fiancée once, but I guess the military always kept me moving."

A different spurt, one that felt like jealousy—which was totally ridiculous—took her. "What happened to the fiancée?"

"She didn't like my job and moved on with a doctor," he said. "Last I heard, they have six kids and are doing well."

The desire wandering through her body provided yet another ache to deal with on top of everything else. The fire crackled, and a log dropped loudly. "You're easy to talk to."

"Nobody has said that to me in my entire life." He probed her temple. "Did you hit your head?"

She laughed and smacked his hand out of the way. "Seriously, though. I do owe you a thank you for saving my life." He'd jumped right into the freezing cold to free her from the branch, endangering his life.

"My pleasure," he rumbled. "I figured I'd get you naked at some point, but this wasn't what I had in mind." A playful tug on her ear accompanied his words.

She embraced the lighter topic. "Are you teasing me?"

"Yeah. Glad you're alert enough to notice. You had me worried for a couple of minutes there." He leaned up to check the fire behind her. Apparently appeased, he settled back down in an impressive ripple of muscle she wished she hadn't noticed.

"I didn't ask. Are you sure you're okay?" she asked.

"Fine. I'll give it another half hour and then I'll stoke the fire again." His body provided a strong and heated wall around her, and she'd never felt so vulnerable and out of her element.

Hypothermia suddenly became the least of her worries.

"You're safe, Ophelia," he said, as if reading her mind. "I promise."

Her body relaxed, even as her mind remained alert. Maybe she should try to talk about business. The idea of that dead body in the snow flashed through her mind. The killing had appeared odd, possibly ritualistic, and Brock knew more than he said. She could tell. "What do you think killed that man? The one from EVE?" She needed to visit the EVE facility as soon as possible to figure this out.

"I don't know," he murmured, no longer seeming so close, yet he hadn't moved.

She sighed. "Yeah, you do. I've never seen anything like it. What kind of animal would do such a thing?"

He didn't answer.

All right. She'd pursue that question later. She had plenty more to work with. "We have nothing to do but talk. Why don't you tell me who you think shot Hank?"

He sighed. "We have plenty to do. I'll stoke the fire now."

Just when she almost got through to him, he shut her out. Well, if that was how he wanted to be, she'd get practical, too. "There must be a radio in one of those bins. Shouldn't we check in?"

He still hadn't moved. "No radio. The batteries freeze, so it's not worth it for the kids to stock them with the other supplies. Plus, they're expensive, and money is tight in Knife's Edge." The firelight danced across his face, hinting at a wildness she'd never encountered in another person. What was it about Alaska?

"Do the kids have some sort of town job, or do they stock the huts out of duty?" she asked.

Brock grinned. "The town hires them to make a little extra money, and they do a good job."

His smile should be bottled and sold back in the city. Her thighs were now becoming too warm while bracketing his. "I wish you'd let me in about Hank." Unable to resist, she flattened her hand over the wound too close to his heart.

"Hank's off-limits, but you can get in any other way you want." He leaned in, his breath warm on her lips. "I know another way we can spend the rest of the night."

Desire, full and languid, spread through her, warming her faster than any fire. Temptation had never been so painful before, but morning always came, and she couldn't do her job with regrets. Although, a guy like him might be worth it. "Not without trust, Brock."

"Fair enough." A veil dropped over his eyes. "We're both warm enough for it to be safe to sleep now. How about a kiss goodnight?"

Well, a kiss didn't take trust. Plus, if Brock sucked at kissing, she could get over this attraction to him and concentrate solely on the job she'd been assigned. "I guess one kiss would be okay."

He settled his broad palms on her bare hips. "Better than okay, I hope."

She lifted a shoulder, trying not to enjoy the feeling of him holding her in place. "You're probably too good-looking."

His upper lip quirked. "Huh?"

She placed her other hand on his chest, marveling at the strength. "Really good-looking guys, especially ones in the service, often don't have to try very hard with the ladies. Maybe you've just skated by." Why he brought out the imp in her, she'd never know.

He smiled, his gaze glittering. "Let's test that theory."

"Sure." She leaned in, pressing her mouth to his, wandering along his lips. Firm and full. When he smiled against her, she felt the sensation in her heart. Light and sweet.

Without moving his hands, he tilted his head, forcing hers to the side. Then he kissed her. Real and deep, full of intent and seeking. No longer sweet. He tasted of male and snow and mint, of everything that was Brock Osprey. Without moving a muscle, he took over the kiss, sending commanding need through her so fast she could only shut her eyes and let him give. And take.

Finally, he released her.

She panted, caught up, realizing belatedly that she'd pressed against him—all of her against all of him. His erection prodded her through his boxers, full and hard.

He swallowed, his eyes a deeper green than she would've thought possible. "How'd I do?" His low and rough voice licked across her skin.

She couldn't talk.

Amusement melded with the lust in his eyes. "I'll take it." He exhaled slowly, his hands still on her hips. "We continuing this or going to sleep?"

She couldn't. Oh, she wanted to, but she couldn't take that risk with him keeping secrets. Yet words still eluded her.

He slowly nodded. "All right. Sleep it is, then." In one smooth movement, he turned her, settled her down to face the fire, and spooned around her, providing warmth and safety.

She stared at the fire, her body hotter than the flames and ready to go. A tree cracked outside as the storm grew louder. That fast, she remembered the danger hunting them. "Who do you think shot at us?"

"You. They shot at you," he said quietly.

That's what she had thought.

CHAPTER FIFTEEN

Brock stacked new kindling and logs in the now-dead fireplace for the next poor sucker who needed fire as Ophelia took care of business outside. He'd already searched the area for the shooter, finding nothing. The storm had cleared, leaving a bright and freezing-cold day. Their clothes had dried through the night, and he couldn't see any evidence of frostbite on either of their bodies.

Once he'd settled her down to sleep the night before, he'd found the box of flares and fired the purple one, letting anybody looking for them know they were okay and not to take drastic measures. Ace and Christian must've believed him because they hadn't shown up, which was good since the storm had raged for hours.

Ophelia walked back inside, wearing her snow gear and his coat. "I'm not taking your jacket today."

"It's clear but cold, and I'm wearing long johns, a T-shirt, and a flannel, city girl. What about you?" He moved slowly in the morning, but a good meal and a workout would get his blood pumping again. As usual, his left leg hurt, but that'd never change. Sometimes, a bullet made itself known forever, and the one that had hit him while on a mission in Afghanistan would always leave an ache. But he'd left that world behind when the Navy honorably discharged him.

She huffed. "Just a sweater." Then she kicked her foot in a move that could only be interpreted as adorable.

Man, he had to get a grip on himself before he screwed everything up. "Exactly how long do you want to argue about this before we get going?" He needed coffee.

She lowered her chin, her skin a healthy hue, and her eyes clear. "Has anybody ever told you how stubborn you are?"

"Most folks who've been around me long enough to have a conversation." He finished repacking the bins with the now-dry blankets and sleeping bags.

She exhaled slowly. "How long did you work as a Navy SEAL?"

He securely shut the bin and turned to face her. They'd talked some before falling asleep the night before, mainly about the town and nothing serious, so the question caught him off guard. "Why?"

She pulled gloves out of his coat pocket and tugged them over her hands. "Just curious. You haven't said, and the meager file I found didn't tell me much. The way you moved yesterday after the shooter engaged seemed natural, as if you've been shot at quite a bit."

He strode across the room and opened the door, his gun at his waist. "I did my job." The last thing he wanted to discuss with her was his military time. Although it was a large part of his life—and one he sometimes missed. He sighed, looking out at the bright and cold-as-shit day. "I led a SEAL team." He moved for the snowmobile, brushing snow off the seat, his skin feeling too tight after sleeping around her all night and not kissing her again. The cold settled around him, burrowing into his bones.

"Impressive," Ophelia murmured, shutting the door behind herself. "You led a SEAL team?"

He paused in readying the seat. "I did. I left because of too many old wounds to move as fast as necessary, and I'm still in contact with my brothers from the team. We lost many, but we survived much." He had no clue why he gave her this. "Did I wake you last night?" He'd thought he'd awakened fast and quietly from the nightmare, but maybe not.

"No," she said. "You've been out for a year?"

"Almost." He straddled the machine, his senses on alert for whoever had shot at them. Nothing disturbed the silence.

She glared at the snow and then stepped away from the hut, gingerly putting her boots in the footprints he'd left in the snow. "You left a year ago, Ace left six months ago, and Christian?"

Where the heck was she going with this? "About two months."

"So, after Hank's death, you each left as soon as your tour ended." She patted her pinkening cheeks. "Yours ended in December and you came home for not only Christmas but for good. Hank died, and then both Ace and Christian retired from the military as soon as possible. That's interesting, right?"

Not really. "We're all around the same age, and we did our duty." Not in the mood to be questioned, he twisted the key, pushed the button, and the engine roared to life.

She pressed on, reaching him. "Except for Damian. Or is his current tour not up yet?"

"Get on the sled, Ophelia." Brock's temper spiked faster than the river had last spring.

She faced him head-on, not afraid in the slightest. "I won't let this go." Then something caught her eye. She lifted her head, delight brightening her expression. "Is that a bald eagle?"

He couldn't look away from her face. To him, she looked intriguing and lovely, which were two words he'd never used about anything or anyone before. "Yeah, that's an eagle." Probably. Tons flew about.

She craned her neck to see better, her sapphire eyes sparkling. "I've never seen one in real life. He's majestic, right?"

"He's a bird of prey, Olly."

Her attention dropped from the sky to him. "I seem to be drawn to that kind of thing."

Did the sight of the eagle leave her unguarded, or was she flirting with him? "You think I'm a hunter, Agent?" His blood started to hum and not from the thought of coffee.

"Oh, you're definitely a hunter, Commander," she whispered, biting her lip like she wanted to solve an interesting puzzle. "Do you think somebody shot at me because I saw that body from EVE or because of the cases I'm trying to solve—including Hank's?"

If that was her idea of flirting, the woman needed to buy a book about the matter. If he spent one more night in her presence, he would lose his mind. Then he caught her meaning, the deeper one, and barked out a laugh. "Was that your casual way of asking if one of my brothers shot at you yesterday because you're investigating Hank's death?"

She lifted a shoulder, clearly challenging him, although she looked miniature in his jacket. "The bullets impacted near me and not you."

"Not a chance did either of my brothers shoot at you." He gestured for her to get on the sled. They'd have to travel past where they'd been fired upon the day before, and he wanted full daylight for the trek.

"How can you be so sure?" She finally straddled the machine.

He handed back her helmet. "Because neither one of them would've missed."

❄

OPHELIA HELD on tightly as Brock drove the snowmobile fast, twisting in and out of treed areas, his body feeling taut and alert. The shooter had waited for them the day before, knowing their path, so they might be waiting right now. The sun shone down as if the storm had never happened, the sky a true blue, and the snow drifting softly and sparkling with life. After maneuvering through the hills, he kept away from clearings and gullies, riding along the river but not close to the rushing water.

When they neared the area where she'd fallen in, she tapped his leg. He ignored her. She tapped harder. Still nothing. Fine. The snow appeared thick enough that she could drop and roll through it, probably stopping before hitting a tree. She released her hold on him, bunching her legs to slide from the snowmobile.

In a shockingly fast move, he twisted and snagged her around the waist with his left arm while also yanking the machine to the right. Using the momentum of the turn, he pulled her around and in front of him, plopping her unceremoniously to face him, straddling him.

It all happened too fast for her to struggle, much less scream. When he pressed the throttle again, the force propelled her flush against him, and she pushed against his chest, her feet fighting for purchase on the footboards.

He drove between trees, turning into a stop in the middle of several spruces and punched the kill switch.

She flipped her face guard up and then reached for his. "What are you doing?"

He ripped his helmet completely free and looked around, his body tense. "Be. Quiet."

She went on full alert, scouting the area. Slumps of snow fell from tree boughs, but the wilderness seemed peaceful. The area *felt* peaceful.

Finally, his body relaxed, and he faced her, his expression

hard. "What did you think you were doing?" He clenched his teeth so hard she heard them grinding at the back of his jaw.

"You ignored my tapping." Wasn't that obvious?

"Yeah. I'm not stopping at the area where somebody fired at us from cover yesterday." He looked around again.

She breathed out. "I'm a federal agent who found a dead body on federal land yesterday. I need to secure the scene, or at least take more pictures since I think I lost my phone in the river. Please let me use your phone. At the very least, I'd like to make sure whoever shot at us hasn't returned."

"No." Brock smacked snow off his helmet. "I'll bring Ace or Christian back out later for the body."

She stiffened, sitting straighter. "That's a nice thought, Big Man, but you're not the law enforcement around here, remember? You're not the sheriff. I am an agent, and I'm calling the shots."

The look he gave her made her want to swallow, so she didn't. Instead, she faced him, wondering if she had a chance in a fight with a Navy SEAL. Oh, she could grapple, but he had skills beyond the norm.

"This isn't federal land," he said mildly, surprising her. "Not your jurisdiction. Sorry, Agent."

He didn't sound sorry.

She moved to get off the sled. "That's okay. I'll just—"

The buzz of an engine caught her attention, and she stilled. He slipped off the snowmobile, taking his gun from beneath his jacket and pulling her off to stand behind him. "Get down."

Why had she dropped her damn gun in the river? She dropped to her haunches along with him, using the sled and the surrounding trees as cover.

An animal bounded out of the trees lining the river, white fur flying, eyes blazing. "Wolf Warrior," Brock murmured, standing and holding a hand out to help her. She ignored his offer, planted a palm on the seat of the sled, and stood all by herself. It would've been a better accomplishment if he didn't look so damn amused.

The animal licked her glove and whined. She patted his already large head, even though he was still a puppy. "Is he a wolf or a dog?"

"Both. I think we're calling him Tika," Brock said.

Two sleds rode into view, following the animal. Christian rode in the front, a shotgun slung over his shoulder and the same dark hat on his head. His snowmobile gleamed black with deep red accents, while Ace's sported blue hues with black stripes. They stopped, both remaining quiet and studying them.

"You okay?" Ace asked.

Brock nodded. "Yeah. Somebody shot at us yesterday. Since you're here, let's take a moment to see if there's anything to find, although the storm probably obliterated any evidence."

Christian tilted his head. "Shot at you? With what?"

"Shotgun," Brock returned, pointing toward the river. "Took cover in here somewhere and was a crappy shot."

"Unless he didn't want to hit you," Ace murmured, jumping from his sled into snow up to his thighs and striding into a bigger stand of green trees Ophelia couldn't identify.

Christian sat back on his sled, removed his glasses and revealed those odd eyes. His helmet didn't have a face guard. "Who would shoot at you?"

"At her," Brock said, tucking his gun back into place.

"Ah," Christian said, his face clearing. "Makes sense."

She frowned. "Hey."

He shrugged. "Nosy people get shot at around here."

She sat on the sled. "I want to go back to the body. We're safe in numbers, right?"

"Body?" Christian asked.

Brock straddled the sled, holding out an elbow so she could swing on behind him. "Yeah. Follow us." He pushed the ignition button and the engine roared again before he turned the machine and drove toward the river. Ice already covered the area where she'd fallen through, but her black coat could still be seen trapped down low.

She shivered at the memory.

Brock stopped the sled.

She pushed off, sinking in the snow and looking at the pristine white mounds. "He's buried?"

"Maybe." Brock moved close to the river and then took several wide steps away before stopping. "The body lay right around here." Slowly, he began kicking snow out of the way in every direction. Soon, a little bit of red ice spread out.

Ace emerged on his sled through the trees, stopping near Christian, who sat on his machine watching. "I found a decent vantage point, but the storm destroyed any evidence of a shooter."

That figured.

More red ice spread out as Brock kicked.

Ophelia's breath caught. "You found his blood." She moved to help, kicking snow as gently as she could. They cleared a decent area but only discovered more red snow sparkling like rubies in the sunlight.

She looked up, meeting Brock's gaze. "The body is gone."

CHAPTER SIXTEEN

After an unsuccessful argument with Ophelia about having the doctor take a look at her, Brock stopped the snowmobile at Sam's Tavern, where several sleds lined up neatly parked outside. Ace leaped off his and strode inside, no doubt wanting a double. Christian had disappeared a mile before town, quietly and without a goodbye.

Brock could use coffee. A lot of it.

Flossy hustled outside, her black coat worn in several places and her boots sliding across the ice before she regained her balance. Brock frowned. The elderly woman needed a new coat, and he'd have to find a way to get her one without ticking her off. He partially straightened.

She shook her hand at them. "Are you two all right? Where did you stay the night?" She paused, and her papery skin dusted with pink. "Oh. Did you stay with Brock, Olly?"

Ophelia made a strangled sound.

Brock shook his head. "We got caught in the storm after taking a tumble into the river, and we waited it out."

Flossy's thin eyebrows rose. "My goodness. Has Doc checked either of you for frostbite?"

"We're fine, Flossy," Brock said. "Just want to get some food and drink before I go back out searching. Olly will stay here with you." He didn't care if Ophelia argued because she needed rest to get over that dunking. There was no reason for her to go out searching, especially since it would be for a body and shooter as well as Wyatt.

Ophelia turned her head and sneezed.

"Bless you," Brock said automatically, focusing back on Flossy. "Is there still food at Sam's, or should we head to the diner?" They both needed warm food, and now. He moved to get off the sled.

Flossy shook her head, her red-feathered earrings shaking. "The food is warm at the diner, and I think Gus made his chili, so go there. But first, the Miller boys found Wyatt. He's at Doc's right now. I heard something's wrong with him, Sheriff."

Brock paused. He wasn't the sheriff and had no right to check on Wyatt.

"Let's go," Ophelia said, tugging him to sit.

Well, she was an FBI agent, and she did need a ride. Good excuse. Plus, maybe Doc could examine her feet for residual frostbite. "You've got it." He sat and twisted the ignition, circling around to head toward Dalika River Road and then driving a block. The town was set in a grid with three roads coming off the river drive with buildings on either side. The hospital, Doc's office, and dentist all shared a heavy wooden building that abutted Dalika River Road and First Street, which ran parallel to Main Street, with Second Street on the other side of Main.

He pulled the sled up front to the double doors and waited for Ophelia to slide off before following her.

She shook snow off her pink pants and sighed before stepping across the shoveled walk and pushing her way in. He followed, kicking snow off his boots on the rubber mat right inside. She did the same.

The waiting room, dotted with folding chairs, appeared

quiet and empty. Someone had painted snowmen on the windows, and Christmas music filtered through invisible speakers. Nancy Phylets looked up from the reception counter and smiled, her red lipstick bright and cheerful. The woman was in her early thirties, smart, and frighteningly efficient, even with a swollen belly, which would be her fourth baby. Probably her fourth son. "Sheriff. It's good to see you."

He sighed.

Ophelia moved forward, lifting her badge from her chest with the chain. "I'm—"

"Olly Spilazi, FBI," Nancy said, tapping papers smoothly into a manila file, her black hair in a no-nonsense bun. "You're sure a pretty one. Look just like that Angie Harmon from that lawyer show. Are you Italian?"

"Yes." Ophelia tucked the badge away. "I'd like to see Wyatt Yankovich, if I could. What's his status?"

Nancy leaned forward, her dark eyes wide. "He's lost his mind. Is babbling something about a knife and blood. It's so weird. Doc is checking to see if he hit his head or something."

Ophelia straightened. "Knife and blood? Anything else?"

"Not that I know," Nancy said.

"Any frostbite?" Brock asked.

Nancy nodded. "Oh, yeah. We have him on a drip with hands and feet already wrapped."

Brock winced. "How bad is the tissue damage?"

Nancy shrugged. "You'll have to ask Doc." Metal file cabinets lined the wall behind her with potted plants spread across the tops, and she turned toward an open doorway to her left to yell. "Doc? Sheriff and the FBI lady are here."

"I'm not the sheriff," Brock said.

"Sure, you are. We elected you." Nancy rolled her eyes. "Bobby said you need to stop being a dork and just take the job." She smiled at Ophelia. "Bobby is my husband, and he and Brock played hockey together in high school. I headed the drama club, and I got the two of them to act in Macbeth. I'll bring you some pictures. It's hilarious."

Ophelia blinked. "Sure."

Oh, man. Brock subtly shook his head at Nancy. He and Ophelia were not dating, and he didn't need to be fixed up. Nancy's eyes sparkled, but she held her tongue. He'd sigh again, but why bother? "This way." He gestured Ophelia toward the open doorway and followed her through. The long hallway led to several examination rooms and one trauma center. "Doc?" he called out.

Just what had Wyatt seen?

OPHELIA FOLLOWED Brock down the hallway and stopped short as a woman emerged from one of the examination rooms, her blond hair in a ponytail and oval-shaped glasses covering her blue eyes. She wore aqua-blue scrubs over a white turtleneck. A stethoscope hung around her neck. "What is all the yelling about?"

"Hey, Doc," Brock said. "This is Special Agent Ophelia Spilazi from the FBI."

Ophelia stepped forward and held out a hand for a firm shake. "Hi." All right. She'd stereotyped, figuring Doc would be a grizzly old guy with a grumpy nature and a heart of gold. This woman looked to be in her early thirties with intelligent eyes and stylish boots lined with fur. "Nice to meet you."

"And you. My full name, which nobody seems to remember, even though I've only been in town since September, is May Smirnov."

Ophelia tilted her head. "You're new to town?"

"She saved us," Brock said. "We've had a series of rotating doctors for a few years, and not one of them has wanted to stay because of the weather. Doc here signed a three year contract."

The doctor nodded. "The signing bonus was a great temptation, and I always wanted to work in a more rural area as a full family practice. I love the snow and quiet." The doctor looked beyond Ophelia to Brock. "Why did you miss poker night last week? My wallet is light, and I wanted a knit hat from that new store in Anchorage. Now I'll miss the next supply plane."

Brock snorted. "If I remember right, Smitty won the pot the week before."

Smirnov pressed her pink lips together, the light in her eyes dancing. "I don't know how, but I think he cheated." She rolled back on her heels and stuck her hands into the pockets of her scrubs.

Just how close was Brock with the pretty doctor? Ophelia ignored a totally irrational spurt of curiosity and cleared her throat. "How is Mr. Yankovich?"

The doctor winced. "Are you asking in an official capacity?"

"Yes," Ophelia said. Hopefully, the doctor wouldn't require a warrant before giving her information.

Dr. Smirnov shrugged. "Fair enough since the sheriff is with you. Wyatt has frostbite on his extremities, and it's too early to tell if I'll be able to save his fingers. We've wrapped all injured skin and are administering an IV with a tissue plasminogen activator. We'll see from there. I've provided him pain medication, and he's currently resting in relative comfort."

"Can we see him?" Ophelia asked.

Smirnov looked at Brock, who nodded. "All right, but I have to warn you, he's not quite there."

Ophelia shoved down irritation at the doctor seeking Brock's approval, but in a small town like this, she remained an outsider. A federal one. "Thank you." Yes, she wore fluorescent pink snow pants that looked like they'd been through a meat grinder, her hair frizzed in every direction, and her bruised face lacked makeup, but she straightened her shoulders and strode into the room with as much authority as she could find.

Her slightly stuffy nose left her hoping she didn't smell too bad.

Brock followed her inside.

Wyatt Yankovich looked tall and lanky with bluish-pale skin and red hair sticking up in tufts. His brown eyes were wide, and his shoulders kept jerking beneath a blanket drawn up to his neck, even though his torso remained elevated in the hospital bed. He slowly turned his head. Red burns from the cold—and probably the wind—marred his entire neck and lower jaw. "Sheriff?"

Brock sighed. "Wyatt, this is Ophelia. She needs to talk to you, okay?" Pressing a large hand to the small of Ophelia's back, Brock gently prodded her toward two purple plastic chairs by the bed.

She took in the machinery beeping quietly around the patient. Brock's hand at her back should be annoying and not reassuring, yet she didn't pull away from him. Her body ached, her eyes hurt, and an exhaustion she'd never felt before kept weighing down her limbs. As soon as she interviewed the obviously frightened kid, she needed to sleep and recuperate from the day. "Hello."

Wyatt looked younger than nineteen. "Brock? What's out there? What happened?" The kid's lips trembled. "Where's my wife?"

May poked her head in the door. "Sylvie is on her way, Wyatt. The Miller boys took a side-by-side out to get her."

Wyatt shuddered. "I hope they're armed."

The doctor exchanged a look with Brock and then disappeared.

Awareness ticked up Ophelia's still-cold shoulders. She sat, trying to look reassuring. "What happened to you, Wyatt?"

The kid sniffed. "I got caught in the storm during the day." His voice lowered, and he looked over her shoulder at Brock, shock slackening his oval-shaped face. "It was still daylight, Brock. They don't come out in the day. Why was he killed during the day?"

Brock drew out the chair next to her. "You're not making sense, Wyatt. You're in shock."

Ophelia sat up straighter. "Who doesn't come out in the daylight?"

Wyatt removed his hands from under the covers, revealing bandages covering them up to his elbows. "I saw the dead EVE man. With his eyes gouged out completely. Gone. Always the eyes." He gulped and then gagged.

"Whoa." Brock looked around frantically. "Do you need a bucket?"

Ophelia leaned forward, her instincts humming. "You saw the dead body? Did you see who killed him?" She fought to keep her voice level. "Did you get any pictures?" Why had she dropped her phone in the river, damn it?

Wyatt looked away from Brock and focused on her for the first time. With his pupils dilated from the pain medication, he finally seemed to see her. "You're the federal lady. Aren't you supposed to be in Anchorage?"

"I brought her here," Brock said quietly.

"Huh." Wyatt glanced down at her bright pink snow pants and then back up to her head. "What happened to you?"

She barely kept from smoothing down her hair. "I fell into a river and had a rough night. What happened to you?"

Wyatt swayed side to side as if he couldn't get his balance, even on the bed. "I faced a storm and then hid from a monster. A real one. It's true, Brock." He shook his head and gulped again. "I thought it was all bullshit, but it's true. They're out there. Just waiting for eyes."

Ophelia's blood pumped faster, and she pressed a hand to the blanket on the side of the bed. "What's out there, Wyatt?"

The kid shook his head. "Ask Christian. I saw him there yesterday. I think. Didn't I?"

Brock jerked. "Christian? My brother?"

Wyatt nodded.

Ophelia stiffened. "You saw Christian out there with the dead man? Before or after the murder?" Or during? Christian seemed to have issues. Had he killed that man for some reason? "Wyatt?"

Wyatt shook his head. "I'm done. Need sleep." He curled onto his side, facing the other way. "Tell me when Sylvie gets here."

Brock stood and placed a hand beneath Ophelia's elbow to help her up. "The kid needs sleep. We can talk to him again tomorrow."

She shook her head, but Wyatt started snoring. Well, all right. She'd question Brock first. "I'd like to stay and speak with Wyatt's wife." Maybe Sylvie knew something about whatever the heck Wyatt had been talking about. Ophelia walked out into the hallway with Brock, nearly running into Dr. Smirnov.

The doctor shook her head. "I spoke with Sylvie on a radio, and she's beside herself. As her doctor, I'm refusing access until she has seen her husband and calmed down. That's only if I don't have to administer a sedative for her."

Irritation forced Ophelia to clench her back teeth. "All right. Please have her call me at Flossy's when she's available to speak, as I've lost my phone." She couldn't wait to jump into the warm pink decorated bed and sleep for hours. "For now, Wyatt is talking about some sort of monster that gouges out eyes. Do you have any idea what that's about?"

The doctor shook her head, no expression revealing her thoughts. "Wyatt is heavily medicated. No doubt he's just talking through the trauma of a night spent in the freezing cold. I don't believe in monsters. Supernatural ones, anyway."

The image of the EVE man's clawed face and gouged out eyes flashed through Ophelia's memory. "Oh, I'm not so sure about that," she murmured. Monsters definitely existed. "I'm going to find this one."

CHAPTER SEVENTEEN

After a night of sleeping like the dead, Brock pushed open the door to the sheriff's office, surprised to find it unlocked. Warmth hit him instantly as he walked inside, and he stopped short at seeing Flossy behind the receptionist's desk, humming to muted Christmas music from a radio behind her as she organized case files. "What are you doing?" He shut out the cold with a shove of his hip to the door.

Flossy looked up, her eyes focusing behind her thick glasses. "Since you've finally gotten your butt to work, I decided to take my old job back. I ran this office for Sheriff Blazerton, you know."

Brock paused. "I'm not the sheriff."

Flossy rolled her eyes. "Stop being an ass, Brock." She patted the gray hair piled on her head and pulled a pencil from above her ear. "We've got a federal agent in town, a bunch of unsolved murders or disappearances, and now a dead EVE man with his eyes clawed out. We totally need a sheriff."

Brock banked his temper. "Then find somebody who wants to be the sheriff."

A swish of sound echoed, and Ophelia walked out of the

conference room. Today, the woman wore a light green sweater and dark jeans. She started. "Oh. Good morning, Brock." The scent of strawberries wafted his way.

He barely kept back a grimace. Instead, he studied her from head to toe. Her eyes sparkled, and her complexion had a healthy glow. "Any residual effects from falling into the river?" he asked. With their health restored, he could take a moment and appreciate the feeling of her naked body against him the day before. Damn, she had some nice curves.

She shook her head, and black hair feathered over her shoulders. "No. A good night's sleep and then one of Flossy's delicious breakfasts have me back on track. How about you?"

His stomach growled. "I'm fine." He hadn't even had coffee yet.

Ophelia wavered and then straightened her shoulders to look even taller. "There's hot coffee in the small kitchenette, and then I'd like to formally interview you, with recording, about Hank Osprey's death. Afterward, we need to find Christian so I can question him regarding Wyatt Yankovich's statement about him seeing Christian around the now missing EVE victim."

"I'm not in the mood for questioning, Olly," Brock retorted. But he was in the mood for coffee. He started to walk toward the kitchenette.

Flossy cleared her throat. "If you're not finally going to admit you're the sheriff, why are you here?"

He paused. "I came to check on Amos. Ophelia upset him the other day."

Flossy nodded. "He's fine. I took scones down to him when I arrived, and he's glad you've decided to get to work. Said it's been lonely not hearing footsteps above his head." She lowered her chin. "There are more scones in the kitchen. For the sheriff."

"There isn't one. But I'm here, and I'm starving." Brock turned without another word and hustled into the kitchenette, downing two of the delicious scones before pouring himself a generous mug of the fragrant-smelling coffee. He didn't think Flossy would come after him with a letter opener for eating the scones, but even if she did, the treat was worth it. Of course, they were strawberry.

He just couldn't get away from the fruit.

As if to prove the point, Ophelia entered the room and refilled her coffee cup. "I've set up a war room in the conference room with the three most urgent cases, and I need to interview you for all three. Now is a good time. I'd rather not call in reinforcements from the federal government, but I will."

The skin at the nape of his neck prickled, and he forced a smile. "There's nothing I like more than a threat first thing in the morning."

The woman didn't blink. "It wasn't so much a threat as a plan of action. Take it as you will."

Not many people met his gaze when he turned growly. The fact that she did had his unwilling admiration for her growing even more. "Fine, Special Agent Spilazi. Let's take a look at your interviewing skills."

"Excellent, Sheriff." With that last zinger, she turned on her boot heel and strode down the hallway to the conference room.

Yeah, he watched her butt as she moved. The woman had a phenomenal ass. He took a deep drink of the coffee, letting the heat and flavor slam into his gut. Then he followed her.

She sat across from him with records, photos, and notepads stacked neatly in front of her. Behind her, she'd used the old chalkboard and taped up four areas showing her cases: Hank Osprey, EVE Victim, Tamara Randsom, and Missing Persons.

He lifted an eyebrow. "Missing persons?"

She nodded, rifling through the notebooks for a clear one on the bottom. "Yes. Statistically, Alaska has more missing persons than any other state in the Union, and several are from this area. I started thinking about the victim wearing the EVE jacket, about Wyatt's allegations, and then figured maybe there's a connection. So, I added another section to my current load." Then she looked up, her blue eyes clear and bright. "After I solve those, there are more cases, as you know. No wonder the FBI assistant director wanted somebody brought into this place."

Brock rubbed the scruff on his jaw. "Alaska has so many missing people because it's Alaska. Some come here to *become* missing. Others succumb to the wilds and the weather. Statistically."

"Maybe," she allowed. "Although if I wanted somebody to disappear, this is where I'd bring them."

"I'll keep that in mind." He took another drink of his vanilla-flavored coffee. How did Flossy create delicious coffee every time? "So. What do you want to know, Agent?"

Ophelia clicked her pen to write. "Let's start with your brother, Christian. Is it possible he murdered the man we found in the snow with his eyes gouged out?"

OPHELIA WAITED PATIENTLY after hitting Brock with the first question.

His smile surprised her. Slow, smooth, and amused. "No."

She blinked but made sure not to look down at her blank paper and show weakness. It didn't help that the former Navy SEAL had probably been trained by the best to withstand interrogation. Nor did it help that he was the sexiest man she'd ever seen outside of movies...and he'd saved her life the other day, getting her naked for survival and being a perfect gentleman the entire time. The feeling of his hard—incredibly hard—body bracketing her all night had given her dreams that should embarrass her. "If your brother requires assistance, I want to help him," she said quietly.

Brock's gaze softened to a mossy green. "If my brother needs help, I'll get it for him." His hand looked big and broad around the large coffee mug. "Christian has never been good with people, and he lives off the grid because it's his choice, not because he wants or needs to hide. If he wanted somebody dead, he'd kill them with either one bullet or a clean slice across the jugular."

Ophelia swallowed. "You're okay with the fact that your brother could be a killer?"

Brock's eyebrows drew down—barely. "Honey? What do you think we did in the Navy?"

"I see. Your contention is that Christian didn't kill that man because the scene felt too bloody and, well, downright strange?"

Brock lifted one powerful shoulder. "Sure. Plus, there's no reason Christian would want that guy dead. It doesn't make sense."

Fair enough. "Wyatt said he saw Christian that day," she reminded Brock.

"Wyatt was out of his mind," Brock returned. "The guy might've seen Christian another time."

She tilted her head to the side. "I don't know about that. It seems to me that if Christian doesn't want to be seen, then he isn't."

"Good point. Maybe Wyatt didn't see Christian at all." Brock kicked back in the chair.

Nice deflection. "That's not where I was going, and you know it." She tapped her pen on the paper. "What was Wyatt talking about? What mythical creatures only come out at night?" Although she'd been exhausted the night before, she'd spent time on her laptop searching for legends about the area and finding nothing. Dangerous wild animals included bears and wolves, but neither were known to just gouge out eyes. "Talk to me, Brock."

"Honey—" he started.

She held up a hand. "You can't charm me, SEAL boy. Don't honey, darlin', or sweet cheeks me. It won't work." Although, she was a complete liar. Something about his rugged voice and the endearments made her go all gooey when she really couldn't afford to do so. "All right?"

"Sweet cheeks?" Amusement glimmered in the impossible green of his eyes.

She gave him her best federal-agent glare.

The amusement deepened. "All right. Here it is. There are legends, told by parents to keep kids from venturing out into the Alaska wilderness at night, about creatures that kill and gouge out eyes. The truth is that most scavenger animals instinctively target soft tissue first because it's easier to consume. This means that areas like the eyes, lips, and internal organs are often the first to be eaten, which is why victims' eyes are usually missing when scavengers have been involved."

It was a plausible explanation. Almost. "The victim from EVE hadn't been dead long enough for scavengers to attack. Whoever killed him took his eyes."

Brock nodded. "Yep."

"That seems ritualistic, don't you think?" she asked, her mind running.

Brock exhaled slowly. "Yep."

"There are more than the average number of serial killers in Alaska, you know," she said, her instincts flaring wide awake.

His frown drew his eyebrows all the way down this time. "How many serial killers are there?"

She pursed her lips. "Not as many as people think, but I believe Alaska has its share."

He snorted. "That's not true. They're all in the Pacific Northwest."

"Not true." She looked down at her still-clean notepaper. "So far, you aren't helping with my cases." She looked up. "I've called the EVE facility and have a meeting scheduled for tomorrow at noon to discuss the victim."

Brock lost his frown. "How the hell did you manage that?"

She wrote the date on the top of her notepaper as well as his name. "I had my immediate boss at the FBI make the arrangements. Personally."

Brock blew out a whistle. "Impressive."

She tried not to warm at the compliment and still needed that additional research on the place. Her contact in DC hadn't gotten back to her yet. "I don't see why if EVE is just a research facility."

"It is and always has been," Brock returned. "They study the ionosphere, and they're not big on visitors. Did they give you any indication about the identity of the victim?"

She shook her head. "I haven't talked to anybody yet. They want to meet in person, whoever they are." Curiosity roared through her. "Can you give me any more information before I go?"

"Yeah. I'm going with you." When she just looked at him, he smiled, all charm. "The ride isn't easy, and you'll need somebody who knows the way. I'm probably the only person in town who will voluntarily take you through that gulley and along the river. It's dangerous this time of year."

What wasn't? It was uncomfortably reassuring to know he'd be accompanying her. She had to get over this dependence on him—after they met with the EVE personnel tomorrow. "I'd like for you to join me," she said, almost primly.

His chuckle warmed parts of her. "All right. Are we done for the day?"

"Ha. I've only been here for a few days, and I'm already finished with the secrets, Brock. I think you suspect who killed Hank, and for the life of me, I can't figure out why you'd want to protect them. Unless it was one of your brothers." Although, the entire town seemed close, almost like family. Maybe he'd protect any of them. Her gut told her he was innocent, even though he'd found the body. Unease filtered through her. Was she being objective?

His head lifted, and his eyelids dropped to half-mast. "I'm not keeping secrets from you. I don't know who shot Hank, but I guarantee it wasn't one of my brothers. We're all trained, and we wouldn't make a mistake like that—considering you said the shotgun blast didn't kill him, and he actually drowned." His voice roughened and became hoarse.

What was he hiding? "Was he dead, already drowned, when you found him?"

"I already answered that question in the affirmative," Brock said.

Oh, he was good, and if she didn't know his background, she'd believe him. He looked earnest, regretful, and honest. But logic ruled, and his answer didn't make sense. Why didn't he want vengeance for his guardian? "You loved him," she said quietly.

Brock nodded. "We all loved him. He was everything."

"Then why don't you want to know who killed him?" she pressed. Something eluded her, but no matter how hard she tried, she couldn't grasp it.

"I've talked all I'm gonna about it," Brock said. "You've interviewed Ace, as well as Flossy, I assume. That leaves Christian."

She blinked. "Yeah. I didn't figure he'd be easy to pin down."

"He isn't, but I spoke with him last night."

She perked up. "You did?"

"Yes. Christian sometimes uses my shop to tweak his snowmobile, and I told him he had to speak with you to avoid more folks landing in town. Figured that would work." Brock glanced at his phone just as the outside door opened loudly. "Although, he's here now. I guess you're up, Agent. Good luck with my brother. He's a peach."

CHAPTER EIGHTEEN

Brock exited the conference room and met his brother near the door. "Thanks for coming."

Christian brushed snow off his black jacket, taking up all the available space in the reception area. "Didn't see as you gave me much choice."

True. Threatening Christian with the arrival of the entire federal government definitely worked. More people in town made the area too busy for the guy. "She's just doing her job. One interview and you'll be done." He looked down at the wild animal sitting patiently by Christian's feet and hid his surprise that Christian had actually shown up.

Flossy fluttered her hands. "Christian, it's so nice to see you in town. There's coffee in the back room, and if the sheriff didn't eat all the scones, there should be a couple left for you." She fluttered her eyelashes. "They're strawberry. Your favorite."

Christian gifted her with a very rare smile, and swear to God, the woman twittered.

Brock shook his head. Why did women, aged twenty to eighty, find his brother sexy? The guy lived as a cranky recluse, wilder than the land surrounding them. "I didn't eat all the scones, Flossy." He didn't bother to correct her about his title because the woman wouldn't listen.

Flossy looked his way. "I'm glad you're finished with your interview. Glennis McGillicuddy just called, and she needs help."

Brock straightened. "What kind of help?"

Flossy shrugged. "Dunno, but she was crying. The old bag is in her nineties, you know."

Christian coughed to cover an obvious laugh.

Brock reached for his jacket hanging on a peg by the door. "That isn't nice, Floss."

Flossy straightened her bony shoulders. "She called my tomatoes *store-bought* last year during the fair, and she's a cranky old bag. Period. To think I'd buy tomatoes. My greenhouse is twice the size of hers. I mean, really." Muttering to herself, she started stacking papers again before turning and inserting different case files into the metal filing cabinets.

Brock pulled on his jacket. Too bad he couldn't do the same with his patience.

Christian looked at him, his eye level exactly at Brock's. "You aren't staying for my interview with the Fed?"

"No," Brock said shortly, readjusting the gun at the back of his waist. "You're on your own." He didn't want to watch his brother answer questions, so he focused on Flossy. "I'll be back after seeing what Glennis needs." He brushed by his brother and opened the door.

"You sure seem like the sheriff to me," Christian said, turning and stalking down to the conference room with the pup at his heels.

Brock slammed the door a little harder than necessary. He stomped down the icy steps, ignoring the constant ache in his left leg. The river road should be plowed by this time in the morning, so he took his truck, driving down the main drag, checking both sides to ensure the stores stayed open and everything looked all right. Just like a sheriff would.

He shook his head, driving around the river and up to a subdivision of sorts set into the forest and surrounded by a cement-block fence that looked pretty covered in ice but remained useless for keeping out deer. He parked in the third driveway, noticing it hadn't been shoveled.

A thrumming started in his temples as he slipped on the icy sidewalk, regained his balance, and then walked up to the small, one-story home with smoke curling from the chimney. He knocked once.

The door almost immediately opened to reveal Glennis, her mascara-caked eyes leaking but her red lipstick firmly in place. "Oh, Sheriff. Thank goodness." She grasped his arm with bony fingers and pulled him into a small living room where the fire blasted heat in every direction.

He entered the house and shut the door, wanting to keep it open with every fiber of his being. It had to be a thousand degrees in there. A white cat with a huge belly sprawled across the top of the floral sofa, its blue eyes watching him lazily. "What can I do for you, Mrs. McGillicuddy?" he asked, his brow starting to sweat.

"It's Ranger." She wore a blue velour tracksuit with bleached white tennis shoes that matched her hair perfectly. Her shoulders stooped a little, but she was still a tall woman of at least five-ten, and she showed some strength as she pulled him through the living room and into the ultra-clean kitchen, where the older appliances sparkled. "He's in danger."

"Danger?" Sweat rolled down Brock's back.

"Yes." She tugged him to the sliding glass door and opened it.

Relief brushed across Brock along with a healthy, cold gust of wind, and he lifted his face in pure gratitude. "All right. Who's Ranger?" The gun still lay reassuringly at his waist.

She pushed him out the back door and pointed to a tall

paper birch tree in her backyard. "He's my other cat, and he's up in the tree. You have to get him down. Please, Sheriff."

Brock froze. "You want me to get a cat out of a tree?" This had to be a joke. It just had to be.

"Yes." Even very thin, the woman had power as she shoved him out the door. "You're the sheriff. You have to get Ranger down before he freezes to death. The little monster ran outside when I opened the door to toss out old water from flowers that'd died, and he shouldn't even be outside. Please, help."

For God's sake. If one of his brothers could see him, he'd never live it down. "I'll be right back." He paused. "If I do this for you, you have to back me with your neighbors that I'm not the sheriff."

"Of course, you're the sheriff." She pushed him again, and he let her. "Now get Ranger. Be careful—his claws are pretty sharp."

Of course, they were.

OPHELIA STUDIED the man across the table. Christian's green eye appeared the same color as Brock's eyes, while his jawline looked just like Ace's. He'd hung his black jacket over his chair, revealing a clean, long-sleeved, blue T-shirt that covered impressive muscles. "Thank you for coming to speak with me today," she said.

Christian tilted his head.

She swallowed and glanced at the sleeping wolf by his side before focusing on Brock's brother. "Who killed Hank?"

If she hoped to surprise him, she'd failed. At least by looking at him, anyway. "Dunno," Christian said, sitting eerily still.

She tapped her pen on the paper, once again having nothing to write down. "Did you kill him?"

"No." He didn't so much as twitch.

"All right. You're a smart guy, Christian. I can tell that much about you. Who do you think killed Hank?"

Christian still didn't move. "I don't."

She paused. "You don't...what?"

"I don't think about who shot Hank," he said, his voice smoother but just as deep as Brock's. "I remember the good times."

She let her instincts take over with the interview. "Do you believe in justice?"

"Yes."

"Vengeance?"

"Definitely." Christian studied her right back, his gaze intense.

She kept her composure, acutely aware of the animal at his feet looking tamer than him. "Don't you want either justice or vengeance for Hank?"

"No."

She waited for him to elaborate, but he didn't say another word. As an interviewer, she recognized somebody with training. He wouldn't fall for any of her usual tactics, so she needed to head in another direction. "Do you think Brock killed Hank?"

"Do you?" Christian asked, surprising her.

She forced a smile. "I'm asking the questions. Would you please answer mine?"

"Brock didn't kill Hank. It's okay for you to date him during this long and no doubt very cold winter," Christian said. "Are we done?"

Heat climbed up her face, but she didn't look away. "Do you think Ace killed Hank?"

"Nope." Christian reached down to pet the animal's head.

All right. "How about Amka?" Ophelia leaned forward. "She's a woman keeping secrets." Yeah, it was a shot in the dark, but she went with it.

Christian smiled, looking suddenly a lot more like Brock. "Amka wouldn't hurt a spider. True story. I've seen her put a moth on a piece of paper to take outside the bar and let free."

Interesting. "Do you spend a lot of time watching Amka?"

"No." The smile diminished, but no anxiety showed on Christian's angled face. It was impossible to read him.

"Does she know you have feelings for her?" Ophelia went with her gut.

Christian stopped petting the wolf-dog. "Agent Spilazi, I stopped having feelings a while ago. Any feelings."

She leaned toward him. "Now, Christian, that's a bald-faced lie. Are you just lying to me, or are you lying to yourself?"

No reaction. Then, a slow tilt of his head. "Interesting question. I wouldn't have thought I was lying to either of us, but if I were, then how would I know?" The man actually sounded curious and thoughtful.

Was he just nuts?

"Okay, let's start with this. Is there any reason somebody would want Hank dead?" she asked, trying for a different angle.

Christian shook his head, and a little snow fell from his black hair to his shoulder. "The world was a much better place with Hank in it. Nobody wanted him dead."

Man, he looked honest. He had quite the skill set.

"Who killed Hank?" she said, more forcefully than before.

"I don't know." His tone of voice remained the same.

Was he messing with her? "Do you want to know?" she asked.

"Not really," he admitted. "A lot of folks hunt in December around here, legal or not, and somebody probably shot him accidentally." For the first time, his gaze flickered, and he covered the action by looking at the pup at his feet.

But she caught it. The flicker. All right. "You know, Christian," she murmured, "you seem like a guy who has no problem meting out justice if necessary. This isn't a case where you're looking for vengeance and want me out of it. This is a situation where you want to bury your head and pretend Hank's death didn't happen." Sometimes, her instincts with people came in handy, even if she didn't understand where the insight came from. Probably growing up in harsh circumstances and learning to protect herself. "There's only one reason I can think of that would keep you from seeking answers for Hank."

"Is that a fact? Just one?" Christian asked.

"No." She placed the pen down next to the pad of paper. "Four, actually—if you didn't kill him. I think you know that Hank was killed by Brock, Ace, Damian, or…Amka. If you thought anybody else shot him, if you had an inkling that a screwed-up tourist somehow murdered Hank in December, when visitors actually don't come here, you'd be all over this case, figuring it out so you could avenge a man you supposedly loved. One who saved you and raised you with love afterward."

The animal at his feet sneezed. "That's an interesting hypothesis, and you're wrong," Christian said evenly. "Nobody would've murdered Hank. We loved him."

"So, you'll take a polygraph test?" she pressed.

Christian looked around the small conference room. "You have one of those handy?"

She smiled. "No, but I know a guy in Anchorage." She didn't, but she'd find one. "How about we fly out the next nice day and hook you up to a machine? If you pass, I promise I'll leave you alone."

His smile lacked the charm of earlier. "I can beat any polygraph, Agent. So, it would be a complete waste of time, even if I were hiding the truth, which I'm not." He stood.

The wolf stood with him, yawning and shaking the fur down his strong back.

"We're not finished," Ophelia said, remaining in place.

"That's where you're wrong." Christian lifted his jacket, partially turning and revealing a pistol at the back of his waist. With the knife strapped to his thigh, he looked every bit as dangerous as she'd suspected. "I've told you all I know, and I'm done being inside for the week."

Was he being facetious? She couldn't tell. "Wyatt Yankovich said he saw you near the dead body the day before yesterday. You know the guy with the EVE jacket who had his eyes gouged out?"

Christian zipped up his coat. "I don't know what you're talking about."

"I think you do." She stood, facing him down. "Did you kill that man?"

Christian turned for the door. "If I had killed him, you never would've found him." He strode down the hallway toward the exit.

"That's just it, Christian," she called after him. "I can't find him. He's gone."

Christian turned to face her, his eyes burning—both colors of them.

She paused. "Does it bother you? Having two different-colored eyes?" Was there a significance to the eye-gouging of the victim the other day?

Flossy gasped. "Now, Ophelia. That's just not nice."

Christian chuckled. "Many things bother me in this world, but my eyes never have. Sorry, Olly. That isn't a motive for me." He studied her for a heartbeat. "I give you my word, on the souls of my ancestors tied to this land, that Brock did not kill Hank and has no clue who did. He looks at you in a way I've never seen, and I want that for him. Peace and something more. You. Give him a chance." Truth rang in his tone.

She couldn't breathe...and she believed him. "So Brock doesn't know who killed Hank. Do you?"

"Take a chance with my brother. You won't regret it." Christian opened the door, stepped outside with his canine companion, and closed it quietly. Then Christian Osprey disappeared as fast as the body had the other day.

Damn it.

CHAPTER NINETEEN

Night blanketed the small town as Brock finally returned to the station after working as a handyman for most of Mrs. McGillicuddy's neighborhood until after supper. The town definitely needed a sheriff. Maybe Ace would think about taking the job and stop drinking.

Ophelia strode outside and gingerly made her way down the icy steps. Her foot slipped, and he caught her by the elbow before she could fall. She'd been there all day? The woman showed clear dedication, no question about it.

He didn't want to release her. "There should be salt in the basement. I'll have Amos take care of the steps and sidewalk." Amos usually enjoyed spreading the salt far and wide. Perhaps he wanted to avoid the federal agent.

She looked up, her blue eyes wide in the light from the entryway. "Thanks. It might take me a little while to get my snow feet under me." She looked down the quiet street, noting the rapidly falling snow.

He grinned. "This is just the beginning. Where are you going?" It was late to be heading out alone.

She rubbed her already red nose. "Flossy found a truck for

sale at Mountain Man's Garage. I called, but nobody answered. Since the garage is just down the sidewalk, I thought I'd walk." The snow fell onto her black leather jacket.

"The garage closes at five, but it's too late, anyway. That was Bob Milt's truck, and it already sold to the Pierce boys." Brock dug a scarf from his pocket and quickly wrapped it around her neck, tying it securely beneath her chin. The blue matched the exact color of her stunning eyes.

Those eyes widened. "You brought me a scarf?"

He shoved his hands into his jacket pockets. "I had a call to Mrs. McGillicuddy's house, and she knits scarves to make extra money in the winter. I figured you needed one." He felt like a dork.

A pretty pink infused her cheeks, and for a moment, she looked confused. Adorable and bewildered. "Thank you."

"Sure." He cleared his throat. "Why did you need a truck?"

"I'd like to find my own way around, and since Wyatt Yankovich is refusing to see me about the EVE case, and his doctor is shielding him in doing so, I want to head out tonight to interview the Randsom family about Tamara Randsom's disappearance." She pursed her lips. "There has to be a vehicle for sale somewhere around here."

He eyed his truck. "There isn't, and soon, vehicles will only be usable right in town and for the first twenty miles of the river road. Other than that, you'll need a snowmobile, RZR, or dogsled. Maybe snowshoes, but not for long distances." He could offer his truck, but he'd rather provide cover for her. Somebody had shot at her the other day. It was probably related to her finding the dead body and being a Fed, but he couldn't be sure. "When did you plan to visit the Randsom homestead?"

Her eyebrows rose, and a snowflake landed on the right one, melting instantly. "Right now, actually. I'd hoped to catch them more relaxed after dinner."

He sighed. "I'll take you."

She paused, looked like she wanted to argue, and then shrugged and carefully strode toward his truck. "I obtained a new phone earlier today at the mercantile and managed to get my number moved over. Even though we don't have much service around here."

He released her elbow and followed, almost running her over when she stopped.

She looked over her shoulder. "I'm so sorry. I didn't think. You've been out of the office all day and probably haven't eaten dinner."

He preferred her prickly side to the sweet because sweet shot right to his groin for some perverse reason. "Mrs. McGillicuddy fed me both lunch and supper," he admitted. "Sandwiches for lunch, and then some delicious meatloaf. I may not need to eat again until next week." He absently rubbed the scratch on his neck from the cat. The meatloaf had helped with the sting.

"Good." Ophelia opened the passenger-side door and climbed inside.

He kicked a chunk of ice off the sidewalk and moved around the truck to the driver's side, sitting and quickly starting the engine to get the heat going. "I don't suppose you called ahead?" He pulled away from the curb.

"Nope. Wanted to catch the Randsoms off guard." She clicked her seat belt into place.

Sounded like a Fed. He flicked on the windshield wipers to keep the snow from piling up.

"Christian swore on the souls of his ancestors that you didn't kill Hank but wouldn't vouch for himself."

Sounded just like Christian. Brock turned up the heat in the truck. "Why don't you concentrate on one case at a time since we're headed out to the Randsom house?"

She shifted her weight in the seat and held her bare hands out for the heat. "I can multitask."

Yeah, she seemed talented and way too dedicated. "Where are your gloves?" He turned the heat up higher, driving away from the town.

"I forgot them at the station." Something she probably wouldn't do again.

Suddenly, a series of bullets impacted the truck. The back tires blew, and the truck skidded across the ice toward the river. "Hold on," he bellowed, throwing out his arm to protect her from the dash.

The impact of Brock's arm hitting her chest smashed Ophelia back in the seat, much stronger than the seat belt already protecting her. The wind blew from her lungs, and she gasped, instinctively reaching for a gun at her waist that wasn't there.

Brock released her and manacled the steering wheel with both hands, his feet working the brakes as the truck whipped around on the ice and bounced off a snowbank with a loud thunk. Her body jerked, and her head whipped forward and back. Faster than she could track, he unbuckled her belt and pulled her across the seat and out his door, crouching and yanking her down. He pulled his gun from the back of his waist.

She sucked in freezing air, her mind clearing, the snow thick beneath her boots as she crouched low enough that her butt became covered in snow. "Extra gun?"

Without looking her way, he plucked a concealed pistol from an ankle holster in his boot. "Glock 26. You have ten in the mag." He handed over the black weapon.

She took it, letting the warmth of the metal seep into her hands. "Location?"

He shook his head. "Other side of the truck. Heard the impact but didn't see anything."

Silence howled around them with the snow falling and the

sky dark. She inched sideways down the truck toward the rear, putting her back to the vehicle and sliding easier. Brock edged toward the headlights, keeping his head down until he reached the front.

Then they waited, in perfect sync.

Nothing. Just silence and more snow. Her breath puffed out, and she took care to turn her head so the telltale sight stayed hidden behind the truck. Her heart beat powerfully inside her chest, and she let the adrenaline rush center her.

Brock leaned his back against the quiet vehicle, closing his eyes. He still crouched, his gun in both hands, his long body looking ready to uncoil at the slightest noise.

She blinked, watching him. The wind intensified, and clumps of snow dropped from the high boughs of fir and pine trees around them, thudding softly on the ice-crusted ground. In the distance, a wolf howled, followed by a cacophony of answering calls, mournful and determined. Ophelia shuddered and gripped her weapon tighter.

Five minutes passed and then ten. Finally, at fifteen minutes or so, she gingerly stretched her shoulders and bounced back on her heels, trying to keep her body from becoming too cold to move quickly.

Brock's eyes opened, and the deep green pierced her. He signaled a plan and then stood, firing his gun over the truck's hood before dropping back down.

No response.

He looked at her and frowned, shaking his head.

She took a shallow breath, not wanting to freeze her lungs. There hadn't been any sounds of a four-wheeler or snowmobile. So, was the shooter still out there?

Brock jerked and looked at their side of the trees, which now concealed the river. He cocked his head slightly to the side and then lifted his weapon, tracking east to west.

She aimed at the forest, trying desperately to hear what he

had noticed. Had the shooter somehow circled around them? They stayed exposed against the truck, but what if two shooters waited? If she moved to the other side, she might be doing what they wanted.

What had Brock heard?

He lifted his chin and let out a barely there whistle with one low note.

An answering whistle instantly echoed.

He motioned for her to lower her gun and then stood. She blinked and slowly pushed to stand, her joints creaking and protesting from the cold. "What's happening?" she whispered.

Christian strode between two sprawling fir trees, the snow up to his knees and the puppy bounding at his side. "Heard gunshots."

Brock launched into motion so fast he was just a blur. One second, he stood down the length of the truck, and the next, he'd grasped Ophelia's arm and hip, moved to the door, and lifted her inside. "Stay there and stay down. If anybody comes near the truck, shoot them." He motioned, and the wolf bounded into the truck with her before he shut the door.

Her mouth gaped. What the heck had just happened?

He motioned something to Christian, who pulled a large flashlight out of his backpack and pointed it beyond the truck and into the forest. Then they moved.

Together, synchronized, they inched forward with their weapons out and ready, their dark forms illuminated by the headlights. As one, they caught a scent and pivoted, their movements fluid and perfectly aligned. Without hesitation, they crossed the road in a synchronized dash, diving deep into the snow and trees with silent precision. Each step mirrored the other, a practiced dance of instinct and trust. Within moments, they melted into the wilderness, vanishing like shadows on a hunt, focused entirely on tracking the shooter.

She gulped, her hands shaking from the cold. The wolf-dog

puppy panted with his nose against the passenger-side window, his wet tail wagging across the leather seat.

Okay. Deep breath and then another. She swallowed and carefully watched outside for movement. Only the falling snow remained visible. She was a trained agent, but she'd worn the wrong boots and didn't have any experience tracking in the snow, so she stayed at the ready in case the shooter doubled back toward the truck. Brock could handle any emergency, and her entire body warmed at the thought. The quiet of the night pressed in, and the windows started to fog. Minutes passed, and she wiped off the glass, looking for anything.

Her mind wandered back to the fact that both Brock and Christian had sounded truthful when claiming Brock's innocence. Or did she just want to trust him? Not once, in her entire life, had somebody jumped into action to shield her.

She didn't need protection, but the feelings that rose from his attempt overwhelmed her at a depth and level she'd never realized. Brock Osprey was becoming way too appealing.

He and Christian emerged from the trees, covered in snow.

She opened her door and jumped out with the animal right behind her. "Anything?"

Brock stepped back and looked at his truck, his broad face grim. "No. The trail leads to a popular sledding slope, so footsteps abound."

Christian lifted a shoulder, and snow scattered. "Wasn't a bad plan, really."

Ophelia tucked the gun into her waist and blew warmth into her hands. "Plan?"

Brock paused and then prowled around the front of the truck. "Suicide Hill is a sledding hill for kids. Well, and adults. It's a long hill, and there's somewhat of a parking area at the bottom. The shooter sledded down and must've had a rig waiting."

Christian dropped to his haunches and ran his hand over the

front tire on the driver's side. "You have three flats. Want to take care of it tonight or tomorrow?"

A muscle in Brock's jaw ticked visibly. "Tomorrow when it's light and not so cold. I'll meet you here and buy you breakfast after."

"Deal." Christian stood and nodded at Ophelia. "That's twice, Agent. We'll find out who wants you dead and why."

Her legs trembled. She needed to get to a store tomorrow and buy long underwear or thermals. "Brock was with me both times. Maybe the shooter aimed at him."

"It's possible," Christian allowed, turning back toward the river and pushing through the snow. "Come on, Tika."

Brock watched him. "You can stay at my place tonight."

"Nope. Need to check on Ace." Then the trees swallowed him.

She shook her head. What an odd man. "Um, what now?"

Brock pointed down the desolate and icy road. "My cabin is that way."

CHAPTER TWENTY

Brock tossed a towel at Ophelia right inside his front door as they both ditched their boots and coats. "You want a warm shower or the hot tub?"

She blinked and hung her coat on the nearest hook. Snow covered her pretty dark hair and her jeans up to her knees. "You have a hot tub?"

"Of course. It's Alaska in the winter." He tried not to think of her nude body in his hot tub. "I don't have swimsuits, just so you know. It's up to you, Ophelia. I want you to stay tonight since there's a shooter out there looking for you, and my cabin is better protected than the B&B. You can shower quickly to warm up, borrow some clothes, and then you're welcome to stay in my guest room." He rubbed snow out of his hair to land on the mat. "Or you can join me in my bed." He didn't need to add the rest.

Her instant chuckle surprised him and then ran right down his spine to land in his groin. "I like that you don't play games."

He wouldn't know how to play that kind of game and didn't care to learn. "I figured you should understand all of your options."

Her smile widened. "I also like that you have absolutely no confidence issues."

Why would he?

She removed her wet sweater, revealing a light green tank top. "I also like that you can handle yourself in emergencies, have a softness for people in trouble, and fill out your T-shirt like a sculptor chiseled you out of stone."

Amusement battled with instant arousal inside him. "I'm getting the feeling that a *but* is coming my way."

"Yeah, you have a cute butt," she drawled, her nipples clearly outlined beneath the soft fabric of her shirt. "This whole situation is complicated, and I believe that you didn't kill Hank."

He cocked his head, noting the goose bumps on her bare shoulders. Oh, he could warm her up and fast, but that was her decision. "You believe me?"

"Yes, I believe that you didn't kill Hank and don't *know* who did," she said, her eyes the clear blue of a mysterious night. "That doesn't make this any less complicated."

"It can," he murmured, moving toward her slowly. "It's just you and me here, Olly. No past, no cases, no facts. Just us." He grasped her delicate chin between his finger and thumb, gently tilting her face and giving her every opportunity in the world to stop him.

Her breath caught, but she didn't pull away. "You protected me tonight. Just like the other night after we were shot at, and I fell in the river." Her voice softened with a thin thread of…bewilderment?

He stepped closer, letting the heat of his body wash over her. Why was she so unaccustomed to a man providing cover? "I know you're an agent and probably a good one, and I know you've had training." He'd never want to take anything away from her. "But this is my town, and I'm used to the wildness of Alaska."

"I know," she murmured.

It was true, but that wasn't all, and he wouldn't hold back. "More importantly, whether you like it or not, you were a woman riding with me both times, and I'm going to protect you. Call me a throwback, call me a chauvinist, even call me an asshole, but that doesn't change the fact that if you're in danger, I'm going to tear any threat apart until you're safe." Giving her that was a risk, but he wouldn't lie to her about who he was in case she wanted in his bed.

Her tongue darted out to wet her bottom lip.

He went rock-hard in an instant. Tension spiraled around them, through him. Keeping his hold light, he lowered his head and brushed his mouth across hers. Her lips were soft and cold, and he licked the bottom one, warming her.

She shivered, and her hands slid up his shirt to his neck as she opened her mouth and let him in.

He dove, kissing her deeper, sweeping his tongue against hers and tasting mint and woman with a hint of strawberries. How the hell did she taste like strawberries? He growled low, grasping her hip and dragging her against him, his mind spinning and his body rioting.

Fire detonated in his gut. He slid his hand around her hip and beneath the flimsy material, stroking the pads of his fingers across her already-heated skin. The woman had gone from shivering to full-on burning, creating a storm in him more powerful than the one outside. He wasn't certain he'd survive it, survive them, but it was too late for caution or reason—at least for him. Hopefully, she'd come to her senses and save them both.

He released her mouth, barely lifting his head.

Her eyes glowed the desperate cerulean of the innermost flickers of a campfire, the hot and tempting blue usually buried deep in the crackling flames. Pink flushed her smooth skin, and in the dim light, she was the most beautiful woman he'd ever seen.

His heart thudded hard, and he took the hit, unable to look away from her. Whatever was happening between them, this new and terrifying sense of need also reflected in her eyes. She felt it, too.

Her hands clenched in his shirt, her fingers curling against his upper chest. Her breath quickened, making her full breasts move beneath the camisole, her nipples so hard he could barely keep from touching her. She licked her bottom lip, her eyes darkening. "If we do this, if we start this, we keep us separate from the case. From everything else."

"I couldn't agree more." In one smooth move, he lifted her against his chest and ignored the warning bells in the back of his head. It was much too late for that.

OPHELIA CAUGHT her breath at his easy strength, sliding her arm over his shoulders. Oh, this was crazy. Her taste in men was terrible, which had resulted in her being banished to the middle of nowhere. Making this mistake might end her career for good.

She didn't care.

At the moment, nothing mattered but the powerful arms holding her and the devastating mouth above hers. She'd never felt so safe and yet so in danger at the same time, and the conflux of opposing feelings hit her like an aphrodisiac. Yeah, she was screwed up.

Who cared?

He carried her into a bedroom that smelled like the forest and Brock. Gently, he sat her on the bed, then whipped off her top and sent it sailing over his head.

She barely got out a laugh before he dropped to his knees, jerked her by the waist closer to him, and sucked one nipple into the inferno of his mouth. Shock and fire rolled through her, and she pressed her hands to the bedspread right behind her butt, unable to do anything else in the moment except arch into his mouth.

He licked and sucked, nipping with just enough bite to steal any breath she might've kept. His shoulders kept her legs wide, and his hands grabbed her ass, partially lifting her as if he couldn't get enough. His tongue was rough and abrasive as he feasted on both nipples, the underside of her breasts, and the hollow between them as if starving.

For her.

She made a sound of protest, unable to think, wanting to get her hands on him.

He lifted his head, his green gaze wilder than any animal in the Alaskan wilderness. "You said yes."

"I meant it," she breathed, reaching for his shirt.

"Good. My way." Keeping her gaze, he pulled at her socks, gently drawing them off and running his hands along her calves.

She reached for the clasp of her jeans, but his hands were there first, ripping open the button and yanking the wet material down. Her jeans and panties joined her tank top somewhere in the room. One wide hand pressed against her upper chest, pushing her down onto her back. He yanked her ankles up and over his shoulders with no warning.

Then his mouth was on her.

She cried out, her eyes closing. The feelings were too intense, and she needed to think, but he went full in on her clit and thighs with his tongue, lips, teeth, and heated breath. The world fragmented, and she sucked in breath as an orgasm blew through her so hard her ears rang.

He didn't stop.

His fingers joined his mouth, his teeth nipping her thighs, his shoulders holding her open for him. Never in her life had she been so helpless in someone's hands as her body gave itself over to him completely, her mind fuzzing into nothing but pleasure. Even so, she shook her head. "I can't. Not again." In fact, one was her limit—if any.

He lifted his head, his eyes burning green. "Wrong." Then his grip tightened, and his mouth sucked her clit into his mouth, his abrasive tongue scraping across her.

She bucked and then tightened, a second orgasm ripping through her and shooting electricity throughout her entire body. Gasping, shuddering, she came down, her heart thundering.

He kept going.

She partially lifted a hand to stop him, but her limbs had gone weak, and she let her arm fall to the bedspread. She shut her eyes, and more pleasure attacked her. Her world, the one only she inhabited, narrowed only to him. His teeth scraped her clit just as his fingers bit into her butt, and she flew again, this time with a weak sigh. Her body shuddered from head to toe. "Brock," she murmured, feeling on fire, alive, yet somehow empty.

He stood, his gaze trapping her as effectively as his hands had. He pulled his shirt over his head, revealing the hard muscles she'd felt, along with scars she hadn't realized he had. So many. Bullets, knives, and gouges. The wild tattoo of the deadly Osprey moved with the play of his muscles as if the bird of prey had a life of its own.

He pushed his jeans down, kicked them out of the way, and watched her.

She felt like prey. The sensation rippled through her with an excitement that didn't make sense but propelled her desire even higher nonetheless. He was built and already hard and big. Very.

His fingers slid inside her, and satisfaction flared across his rugged face. "You're ready."

She nodded. "I am."

"Me, too." He leaned to the side and yanked a condom out of his bedside table, ripping open the wrapper and quickly rolling it over himself. He set a knee on the bed, slid a hand beneath her ass, and lifted her to him. Then he pressed into her, stretching her, burning her, overtaking her and not pausing.

His invasion was intense, and her body was forced to accept him. Inch by inch. At the back of her mind, she knew he'd prepared her for this, which softened her even more to take him. All of him. His fingers dug into her hips, and he levered completely over her, overwhelming her. He wasn't gentle, and it felt like he gave her all of him.

She wanted that. More than she'd realized.

He drove all the way inside, and her body arched, her head going back. He was huge. The feeling was beyond intense. Then he started to move, hard and fast, controlling every movement, maybe even her breath. She grabbed the tense and corded muscles in his arms, holding on for all she was worth.

He powered inside her, hard and strong, slamming deep.

She lifted her knees, giving him more, her inner thighs smashed against his hips.

He still watched her, his thrusts ruthless, his hold unbreakable. Again and again, he hit a spot deep inside her she hadn't realized was there, forcing spirals of raw pleasure to take her away. Ache and need and something else, something desperate, attacked every cell in her body and every thought she might've had.

There was no warning as the volcano erupted, blowing inside her and clenching her inner muscles so hard it hurt. His cocked swelled, fighting to stay deep, his body shuddering as she pulled him with her and drained him. She rode the wild storm and finally came down with a soft whimper, her body relaxing.

His forehead dropped to hers as he jerked more inside her. Then he kissed her, a bare, gentle brush against her mouth, and tears pricked the backs of her eyes.

She closed them and felt her heart beating too fast for reality.

He rolled off her, tugging her into his side. "I like your butt, too."

She burst out laughing, even though sleep was already calling her home. "Night."

"Oh, baby. We're just getting started." Then he kissed her again.

CHAPTER TWENTY-ONE

Brock walked out into the snowy dawn to see his truck already next to his metal shop with Christian and Ace changing the last tire. He strode toward them, his body satiated but his mind...not so much. "You two are out early." His breath left puffs in the freezing air.

Christian stood, his dual-colored eyes serious. "Tika was cold. I let him inside. He should be by the fire, which I stoked."

Brock nodded, not having noticed either. All right. Maybe his mind had completely unraveled.

Ace held a tire iron in his hand, his eyes clear for a change. "Your woman is a screamer."

Brock coughed, and his ears rang. "You were outside?"

Christian nodded. "I checked on Ace last night and found him brooding on his back deck, so we decided to try and track the shooter. Then we returned here, figured out you had company, and thought we should cover the perimeter."

Ace grinned. "Yeah. You didn't exactly seem focused on watching for threats."

That was the damn truth. The only thing, the only person in his world last night had been Special Agent Ophelia Spilazi.

"Thanks." He warmed, full-on, almost back to being with his brothers like they'd been before Hank died. He needed them, and they needed him. Maintaining distance between them wouldn't cut it any longer.

Except he'd just slept with the agent leading the investigation into Hank's death.

He shook his head.

"No shit," Ace agreed, snow falling onto his dark hair. "You keeping her?"

After last night, Brock wasn't sure he could let her go. But they had the case between them. "I don't know." He walked around the side of the truck to view the bullet holes. He flushed with anger, centering himself in the moment. "I am going to find the person who shot at her." And rip off his head.

Christian nodded, probably at the unsaid part. "The storm covered all tracks, which we expected. Also, no shell casings, which is impressive that whoever shot at you had time and could find them all in the snow before taking off. I don't think we're dealing with a moron, although he hasn't hit his target yet."

Brock didn't like the *yet*. "Did you find anything at the bottom of the hill?"

"No," Ace said quietly. "We can ask in town if anybody saw a car or truck come through, but you know that parking area leads to a back road headed north. The guy could've gone anywhere around the river."

"Or to several subdivisions," Christian added.

Brock sighed. "Okay. She can't stay at the B&B because it'll put Flossy in danger. She'll have to stay here."

Christian's lip twitched, and he almost smiled. So close. "I assume there's a place for her to rent somewhere around here. She's a Fed, Brock. She can take care of herself."

"She doesn't need to," Brock countered instantly.

Ace sighed. "He is so keeping her."

Christian's gaze narrowed. "How? How can you possibly think of keeping an FBI agent? After...everything."

Brock wiped snow off his face. "Stop talking about her like she's a wayward puppy. I like her." He kicked a chunk of ice out of his way. "She needs protection right now, whether or not she's trained. Nobody is trained for Alaska like us."

Ace stepped closer to him, his eyes burning. "I know she's not a puppy, just as I know you've never been able to turn away from any woman or stray who needs covering. Just ask yourself if that's what's going on here. Is your hero-savior complex causing you to like her? She's a fucking Fed, Brock."

"Hero-savior complex?" Brock snorted, his temper igniting instantly. "Seriously? You turning into a shrink, brother? Is that why you don't look hungover for the first time in too long, or is it because Christian dragged your ass away from the bottle?"

Ace moved for him, obviously looking for a fight.

Brock was more than happy to give him one. He tensed his legs for the hit.

Christian instantly put his body between them. Fuck, he moved fast. "Knock it off. We don't have time to fight each other. Somebody is shooting at your Fed, there's a missing dead guy from EVE without his eyes, and I can't get ahold of Damian. Get your heads out of your asses."

Ace stepped back first. "That's a lot of words for you, C."

"No shit," Christian muttered, edging a safe distance away.

Brock stilled. "You can't reach Damian?"

"No," Christian muttered. "We always check in once a month, and I haven't heard anything for six weeks."

"He's probably on a mission," Ace said, not sounding sure. He scrubbed his hand through his shaggy hair, scattering snow and ice. "I hate it when he goes dark. If he needs backup, we won't know it." Stepping away, he shook more snow off his thick jacket. "Speaking of backup, what's your plan with the agent?"

Brock shook his head. "She wants to interview the Randsoms today, and somehow she got an appointment at EVE for this morning."

Christian's eyebrows lifted. "EVE? No shit? She's got some pull."

"So you're going to be the sheriff?" Ace asked.

Brock's ears heated. "No. You know I'm not." He didn't need to go into the why—in fact, he didn't want to. Not yet. Not now. He cleared his throat. "Wyatt said he saw you close to the EVE victim, Christian. Were you there?"

Christian frowned. "No. I've seen him out fishing before, and he's seen me out hunting, but not this past week. My guess is that he's just mixed up after freezing his ass off out there for a night."

"All right." Brock had no reason not to believe his brother.

Ace braced his shoulders. "Don't you think it's time we talked about—?"

"Brock?" Ophelia opened the front door and stopped short at seeing the three men. She wore one of his T-shirts with her long legs and adorable feet bare. The woman was the sexiest thing in existence. Her face turned a lovely pink. "Oh. Um. Good morning." Then she shut the door and disappeared.

Ace barked out a laugh.

Christian nodded, his eyes sparkling. "Yeah, I get it."

"No shit," Ace agreed.

Brock sighed.

After a breakfast of waffles with blueberry syrup, Ophelia called the hospital while Brock showered, and the doctor relayed that Wyatt refused to speak with her. So, she booted up her laptop and rapidly typed an affidavit to obtain a warrant to hold Wyatt Yankovich as a material witness in the EVE murder victim case. Signing it electronically, she fired it off to the Assistant U.S. Attorney in Fairbanks, who would make the motion to a judge. Hopefully today.

Rolling her neck, she tried to ignore the headache holding Wyatt would cause. The town wouldn't like it, but since he refused to speak with her, she had no choice.

Standing, she wandered over to an old collage of pictures in a faded wooden frame on the wall near the door. Pictures of Brock playing football, Christian on a motorcycle, and Ace wrestling with Damian took up squares. As did a couple of Hank working on an engine and fishing. Frowning, she leaned in and squinted at a ball cap on his head. The symbol appeared familiar.

"You ready?" Brock strode into the living area, his hair wet and his hard body in jeans and a T-shirt.

"Is that the EVE symbol?" she whispered.

Brock paused and looked over her shoulder. "Maybe? I don't know. The picture is old and faded."

She turned and looked up at his chiseled face. "Did Hank work for EVE?"

"No." Brock's gaze warmed. "You're always working, aren't you?"

"Brock," she murmured.

He removed her jacket from a hook to hold out for her to shrug into. "Hank worked with diesel engines in the service, and EVE runs on those, so I think he contracted with the facility a couple of times through the years when they had an emergency. Nothing major. He didn't really work there."

Yet…now Ophelia had a connection between Hank and EVE, a possible one with Tamara Randsom with her environmental grant, and the disappearing victim in the snow. Could EVE be involved with all three? Anticipation lit through her. "Let's get going."

"Sure thing." He reached for his truck keys.

She followed him out to his powerful looking truck and engaged the seat warmers immediately. They drove in silence for almost an hour around the river and through a canyon with hard edges of snow up both sides. "How likely is an avalanche?" She decided to finally breach the peaceful quiet between them.

"We're okay for at least one more snowstorm. Then all bets are off." His sunglasses hid his expression as the sun finally blazed across the stark white world outside. "The EVE facility likes to stay remote, so they don't do anything to clear the roads, and the town doesn't have the resources."

She settled her hands on her clean and dry jeans, having washed them earlier that morning. The shirt was Brock's, and she'd tied the white button-up at her waist over her tank top, going for casual. It wasn't her usual uniform to interview suspects, but at the moment, she didn't have much choice. "If you're not the sheriff, why are you escorting me?"

"I'm not the sheriff, and you keep getting shot at," he rumbled, his hands more than capable on the wheel.

Looking at said hands, a flush wandered through her entire body. Yeah, he definitely knew how to use those hands. And his mouth. And the rest of his body. Never in her life had a man taken over *her* body, and he'd done it effortlessly. Even now, hours later, she tingled. He'd marked her, in several places, leaving light nips or whisker burn. She wore him right now. The thought flipped her abdomen over. She cleared her throat. "Why don't you just give in and be the sheriff?"

His hands tightened on the steering wheel, but other than that, he didn't react.

She tapped her bottom lip, thinking it through. "You like helping people, and you're a bit of a control freak with danger." He'd make the perfect sheriff. "The only reason you're not interested is…" Her mind ran through all the facts. "Oh."

He turned the truck out of the canyon onto a road next to a wide field covered in a massive antenna array field. Thousands upon thousands of them glinted in the weak sun. "I'm just not interested in the job."

"Wrong." Oh, he was definitely interested. She turned to study him even closer. "You can't take the vow and do the job because you know who killed Hank." It was the only thing that made sense. While she didn't know him nearly as well as she wanted to, Brock Osprey was all about honor, duty, and badassery. And she'd slept with him last night—although they hadn't slept much. He wouldn't be able to ignore his duty, and there no was doubt his loyalty stayed with his brothers. "Who killed him, Brock?" she asked softly.

"I don't know." He glanced at either side of them and seemed to tense. "There's too much man-made crap around here."

"If you don't know, who do you suspect?" Her blood flowed faster as she caught a scent in the case.

He shook his head. "I suspect a hunter." The man made a decent liar, but he'd been inside her the night before. They'd bonded, whether he liked it or not.

"I can tell you're lying," she murmured. "The only reason you won't take the job is because you'd be torn between your duty and your family." Unless the murderer was somebody from town, but he didn't seem close to anybody except his brothers. "Which of your brothers killed Hank, and why?" Then another thought caught her. If Brock had found the body, he might've helped cover for one of them. "Are you an accessory after the fact?"

He swung his gaze to her. "Of course not." He tipped up his glasses, revealing those green eyes. "Give me a break."

Okay. That seemed like the truth. Relief wandered through her, considering she'd gotten naked with him the night before, and he now knew her body better than she did. Brock had been very thorough. She stared at the antenna field. "There have to be almost two hundred of those."

"I guess. I do know the array field is spread over more than thirty acres." He halted the truck near a wide gate with a guard house.

She leaned to peer around him as two men walked out, both dressed for warm weather, the second guy holding an assault rifle. All right. Serious firepower there.

"ID?" the first guy, a mammoth in a black jacket, asked. Military-issued dark glasses covered his eyes, and a hat covered his head, but he looked to be in his late twenties and held himself like he could fight.

She handed her badge to Brock, and he gave it to the guy, along with his license.

The man disappeared inside the building for a few minutes and then returned to give them their IDs and two badges already on neck lanyards. "Wear these before you approach the main door."

She took hers and studied it. The black badge had *EVE Visitor* emblazoned across it in dark red letters, along with several visible chips and holographic stamps. Impressive for a place in the middle of nowhere that supposedly studied the ionosphere. She pulled the lanyard over her head and settled the badge below her chest. The chips must track them throughout the facility.

Brock tugged his over his head and then drove past the gate and down the long drive to the sprawling cement block and metal building comprised of three stories. Aboveground, anyway.

"Have you been here before?" she asked, lowering her voice for some reason.

"Nope." He pulled the truck into a parking lot and stopped the engine. "The folks who work here live here and rarely come into town. We don't cross paths much."

She held out her badge. "You have to be curious about this. I mean, come on. They study the *ionosphere*?"

He flashed a grin. "I really think they do, and growing up,

there were so many scary stories about this place, we stayed away. Sometimes, the scientists pop into town, and they're all pretty dorky. Not scary." He opened his door and hustled around to open hers, assisting her down the long distance to the ground.

Her instincts hummed, and she walked with him across the plowed area to the front door, which he opened easily to reveal a large, industrial-looking waiting room. A man waited in front of a metal reception desk with two armed guards sitting behind it. He stood to about six-foot-three and had thick black hair and the darkest green eyes she'd ever seen. His suit looked expensive, his body hard, and his gaze extremely intelligent. There was something familiar about him.

He looked past her to Brock and then smiled. "Hello, brother."

CHAPTER TWENTY-TWO

Brock rocked back on his heels and quickly recovered, eyeing his brother. "Damian." He grasped Ophelia's arm and strode forward, his mind reeling. "What are you doing here?"

Damian held out a hand. "Special Agent Spilazi? It's nice to meet you."

She shook his hand, her gaze going from Brock to Damian and back, her tone hesitant. "You, too."

He gestured them toward a bank of three elevators. "Let's go up to my office."

Brock's hands heated, but he walked toward the nearest silver-fronted elevator and held his questions until he got his brother alone. What the hell could Damian be doing at EVE? Brock already felt off balance from his too-intense night with Ophelia, and her strawberry scent was driving him crazy again. It had taken all his self-control not to pull over to the side of the road and kiss her on the way.

He'd only had one night with her, one taste, and he needed more with a craving that should cause him concern.

The doors glided open, and the silent ride up bristled with

tension. Damian led the way through a small waiting area and down a long hallway with thick carpet to an office in the back corner. He nodded at a woman at the desk outside and opened his door. "Come on in."

Brock followed Ophelia into a room with concrete walls, mainly steel and glass furnishings, and a wide window facing Knife's Edge Mountain and the peaks beyond. The office contained no wood except for the desk's top—a thick wooden slab held up by sharp-cut concrete columns. The room looked industrial, luxurious, and stark.

Damian gestured them away from the desk to a corner with a black leather sofa and two chairs. "Please, have a seat." He took one of the chairs.

Brock dropped onto the sofa and kept himself between his brother and Ophelia, the sense of being unbalanced pissing him off.

The woman from outside poked her head in. She had to be in her early sixties with salt-and-pepper hair, blue eyes behind glasses, and a no-nonsense look. Her impeccable black suit gave her a refined appearance. "Would you like coffee, tea, water, or any sort of soft drink?"

"It's cold out," Damian said. "Please bring coffee, Elisa."

"Of course." The woman silently disappeared.

Brock cocked his head, trying to keep his temper from blowing. Nope. Too late. "What the holy fuck are you doing here, Damian?"

Damian sighed. "I'm just getting settled. I planned to call you, but everything happened so fast. I was honorably discharged, offered this job, and had to get up and running within a week. It's been crazy."

Was that it? Somehow, Brock doubted it. Damian didn't want to talk about what'd happened with Hank any more than he did. Brock looked around the office, noting the absence of a desk plaque. Okay. So, Damian *had* just arrived. "What exactly is your job here?"

Damian's suit looked like it cost more than Brock's truck. "I'm the head of security."

Well, now. Curiosity prickled through Brock. "So, you can get into any department?" Oh, the tales they'd invented about this place while growing up.

Damian grinned, obviously remembering the best gory stories. "Most of them. There are a couple of labs with proprietary machinery. It's my job to keep them protected and not infiltrated. Even by me." His tone remained level and his smile in place. Anyone who didn't know him could easily believe he had no issue with the situation.

Brock knew him, and Damian was not pleased. "Interesting."

Elisa strode efficiently inside with a silver tray bearing a coffee carafe, mugs, and condiments. She placed it on the table. "Would you like me to pour?"

Brock watched her and pressed his lips together to keep from smiling.

Damian stopped smiling. "No, but thank you."

The woman walked out without a word.

Brock snorted. "She doesn't like you."

Damian took the carafe and poured three mugs, handing two over. "No kidding." He didn't sound too bothered by the fact. "The last head of security was fired, and I think they dated each other for a long time. Well, not fired. Forced into retirement. They wanted somebody more on the cutting edge of security, and the guy couldn't figure out his cell phone."

"Unlike you," Ophelia murmured, blowing on her coffee. "You're cutting-edge?"

Damian gifted her with his most charming smile. "Rumor has it."

Brock took a deep drink, letting the hot liquid burn his throat. "Why haven't you contacted Christian? He's worried."

Damian rolled his eyes. "If C was worried, he would've already hunted me down. You know that."

Truth. Christian could hunt and track anybody, even someone with cutting-edge security. "If you don't return his call, he's going to find you," Brock warned. "When he's done dogging Ace."

Damian sat back, concern in his deep eyes. "I know about Ace's plane wreck, but I didn't realize he still suffered. How bad is it?"

Brock shrugged. If Ace wanted to talk about it with Damian, he would. "Call him and find out."

Damian sighed. "Point taken."

Ophelia took another drink, her pretty eyes missing nothing. "I'd like a tour of the facility."

"I'm sorry, but that's not possible." Damian studied her and then looked back at his brother. "Even if the local sheriff is here with you."

Damian had been in touch with somebody. Or maybe the gossip from town had reached EVE. "I'm not the sheriff," Brock said evenly. "Won't be, in fact. But Ophelia needed an escort, and here I am."

One of Damian's dark eyebrows rose. "The lovely FBI agent required an escort?" He looked back and forth between them and apparently saw something interesting. "Well, now. What a conundrum."

Oh, Brock might actually hit him.

OPHELIA WATCHED the interplay between the brothers, trying to find the source of the tension. Conundrum? Definitely. "What exactly is this place, Damian?"

He waved a hand in the air. "This is a scientific research facility dedicated to studying the ionosphere—the layer of the

Earth's atmosphere that's important for radio communications, GPS systems, and satellite operations."

"That's the line I've heard," Ophelia murmured. "Is that true?"

"Of course. The work here focuses on understanding natural phenomena like space weather, solar flares, and how they affect our modern communication infrastructure." Damian smiled, all charm. "Much of our research is done openly, with universities and scientists from around the world contributing to studies aimed at improving things like navigation and emergency communication systems. While we use powerful radio signals for research, these transmissions are directed toward the upper atmosphere and can't affect the Earth's surface or people directly. Our goal is scientific progress, not secrecy."

Now that sounded like the company line, and she'd worry about it later. "Did you kill Hank, Damian?" she asked out of the blue.

Damian didn't so much as jump. What was it with the Osprey brothers? They were unflappable. "No. I assume a hunter caught him by mistake," he said smoothly. Way *too* smoothly. Brock's rougher edges were easier to deal with, and not just because he kissed like a god.

Ophelia couldn't help but sigh. How freaking frustrating. "The mysterious and so-sad hunter seems to be the party line."

Damian took another drink. "It's the truth."

The man was a good liar, but drinking before speaking was a tell. "Did Ace kill Hank?" She purposefully kept her voice soft.

Damian met her gaze over his mug. "I fear somebody poaching, out hunting outside of the legal season, accidentally shot Hank and became too frightened to admit it, Agent. Since they were breaking the law. That's my final statement on the matter."

She swallowed. "You and your brothers are like a solid wall crumbling from the inside, you know that?"

Brock stiffened next to her.

Damian tilted his head. "Meaning?"

She went with her instincts, even though she didn't have the facts. "Brock won't accept the sheriff position, Ace is drinking himself to death, Christian is in a category of his own, living in the wild and stalking the shadows, and you took a job in your own backyard and didn't bother to tell any of them. Something is wrong between you four, and the only thing that makes sense is that it's about Hank's death. You know who killed him." She struggled to determine if Damian might be the killer. After meeting each of the brothers, she couldn't get a handle on who might have harmed Hank.

"Hmm." Damian looked at her again as if really seeing her. "She's smart, Brock." Was that approval in his tone?

Fire flashed through her, singeing the tips of her ears. "I'm also right in front of you, Mr. Osprey. I strongly suggest you speak directly to me."

His lips twitched. "I apologize, Agent. It's just rather rare that any of us approve of our brothers' women, and I wished to give him a compliment."

And piss her off. On purpose? She watched him carefully. Was he waiting for her to protest the archaic language? "While you might have made your last statement, I'm nowhere near done, nor have I been distracted from the matter in any way. I'm surprised I need to remind you that lying to a federal agent is a felony."

Damian laughed out loud, the sound dark and rich. "I appreciate the reminder. You're going to be fun to have around, Olly."

Great. Now everyone called her Olly. Wait a minute. Where had he heard that? What kind of pipeline into the town did he have? "You said you just arrived. Who have you been speaking with in town?"

He shrugged. "Nobody, but word gets around, even for those who have just arrived. I already heard that my brother is involved with an FBI agent."

"We're not dating," she muttered. She wasn't sure what they were doing, but it seemed more intense and less intimate than mere dating. Time to switch tactics, although that didn't seem to work with these guys. "Will you identify the deceased EVE male we found the other day, and explain to me why his body disappeared?"

Damian drummed the fingers of his free hand on his perfectly creased slacks. "I have no knowledge about that poor sap, and he did not work for EVE."

She kept track of his reactions as well as Brock's. "The deceased wore an EVE jacket."

Damian finished his coffee and placed his cup on the tray. "If you had a body or a picture, we might know more. All I can tell you is that we're not missing personnel, and based on the description sent to me from the FBI assistant director requesting this meeting, the deceased isn't a former employee. I'm sorry I can't be of more help."

"I'd like to look through your personnel files." She put her cup on the tray as well.

Damian sat back, overwhelming the leather chair. "No. Sorry." He sounded properly regretful and full of it.

"I can obtain a warrant." She kept his gaze.

His cheek creased as if he wanted to smile again but held back. "No, you can't. Even if the deceased body, the one that somehow disappeared, did *wear* a jacket embroidered with our logo, he could've gotten it anywhere. Many of our employees donate clothing every winter to the local care units."

She kept control of her temper. "Why would his eyes have been gouged out?"

"Animals?" Damian murmured.

"Not enough time," she countered. "There are rumors about such killings around here."

Damian shook his head. "Those are tales told to keep kids out of the wilds in the winter, where the threats are the weather and animals. I don't know why anybody would gouge out eyes, but I'm not a criminalist, Agent."

"You were in intelligence?" she asked, already knowing the answer.

He nodded and looked at his brother's empty mug. "More coffee?"

"No." Brock placed his cup next to the others. "What's the problem with us looking through the personnel records here? This is just a research facility, right?"

Ophelia masked her surprise at having Brock help her out.

"Right," Damian answered. "But we have world-renowned scientists, and like I said, proprietary machinery. So, we have to keep confidentiality at the forefront. It's my job, Brock. Get a warrant, and I'll hand over the records."

"Will you?" Ophelia murmured, trying for any reaction from the man.

No reaction. Just one word. "Yes."

So far, she had completely struck out with all of her cases. "I don't suppose you knew Tamara Randsom?"

"Not really. We crossed paths occasionally, when I came home on leave, but I've been off on missions for years. I am sorry to hear of her disappearance and don't have any information about that case." Damian glanced at a military-style wristwatch. "I don't mean to be rude, but I have a conference call in a few minutes and have told you everything I know."

"Did Tamara work here at EVE? Even in a contractual capacity?" she asked.

Brock turned to stare at her, and she kept her focus on Damian.

He didn't blink. "Not to my knowledge."

She gave him her most professional smile. She might be able to connect Hank, Tamara, and the recent victim by the river to this place. What the heck did that mean? "Tamara worked under grants as a U.S. Geological Survey Scientist. Surely she spent some time here at EVE? Would you mind terribly digging into personnel and independent contractor files for her history?"

"I'll have Elise conduct a search and get back to you. Please leave your phone number with her before you leave." He glanced at his watch again. "If there's nothing else—"

"Why do you think somebody shot at me?" She purposefully ignored the hint.

He blinked. Finally, some sort of reaction from the security specialist. "How should I know?"

"You worked in intelligence, and now you're in security. Your background is impressive, and I haven't gotten my hands on most of your military records. Yet." She let the last word hang for several moments. "So, tell me. Why would someone try to shoot me not once but twice?"

Damian studied her, his gaze hooded. "I don't think that's the question."

Her heartbeat accelerated. "What's the question?"

He scrutinized her for several long moments. "The question is—why did they miss?"

CHAPTER TWENTY-THREE

Brock could barely wait to get his brother alone, which would happen soon. The drive to the Randsom home passed in silence, and it came as no surprise to find the homestead deserted for the day. The clear, sunny day invited time spent on a four-wheeler or snowmobile.

Ophelia noted the deserted place with her lips pursed and then had been quiet all the way back to town. After lunchtime, Brock walked behind her up Flossy's front steps, and the older woman met them at the door.

"I heard you got shot at again last night," Flossy said, looking up, her eyes wide.

Ophelia nodded. "I did." She sounded more resigned than frightened. "Are there any places for rent in town? I should stay somewhere else."

"Don't be silly." Flossy took her arm and pulled her inside. "We have good locks, and I own a shotgun. You know how to shoot, right?"

Ophelia smiled. "Yes, I know how to shoot. I don't want to put you in danger, Flossy."

Brock followed the women inside, where heat blasted him.

He wanted Ophelia back in his bed. They'd started something, and he didn't want it to end. What did she want?

"I can make you two a late lunch if you want," Flossy offered, wrapping her gray cardigan tighter around her small waist. "The station was boring with both of you gone, and Amos is in a mood, so I came home for the afternoon." She squinted up at Brock. "I hope that's okay."

He wasn't the damn sheriff. "You can do anything you want, Flossy." Why couldn't he get through to everyone? Oh, yeah. Maybe because he kept acting like the sheriff just to protect a tall agent who smelled like strawberries. He battled between his need for her and his loyalty to his brothers, a dull ache settling in his gut. His appetite deserted him.

Flossy bounced back on her fur-lined boots. "Good. Olly, why don't you take the afternoon off, too? There's a quilting party this afternoon over at Delores's house, and nobody will know you're there, so you won't get shot at. Let's go have some girl fun."

"No," Brock said, keeping his wet boots on the mat.

Ophelia turned to face him, her eyes so blue it hurt to look at them. "Why do you keep trying to protect me?"

Because of how she looked at him when he did—like he was some damn hero. He'd stopped being a hero years ago—if he had been one even then. But the way she studied him with softness and vulnerability in her eyes made him want to be one again. Plus, the woman needed some serious cover, and he could provide that. "You need to be careful until we find the shooter."

Flossy smacked him on the arm. "She's fine. Nobody will know she's with me. It's not like she's a regular at the quilting parties."

Well, that was true.

Then Flossy turned to Olly and sweetened the deal. "Loretta

Randsom will be there. Don't you want to talk to her about Tammy Randsom's disappearance?"

Ophelia went on full alert. "I really do. Definitely."

Brock knew when he was outnumbered. "All right. I'll take you both to Delores's house and then pick you up. What time will you be finished?" He reached for Flossy's jacket on the nearest hook.

"Right after supper." The elderly woman shrugged into the coat and then looked at him, her chin firming. "You're being awfully bossy, Sheriff. What exactly happened between you two last night? I know you stayed at your cabin." She buttoned up, looking from him to Ophelia and then back. She plucked a huge bag off the floor. "Not that it's any of my business."

"You're right. It's not." Brock opened the door and ushered both women outside, scanning the neighborhood for threats. He caught sight of Christian on the other side of the street and made a sign that they needed to talk.

Christian strode around the building and across the road, jumping into the back of the truck with his canine companion.

Ophelia helped Flossy into the front seat and then took the back seat next to Christian, reaching out to rub the wolf-dog's ears as he sat on Christian's lap.

Life was getting weird.

"We're dropping the ladies off at Delores's." Brock sat and started the engine.

Christian nodded, already taking point out the window.

Whoever had shot at them had done so under the cover of darkness, and it was doubtful they would try it during daylight when Brock could track them.

Ophelia's phone buzzed, and she lifted it from her pocket to look at the screen. "I have to take this." Then she pushed a button and pressed the phone to her ear. "Spilazi."

Curiosity had Brock watching her expression in the rearview mirror while also keeping an eye on the snowy road.

She looked out the window. "No, sir. Yes, I filed the first report yesterday afternoon before heading to the Randsoms, but a shooter engaged me and I didn't make it to interview them. No, we don't know. Yes, at the bottom of the river." Her shoulders slumped. She must be talking about the gun she'd lost.

He tried to smile at her through the mirror, but her gaze remained outside.

She straightened in her seat. "No, sir. I've interviewed all four of them. So far, there isn't a likely suspect."

Christian tensed but didn't look at her. Hank's case truly mattered to her boss.

Brock fully turned back to the road.

She continued. "I'm well aware of that, sir." Then, she fell quiet for several moments. "I'll send those so you have them first thing in the morning. Yes. I understand. I'm still waiting for work history on Tamara Randsom, and would you please have somebody conduct a search for any payments made to her and to Hank Osprey by EVE? Also, I need a deep dive on odd killings in this area, all of Alaska really, where the victim had their eyes gouged out."

Brock barely bit back a sigh. For goodness' sakes.

"Thank you." She slipped the phone back into her pocket.

Brock eyed her in the mirror again and had the oddest desire to enfold her in a hug. She looked fragile in the back seat next to the panting wolf-dog. Determined and somewhat pissed but still vulnerable. Why did this woman affect him like this? He switched his line of sight and caught Christian's knowing gaze in the mirror.

There had been a hint of desperation in her movements but not in her tone. Why exactly had Ophelia been sent to the middle of nowhere? Obviously, he needed to push her for more information about herself.

He drove out of town and along the river road, his mind working until they reached the subdivision. He passed Mrs.

McGillicuddy's house and drove around a curve, stopping at a lime-green one-story home with a few rigs in the driveway. "We're here."

OPHELIA CARRIED Flossy's stuffed-full bag inside a pretty dining room with a soft-looking quilt spread across the table. A white smocked tree sat in one corner with various Christmas decorations, including several elves on a shelf, adding a festive vibe to the home. Four women looked up at her, and she recognized two of them. "Hi, Doc. Hi Monica."

"Hi, Olly." The doctor sat at the far end, stitching what looked like a wild wolf. "You already met Monica at the tavern. This is Delores Jerky and Loretta Randsom. Ladies, meet FBI Special Agent Ophelia Spilazi."

Ophelia's hands felt damp. She lacked the girly skills to knit. "Hi."

"Hi," Delores echoed. She looked around seventy, with steel-gray hair braided down her back and darker skin marked by laugh lines spreading from her deep black eyes. "Welcome to my home." She gestured for Ophelia to take the seat next to her.

Ophelia sat, and Flossy took the head of the table on her other side.

Monica grinned. "I need to go through some of my boxed winter clothes for you. It's nice having another woman with decent height around here."

Ophelia chuckled. "I agree. I never could share clothes with many friends. Too gangly."

"Ditto, sister," Monica said, her hands full of quilt, a beautiful solitaire diamond sparkling on her ring finger.

"What a lovely ring," Ophelia said.

Monica smiled, glancing at her ring. "Thank you. David bought it in Anchorage, and it's exactly what I've always wanted. The plow business pays well, and I make good tips at the diner. I'm hoping we can save enough to go to the Caribbean for a honeymoon after the wedding." She looked up. "I also hope you're still in town to attend in August."

Would she be? Did Ophelia want to stay in Knife's Edge? She did like the charming small town, and she wanted to find those missing persons. But if she arrested one of the Osprey brothers, the town would most certainly turn against her.

Loretta sat across from her. "Hi." The pretty blonde had sparkling brown eyes and a genuine smile. "I hoped we'd get a chance to meet."

"Me, too," Ophelia admitted. She couldn't just launch into her questions now, but maybe she could ease some information out of the woman. "I have to admit that I've never quilted before. I might just have to watch."

Flossy smacked her arm. "Don't be silly. The only way to learn how is to do it."

"Same with shooting," Ophelia murmured.

Delores reached for a stand-up tray next to her. "Red, white, or pink?" She gestured to the three already open bottles of wine.

"Red," Ophelia said automatically.

Delores poured everyone glasses, apparently already knowing what the others wanted. Full glasses—to the brim of thick and tall wineglasses.

Ophelia took hers and smiled. "I didn't know quilting involved copious amounts of wine."

Flossy had to hold her glass with two bony hands. "When the fabric patches become blurry, we stop quilting."

"And keep drinking." The doctor snorted, accepting her glass of white wine.

Ophelia laughed. "Can I ask how Wyatt is doing without sounding like an agent, Doctor? Just sounding like a...person?"

"Call me May, and of course you can. He's much better, and the frostbite doesn't look permanent. I think he'll keep his limbs." May smiled and took a healthy drink of her wine. "He's still babbling about monsters in the woods, although he didn't see any."

At least he was still in the hospital. Ophelia had contacted the attorney in Fairbanks but he wouldn't be able to get a hearing until Monday. Once the judge signed the warrant, Ophelia could take Wyatt into custody.

Delores leaned forward. "Are you any further on the case? Who killed that EVE guy?"

Ophelia shook her head. "No clue, and according to the folks at EVE, he didn't work there. Their theory is that he acquired the coat with the logo on it from somewhere else."

"Right," Flossy muttered. "Tons of secrets out there, I'm tellin' you."

Including the identity of the new head of security, a fact Ophelia would not share. "Do you all really think that place just studies the ionosphere?" She couldn't wait until she received the information about EVE from DC. If she received the information.

"Who the heck knows," Delores said.

Flossy took out her supplies and handed over a blue square of material with a majestic eagle already stitched on it. "You can stitch this to the quilt. He reminds me of Brock."

"Thanks." Ophelia looked at the material. Brock as an eagle? Made sense, somehow.

Flossy removed another square. This one had a bunch of owls scattered across it, looking like a bunch of kindergarteners. "I've always had fun with the rumors about EVE, but to be honest, I've never seen anything odd. Sure, the talk is crazy, but life gets boring out here in the winter when we're not trying to survive."

Doc nodded. "I've only been here a couple of months, but I haven't seen anything out of the ordinary either."

"Me neither," Loretta said, leaning over to carefully stitch her square to the bigger pieces.

Flossy nudged Ophelia in the arm. "I listened to your conversation in the truck. Was that your boss?"

Ophelia nodded. "Oh, yeah. That was my boss."

Flossy grimaced. "Are you in trouble? Is that why they sent you all the way out here?"

Might as well tell the truth. "Yes. I had the same partner for a year, and it turned out he had a gambling problem and ended up stealing money and getting in deep with the wrong people."

"How is that your fault?" Monica asked, her brow furrowing.

Ophelia's stomach cramped. "He was my partner, I'm an FBI agent, and I didn't see it. Plus, well…"

Loretta twittered. "You were more than partners with this man."

Ophelia nodded. "Yep. That's also against the rules." She'd thought he was the one. Boy had she been wrong. "So, I'm on my last chance here, according to rumors at the Bureau." And what her boss had said.

Loretta winked at her. "I've been accused of murder, so I don't really pay attention to rumors because they're usually wrong."

Ophelia coughed and set down her wineglass. "Huh." She didn't know what else to say.

Loretta laughed. "Go ahead. You know you want to interview me, and I don't have anything to hide. Feel free."

Ophelia paused, wanting to do her job but also needing to relax. "You have a right to a lawyer."

Loretta's louder peal tinkled like bells. Her brown eyes sparkled. "Thanks, but I don't need one. Tamara Randsom was a cranky woman who didn't like anybody, including Leo. I don't think she abandoned her kids, but she definitely left him. Their divorce went through and she moved out to the Tundra Haven complex."

Ophelia paused in watching Delores's hands. Finally. Some relevant facts. "A complex?"

"I guess a long stay motel that folks used as apartments?" Delores murmured. "Yeah. That's how I'd describe the place."

Monica nodded. "Tammy lived at the Tundra for at least a month."

Ophelia tried to keep her tone level. "Tell me about the Tundra Haven. Did Tammy live with anybody? Who owns the place? What happened to her belongings after her disappearance?"

Loretta held up a hand. "Whoa. Slow down. I had a drink earlier today. Let's see. She lived alone as far as I know, Jarod Teller owned the complex, and her belongings burned in the fire that demolished the whole place."

Fire? Ophelia sat back. "How long after she disappeared did the fire occur?"

Loretta twisted her lip. "The fire took place sometime in the spring, maybe May? I don't know exactly when Tammy disappeared. Nobody does. She partied a lot in town from what I heard, and it's not like she and Leo had a custody arrangement in place. He kept the homestead and kids, and she took them when she finished partying and acting like a teenager. That's what he said, anyway."

Ophelia sat back and watched Loretta's facial muscles. She seemed to be telling the truth. "Does Leo have any idea where she is?"

Loretta shook her head. "No, he doesn't. He also thinks she never would've left the kids, so something bad probably happened to her. But neither of us hurt her, and we have no idea who did." She sighed. "We've searched our property for any sign of her but have found nothing. Sometimes people disappear around here, and we don't know if it's because of animals, the weather, or something worse." She bit her lip. "I wish she had just taken off and would come back and see the children someday, but it doesn't feel like that's possible."

"Is there any chance she died in that fire?" Ophelia asked.

Flossy shook her head. "Oh, no. I don't remember the exact date of the fire. When the insurance guy found out we lacked a fire marshal, he had a buddy from Anchorage come here with his cadaver dog, and we all searched the rubble for valuables that might've survived for those who'd lost their homes. The expert and dog confirmed that there were no human remains. Thank goodness."

Ophelia sat straighter. "You wouldn't have the names of the insurance adjuster or his buddy?"

"Nope," Flossy said. "I'm sure Jarod does. He did get a big payout, I think. Don't know the amount." She patted her gray hair. "If you ask me, Tammy just didn't want to stay in Knife's Edge."

Delores nodded. "Yeah, I agree. Tammy always acted too good to live here and didn't make friends. She didn't care much for Leo and wanted to live in a city—a real one. But she loved her kids and wouldn't have just left them."

Ophelia studied how Delores moved the quilting needles. "When was the last time you saw Tammy, Loretta?"

"I think it was during the kindergarten graduation," Loretta said, pursing her lips as she thought. "I'm pretty sure."

So the day of Tamara's last social media post.

Loretta resumed stitching the quilt. "Leo heard that Tammy, ah, sowed her wild oats. That she slept with a few men from town."

"Who?" Ophelia asked.

Loretta shrugged. "Leo didn't say who and I didn't ask."

Delores cleared her throat, her hands stitching fast and sure. "I heard she was having a good time, as well. It's too bad the Tundra burned down."

Wasn't it, though?

CHAPTER TWENTY-FOUR

Brock hunched into his jacket and hopped out of his truck just as David easily carried a giggling Monica over his shoulder out of Delores's house.

"They got into the wine," David said, opening the plow truck's door and gently tucking in his fiancée. After securing her seatbelt, he shut the door and snorted. "A lot of wine."

Shaking his head, Brock strode up the walkway and knocked on the door as the chilly air burned his skin, biting back a smile at the peals of laughter from inside. The plow truck ignited behind him and David drove off, leaving the surrounding area quiet.

The hair on Brock's nape stood, and he went on full alert. He looked around the normally peaceful subdivision, seeing quiet houses surrounded by darkened trees. Somebody lurked out there. He didn't know who, but every instinct he had told him somebody watched him right now.

It wasn't Christian. He knew Christian. Oddly enough, he knew what it felt like to be hunted by C. It wasn't his brother watching from the woods.

The door opened, and he pivoted as heat blew from the

small home. Ophelia stumbled out with Flossy on her heels, both women laughing and already bundled up for the frigid night.

"Thanks for coming to get us." Ophelia looked up, her cheeks rosy and her eyes bright. "We had a little bit of wine."

Flossy snorted and nudged Ophelia aside with one skinny elbow. "We had a lot of wine." Thick material tumbled out of her hands to land on her boots.

Brock leaned over and snagged the partially finished quilt before it could get too wet. "Flossy, be careful." He lifted the squares, noting a large salmon taking center stage in one of the squares. "That's a big fish."

Flossy giggled. "Yeah, I know." Then she looked around the darkened subdivision and up at the snowing sky. "Hey, we've got to get going. I have to work early in the morning." The elderly woman slid her hand beneath his elbow. "Let's go, Brock."

He paused. "Who else needs a ride home?"

Flossy snorted. "Nobody. Loretta drank mostly water after just one glass of wine so she could drive home. Doc is sleeping on the couch right now, and Delores lives here. You should know that. Geez."

Wow. Tons of wine. Brock reached for Ophelia's elbow to assist both women down the stairs and toward the truck, which he'd left idling in the driveway. Even so, he scrutinized the forest on the other side of the subdivision to the north. The sense of somebody watching him had gone. Nobody was out there. Perhaps his imagination was fucking with him. "Let's get you two in the truck," he said calmly, hustling them both into the warm cab before looking again at the forest. Nothing moved.

They were halfway home before Flossy finally kicked her feet toward the heater. "Oh, man, Brock, you should have seen Olly interrogating Loretta. It was actually a lot of fun."

Ophelia snorted from the back seat. "I did not interrogate anybody. I just asked her a couple of questions. Frankly, she volunteered a lot of information."

Brock looked through the rearview mirror at Ophelia, who had settled in quite nicely. "What do you think? Do you believe she harmed Tammy?"

Ophelia shook her head. "No, not really. I can't say for certain, but she seemed to be telling the truth. Although..." She looked out into the darkened night. "I have to say, everyone seems to allow for odd happenings around here. What exactly are you people afraid lurks in the woods?"

Brock shrugged. "There's a lot of danger out there, but nothing supernatural. The cold will destroy you faster than anything else." He turned off the river road and headed down Main Street, driving slowly to Flossy's place. He jumped out and helped the elderly woman to the door as Ophelia brought all their quilting supplies.

Flossy moved inside and toed off her boots, her thin hand holding the material that showed a massive moose. "I stitched the owls and fish but didn't get a chance to add the moose. Maybe I'll only have one glass of wine next time." She wavered slightly.

Brock turned toward Ophelia. "So. Are you staying here or with me?"

Ophelia handed the remaining quilting supplies to Flossy. "Oh, I'm staying with you, but first we're going to have a drink at Sam's."

The woman wanted to grab a drink? "All right." Then he grasped her arm to help her across the ice to the truck while scanning the surrounding area for threats. Soon they headed down Main Street again toward Sam's. "It seems like you had a good time at your first quilting party." He kept an eye on a strengthening storm, evidenced by the wind beating the trees down around them.

She grinned. "Oh, I had so much fun. Who knew quilting could be enjoyable? I don't have a lot with friends, to be honest." Her voice quieted at the end. "I guess I've been busy with work and haven't really worked on forming good friendships."

Yeah, she came off adorable when tipsy—and sounded a little lonely. He could relate, especially since he didn't feel in sync with any of his brothers. He didn't know how, but he needed to fix that. Somehow.

Before he knew it, they walked inside the bar. Heat slammed into him along with the din of noise. At this time of night, Sam's only had a few regulars at the bar, along with a couple of people playing pool. Amka waved a greeting from behind the bar, and he waved back. Then he caught sight of Leo Randsom over in the corner and awareness dawned. "Ah, I get it. Leo Randsom is here. All right, let's do this."

Ophelia tromped toward Leo's table.

He sat alone with a drink in front of him. As he looked up, his eyes stayed clear, his graying beard rugged and bushy. "Hey, what's up, Brock?"

Brock nodded his head toward Ophelia. "I think Olly has a couple of questions for you."

Leo grinned. "Yeah. Loretta texted from the quilting party and said you'd probably be by."

Ophelia took out a seat. "I already talked to Loretta, and I wanted to get your take on what happened to your ex-wife."

Leo kept his hand flattened on the table with his beer to the right. "I wish I could tell you something or say I know anything. All I know is that Tammy was unhappy, wanted to leave, and took off. Before you ask, I do not think she would've left the kids. I think something happened to her, and we don't know what."

Amka hustled over with a pitcher of beer and ice-covered mugs. "Hey, you two. There's a storm coming. What are you doing out right now?"

Brock gratefully took the mugs and poured two glasses. "We're just working." He looked around for Jarod. Ophelia had mentioned she wanted to interview him during the drive to the tavern. "Where's your business partner?"

"Who knows?" Amka muttered.

Ophelia grasped her arm before she could leave. "I'm curious about the Tundra Complex. I heard Jarod owned it and that it burned down."

Amka nodded. "Yes. The old place had faulty wiring, but at least nobody was hurt in the fire. I don't know much more about it than that. Jarod owned it. If he comes back in, I'll let you know." She hustled off to bus another table.

Brock couldn't figure Amka and Jarod out. Amka struck him as intelligent, and he trusted that she'd ask for help if necessary, but what if fear stopped her? She didn't appear frightened, but something felt off, and he wanted to help. He handed one of the beers to Ophelia.

She took a sip, her gaze on Leo. "Okay, so your divorce from Tammy went through last March. When did you start dating Loretta?"

Leo nodded. "I started seeing Loretta that March and married her in July. She's the one. Don't look at me like I'm a jerk. Tammy cheated on me a good year before we even filed for divorce."

Brock took a drink of his beer. He'd heard rumors but never paid attention to them.

"With whom?" Ophelia asked.

Leo tipped back his beer and swallowed several gulps. "The summer of *last* year, when we were still married, I followed her a few times and staked out the Tundra Complex."

"What? I thought the Tundra served as an apartment complex," Ophelia said, her brow furrowing.

Brock nodded. "The Tundra had about twenty suites and served as a long-stay motel. But Jarod rented rooms by the hour to make extra money." He didn't judge what others did, but the by-hour situation never made sense to him.

Leo looked down at the table. "That summer, I caught Tammy taking tourists there. You know. A guy from a fishing or hunting tour." He moved uncomfortably. "I should've divorced her right there and then, but I worried about the kids. Then earlier *this* year she wanted a divorce, so I gave it to her."

Ophelia narrowed her eyes. "What are you leaving out?"

The woman had excellent instincts. Brock enjoyed watching her work.

"Nothing that is relevant to your case," Leo said.

Ophelia waited until he looked up at her. "That's up to me, don't you think?"

He glanced at Brock, who nodded at him.

"Fine, but it's not relevant. Last year, during the summer when I was following my wife around, I saw Hank leaving that place a couple of times."

"Hank?" Brock shook his head. He'd had no idea. "Why would he have been at the motel? The man had his own cabin." As far as Brock knew, Hank hadn't been romantically involved with anybody in eons.

Leo shrugged. "I don't know. Maybe one or more of you guys came home for leave that summer, but I don't remember. Maybe that's why Hank kept any liaisons away from his place. Or he just wanted privacy. Who knows? I don't know, and I don't care. Frankly, I wouldn't know if I hadn't been staking out the Tundra to see who my wife was fucking."

Ophelia cast Brock a look and then refocused on Leo. "Is there any chance Hank and Tammy had relations?"

Heat flushed down Brock's back. "Hank would never have slept with Tammy since he considered Leo a friend."

Leo nodded. "Totally agree. They weren't there together."

Ophelia put her palm to her forehead. "Okay. So what? Eighteen months ago, in the summer, Tammy had liaisons with tourists, none of whom you know."

"Not just in the summer," Leo groused. "She kept it up until we got divorced. But at least her taste improved after that."

Warning ticked down Brock's back. Why? He didn't know. "What are you saying?"

Leo looked miserable. "This May, after you left town, Tammy and Ace had a thing. It might've only been one night or weekend. She was now living at the Tundra, and I dropped by the kids' spring soccer schedule and found him coming out of her place. He still had bruises from the plane wreck and wouldn't meet my eyes." Leo glanced up, sweeping his hands wide. "I didn't give a shit. Felt bad for the guy, to be honest."

Brock's eyebrows lifted. Ace had slept with Tammy? That didn't sound like Ace, since he and Leo were friends, but he had gone through a rough time after the plane wreck, which they still hadn't discussed in any detail. "What the hell?"

Ophelia sat back, looking like her nice buzz disappeared. "Brock?"

"I didn't know that," he said.

Ophelia focused on Brock. "When did Ace return to town after his plane wreck?"

Brock crossed his arms. "I left on the first of May, and apparently my brother came home on the fifth. Obviously, if I knew he was coming home, I would've stayed. I didn't know, and I went off the grid until last week."

Leo nodded. "Don't blame you. Walkabout is a good way to handle stress, and getting out of the service seems stressful. My brother was a Marine, and he went through the same thing."

Brock didn't regret his time wandering the wilds, but he wished he could've been there for Ace.

Ophelia lowered her chin. "Leo? What's the timeframe between when you caught Ace with Tammy and the Tundra burning down?"

Leo shrugged. "Maybe a week? Shit, I don't remember. I didn't torch the place because my ex-wife had sex there, and I can't even pinpoint when she disappeared since she refused to agree to any sort of custody schedule. May was a rough month for Knife's Edge. I guess Tammy disappeared, the sheriff keeled over in the middle of church, and then the Tundra burned down. We were all scrambling, I guess."

Brock glanced at Ophelia. "I heard that everybody got out and nobody died in the fire, so that's good."

"Leo? While you staked out the Tundra, did you see anybody else of interest?" Ophelia asked.

Good question. Brock sat back to watch her work.

Leo finished his beer. "No. After we divorced, I saw her with Ace, with Fred Jeronimish, and still with Jarod." He glanced under his lashes at Amka behind the bar. "Fred moved down to the lower forty-eight, but if you want more info, I'd talk with both Jarod and Ace. Sorry, Brock."

A stone dropped into Brock's gut. He really didn't like this.

Leo kicked back his chair and stood. "All right, I'm done with this interview. If you want to ask me anything else, talk to my lawyer. All I'll tell you is that I have no clue where Tammy is, and considering she hasn't tried to contact the kids in any way, she's probably dead. That's it. Sorry. I truly am." He turned and lumbered toward the bar to pay his bill.

Ophelia took another sip of beer. "You know, every time I think I have a line on either of these cases, they go in the opposite direction of what I expect." She gently placed the mug back on the table. "Well, let's go talk to Ace."

The door opened, and Christian walked in, snow in his hair.

Brock instinctively stood.

Christian moved toward him. "I was out night hunting once it got dark and I think I found Tamara Randsom's body up by Gravewatch Peak in an old warming hut." He glanced at Ophelia, keeping his voice to a low whisper. "It looked like something clawed her to death...and gouged out her eyes."

CHAPTER TWENTY-FIVE

The nighttime snowmobile ride took nearly two hours, and by the time Ophelia stretched off the back of Brock's sled, she regretted insisting on seeing the scene for herself. Her legs were stiff, her spine ached, and her bones felt bruised from the constant jarring over rugged, icy terrain. They had to be at least 4,000 feet above sea level. The air felt thinner, colder—like even breathing here required effort.

Brock knew the area well, and with his headlights, the ride had felt safe.

At least Ophelia had sobered up as midnight approached. Regardless of the late hour, with one body already having disappeared on her in the Alaskan wilderness, she needed to view the scene and take pictures to document this one.

The moon tried to break through the thick clouds but didn't have the strength to illuminate much. The snow had finally stopped falling, but the sky had cleared just enough for the cold to deepen and settle into the landscape like a predator. She shivered as Brock straddled the sled beside her, reaching out to steady her with a gloved hand around her elbow. His firm touch grounded her.

Christian had zoomed ahead and set up impressive flood lights aimed toward the dilapidated structure.

Ophelia studied the ramshackle hut ahead. The place looked even older and more weathered than the one where they'd spent the night. The wood was warped and splintering, the roof sagging under the weight of accumulated snow. The kicked-out path to the door was rough, as if whoever made it had cared more about speed than creating something usable.

"This place has been abandoned for years," Brock said, his breath fogging in the icy air. "We don't use it anymore. There's a better one about a mile east."

Christian's snowmobile sat parked to the left of the hut, the engine still ticking as it cooled. Christian himself emerged from the shadows of the entrance, shouldering the weather-beaten door open. The top hinge caught, and he had to shove harder to get it to swing wide. "This is not a good scene."

Ophelia's spine stiffened, and her head snapped up. "I'm an FBI agent, Christian. I've seen dead bodies before." Her breath puffed white in front of her face as she spoke.

Christian lifted a shoulder, his expression unreadable. Somehow, despite the unforgiving weather, he looked completely at ease in his black snow pants and matching jacket. Not even his nose or ears were red. The cold seemed to slide right off him.

Would she ever get used to this? The cold here wasn't like anything she'd ever known. It felt alive, relentless. She figured it might take years to adjust.

Taking a steadying breath, she plowed forward, sticking to the rough path. Even with the trail, the snow reached her knees in some places. Every step took effort.

Christian stepped aside to let her pass, and she ducked into the hut. Inside, the temperature somehow felt even colder, even with a large floodlight scaring all of the shadows away. The wind had worked its way through the cracks in the walls, and patches of snow and ice coated the floor. The place was an empty shell—just rotting wood, dust, and silence.

Her gaze landed on the body propped against the far wall.

A woman.

Her legs stretched out in front of her, stiff and awkward. What remained of her pants clung to her thighs in frozen, threadbare patches, faded from exposure and shredded near the ankles. Her jacket hung in tatters around her shoulders, its original color long lost to dirt and time. The fabric was frayed and paper-thin, brittle in some places like it had been gnawed or rotted through.

Her hair—what little was left—hung in sparse, brittle strands around her scalp, a dull, lifeless brown that looked matted and clumped from where the weather and animals had gotten to it. There were strange gaps where patches had fallen away or had been torn out entirely.

Ophelia swallowed hard, forcing herself to move closer despite the chill creeping up her spine.

The body was leaning at an unnatural angle against the far wall, half slumped, as though she'd been dropped there. Ophelia's gaze swept over the remains. Her arms lay limp at her sides, the sleeves of her jacket barely recognizable, the fabric shredded and frozen into the shape of the wall. What skin remained on her arms was stretched taut and thin, cracking along the joints where the ice had settled.

The woman's torso was partially exposed, the remnants of her shirt stiff with frost. Beneath the layers of ice and fabric, her ribs protruded slightly, as if the skin had dried and shrunken around her bones. Ophelia's breath hitched as she caught sight of her face—or what had once been her face. Then she lifted her phone and took pictures of the scene from every vantage point.

"She's partially frozen, partially not," Christian said from behind her, his voice grim. "Probably killed in the summer, decomposed for a while, and then froze when the temperatures dropped."

Ophelia barely registered his words. Her eyes remained locked on the hollow sockets where the woman's eyes should have been. The void there was haunting, as though the skull itself had secrets it was refusing to share.

She felt Brock step closer, his steady presence a silent reassurance. His warmth radiated through the frigid air, but she forced herself not to lean into it. Instead, she took another step forward and crouched down for a better view.

The skin on the woman's face was like thin, cracked parchment, discolored in places where frost had taken hold. Her lips had curled back slightly, leaving her teeth exposed in a macabre grimace. Her cheekbones jutted out sharply, skeletal but still oddly human beneath the frozen ruin of her flesh.

"Rodents?" Ophelia tilted her head, her voice quiet but steady.

Christian nodded grimly. "Could be. Scavengers, maybe birds. There's no way to know for sure until Doc takes a look."

She pointed to the woman's skull, narrowing her eyes at the faint, uneven depressions along the side. "There are dents here."

Christian crouched beside her, his expression dark. "Blunt force trauma, maybe. Or it could be bullet wounds, depending on how things broke apart. Hard to tell with the way she's been left like this."

"There's dried blood on the floor," Brock added, nodding toward the dark stains just visible beneath the layer of snow and dust. The stains had spread outward in uneven streaks, frozen over in thin layers of ice, but still unmistakably red-brown.

Ophelia scanned the rest of the room. It was barren—no furniture, no tools, no signs of human life. Just dust, ice, and decay.

Her stomach twisted, but she kept her voice calm. "I don't suppose we can get a forensic team out here?"

Christian snorted, shaking his head. "Not until May, probably."

Her head snapped toward him. "May?"

He shrugged, glancing at her. "Yeah. That's usually when Knife's Edge connects to the outside world again. It's almost impossible to get anyone out here during the winter. Even if they tried, it'd be a death wish."

He turned toward the door, angling his head like he could already hear the distant whisper of the next storm. "Another one's coming in about an hour. I talked to Amos this morning—this one's gonna last a few weeks."

Brock nodded in agreement. "We'll be lucky if we can get word to Anchorage, let alone send anyone in or out."

Ophelia clenched her fists, frustrated. They had a dead woman lying here—evidence frozen in time—and no one to properly examine her.

"So, what do we do?" she asked, her voice tight.

Christian's voice remained matter-of-fact. "Doc will freeze the body. Which ain't exactly hard to do around here."

Ophelia forced herself to stand, brushing the snow from her knees. Her legs shook, though not from the cold. She turned to Brock, searching his face for any sign of doubt.

He met her gaze, his jaw tightening. "We take her to Doc first. See what she can tell us."

She nodded slowly. "Let's do it." She paused, swallowing the lump in her throat. "Then we need to notify Leo."

Brock's shoulders tensed, and for a moment, he didn't speak. Finally, he exhaled and gave a short nod. "Yeah. He deserves to know."

Christian gestured to the lights. "The rescue toboggan is attached to my sled. Help me load her up and pack the lights, and then you two go back and get some sleep. It'll be slow going for me with the body, and I won't be able to just take her over the hill."

Brock glanced at Ophelia, obviously torn.

She lifted her chin. "I'm fine. We should go together."

"No," Brock said finally. "We're talking about hours of difference. I'll take you to get some sleep at my place. Period."

She didn't have the energy to argue with him.

The wind howled outside, as though reminding them of the storm barreling toward them. They didn't have much time.

Ophelia took one last look at the woman's lifeless form, committing every detail to memory. Whoever she had been, whatever had led her to this place—Ophelia was going to make sure her story didn't end here, in the cold, forgotten and alone.

CHAPTER TWENTY-SIX

Before her morning coffee, Dr. May Smirnov finished tying off the last suture on Ace Osprey's stubborn head wound. The thin line of stitches was neat despite his insistence on moving every time she touched his scalp. She usually arrived at work before dawn, so today was no exception, although she'd slept much better than usual on Delores's couch and might've slept even longer had Brock not radioed her about a body coming in. She'd reluctantly moved off the sofa and headed into work, calling and awakening the forensic pathologist in Anchorage once she had cell service close to town.

Ace had been waiting for her, bleeding as he leaned against the building. Moron.

"Now, tell me again how you managed to slice open your hairline," she murmured, focusing on snipping the final thread rather than the subtle, earthy scent clinging to him. The last thing she needed was to be distracted by a patient—especially one like Ace.

He grinned, the corner of his mouth tilting in a way that sent a jolt through her nerves. "I tripped and fell. It's that simple, Doc."

She arched a brow, unimpressed. He also smelled like whiskey. "Nothing is ever that simple."

He shrugged but didn't lose the grin.

She tossed the suturing tools into the metal bowl with a sharp clang. "Did you know the Surgeon General updated the guidance about alcohol? It's a toxin—never good for you, not even in small doses." Her voice came out sharper than she intended, but she blamed the way he was watching her.

"Yeah, I heard." He reached for his coat. He shrugged it on with ease, despite the height of the examination table forcing him to sit taller than usual. She winced internally. The clinic's old, cheap equipment didn't make things easy—she'd had to stand on a step stool just to reach him, which irritated her more than it should have.

His green eyes caught the sterile light, sparkling with amusement. His unkempt hair, streaked with deep brown, was in desperate need of a cut. She felt an almost overwhelming urge to push it back and trim it herself—an impulse she fought off with a professionalism that was becoming harder to maintain.

She wasn't here to take care of him in that way. She was his doctor. Nothing more.

A sudden crash sounded from outside. The loud bang reverberated through the small clinic.

She jumped.

Ace's gaze immediately sharpened, narrowing as he studied her. "That's just snow falling from the eaves. You okay, Doc?"

"Oh, yeah." She forced a laugh that sounded hollow to her own ears. "Loud noises and all that." She tried to shake off the feeling of being exposed and turned back to make a notation in his chart.

The truth was, she hated loud, unexpected sounds. They took her right back to moments she didn't want to remember.

Ace's focus followed her as she scrawled her notes in his thickening chart.

"You know," she began, keeping her tone light, "as your doctor, I'd recommend looking into mental health support. There are several excellent professionals you could Zoom with. You could even use my office if you wanted."

One side of his mouth lifted into a sardonic grin. "You think I need my head shrunk?"

"Definitely," she retorted, smiling despite herself. "You're stitched together more often than not, and you've been coming in here more frequently, according to your medical records. Something's off. Whatever happened with that plane crash, Ace? You haven't dealt with it. You need to."

The grin faded from his face, replaced by something quieter and more serious. He crossed his arms, leaning back just enough that the table creaked beneath him. His gaze locked on hers, steady and probing. "What about you?" he asked quietly.

Her fingers froze over the chart. She blinked. "What?"

"What are you dealing with, Doc?"

The question was so unexpected, so direct, that she felt like the floor had shifted beneath her feet. She looked away, but the weight of his stare didn't let up.

They'd run into each other around town more than a few times, enough for her to know his habits and his quirks. And any time he got himself injured—which was more often than not—he showed up at the clinic. But never once had he asked her a personal question. Not like this.

"I don't know what you're talking about."

He didn't look away, his gaze steady, peeling back her layers. "I think you do. Loud noises, huh? What else bothers you?"

She turned to face him fully, trying to muster the confidence she always felt in the exam room. "Nosy patients," she said flatly.

"Fine, but if you need help, I can sober up." He winked. "Do you need help?"

Charming, sexy, and wounded. A total disaster, basically. "No. Just pay your bill on time."

He sobered, looking dangerous instead of damaged. "I'm here if you need me."

Her throat tightened. "That's kind of you," she murmured. "I don't need help—of any kind. Stop drinking. Listen to your doctor."

"You're not my doctor," Ace said lowly. "Just because you patch me up once in a while doesn't give us a doctor-patient relationship, May. Don't forget that."

She couldn't breathe. "What are you saying?"

"The words make sense. I'll lock the front door on my way out." Ace's jaw flexed. "You need to be more careful opening the place by yourself so early in the morning."

"Brock and Ophelia will be here in a few minutes, if you want to wait for them," she offered.

His expression blanked. "Yeah, Christian left me a message when he hit town and probably called them as well. I'm sorry about Tamara. I'll see you later, May." He loped out of the examination room and down the hallway, disappearing. The tension in the room relaxed. How odd.

She shook herself out of it and cleaned the room, sterilizing it. Then she moved into the hallway, ready to make that coffee.

The knock on the clinic's front door was sudden and sharp. She jumped again, her shoulders jerking before she could stop herself. Oh for goodness' sake. She knew they would be coming. Clearing her throat, she pressed her hand to the door, willing herself to stay in the present. She wasn't that person anymore. She was in control.

She opened the door. "Sorry. I forgot that Ace locked this."

"Hey, Doc," Ophelia said as she entered the reception area, her voice steady. "Ace? Why was Ace here?"

Damn it. She shouldn't have said anything. "Um, forget I said that." Did she just violate HIPAA?

Ophelia's eyes narrowed. "Okay. For now, we put the body in the hospital operating room instead of your office."

The small-town hospital sat snugly between May's clinic and the dentist's office, the three businesses sharing a single operating room when surgeries or emergencies cropped up. The room had seen its fair share of chaotic injuries, but nothing like this.

"Sounds good," May said, tying back her hair with quick precision. "I already contacted a forensic scientist colleague in Anchorage and we'll see what we can do from here. But we'll still need to send the body to the city when we get the chance." But now wasn't the time to dwell on that.

Taking a deep breath, May strode with Ophelia through the hub of her office and into the operating room. Brock already waited, his expression a mix of grim resolve and shared grief.

"You acting here as the sheriff?" she asked Brock, her tone more brisk than she intended.

He exhaled. "I don't know. I'm not the sheriff, but I'm the best we have right now."

"Well," she said firmly, gesturing toward the door, "you two need to leave, please. I need to keep this place sterile."

Ophelia frowned, but Brock gave a short nod.

"I mean it, Agent," May added, emphasizing Ophelia's title on purpose.

Ophelia blinked, then finally turned and followed Brock out.

The room fell into silence as May turned to the body on the table. Her heart clenched. She'd never met Tamara. What a waste of a young life—and those poor kids left behind without their mother.

She took a moment to ground herself, then booted up the computer. She still needed coffee, damn it. The internet was unpredictable at best, but for now, it held. She initiated a call to the forensic lab in Anchorage, and a familiar face appeared on the screen.

Dr. Elijah Porter. He was younger than most forensic experts she'd met, probably mid-thirties, with close-cropped auburn hair and wire-rimmed glasses that magnified his intelligent, steady gaze. They'd crossed paths at a conference two weeks previous when she'd ventured as far as Anchorage, where he'd given a sharp, no-nonsense presentation on managing evidence preservation in extreme environments.

"May," Elijah said, his voice calm. "Thank you for calling me in on this. What have you got?"

"A body," she said plainly. "We're isolated, and the weather's about to trap us here for a few weeks. I need to conduct a partial autopsy remotely."

His face tightened, but he nodded, all business. He'd asked her out in Anchorage, and she'd pretty much run away. "All right. Let's get started. Walk me through the scene."

May switched on the overhead light and angled it to better illuminate the body on the examination table. The harsh light cast long shadows over the sterile metal surface. She scanned the area beneath the body and along the sides of the table for any fluids or evidence that might have seeped out during transport. A faint, reddish-brown stain clung to the edges of the table, likely from thawing during the move.

"Residual fluid," May murmured as she leaned in closer, swabbing the edge of the stain with a sterile cotton swab. The cold antiseptic smell in the room mixed uneasily with the faint metallic scent clinging to Tamara's remains.

Elijah's image on the screen flickered as he adjusted his view. "That tracks. If she died in June and was exposed to the heat for weeks, most of the blood would have pooled, dried, or been absorbed. What you're seeing now is from the thaw after she was moved. She bled out when it was warm."

May's stomach tightened as she took in the full picture. "So the environment sped things up and then preserved her."

Elijah nodded. "Apparently."

May retrieved forceps and lifted a strand of brittle hair near the back of the head. The strands broke apart as she touched them, crumbling into small, dry pieces. She carefully placed the largest intact pieces into a collection bag. The rest would be useless for further testing.

She adjusted the light again and leaned toward the ragged fabric of Tamara's tattered jacket. "I'm taking fiber samples from the clothing remnants," she said aloud for the recording. She gently sliced away a portion of the frayed sleeve and placed it in a labeled evidence bag.

Elijah leaned closer to his screen. "Show me the skull."

May repositioned the camera to highlight two dents in the skull. The larger one was jagged and deep, while the smaller one was almost circular.

"Blunt force trauma," May murmured as she traced the edges of the depression with a sterile probe. "But different shapes—could they both come from the same weapon?"

"Maybe," Elijah replied thoughtfully. "If it was something irregular, like a crowbar, or if the killer changed the angle of the strikes. But it could also be two different weapons."

May leaned in further, noting the splintering along the edges of the larger depression. "Whatever they used, they hit her hard enough to fracture the bone. This wasn't an accident. No fall does this."

Elijah nodded slowly, his expression grim. "This was deliberate. You can confirm the manner of death as homicide."

The words settled heavily in the room. May felt a chill that had nothing to do with the temperature. Tamara hadn't slipped and fallen. She hadn't gotten lost or injured. Someone had attacked her—brutally.

May shifted her focus to the hollow orbits of the eyes. The edges of the sockets were uneven and frayed, as if something had chewed at them.

"The orbits are empty," she noted quietly. "The edges aren't clean. Could scavengers have done this?"

Elijah narrowed his eyes at the feed. "It's consistent with

scavenger activity, especially if she was left exposed during the warmer months. Rodents, birds...But there's no way to know for sure without testing the tissue inside the sockets."

May swabbed carefully along the edges of the eye sockets, collecting any residue that might offer clues. She sealed the swab in a vial and added it to the evidence tray.

She adjusted her view of the body, taking in the dried remnants of blood near the scalp and the frostbitten discoloration along the arms and torso. Even with the preserved tissue, the signs of early decomposition from the summer heat were still visible—the papery thinness of the remaining skin, the way some of the muscles had shriveled.

"You're doing a good job," Elijah said.

"Thanks." May took a slow breath, trying to focus on the task at hand rather than the grim circumstances. "Is there any chance we can get her body to Anchorage?"

Elijah's expression darkened. "Not for weeks. Not with that storm coming in. But you're already doing everything we would do at the lab."

She gave a brief nod. The evidence had to be preserved as best as possible until transport became feasible. Freezing the body again would slow further decay, but it wouldn't stop everything.

"Understood," she said, pressing her lips into a tight line. She noted the samples she'd collected—tissue, fibers, hair, and residue—and organized the sealed vials and bags in the evidence tray.

"Good work, May," Elijah said after a pause. "I'll make sure this case is flagged as a priority once we can receive the body."

May exhaled slowly. "Thank you."

He grinned, now off duty. "Maybe you can escort the body and we could get that drink this time."

She forced a smile, having no intention of leaving the safety of Knife's Edge again. Ever. "That would be lovely."

"Good." Satisfaction tilted his lips. "I'll see you then." He ended the call.

She stood there for a long moment, staring at Tamara's lifeless form. Finally, she peeled off her gloves and disposed of them before walking to the hospital reception area, where Brock and Ophelia waited on black leather chairs. "It's done," May said softly. "Cause of death is homicide."

CHAPTER TWENTY-SEVEN

Brock's gut twisted like a steel coil. Someone had killed Tamara—brutally—and he hadn't seen it coming. He'd been half-living since Hank died, trudging through the motions, barely paying attention to the world around him. That had to stop. He shouldn't have left town for so many months, but he'd needed the time. To heal.

Poor Tamara.

True, most of the town—including Leo—had figured Tamara had simply gone off to party somewhere else, wanting to escape the weight of responsibility. But someone should've looked deeper into her disappearance. Someone should've cared enough to ask more questions.

He now sat in Leo's home next to Ophelia on a loveseat, facing Leo and Loretta sitting on a matching sofa as he gave them the notification.

The man's face crumpled. Tears filled Leo's eyes along with shock. Loretta had clutched his hand, pale and trembling.

"I don't know how I'm going to tell the kids," Leo muttered, shaking his head.

"We'll tell them together," Loretta said softly, her voice

steady despite the tears. "I think...I think we all knew Tamara wasn't coming back. But having it confirmed...it's terrible." She looked up at Brock, her expression fragile but fierce. "Who would do this to her? It doesn't make sense."

Brock's eyes felt like somebody rubbed sandpaper in them. He and Ophelia hadn't slept in over twenty-four hours. "I don't know." He kept his voice low. He didn't mention the missing eyes. Their removal hadn't caused Tamara's death, and Leo didn't need to know that haunting detail. "We'll find out, though," Brock promised.

Leo's expression shifted. "So...you're taking the sheriff's job?"

Brock didn't answer.

Ophelia cleared her throat, her presence calm but commanding. "We'll need to interview you both later—once you've had time. But, Leo, I'd like you to walk me through the last time you saw Tamara."

Loretta began to speak, but Ophelia raised a single finger, stopping her mid-sentence. "No, thank you, Loretta. Just Leo, for now."

Brock leaned back against the wall and crossed his arms. He knew what Ophelia was doing—she didn't want to give them time to get their stories straight. He understood that from a law enforcement perspective, but as a neighbor and friend, it grated on him.

Leo scrubbed a hand over his face, pressing his ring fingers into the corners of his eyes. "I honestly don't know," he admitted. "It was sometime in May. She'd come and go. Sometimes she'd show up to take the kids for a weekend. Sometimes she'd call—if there was cell service." His shoulders sagged. "But I can say for sure I saw her at the kindergarten graduation mid-May. But she did not attend the Knife's Edge annual town meeting on June first, and I thought it odd. We elected Brock sheriff that day."

Brock's jaw clenched. "I should've attended that meeting," he muttered.

"Yeah." Leo gave a dry, humorless laugh. "Maybe you could've convinced everyone to elect Ace instead. Too late now."

"You might as well be sheriff," Loretta said softly. "We're all treating you like one anyway."

If Brock could take the job officially, he would. But not yet.

"So, the kindergarten graduation," Ophelia prompted. "That's the last time you know for sure you saw her?"

Leo nodded. "It all blends together after that. I may've seen her when she came to get the kids, but I don't remember clearly."

Her eyes shifted to Loretta. "What about you?"

Loretta's cheeks flushed as she twisted her hands in her lap. "I saw her at the graduation as well. Leo and I sat together...holding hands. It angered her. She glared at us and flipped me off as she walked out."

Leo's eyebrows shot up. "She did?"

"Yes." Loretta shifted uncomfortably on the sofa next to her husband. "I didn't say anything because—well, you two already didn't get along. And I figured seeing you happy...when she hadn't figured things out yet...probably made her furious."

"I get it," Leo murmured. "We're all human."

Ophelia studied the two of them carefully. Loretta looked young and fresh beside Leo, her long hair in a neat braid trailing over her shoulder. But Leo's broad, calloused hands gripped his knees tightly, the muscles tense.

"Did either of you hurt Tamara?" Ophelia's question was blunt, delivered without hesitation.

Loretta's jaw dropped, and Leo leaned back in disbelief.

"Of course not," they said in unison.

Loretta's eyes glistened with fresh tears. "We would never do that."

"She has—had—children," Leo said, his voice cracking. "Even

if I was some kind of asshole who'd hurt a woman—which I'm not—I'd never do that to my kids. They always come first."

The truth in his voice was palpable, but Brock had seen enough in life not to put blind faith in anyone.

"Okay," Ophelia said, her tone softening. "I need you both to put together a detailed journal of the time between the summer you discovered Tamara cheating on you, your divorce, and her disappearance. Write down everything—every time you saw her, every person who was around her, anything she said or did. Can you do that?"

Loretta nodded silently, wiping at her eyes.

Leo didn't answer. He just stared, his eyes filled with simmering anger.

Brock held his gaze for a moment, then shook his head and stood. "Questions have to be asked, Leo. I'm sorry for your loss."

Leo's face twisted, but he said nothing as Brock stepped past him and escorted Ophelia out.

They made the snowmobile ride back to town in silence, save for the hum of the engine and the occasional rush of wind tearing past them. Brock had insisted Ophelia sit in front of him to shield her from the worst of the cold. He kept his arms braced around her, his legs snug against the outside of hers to keep her steady and as warm as possible. She sagged against him, probably half asleep.

He tightened his hold on her, making sure she stayed somewhat awake.

She nodded, then tilted her head back just enough to clunk the top of her helmet against his. The playful gesture was so unexpected that he chuckled. Even with the cold trying to freeze them both solid, that small movement warmed him more than the layers of gear ever could.

He felt the shift in his blood—an unmistakable heat spreading through his veins like a shot of fine whiskey. Having her this close, her body tucked against his, made him forget for a moment how brutal the day had been. His legs tightened involuntarily as if to pull her closer.

Would he always feel this way around her?

That thought made his chest ache in a way that had nothing to do with the cold. Would there even be an *always*? He'd been running on autopilot since Hank died, trying to keep his brothers and himself afloat. His life was still a mess. Until he figured out how to patch himself up, he had no right to consider something more with her. But the other night—the way she'd whispered his name, soft and raw—had stitched something together inside him that he hadn't even realized was broken.

He pulled into town and parked on the curb in front of Sam's Tavern. Ophelia swung her leg over the seat and stood with surprising grace despite her obvious fatigue.

Brock slid off behind her and stepped forward to undo the chin strap of her helmet. His fingers brushed her jawline as he lifted it off, and she shivered. "You sure you're up for this right now? We both need sleep."

"Yeah, I'm sure. We really need to talk to Jarod. I'm curious about the timing of the Tundra Haven fire." Her voice was steady, but the tension in her shoulders betrayed her reluctance. "Then Ace. Please call him again."

If Ace didn't want to be found, he wouldn't be. "I will," Brock said, knowing it was useless. Ace would get back to him when he wanted.

Ophelia shifted her weight and let out a slow breath. "I think I should speak with Jarod alone."

Brock straightened to his full height, and pulled off his own helmet, holding it at his side. "Excuse me?"

Ophelia turned to face him fully, snowflakes clinging to the strands of hair that had escaped from beneath her hat. One flake landed on her nose and melted instantly.

"I think," she repeated, "he'll be flirty and more forthcoming if you're not there. If you are, he'll try to act tough and macho." She hesitated, then added, "And Brock...you haven't officially decided to be the sheriff."

He flinched slightly, but she didn't back down. Her eyes locked with his, her chin lifting in quiet defiance. "You're acting like it. People are treating you like it. But until you make that commitment, you're not."

The challenge hung in the air between them. He wanted to argue, to tell her she was wrong—but she wasn't. He growled low in his throat. "All right," he said, his voice rougher than he intended. "You can talk to Jarod. But if he gives you any trouble—"

She cut him off with a wink which was cute, even with the exhaustion evident in her pretty eyes. "I know. Plant him on his ass."

A grin tugged at his lips despite the weight pressing down on him.

"Trust me," she added, stepping toward the tavern doors. "I'm looking forward to it."

"I do." Brock sucked in freezing air, forcing himself to awaken completely.

She turned suddenly to face him, still outside, her face reddening from the air. "Ace is hiding from us, Brock. I like you. A lot. But you have to realize that there's more than a decent chance that I'm going to have to arrest your brother. Even if I can't prove it yet, I think I have enough to arrest him on suspicion of murder."

No, she didn't. She had enough to try and that would normally scare somebody. Not Ace. "Ace didn't hurt Tamara." He knew to his soul that Ace would never harm a woman.

"What about Hank?" she whispered. "You know as well as I that he left Doc's earlier to avoid us. There was no reason for her not to tell him that we were bringing in a body, so I'm sure she did. And he did not stick around."

"We don't know that," Brock said, his gut churning.

Where the hell was Ace?

CHAPTER TWENTY-EIGHT

Ophelia couldn't feel her legs. She needed a massage—a long, luxurious session where someone worked out every knot until she could remember what warmth felt like. "Let's do this so we can get some sleep." When was the last time she'd been up for more than twenty-four hours? She couldn't remember, and the world felt fuzzy.

"Agreed." Brock pushed open the door just as David and Monica walked out, bundled in their winter gear.

"Hi," Monica said, her voice softening as she caught sight of them. "Amka made her orange scones today, so we stopped by for breakfast. Oh, Lord. I'm so sorry." She lowered her voice, sympathy etched across her face. "I heard about Tamara. Do you know who did it?"

Ophelia shook her head. "How in the world did you hear already?"

"Ace was here for scones," David said. "He mentioned that Christian called him. It's so sad."

Ophelia cut Brock a look. She *knew* that Ace was avoiding them. Dread skittered down her back. This was going to be a disaster. Her mind fuzzed from lack of sleep and she studied the couple.

"You two look exhausted," Monica said gently, wearing black jeans, fur-lined boots, and a red sweater that made her look both festive and warm.

David nodded, dressed in his usual jeans and a flannel shirt, though the bright red color stood out against the muted gray and white of the winter scenery. "Get some sleep. For now, I need to plow closer to EVE today. They're having electrical problems again, but I don't think the road's passable."

"No, it's not," Brock said. "Don't hurt yourself or put yourself out. They built their facility way out there on purpose, and they've got their own plane."

David shrugged. "All right. I'll take it as far as Raven's Pass but no farther."

"Good plan," Brock said. "We don't need to gather another search party together already."

David grinned, looking boyish despite the weight of the conversation. "No worries. I've got a wedding to plan."

Monica elbowed him. "It's already planned. All you need to do is show up."

David gave an exaggerated sigh. "I'm not convinced about the vanilla cake. I think I want butterscotch."

Monica's eyebrows rose. "You want a butterscotch wedding cake?"

"Sure, why not?" David asked, unbothered.

Monica glanced down, thinking. "Well...we could do one layer of butterscotch, I guess. I've just never seen that before."

"There you go," David said, grinning. "See? I'm helping."

Monica rolled her eyes but smiled anyway. "Oh—Ophelia. I went through some of my winter boxes and found a parka I think will fit you. It's a little longer in the arms so will fit you, but I don't wear it anymore. I gave it to Amka to save for you when you came in."

Ophelia's heart warmed. "Thank you. That's so nice of you."

Monica waved a hand. "Don't worry about it. I'm sure I've got extra snow boots somewhere too, but they might be out at the shop where David keeps the snowplows. We'll head out there later this week and I'll dig through them."

"That'd be great, but there's no hurry. These are surprisingly warm." Ophelia looked down at the snow boots Amka had given her.

David draped his arm over Monica's shoulders. "Come on, hon. We've gotta go." He steered her toward the lumbering snowplow across the street.

"I need coffee." Ophelia walked inside and spotted Jarod by the fireplace, a mug cradled in his hands, steam curling upward.

Amka bustled behind the bar, wiping it down with precise, almost obsessive movements.

"That guy really doesn't do a damn thing, does he?" Ophelia muttered under her breath.

"Nope," Brock said. His voice dropped. "You need me?"

She shook her head. "Not yet."

Brock's expression tightened, but he nodded. He stepped toward Amka at the bar as Ophelia wound her way through the tables toward the fire.

Jarod looked up as she approached, his brown eyes darkening as a slow, deliberate smile spread across his face.

"Well, hello, Agent." He kicked the chair across from him out with his foot. "Why don't you sit your pretty self down?"

"Gee, thanks." She pulled out the chair and lowered herself into it. The warm scent of whiskey drifted toward her, mingling with the smell of wood smoke. She glanced at his mug. "Hot toddy?"

He nodded. "Would you like one?"

Ophelia hesitated, then sighed. "No. I need coffee." And three days of sleep.

Jarod raised his hand. "Hey, Amka—coffee over here."

"I can get it," Ophelia muttered.

"No, no. I've got it," Amka called, waving her hand as she hurried toward them, the white apron around her waist cinched tightly. She set the steaming mug down in front of Ophelia and patted her arm. "This will warm you up, Olly."

Ophelia managed a smile. "Thanks."

Jarod watched Amka walk back to the bar, his gaze lingering.

"You're an interesting couple," Ophelia said.

Jarod's grin widened, but something flickered behind his eyes—something Ophelia couldn't read. "Thank you."

Ophelia couldn't feel her legs anymore. The warmth from the fire nearby barely made a dent against the cold that had settled deep in her bones. She wrapped her fingers tighter around the mug, the heat seeping into her palms as she watched Jarod's smug smile stretch across his face.

"We're a great couple," Jarod said with a lazy grin. "She's a bit of a worker bee. Not exactly a queen, but you do what you gotta do." His teeth were white and straight, almost unnaturally perfect.

What an annoying statement. "What does that mean?" Ophelia asked, keeping her tone neutral.

"It means you're a queen." He winked. "But you probably already knew that."

She fought the urge to roll her eyes. She might actually have to put this guy on his ass. The thought made her lips twitch into a small, involuntary smile.

Mistaking it as interest, Jarod's grin grew wider. "So...you wanted to see me?"

"Actually." She placed her mug on the table carefully. "I want to talk to you about Tamara Randsom."

His expression sobered in an instant. "Yeah," he muttered. "Heard you found her dead." He shook his head slowly. "I figured she'd run off with some rich guy and headed to the Caribbean or somewhere warm." His eyes shifted toward the windows, as if imagining sunshine and turquoise waters. "That's what I'd do."

"Then why are you here?" Ophelia asked, filing away his statement for later. She made a mental note to run a full background check on him.

Jarod's head lifted, his gaze sharpening as he stared at her for a long beat before flicking purposefully toward Amka, who was busy cleaning glasses behind the bar. "Love," he said simply, his voice softer. "This is where she lives. This is where she wants to be. If I could get her to move to an island, believe me, Chickie, I would."

Ophelia blinked. "Did you just call me *Chickie?*"

His grin didn't falter. "Yeah."

"How old are you?" she blurted.

He raised an eyebrow. "Twenty-nine. How about you?"

"Twenty-eight."

"Ah. I'm older." His grin widened. "What do you think about older men?"

Right now, she thought he was a complete ass. "When was the last time you saw Tamara Randsom?" She steered the conversation back on track.

He shrugged and took a slow sip of his drink. "Probably sometime in April or May."

"Before she disappeared, you were her landlord, correct?"

He sat back, draping one arm over the back of his chair. "Yep. I owned the Tundra."

"How long did you own the Tundra?"

"For about five years," he said. "Inherited it from some aunt I barely knew. That's when I moved up here."

"Did it make good money?"

He lifted a shoulder lazily. "It brought in some cash, but the place needed more repairs than you'd think. There wasn't great money in it." He paused, eyes glinting. "The hour-by-hour stuff was good, though. Not a lot of that around here."

"Yeah, so I've heard." Ophelia leaned forward slightly. "There are a few rumors…like you and Tamara had a relationship."

Jarod's expression tightened for the first time. "Oh no," he said smoothly. "We didn't have a relationship."

"Did you have sex?" she asked bluntly.

He smiled again, the charm sliding back into place like a mask. "Agent, I don't kiss and tell."

"Is that a yes or a no?" Ophelia's voice hardened. "Keep in mind that lying to a federal agent is a crime."

Jarod's smile disappeared. "Then I plead the Fifth."

She took that as a yes. "When was the last time you and Tamara were together?"

"I didn't say we were," he said evenly. "And again, I'm pleading the Fifth."

Ophelia inhaled slowly through her nose, forcing herself to stay calm. "Do you know if anyone else was involved with Tamara?"

Jarod looked away, pretending to think. "Fred Jeronimish, for sure. They went on a couple of dates in town before he left."

"When did he leave?"

"May, maybe? About a month before she disappeared." Jarod took another sip of his hot toddy. "She was missing him, though. Drank a little too much, feeling sorry for herself. But I'm sure she found someone to take his place." He winked again.

Ophelia resisted the urge to punch him. "Anyone else?"

Jarod leaned back, crossing his arms. "Osprey. Ace, I mean. They shared a weekend. I remember that one."

She kept her face neutral. "Anyone else?"

Jarod shrugged. "Probably. She picked up guys from town sometimes. I remember there was a fishing crew here one weekend from Anchorage. Pretty sure she banged at least two of them."

Ophelia's stomach churned, but she kept her voice steady.

"It's my understanding that Hank Osprey might have used the complex as a motel from time to time."

Jarod blinked, then nodded. "Yeah, he might have."

"Who did he see there?"

"I have no idea." Jarod's face darkened. "Hank paid me by the hour and told me if I was anywhere near the place while he was there, he'd kill me—and I believed him. So I stayed away. I don't know who he saw. Could've been Tamara, for all I know. Or maybe he did something spy-like with the military. Or whatever. But believe me, that was not a man you messed with."

Ophelia's spine straightened at the raw honesty in his voice. "So, you're telling me that Hank Osprey met someone at that complex a summer ago, and no one knew who?"

Jarod shifted uneasily. "I'm not even sure he met someone. Could've just needed time alone. I don't know."

"How did the Tundra burn down?"

"Faulty wiring," Jarod said, lifting his shoulders again. "That place was a wreck. Hard to keep up. I don't miss it."

She didn't like how his gaze flicked away. "But it was the only motel in town. When you got hunting or fishing tours, you made money, right?"

"Yeah, some." He rubbed his thumb along the rim of his mug. "Insurance gave me a hundred grand. I considered going somewhere warm, but..." His gaze moved to Amka, where she chattered with Brock at the bar. Jarod's gaze hardened.

Ophelia raised an eyebrow. "Do you still have the money?"

"Most of it," Jarod replied. His grin returned. "I'm thinking of taking a trip to Anchorage for the weekend. I'm sure you have research to do there."

She blinked. "Did you just ask me to go to Anchorage with you?"

Jarod leaned forward, eyes gleaming. "Is that an offer?"

Ophelia's jaw tightened. "Absolutely not."

His expression didn't waver.

"Did you kill Tamara Randsom?" Ophelia's voice dropped to a cold whisper.

"Of course not," Jarod said smoothly.

"I need the name of your insurance adjuster as well as his friend from Anchorage who brought the cadaver dog to town."

Jarod sipped his drink. "Gosh darn it. I don't remember."

"It's a felony to lie to a federal investigator," Ophelia said.

He swallowed. "I'm not lying. I don't remember the adjuster's name, and I'm not even sure he introduced me to the guy with the dog. Sorry."

Ophelia dug deep for patience. "All right. Give me the name of your insurance agency."

His brow crinkled, and he looked up at the ceiling. "Darn it. Don't remember."

What a jerk. "That's suspicious. Did you harm Tamara and then burn down your own complex?"

"Of course not."

Fine. Ophelia would obtain a subpoena for his financial records, and she'd also contact the Alaska Division of Insurance Agency for their records. "Did you hurt Tamara in any manner?"

He smirked. "Tammy was a good lay. Why would I kill her?"

Her hands curled into fists beneath the table. "Why are you engaged to that lovely woman if you so obviously can't commit?"

"We're not married yet." He leaned toward her, his gaze intense. "I'm not the only one who can't commit."

She kept herself still and in control. "Meaning what?"

He shrugged, slyly licking his lips. "Guess who else used the Tundra for some nookie?"

She didn't want to hear this. "Who?"

His focus flicked to the bar and back. "David Laurence dumped Monica Luna on Thanksgiving of last year. She rented a room from me for two months."

Relief filtered through Ophelia. His sly look had thrown her off. "All right. So Monica lived at the Tundra. What's your point?"

"My point? Your so loyal boyfriend, who I'm sure tells you everything, stayed the night with her that December. You know what, Agent?" He leaned even closer to her, the whiskey on his breath wafting over her face. "They were together the night... and morning of Hank Osprey's death."

Her stomach dropped.

Satisfaction filled Jarod's gaze as he now sat back. "Now, I have to wonder. Why wouldn't Brock give you his alibi for that murder? Perhaps she was his accomplice?"

CHAPTER TWENTY-NINE

The heat of the tavern pressed in close as Ophelia stared at Jarod, keeping all expression off her face. "I'll ask you again, and keep in mind I can help you if you're honest with me. Did you kill Tamara?"

"Nope. Maybe Brock did." Jarod smiled. "Perhaps she found out about Monica? Or maybe Brock dated her as well—most men in town did. Maybe she got too clingy and he killed her. That's my bet, Agent."

She forced her own smile, so tired her ears rang. But fury flowed through her blood, so she could at least focus. "Doesn't track for me, Jarod." Yet it did. Maybe. A little. "What if Tammy threatened to tell Amka about your affair? You know, the one that continued after you and Amka became engaged?"

Jarod lost the charm. "Like I said, I'm not married yet. Amka understands that. I sure as hell wouldn't kill somebody over it."

Ophelia faked a wince. "It's the timing, you know? Tamara disappears and we now know was killed. Then her place burns down? All evidence in it gone? Even worse, you own the place and end up with a big, fat settlement payment?" Man, she was pissed. Furious. But she wouldn't let this asshat know he'd gotten to her. "Sounds like motive to me."

He rolled his eyes. "You've got nothing."

Nothing. That was true. She frowned. "Who investigated the fire?" Sheriff Blazerton had died by that time.

Jarod shrugged. "The insurance folks sent out a guy, but the place burned to the ground. No foul play, Olly."

It was really too bad the sheriff had died. She stood and leaned toward Jarod. "I don't know about that. I'm going to do a background check on you that will tell me your favorite cartoon character when you were a toddler. You're my number one suspect for Tammy's murder, Jarod. You might want to find yourself a good lawyer."

"Say hi to your boyfriend for me," Jarod drawled.

"Count on it," Ophelia said sweetly, turning her back on him to see Brock on a stool with his back to her, broad shoulders taut under his worn flannel shirt.

She made her way to the bar, masking the storm brewing in her chest with an easy smile. Brock still hadn't noticed her, but Amka caught her eye.

"Hey, Olly. You hungry?" Amka asked.

Ophelia would puke if she tried to eat anything right now. "No, but thank you." She sat on a bar stool next to Brock, not looking at him. "I hate to ask you this, but did you know that Jarod and Tamara Randsom had an affair that possibly started a year and a half ago and lasted until her disappearance this last May?"

Brock turned toward her. "You think this is the place?"

"Yes." Ophelia would ask Amka in for a formal interview, but she wanted answers before Jarod had a chance to speak with his fiancée. "I'm sorry if that hurts you." She was too tired to be smooth.

Amka's chin lifted. "I heard rumors but didn't know the full truth."

"Did you kill Tamara?"

"Ophelia," Brock growled. "What are you doing?"

She kept her focus on Amka. "My job. Amka?"

The woman's dark eyes flashed. "No. I didn't kill Tammy."

"Do you think Jarod did?"

Now something undefinable flashed in those eyes. "No." Her gaze flicked to his table. "He's not a killer." Did her tone lack conviction?

"When did you become engaged?"

Amka swallowed. "On New Year's Day."

Brock stiffened.

"Where were you when Hank died, Amka?" Ophelia asked.

Amka's eyes widened. "That day was normal for me until I heard about Hank's death. I came right to work, and the sheriff told me when he came in for a drink around lunch."

Ophelia frowned. "The sheriff drank during the day?"

"Sure," Amka said. "He and Hank had been friends for decades. Hank's death tore the sheriff up."

"Did you kill Hank?"

Amka stared at her. "Are you nuts?"

Maybe. "Yes or no?"

"Of course not."

Ophelia continued smoothly. "When was the last time you saw Tamara Randsom?"

Amka twisted a bar towel in her hands. "I think I saw her during the kindergarten graduation. I don't remember seeing her after that."

Ophelia's eyebrows rose. "Did the entire town attend that graduation?"

"Yes," Amka said simply, looking at Brock for confirmation. "We all do. It's an event."

"Did Tamara leave the ceremony with anybody?" Ophelia asked.

Amka shook her head. "No. I remember seeing her flip off

Loretta and leave on her own. I have no clue where she went after that."

"What about you?" Ophelia asked softly.

Amka swallowed. "I came back to work. As usual."

"I see." Ophelia looked at her watch. "I'd like to formally interview you on the record in the matter of Tamara Randsom's death. Say tomorrow at the station around three in the afternoon?" That should give her enough time to obtain a preliminary background check on the woman. Ophelia wanted to get all of her ducks in a row before she called in Jarod.

"Do I need a lawyer?" Amka asked.

Ophelia shook her head. "Not if you didn't do anything wrong." She pushed off the stool. "Brock?" She kept her mask firmly in place. She brushed a hand over his arm as if everything was normal. "Time to go?"

He nodded, though his eyes narrowed slightly. "Sure."

Outside, the cold Alaskan air was sharp against her cheeks. Snow swirled in slow drifts under the glow of the streetlamp. The town felt quiet, the kind of quiet that pressed in and left too much room for unspoken things.

"Let's go to the station," she said casually, though her words were a tight thread in the cold air. She would confront him there.

Brock studied her. "Sure. I don't want to leave the sled here." He slid his leg over and held out his arm.

She hesitated for just a second before she smiled, accepted his help, and swung behind him. He handed back her helmet, which had been hanging on a handlebar. She pulled it onto her head and secured the strap.

He did the same and started the beast.

Fury rolled through her. She wrapped her arms around Brock's waist, feeling the familiar heat of him through his jacket.

The engine roared as they shot forward, the snow spraying

out behind them as they sped down the street. But when they reached the end of the main street, he didn't slow down and flip around. He kept going, his body a hard wall as he took the river road away from town.

Her fingers tightened around his waist, anger simmering in her chest. Apparently she wasn't in a playing poker state of mind and hadn't fooled him with her casual request. Damn, she needed sleep.

By the time they pulled up in front of his cabin, she was seething. The second he killed the engine, she jumped off and spun around. "What the hell, Brock?"

He tugged off his helmet, his face already stormy. "I could ask you the same thing."

"I said I wanted to go to the station."

"I heard you," he said bluntly. "But we're both exhausted, and obviously something has you furious. So we're talking about it here, away from everyone else. Period."

She shoved her helmet into his chest, forcing him to grab it. "Fine." She stomped to the front door and shoved it open to yank off her coat and hang on a hook. Then she kicked out of her boots and moved closer to the grand stone fireplace in the great room. She needed space. She needed answers. And she needed them now.

Brock followed her inside, shutting the door hard enough to rattle the windows. "All right." He threw his helmet onto the table. "We're here. Out with it."

She whirled on him, anger blazing in her eyes. "You should've told me."

"Told you what?" he asked, his voice hard but cautious.

"Monica," she bit out, every syllable like a slap. "You spent the night with her last December. She was your alibi for Hank's fucking murder."

Brock's eyes darkened, his nostrils flaring. "Jarod obviously knew that. How?"

"Does it matter?" she asked, stepping closer. "Who the fuck cares what Jarod knows? Monica can provide an actual alibi for you, and you still kept your night a secret. Why? Are you in love with her?" The last question shocked her. She hadn't meant to ask that.

"Of course not," he said, his voice tight, like he reined himself in. "We're just friends. The night was stupid and we both regretted it. Nobody knows. Well, I thought nobody knew. David doesn't, and I see no reason to hurt either one of them."

Fury felt like acid in Ophelia's throat. "You let me walk around in the dark, Brock. You let me think I had the whole story when I didn't."

"I made her a promise and wanted to keep her life from getting ripped apart." He scrubbed a hand over his face, frustration bleeding through his composure. "Her presence when I found Hank's body doesn't change anything."

"Oh, you're wrong about that," Ophelia hissed.

He crossed the room in two strides, standing close but not touching her. His energy was like a storm—electric and overwhelming. "I wasn't trying to keep you out," he said. "But you and I both know Monica wasn't the point. She didn't see who killed Hank. She didn't have anything to do with it."

"She had something to do with you," Ophelia shot back. "And that makes it my business."

His jaw tightened, the weight of everything unsaid between them filling the space like a vacuum. He looked at her, really looked at her, and something flickered in his eyes—pain, regret, something else. "You're right," he said finally. "I should've told you."

Her throat tightened. "Why didn't you?"

He hesitated, then finally said, "Because I made her a promise, and I didn't think it mattered. The night with her didn't mean anything to me. The morning did, but I didn't kill Hank. You know that." His voice turned rough, raw. "Then you and I happened so fast, and I figured we had a clean slate. We both know I didn't kill Hank, so why break a promise? Because my night with you mattered. Completely."

"You could've trusted me."

He levered back slightly. Barely. But enough. "Yeah, I could've with that."

With that.

"It's always going to be between us," she whispered. Tears burned the backs of her eyes, but she forced them back. She wouldn't cry. Not here. Not now. "Whoever killed Hank. That's always going to be between us. We both know it."

His hand lifted like he wanted to touch her but stopped halfway. "Not if we don't let it."

She swallowed hard. "I don't trust you."

"Yeah, you do. I fucked up by not telling you about Monica, but you trust me."

Did she? God, she couldn't think. "What else are you keeping from me?"

"Nothing. You have my word."

"That doesn't mean anything." Yeah, she aimed to hurt with that one. "Now, I want to go to Flossy's."

He tucked his thumbs in his jean pockets. "No."

Her head snapped up. "Excuse me?"

His green gaze bore into her. "I said no. In case you forgot, somebody has been shooting at you. You're in danger. Right now, you can barely stand, much less defend yourself. So you're staying here until you get some sleep. You can have the guest room."

She couldn't argue with his logic, even though she wanted to kick him in the head. "Fine. It better have a lock." She strode past him to the hallway, heading into the guest bedroom, which did, indeed, have a lock.

She'd figure out if she should arrest him or just shoot him after a few hours of sleep. Yeah. Good plan.

CHAPTER THIRTY

The smell of bacon awoke Ophelia from a dream where she'd found herself running through thick snow between ominous trees, chasing something. Or someone? She liked the idea that she chased instead of fled in the dream.

Yawning, she stretched and then caught herself, looking around. Brock's house felt like home. Then she remembered the day before.

He'd lied to her. By omission, anyway.

Yeah, in the light of the morning, she could see his point of view. He didn't want to hurt David or Monica...and things had progressed quickly with Ophelia.

Could she move past that?

Could he if she arrested one of his brothers?

Did she even want to try? Never in her life had she felt like this with a man, safe and slightly irritated, and she knew to her soul that he was a good man. Loyalty did matter. She forced herself out of bed to the attached bathroom, noting her hair was a tangled mess around her face.

A packaged toothbrush was next to a travel sized tube of

toothpaste, and she used both before washing her face and quickly braiding her now wild hair down her back. Her phone buzzed and she looked down to see that the warrant to hold Wyatt Yankovich had been granted by a federal judge. Excellent. She'd drop by the hospital after meeting with Monica and execute the warrant.

It was time Wyatt spoke with her again. Oh, she couldn't force him, but being served with a warrant usually did the trick.

Feeling like she finally caught a break, Ophelia padded barefoot on the cold wooden floor out the room to find Brock in the wide kitchen setting out two plates on the round table near the back door.

"Morning," he said, his gaze a dark green. "Coffee?"

"Yes," she said, moving gratefully toward him as he handed her a full mug. She took a strong gulp and let the heat fill her stomach. "Thank you."

He gestured her toward the table before bringing over the bacon and a large plate of scrambled eggs heavily ladened with cheese. In the soft morning light, he looked large and dangerous in his faded jeans and ripped T-shirt that appeared to have a bear across the back. "I thought about us a lot last night. I screwed up, and I'm sorry. I won't do it again."

She rubbed her chin and sat at the table, her stomach growling. A badass Navy SEAL who could apologize? "I'm a bit unsettled with you right now." But her body wanted to jump him. It wasn't fair. Nobody should look that sexy in the morning.

"Yeah." He sat and took a deep drink of his coffee. "That's my fault. I'll make it up to you."

Saving her life by jumping into a freezing river went a long way. "Maybe we should cool it for a while, at least until I figure out who killed Hank," she murmured, scooping eggs onto her plate, her mind befuddled. "We can't work that case together any longer." Not that he'd taken the sheriff job, because he still hadn't.

He reached for the bacon. "That's a good idea. Sorry again. I honestly didn't want to hurt Monica or David and had banished that night and morning from my reality. Still should've told you, though." He munched on a piece, his jaw hard. "Although if this case gets out, that info may end up public, whether we like it or not now."

True. In a trial, a defense attorney would run with it. But she couldn't worry about that. "Why didn't Sheriff Blazerton include that info in the file?"

Brock shrugged. "He knew I didn't kill Hank, and also, Monica was his niece. That must be why."

Fine. "I need to speak with Ace. Could you send me his cell number?"

Brock glanced at his phone sitting on the table. "I texted him earlier and asked him to stop by. Hopefully before he's drinking."

She paused in eating more eggs. "How bad is Ace's drinking problem?"

Brock shook his head. "I don't think he's a raging alcoholic, but I do think he's using booze to deal with a plane crash he had last year. It's his story to tell, and frankly, I'm done waiting for him to tell me about it." His gaze darkened. "That was off the record, Agent. Don't even think of using that information to push his buttons during an interview, or I'll tell him to take to the woods with Christian. Got it?"

His over-protective side could be both sexy and a total pain in her ass. "I've got it, so long as the plane crash doesn't have anything to do with my investigations."

"He crashed a military jet, so I think you're safe," Brock said wryly.

"Did this occur before or after Hank died?" Most situations in life were somehow related, she'd learned.

Brock finished off his coffee. "After and it had nothing to do with Hank's death. If Ace piloted a plane, he remained fully cognizant and in control of the situation. Period."

"Fair enough." She took another bite of the delicious eggs. "What do Ace and Christian think about Damian working for EVE?" She had no doubt Brock had told them and wanted to know their opinions before she interviewed them again.

Brock took more of the eggs and watched as the cheese stretched and then landed on his plate. "They're happy that Damian is back in Alaska, and I believe they're looking forward to the four of us getting together sometime soon." His tone remained level and calm.

Hmmm. Something told her that didn't cover everything, but she remained on the outside, watching the four brothers handle things in their own secretive way.

The front door opened and Ace walked inside, kicking off snow gear.

Ophelia hid her surprise that he'd actually shown up.

Brock glanced his way. "Coffee's hot and we have eggs and bacon left."

"Ate at the diner." Ace strode on thick gray socks to the kitchen and poured himself a mug of the steaming coffee. He looked at Ophelia in that same direct way Brock had. "Understand you heard I had an affair with Tammy Randsom. I did. We hooked up after she and Leo divorced."

Brock sighed. "I wish I hadn't gone out of town for so long."

Ace shrugged. "Not your fault. I came home after the plane crash and was still mourning Hank. It's an understatement to admit that I did not find myself in a good place. The affair lasted two weeks, and it turns out she also dated Fred Jeronimish at the same time." He tipped back the mug and finished the entire contents. "It ended when I discovered that fact. Also, she and Jarod tore up the sheets some, which absolutely pissed me off on Amka's account."

Ophelia lifted her head. "Did you tell Amka?"

Ace stared into his mug. "Yeah. I felt like a snitch and a shitty guy, but we've known Amka her entire life, and I couldn't let her marry that asshat. Yet they didn't break up." His frown drew down his dark eyebrows. "Sometimes I just don't understand people."

Ophelia made some mental notes to prepare for her upcoming interview with the bar owner. How angry was Amka with Jarod...and Tammy? "How do you feel about Damian being home?" Ophelia expertly switched topics, wanting him off balance. Somehow.

Ace glanced through the sliding glass door to the snow piled on the wide deck. "It's good to have D home. Although, if he doesn't actually head here into town, Christian is going to infiltrate EVE, and it's not going to be pretty." He said the last as if directly to Brock. "As the sheriff, you probably have some sort of duty to cooperate with the EVE folks, right?"

Brock just glared at him.

Ophelia pushed forward before Brock could argue about his job position. "Did Christian kill Hank?"

Ace didn't even blink. "No." Rolling his neck, he leaned back against the counter. "I know C seems like an oddity to some people, but he's a good guy. Yeah, he prefers wilderness to structures and animals to people, but he's been through some shit in his career, and he's coping better than most. One thing he would never do is kill family. Period."

"I think you killed Hank and are drinking yourself to death out of guilt," she asked softly.

"You're wrong." Ace met her gaze levelly, his green eyes a shade off of Brock's. "I understand your line of thinking, but you're just way off. Honestly. A hunter, probably some jackass out for fun from the lower forty-eight and on vacation, way out of his depth, accidentally shot Hank. Either he or she didn't realize it, or they did and ran away like scared cowards, but nobody around here killed Hank."

He was lying. Ophelia could point to no obvious evidence of deception, but she knew, she freaking knew, that he wasn't telling the truth.

She smiled. Her most genuine, casual, feminine smile. "You're full of shit, Ace."

He blinked. For the first time, he showed surprise as his gaze cleared and his eyes widened just enough to be noticeable. Brock jerked back, for once exhibiting a reaction not deliberately calculated. Yeah. They hadn't expected her to catch the deception or call him on it.

Brock cleared his throat.

Ophelia held up a hand. "You've all been lying to me. Why, I don't know. All four of you were in town when Hank died, and Brock is the only one with an alibi. An alibi I need to follow up with later today." She would not take the man with her, either. "Now start talking, or you both could end up being charged with lying to a federal agent, which comes with prison time, if I remember right."

Neither man said a word. How irritating. Not a lick of this made sense. She could tell they'd all loved Hank. "I need to borrow your truck today until I can find one to buy," she murmured.

Brock's eyebrow lifted. "Why?"

"To go somewhere. You and I are not on the same page on this investigation, and you're not even admitting you're the sheriff. So I'm asking you as a friend to borrow your truck."

"As a friend?" His eyes burned an unfathomable green. "Is that what we are?"

She had no clue how to define what they were. "No."

"You seem to be forgetting that somebody has been shooting at you." He stood and started collecting the dirty plates. "I'm happy to drive you since we've got about a day or two before most of the river road becomes impassable by truck. I take it you want to interview my alibi for the day of Hank's death?"

"Yes," Ophelia said.

Brock shrugged. "Monica and David live in the opposite direction of here, on the other side of the river. I'll drive you and wait in the truck for as long as you need." He took the dishes to the kitchen.

She hid her surprise at his acceptance of her goal for the day. "Ace? I suggest you meet with an attorney soon."

"Not necessary," Ace said, taking his mug to the sink, eyeing his brother. "You really going to take your current, um, girlfriend to meet your ex?"

Brock started doing the dishes. "Monica and I didn't date, and from the tone of the agent currently wearing my T-shirt, we aren't either right now." While his voice remained level, a muscle ticked in his strong jaw. "I hate that this one mistake may screw up Monica's life. David shouldn't have to know."

So they were back to 'agent' again. Fine. That worked for Ophelia. The sense of betrayal felt real. She'd almost considered Monica a friend. But she could also understand a mistake and wanting to keep it from David. Maybe. Honesty mattered. Ophelia would have to dig deep for objectivity considering she could be the current lover. Maybe. At the moment, maybe not.

So she jumped in with both feet. "After I speak with a couple of witnesses today, I'd like to organize a meeting with the four Osprey brothers at the same time. Can you arrange that for me?"

Neither Osprey brother looked at each other. Both stared at her, and neither showed an ounce of emotion. She couldn't get a read on either one of them.

Not even close. Yeah, she really needed to find her own vehicle somehow in town. She made a mental note to call Flossy and see if she could help.

For now, it was time to discuss Monica's one night stand.

CHAPTER THIRTY-ONE

Monica Luna stood eye-to-eye with Ophelia in her bare feet—a rare occurrence, given Ophelia's height. While both women were tall, Monica had a full-figured frame, her generous curves filling out her beige sweater and dark jeans as though they'd been tailored for her. She was stunning, with striking blue eyes, thick brown hair, and full pink lips. This time, however, Ophelia found herself resenting that beauty.

"I'm sorry about this, Olly." Monica looked pale today. Her gaze moved beyond Ophelia to Brock waiting in the truck and she gave a hesitant wave. "I screwed up." Then she stepped to the side. "Come on in."

"Sorry? You knew I was coming?"

Monica nodded. "Brock texted me a heads up."

Well, that just figured. Ophelia stepped inside the warm home, somewhat surprised Monica and Brock had managed to keep their one night a secret. There seemed to be no secrets in Knife's Edge—except those involving murders. "Thank you." She kicked off her snow boots in the small alcove and handed over her coat. Dots of snow still flecked the collar. "When is it going to stop snowing?"

"Around May," Monica said quietly, hanging the coat on a series of angled hooks. "Can I offer you coffee?"

"Sure." Ophelia followed her into a wide living area with a flatscreen mounted above a stone fireplace that was crackling happily. "I'm not arresting you and you're under no type of detainer, but you have a right to have a lawyer present if you want."

Monica hitched into the adjoining kitchen, which had been painted a cheerful yellow. "That's okay." She filled two mugs with coffee and strode around a wide island. "Let's sit by the fire." Monica carried two thick red mugs around a denim sofa and sat in the adjoining chair, shoving aside a bright yellow throw pillow that made the room feel lived-in and warm.

Ophelia followed, curling into the corner of the couch and letting the fire's warmth seep into her. Monica's house was full of personal touches—handmade quilts draped over chairs, shelves packed with books and framed photos, and a faint scent of vanilla lingering in the air.

"David's working long hours with the snowplow." Monica wrapped her hands around her mug. "I regret my drunken night with Brock because we're just friends and it was stupid. But you two weren't dating at the time, and neither were David and I."

Ophelia appreciated the frankness. "I understand." She paused, studying Monica. "You don't think you should tell David?"

"No." Monica's gaze drifted around the room before settling back on Ophelia. "He'd broken up with me at the time—not sure if he wanted to get serious. And I don't think it's his business. Why make things difficult around here? Brock and I got drunk, got naked, and both regretted it."

Ophelia swallowed the bitter taste rising in her throat. Did he whisper soft words into the woman's ear after sex? Did he hold her the same way? She shoved down the thoughts, forcing herself to focus on the investigation. "Tell me about that morning."

Monica shrugged, the steam from her mug wafting up. "I lived briefly at the Tundra Complex before David and I got back together, and it's on the opposite side of town. We'd taken my snowmobile from the bar the night before, so I had to give Brock a ride back to the tavern to get his. It was so freaking awkward because we both knew we'd made a big mistake. We were later than we liked getting back and didn't want anybody to see both of us on my sled, so we went the roundabout way by Crocker's Creek." She paled even more. "That's where we saw Hank."

Ophelia forced her gaze down into her coffee, pretending to be unaffected. "What did you see?"

Monica gulped, her eyes getting a faraway look. "He lay in the river, face up, obviously dead. Blood still poured from his chest." She placed her mug on the coffee table and rubbed her arms as if she couldn't get warm.

Ophelia looked around the cozy house, trying to shift the conversation. "Then what?"

"Brock pulled Hank from the creek, and we had to leave him there to ride into town and tell the sheriff."

"The sheriff saw the scene?"

Monica nodded. "Yeah. Of course."

So where did the pictures go? Or had Blazerton taken any? "Why would the sheriff keep your name as well as Brock's out of his report? Who found the body is always important."

Monica reached for her coffee. "The sheriff was my uncle on my mom's side. He knew Brock and I didn't kill Hank, and he didn't want to mess up my life because of David. Family matters around here, Olly."

Obviously. Ophelia took in a deep breath. "Did you see anybody around the body?"

"No."

That tracked. "Who do you think killed Hank?"

"Somebody by accident, I'm sure." Monica shook her head. "Everyone knows you're looking at the Osprey brothers, but it doesn't make sense." She rubbed a thumb along the edge of her cup. "I attended the funeral. All four of those men—so trained and deadly—and yet in that moment, they all became little boys again. Lost ones. I've never felt such pain in a room."

Ophelia's throat tightened at the thought of the Osprey brothers grieving like that—each of them powerful, dangerous, and still utterly human.

"Then why are they all blocking my investigation?" Ophelia blurted out, the words sharper than she intended.

Monica's expression shifted, her lips turning down in a frown. "Because it hurts…and it's over."

Ophelia opened her mouth to argue, but Monica pressed on.

"They're finally healing, Ophelia. They've all come home again. Ace, Christian, Damian, and even Brock—they scattered after Hank died. And now, they're trying to be brothers again." Her voice softened. "A hunter killed Hank, and you're just stirring up the pain."

Ophelia's hands tightened around her mug. "I don't think it was that simple."

Monica sighed. "I know you don't. But you're an outsider here. When you poke at old wounds, the people who stayed behind are the ones who bleed."

The fire crackled as the silence stretched between them. Ophelia understood Monica's words, but that didn't change what she knew deep down—Hank's death wasn't random.

And someone in this town was hiding the truth.

Ophelia's eyebrows rose on their own. "How did you know Damian returned to town?"

Monica chuckled. "I heard from Amka at Sam's, who heard it from Flossy, who heard it from…"

"I've got it," Ophelia said. "Gossip in a small town, right?" But had there been an inflection in Monica's tone? "You stressed Flossy's name. You seemed like friends when we quilted together."

"We are now, but she didn't like me when David dumped me. They're second cousins." Monica took a deeper gulp this time. She leaned forward. "She knew I slept with Brock since she worked at the sheriff's station and was there that morning when we reported the death."

So even Flossy could keep a good secret. Interesting. "You're friends now."

"Yeah, she forgave me, but she was pissy for a while. She even stitched a vulture into the quilt she entered in the spring fair, and I know it represented me, but she won't admit it even now."

Ophelia winced. "That had to hurt."

Monica snorted. "Not really. Her idiosyncrasies are endearing. Now Flossy creates these little robin decorations to represent me. I think she realized that David was the one to temporarily end things between us. She's even growing the flowers for our wedding in her greenhouse. Life is weird."

"Maybe," Ophelia agreed, though she had trouble imagining what it felt like to have someone craft an evil bird in your honor. "Who else knows about your night with Brock and that you possibly found Hank's body?"

Monica shrugged. "You never know in a small town. We did see Amka opening the tavern when we drove by on the snowmobile, so I'm sure she figured it out."

Ophelia paused. "I thought you said you got a late start."

"Yeah. That's why we tried to avoid town."

"What time does Amka usually open the tavern?" From what Ophelia had understood, Amka opened early. Very.

Monica tapped her finger on her lips. "Huh. Usually crack of dawn for those early fishermen, even the ice fishermen, to fill their thermoses with spiked coffee. I guess she got a late start that day, too."

Which would explain how Jarod knew about the affair. Amka must've told him. Yet another issue to discuss with Amka. "How well did you know Hank?"

"As well as anybody in town," Monica said easily, taking a sip from her mug. "I talked to him a few times at the doctor's office. I was having thyroid issues and had to go in once a week, and Hank hung out in the waiting room now and then. He gave me some great tips to find good fishing holes up Crocker's Creek."

Ophelia leaned into another bright yellow throw pillow, her body going on alert at the mention of the doctor. "Who was the doctor at the time?"

"A dorky guy named Sheriton Zimmer who definitely missed living in sunny California. He couldn't wait to serve his three months and leave. It's amazing we got Doc May to sign a three-year contract."

Ophelia steered the conversation back as her blood hummed. "Why was Hank seeing the doctor?"

"Dunno," Monica said with a shrug. "But he'd definitely lost weight and didn't look as robust as usual that Christmas season. A bad flu hit a bunch of the older folks in town, and Hank had just turned seventy, you know?"

Facts shifted around in Ophelia's head like puzzle pieces sliding into place. Hank's age, his health, his routine...something wasn't lining up. He'd been a man of habit, strong-willed and private. Why hadn't anyone mentioned health issues before now? "Is there anything else you can tell me about Hank's death?"

Monica's fingers tightened slightly around her mug. "No."

Ophelia didn't have any other questions regarding Hank. Right now, anyway. "You said you lived at the Tundra. So did Tamara Randsom. Did you cross paths?"

"Oh, no. I moved back in with David in early February when

we reconnected, and he proposed. I don't think Tammy moved out there until after that. Before you ask, I have no clue who would've killed her." Monica cleared her throat, as if shaking herself loose from the tension. "Look...I'm sorry if my drunken night with Brock caused any awkwardness between you and me. I enjoyed quilting with you." She offered a tentative smile. "I hope we can move on."

Ophelia blinked, caught off guard by the offer.

As an olive branch, it wasn't a bad one.

"Of course," Ophelia said, returning the smile. "I enjoyed quilting too." She felt a small measure of relief that Brock had an alibi, even though her gut had never pegged him as Hank's killer. "And none of this is really relevant to the case right now...I don't think." She paused, choosing her words carefully. "I'll do my best to keep your name out of the report, but I can't guarantee that the truth won't come out."

Monica gave a relieved nod.

Ophelia sipped her coffee, letting the warmth ease the tension in her chest. Whoever killed Tammy—and Hank—had left a tangle of lies and secrets in their wake. She wasn't sure how long it would take to unravel, but one thing was certain—she needed the truth.

"I don't want to interfere at all." Monica shifted on the sofa. "But the buzz around town is that you and Brock are serious. I've never seen him look at anybody like he does you, and as his friend, I hope you give him another chance." She finished her coffee. "I learned the hard way that you have to fight for love, and you have a really good chance with Brock. He's a good man, Ophelia. Loyal to a fault—even with friends. Please just say you'll consider it."

"I will," Ophelia meant it but she feared that Hank's death would always be between them, if she discovered his killer...or if she couldn't. The truth lurked somewhere, in plain sight, hiding behind familiar faces and friendly smiles. "Thank you."

Monica perked up. "Oh. Speaking of buzz around town, I heard you're looking for a vehicle to buy or rent."

Ophelia placed her mug down on a coaster on the coffee table and straightened. "I do. Please tell me you have something."

"I have an older Jeep that we just don't need, and I planned to wait until spring to sell it, but it's yours if you want it."

"I want it." Ophelia finally relaxed. She needed to pursue the investigation herself and now had a different theory that finally clicked the obscure facts into place…and led her right down the path she'd already been pursuing. But now she might know the *why*, if not the who. "Is that Jeep ready to go?"

CHAPTER THIRTY-TWO

The Jeep needed new snow tires, so Ophelia kept her speed slow as she maneuvered from Monica's toward town. The icy road shimmered beneath the thin midday sun, and even with four-wheel drive, the ride felt precarious. Brock had definitely been irritated when she'd secured her own transportation.

She could still picture the way his jaw had tightened, his arms crossed over his broad chest. He wanted to protect her from whoever kept taking potshots at her. Sweet, sure—but also frustrating. She was a trained federal agent. She didn't need anyone, not even Brock Osprey, playing bodyguard. She knew how to return fire, and she still had his spare weapon on her.

Besides, the guy seemed like a bit of a control freak. While that made things dangerously attractive between the sheets, she couldn't let it interfere with her job. She had a duty to the case, not to him. Especially since she almost had enough to arrest Ace on suspicion of murder. Maybe. She needed somehow to tie him to the crime scene first. Another thing to talk to Amka about. Perhaps she'd seen Ace that morning.

Even so, Ophelia's body flushed at the memory of the night she'd shared with Brock. The way his voice deepened when he murmured her name. The way he moved, deliberate and unrelenting.

"Get it together, Spilazi," she muttered, forcing herself to focus as she dialed a number with one hand, her other hand steady on the wheel. After navigating several layers of bureaucracy, she finally reached FBI Assistant Director Bill Burrington.

"Find Hank's killer?" Burrington's familiar gruff voice barked through the line.

"No, sir," Ophelia said, sitting straighter against the worn leather seat. "But I think I'm close. I've got nothing solid on the Tammy Randsom murder, and the body in the woods...well, it disappeared."

Burrington sighed, the weight of disappointment hanging in the silence. "Sounds like sending you to Alaska was a waste of time."

Ophelia's grip on the phone tightened. "I said I'm close, sir. The warrant to take Wyatt Yankovich into custody as a material witness finally came through, and I'm on the way to serve it. For now, I'd like a search warrant for the EVE facility. Even though I believe I've found a different avenue to pursue for Hank's murder, I can tie all three of my current cases to EVE. My research request hasn't even gone through yet."

Burrington chuckled—low, dry, and unimpressed. "You want a warrant to search a private facility located in the middle of nowhere that has top-secret governmental contracts?"

When he put it like that...

"Yes," she said, determination thick in her voice. "They're just studying the ionosphere, right?"

"You'd be surprised what the ionosphere can do," he replied. "You don't have enough for a warrant to search a public restroom, much less a now private installation with governmental contracts. And trust me—I hit brick walls trying to dig up more intel on that place. You need to let it go. Get me Hank's killer by the weekend, or I'm pulling you home where you can quietly retire. He was my friend, and I want justice for him. Find Hank's murderer. Understand?"

Darn it. "Yes, sir. Also, would you mind requesting a warrant for Jarod Teller's financial records and one from the Alaska Division of Insurance Regulators regarding a fire that took place last May here in Knife's Edge? I feel like you'll get a faster response than I did with the Wyatt Yankovich warrant."

"Fine. I'll get somebody on it." The line clicked, cutting her off.

Ophelia's heart sank. One mistake—sleeping with a co-worker who turned out to be a self-serving jackass—and her career had been dangling by a thread ever since. The only way to redeem herself was to bring home a win.

The hollow silence in the Jeep felt louder than the wind outside.

She pulled into the parking lot of the doctor's office, wondering if she could take months of icy winter with little light. Gingerly, she stepped out of the vehicle, the icy air immediately stinging her cheeks. She looked around instinctively, scanning for any sign she'd been followed. Nothing. Satisfied, she ducked her head against the frigid wind and hurried toward the entrance. At least the snow had stopped.

Even so, it was nearly noon, and darkness would be creeping back within a couple of hours.

So different from D.C. But at least in July, it would be light all day and night. Just think of what she could accomplish with endless sunlight.

She pushed open the door to the doctor's office and stepped into the warmth. A young man sat behind the reception desk, his eyes fixed on a computer screen. The waiting area held deep green leather chairs, scattered toys, and a mounted television playing a daytime soap. The place looked more like someone's cozy living room than a medical clinic.

The man behind the desk looked up, his eyes dark and sharp against his pale skin. He couldn't have been more than twenty-one or twenty-two. His AC/DC T-shirt seemed out of place in such a quiet setting. He hadn't been on duty last time she'd been here since it'd been so early, probably.

"Hi. You must be Agent Spilazi. I'm Lance. How can I help you?"

"Hi," Ophelia said, walking toward him. "I'd like to see the doctor."

He glanced at the screen in front of him and nodded. "She'll be free in a couple of minutes. But if you're here for an appointment, I'll need you to fill out a new patient form."

"I'm here on business." She debated whether to flash her badge.

"Oh. In that case, you can head straight back." Lance gestured toward a door to the right of the desk. "Go all the way down the hallway to the last door on the right. She's in there eating lunch."

Ophelia hesitated for a moment before nodding. So informal. "Thanks."

She walked down the hallway, passing two examination rooms and a couple of closed doors until she reached the last open doorway. She knocked lightly on the frame.

May looked up from reading her tablet, a half-eaten sandwich resting on a brown paper bag next to her keyboard. "Ophelia. Come on in."

Ophelia stepped inside and sat in one of the guest chairs, which matched the green leather ones in the reception area. May's blond hair was tied back in a ponytail, and her smudged glasses framed sharp blue eyes. Her lab coat hung neatly on a hook by the door, and she wore a thick white sweater over jeans.

"I like your office," Ophelia said, glancing around. A large window framed snow-laden trees, while a credenza held framed diplomas and a stack of neatly labeled files.

"Thanks." May folded her hands neatly in front of her. "What's up?"

Ophelia pulled out her phone. "I have a warrant to secure Wyatt as a material witness. It's on my phone but I can print it out if you'd like."

May winced, a flicker of something in her eyes—sympathy or regret, maybe both. "I thought you heard. Wyatt and Sylvie headed out on the EVE delivery plane for Anchorage and then to Hawaii this morning."

Ophelia's stomach tightened. Damn it. "How in the world did they afford that?"

May shrugged. "Heck if I know. Maybe they used credit cards or sold something off. People do strange things when they need to escape."

Or when they need to disappear for other reasons. "How often do locals hitch rides on the EVE supply plane?" Ophelia asked, watching May carefully.

"To my knowledge, not often," May replied, her brows furrowing. "That's what makes it so unusual. I'm not sure how it happened, but the whole town had gotten involved in searching for Wyatt when he disappeared. Maybe Damian pulled some strings." She took a breath, then added, "After Wyatt told me about the trip, I also called Damian this morning and requested the use of his plane to transport Tamara Randsom's body and all collected evidence to the medical examiner's office in Anchorage. He agreed—kindly, I might add—but the plane won't be back for a couple of weeks. So at least that's progress."

Ophelia absorbed the information, her mind racing. The EVE facility's connection to the town seemed deeper than she'd realized, and it wasn't just about the plane—it was the level of influence they seemed to wield. She made a mental note to visit Damian again soon. For now, as soon as she left, she'd have the FBI in either Anchorage or Hawaii pick up Wyatt, depending on his location. Ditching town wouldn't work for him. Nice try, though.

"Well," she said, her voice thoughtful, "at least we know that locals—people who belong here—might catch a ride if they need to."

May's pink lips curved into a soft smile. "Brock brought you here, which makes you one of us now, even if you don't want to admit it. So, whether you like it or not, you belong."

The thought warmed Ophelia faster than the heat blasting up from the floor vents. She leaned back, her shoulders relaxing for the first time that day. "I've never belonged anywhere," she admitted before catching herself. Something about May—the calm in her voice, the kindness in her eyes—invited honesty.

"That's sad," May said softly, her brow furrowing in concern. "Although...I know what you mean. Sometimes you think you belong somewhere, and it turns out you're dead wrong." Her gaze drifted for a moment before she shook her head, focusing back on Ophelia. "So, Olly. What else would you like to know?"

Ophelia's tone lowered. "Did Hank Osprey suffer from an illness?"

One of May's light eyebrows rose. "Excuse me?"

"He sought medical care regularly before his death. Why?"

May swallowed, visibly bracing herself. "I can't discuss a patient's care. You know that."

"I'm dealing with an obvious homicide," Ophelia countered gently. "Come on, May. I can get a warrant in an hour for a dead man's records, and you know it. So help me out here. I'm not letting this go."

May's face paled slightly as she pushed her sandwich to the side. She exhaled slowly. "I know you could get a warrant. That's true." She blew out air and turned to her computer, a bulky piece that obviously needed updating. "I'll see what kind of records the former doctors might've kept." Her fingers flew quickly across the keyboard and she brought up several documents, leaning forward to read. "Well, crap."

Ophelia sat straighter. "What?"

May turned, her brows up, her eyes soft. "One of the former doctors treated Hank for stage four pancreatic cancer. The disease progressed far enough that the only plan seemed to be to keep Hank comfortable."

Surprise and sorrow blew through Ophelia like a punch to the chest, even as the doctor confirmed Ophelia's new theory. "That's terrible."

May nodded, her eyes glimmering with genuine sadness. "Yeah. The doctor noted that Hank probably hadn't been feeling well for a while but didn't seek medical intervention until it was too late. And then...well, he refused to spend his last month of life in a hospital." She paused. "The doctor prescribed pain meds that hopefully eased his suffering."

"Did the Osprey brothers know?"

May shrugged, her expression unreadable. "That isn't mentioned in the notes. However, from what I've heard about Hank just in my time here, I wouldn't be surprised if he kept the diagnosis from them." Her intelligent gaze locked onto Ophelia's. "A fact I'd be more than happy to testify about if it ever came to that."

Ophelia's mind spun as she processed the revelation. She felt for the Osprey brothers—especially Brock. "Understood," she murmured. After a beat, she asked, "But...in a trial, you'd also be asked whether Hank's death could've been considered a mercy killing. The four men who loved him would've wanted to ease his suffering, wouldn't they?"

May pressed her lips together and glanced away, unwilling to respond.

"That's what I thought," Ophelia said, the weight of the unspoken confirmation pressing down on her.

Mercy or not, it still counted as murder.

And someone would have to answer for it.

CHAPTER THIRTY-THREE

Brock's stomach rumbled as he parked his rig outside Sam's. The bar offered clam chowder today, and his hunger gnawed at him. The temptation to text Ophelia and invite her to meet him almost had him reaching for his phone. Yet the stubborn woman had headed off on her own to talk to Doc and flat-out refused to let him accompany her. Yeah, she was still pissed. He couldn't blame her.

The warmth of the bar hit him immediately, carrying the familiar scents of fresh bread, seafood, and wood smoke from the fire near the corner. His eyes adjusted to the dim interior, scanning the tables until they landed on a man sitting near the fire, leaning over several muted red file folders.

Brock forgot all about the text as he crossed the room and pulled out a chair.

"Hi, Brock," Damian said without looking up, his voice as smooth as ever, but with an edge Brock didn't miss.

"Hi." Brock gestured toward Amka, who was wiping down the bar with long, purposeful swipes of her cloth, then leaned on the table, folding his arms. "What are you doing here?"

Damian closed the top file folder with a quiet snap and

finally looked up, his sharp gaze hooded beneath thick lashes. His face appeared unreadable, as though it had been carved from stone. "It's clam chowder day."

Brock's lips tugged into a reluctant half-smile as he took in his brother's appearance. Damian's tailored gray suit fit like it had been made for him—because it probably had. The crisp white shirt beneath his jacket was starkly clean, unwrinkled, and practically glowing under the dim lighting. His silk tie was a deep emerald green, knotted so precisely that it looked like it had been tied by a machine.

"You're a little overdressed for clam chowder day."

Before Damian could respond, Amka arrived with a steaming bowl of soup and a frosty beer, setting them down with practiced ease. She offered Brock a small smile. Her faded jeans hugged her hips, worn in at the knees, and her light flannel shirt was rolled up at the sleeves, showing slender, strong forearms. Strands of dark hair had escaped her ponytail and framed her face. "Here's your chowder," she said lightly.

"Thanks." The delicious smell made his stomach rumble.

"I have a to-go thermos for Christian if you see him. He loves clam chowder day." She didn't wait for an answer, gathering the dirty dishes from the next table in one fluid motion before heading back to the bar, her boots thudding softly against the wooden floor.

"That's interesting. What's up between them?" Damian pushed the file folders aside as he reached for his beer. The amber liquid shimmered as it sloshed in the glass.

Brock watched Amka for a beat longer before answering. "Nothing. Christian's a wild animal right now who barely comes into town. She feeds all the wild animals." He shrugged. "True story. The woman even feeds the squirrels during the summer."

Damian chuckled, the sound low and brief. "Soft-hearted, huh?"

"Something like that," Brock muttered.

Damian took a sip from his glass, his brow lifting in a familiar arch. "How's it going with the Fed?" He leaned back, a lazy grin spreading across his face, the kind of grin that could either charm or infuriate, depending on who was on the receiving end. "You two sleeping together?"

Brock took a long pull from his beer, the cool liquid sliding down his throat and dulling his temper—though not by much. The cold bitterness of the beer felt good, but his irritation simmered beneath the surface. His jaw clenched slightly as he set the glass down with a dull thunk against the wooden table. He studied Damian for a long moment, weighing his words carefully. "The Fed is pissed off at me right now. How's your ex-wife?"

Damian's lips twitched as he set his glass down, but the smile didn't reach his eyes. "Couldn't tell you. Last I heard, she was running a CIA op somewhere in Taiwan."

Which meant she probably wasn't in Taiwan at all. If Damian mentioned it out loud, she was likely halfway across the world in some location too classified to admit.

"Someday," Brock said, eyeing his brother, searching for cracks in his calm exterior, "I'd like to hear the full story about your Stella."

"There's no story," Damian replied with a nonchalant shrug, though the slight tension in his shoulders betrayed something deeper. He leaned forward slightly, folding his hands in front of him. "You should take the sheriff job, Brock. There's no reason for you not to. The town needs a sheriff, and you're the best person for the job."

Brock resisted the urge to sigh. The weight of the town's needs felt heavier than it should've. "Yeah, I don't think so. I'd have to coordinate with the FBI, and I don't want to do that."

Damian's second eyebrow rose this time, and he gave a

small, almost imperceptible smile that was both knowing and infuriating. "Consider that taken care of, then."

Brock paused, his spoon halfway to his mouth. What the hell did that mean?

Irritation pricked along his skin like static electricity, but he pushed it down and dug into his clam chowder. The taste, as always, was phenomenal—rich with fresh clams, potatoes cooked just right, and Amka's signature seasoning.

But even the best chowder couldn't mask the tension thickening the air at the table.

"The clam chowder is excellent," Brock said, watching Damian closely. "But not delicious enough to bring you all the way into town. So...what's up?"

Damian ran a hand through his perfectly styled hair, the dark strands falling right back into place as if even his hair knew better than to defy him. "I thought I'd just pop into town and visit my home."

Amusement tugged at Brock, and he set down his spoon, leaning back slightly. "Christian got to you."

"Yeah. You could say that." Damian took in one long pull of beer, his shoulders one long line of tension.

Brock chuckled, shaking his head. "You work in one of the most secure facilities in the world, yet our brother somehow sent you a message? What did he convey?"

"That if I didn't come into town today, he'd take down the secure facility in a way I wouldn't appreciate." Damian's lips tilted into an unwilling smile, the expression equal parts exasperation and fondness. "While I'm fairly certain my new protective measures would've held, it's clam chowder day, so I figured...why not?"

Brock laughed under his breath. It was such a Christian thing to do—threatening something insane while counting on their sense of obligation to reel him back in.

"Has he made an appearance?"

Damian shook his head. "Nope. I sensed him outside when I came in, but he hasn't made the move yet." He tapped the table lightly with two fingers. "Is it just me, or is he getting even more antisocial?"

"I don't know," Brock admitted. "He's always preferred the outdoors, but there's something else going on with him. Not sure what." He paused, letting the thought linger before leaning in. "Have you figured out the identity of the victim who wore the EVE jacket?"

Damian's expression grew serious, the earlier humor fading like a distant echo. "No." He met Brock's gaze squarely. "I told your woman the truth. We aren't missing any employees—or contractors. Not a single one."

Brock's eyes narrowed as Amka returned to deliver another frosty beer, clearing Damian's nearly empty mug. Damian's gaze followed her as she moved across the room, her ponytail bouncing slightly with each step. "She gets more beautiful every year, doesn't she?"

Brock grunted, a noncommittal sound, though he didn't argue.

Damian leaned in conspiratorially, his voice dropping slightly. "I heard a rumor she got engaged to Jarod Teller." He rolled his eyes, an exaggerated gesture. "That guy's been a jackass since day one. What's going on there?"

Brock lifted a shoulder, keeping his tone neutral. "If I could explain, I would." His gaze sharpened. "But stop changing the subject. You know more than you're saying about the dead guy."

"I know more about most things than I can ever reveal. Treason and all that," Damian said smoothly, taking a deep drink from his beer. The knot of his emerald tie stayed perfectly in place, undisturbed despite his movements. "But in this case, I truly have no idea about his identity. There's no missing employee at EVE. Everyone is accounted for, and we haven't had any turnover for at least a year."

Brock stared at his brother for a long moment before asking, "What are you even doing working for EVE, Damian? You wanted out of active duty—or active intelligence, or whatever the hell you've been doing for the last few years—but EVE? If you're there, they're not just studying the ionosphere."

Damian finished his soup, wiping his mouth with a napkin in slow, deliberate movements that spoke of control. "The ionosphere is important, Brock. Understanding it is critical to protecting the world's food supply. What we're doing is worthy of my time." His smile sharpened, but his eyes remained shadowed, as though some private thought lingered behind them. "Of course, I'm not the director of the entire facility. Yet."

"Fair enough," Brock muttered, tired of the endless game of half-truths. He let the silence stretch between them until it felt almost suffocating, the only sounds in the bar the low murmur of conversation and the soft crackle of the fire. Finally, he dropped the bomb. "Did you kill Hank?"

Damian paused, his beer mug halfway to his mouth, the amber liquid catching the firelight. His gaze snapped to Brock's face, sharp and unwavering. "No. Did you?"

"No." Brock searched his brother's expression and felt absurdly pleased that he couldn't read it. Damian had always been the most composed of the brothers, his poker face legendary. But Brock knew one thing—Damian wouldn't lie to him in this situation. Treason? Sure. Murdering Hank? Never.

"Hank was dying," Brock said quietly, the words tasting bitter as they left his mouth.

"Yes."

Brock lowered his voice further, almost a whisper. "Anybody who killed him just helped him end the pain the way he wanted." His throat tightened as the weight of the thought pressed down on his chest. "But who would Hank ask?"

"I'm aware." Damian set his glass down with a muted clink, his body visibly relaxing as if relieved to finally discuss what had been sitting like a stone between them. "If it wasn't you, and it wasn't me...who's your guess? Christian?"

"Maybe. But Ace has been in a rough place since Hank died. It could be guilt." Brock's fingers tightened around his spoon until his knuckles turned white. "Hank died by drowning and being shot. I fucking found him." If Monica hadn't been with him, would he have still notified the sheriff? The question might never be answered because he truly didn't know.

Damian lifted a powerful shoulder beneath his perfectly tailored suit jacket, a movement as calm as if they were discussing the weather. "I would've probably turned away after the shot. Out of pain or instinct, maybe both. I read the autopsy report. Hank's lungs barely had water in them. My guess? He was shot, fell into the river, sucked in one or two breaths, and that was it. In my mind, he died of cancer. Period."

Brock didn't ask how Damian had gotten ahold of the autopsy report—he didn't need to know. "Agreed. Cancer killed Hank." The diagnosis alone had been a death sentence, one none of them could've beaten.

The outside door opened with a loud creak, letting in a gust of icy wind that scattered snowflakes onto the wooden floor.

Damian straightened, his polished demeanor sliding back into place like armor. "Christian's here. Let's ask him if he fired that deadly shot."

CHAPTER THIRTY-FOUR

Ophelia caught sight of Christian walking into Sam's Tavern, so she parked by the curb and jumped out of the Jeep to hustle after him, her boots sliding across the icy ground. The frigid air cut through her coat, but she maintained her balance and entered the warm establishment right after him, noting him stalking toward both Brock and Damian. The rustic interior smelled of cedar and butter, the heat from the fireplace chasing the chill from her bones. Brock's gaze instantly lifted and met hers.

A shiver wandered through her, sending warmth skittering through her veins. Damn, he was sexy. His broad shoulders stretched the flannel shirt he wore like it had been custom-made for him. Whatever he and Damian discussed looked serious, as both men had nearly identical frowns—the kind that hinted at some long-buried family truth.

She plastered on her best smile and followed Christian. "This is fortuitous."

Christian didn't so much as twitch. Instead, he pulled out a chair for her with a deliberate motion, his expression unreadable. Had he known she walked right behind him the entire time? If so, he gave no sign. Nonplussed but slightly impressed, she sat across from Brock and waited until Christian had taken the chair next to her, his frame tense yet controlled.

"Glad you came into town, Damian," Christian said, his voice rough, though not unkind. His dark hair had been tied back at the nape with what looked like a regular rubber band—functional, not stylish.

Damian angled his head toward the empty soup bowl in front of him, looking every bit the polished, big-city professional in his tailored suit and power tie. He stood in stark contrast to his brothers, who filled out their flannels and jeans in a way that could grace any high-end catalog.

"It's clam chowder day," Damian said with a shrug, though the slight twitch at the corner of his mouth suggested more than the simple statement let on.

Amka wiped her hands on a dishtowel and walked toward them. The pretty woman looked harried, her dark hair twisting out of a ponytail, and her cheeks flushed from the heat of the kitchen. Despite the chaos around her, her red flannel shirt and jeans remained free of the stains that had collected on the towel she held.

"Soup?" she asked, her gaze flicking between Christian and the others.

Christian's eyes—one black and one green—glanced toward the door and back again, sharp as knives. The tension in his shoulders didn't ease as he tapped the table with his fingers before finally nodding.

"In a to-go container, Christian?" Amka asked, waiting until he nodded to smile at Ophelia. "Olly, if you're not allergic to clams or seafood, you'll like it."

"Sure, and with a soda, please," Ophelia said, her curiosity piqued by the quiet interplay. She noted the flaring of Christian's dual-colored eyes, their intensity fixed solely on Amka as if nobody else existed in the room. In any room.

The woman's flush deepened, and she quickly turned back toward the kitchen, her tennis shoes silent on the polished wood floor.

Damian cleared his throat. "You wanted me in town, C. Here I am."

Fascinating. How much would they discuss in front of her? Ophelia leaned back. She knew when to stay silent and observe, a skill that had served her well during her time with the Bureau.

Unlike Christian, who seemed intent on ignoring her entirely, Brock's attention locked onto her like a physical weight. His dark green eyes bore into her, steady and unrelenting.

She reminded herself that she was an armed federal agent—trained, capable, and not easily shaken. Yet the heat that climbed into her cheeks betrayed her composure. She stared back, irritation flaring at her own reaction. "You have something to say?"

Brock's rumbling voice came low and even. "How did it go with Doc?"

Damian sat back, tossing his paper napkin into his empty soup bowl with a soft thunk. "Do you two need privacy?"

"No," Ophelia answered quickly.

"Yes," Brock drawled at the same time, his lips twitching slightly.

Christian snorted, shaking his head.

Damian's expression remained impassive, but a new tension seemed to roll off him in waves. Whatever undercurrents existed between them, he didn't like it.

Ophelia felt her cheeks warm even more. What *were* they doing? Why would her relationship—or lack thereof—with Brock irritate Damian? Was it because he'd killed Hank and didn't want Brock getting too close to a federal agent? If they were even dating. They weren't dating. Were they?

Christian blew out a long breath and pointed his spoon at

her. "Man. I felt like I just watched a movie play across your face, Olly. You should never play poker."

Shoot. She'd lost control of the conversation she'd never controlled in the first place. "I didn't mean to interrupt your family gathering." Total lie. She'd meant to sit down, fully aware they wouldn't ignore her. By the quick flash of amusement across Brock's face, he knew it, too. "Pretend like I'm not here."

She leaned back as Amka approached, balancing bowls of soup with practiced ease. A bowl of clam chowder and a soda landed in front of her with a clink. The aroma of creamy broth and fresh herbs teased her senses.

Amka placed a plastic container with the lid to the side as well as a soda bottle in front of Christian. "Silverware is wrapped in the napkins in the center of the table, if you want to eat any here." She gave him a small smile before bustling away toward another table.

Damian's sharp features tensed. "Christian? You wanted me in town, so here I am. What did you want to say to me?"

Christian didn't look up as he unwrapped a napkin, claimed a spoon, and sampled the soup. "It's Ace."

Brock's brows drew together. "What about Ace?"

"He's unraveling, and I'm done with it." Christian's spoon scratched softly against the interior of his bowl.

"I thought he seemed better," Brock said, taking a swig of his beer, though his posture remained stiff.

Christian continued eating, slow and deliberate. "He's been going out to the cemetery and drinking with Hank." He paused, then added, "Well, drinking alone. Passing out on Hank's headstone."

Brock's arms crossed tightly over his chest, his frown deepening. "Hank isn't even buried there. We cremated him and scattered his ashes in the river."

Damian's smile looked strained as he leaned back in his

chair. "That's illegal, I'm sure, Agent Spilazi. So, what Brock meant is that someone scattered the ashes."

Christian didn't react, but Ophelia caught the slight twitch at the corner of his mouth—his version of acknowledgment.

"Just like someone shot Hank." Ophelia's voice cut through the tension as she sampled the soup. The delicious warmth slid down her throat, chasing away the cold from outside and providing a momentary sense of comfort.

Nobody answered her. She set down the spoon and turned to look directly at Christian. "When you say you're done with it, what does that mean?"

She already suspected that he wouldn't admit if Ace had been the one who fired the shot that ended Hank's life. But right now, he felt like the most likely suspect.

The silence stretched. Brock's jaw ticked. Damian's eyes darkened.

And yet, Christian's gaze remained steady—fixed somewhere far away, where none of them could follow.

"I'm going to dry him out," Christian finally said, putting the lid on the soup. "He's not going to like it, and neither am I." Christian pushed back his chair and stood. His movements were deliberate, each one as controlled as the man himself. "Damian? I've given Brock a week. There has to be some sort of detox unit in that mystery facility you now run." He gently slid the chair back into place, economical in every movement.

"Where is Ace?" Ophelia asked, eyes narrowing.

Brock scrubbed both hands down his angular face, exhaustion etched into every line. "I don't know. I thought he planned to help plow the river road today."

"He's drunk at his place," Christian said bluntly, reaching into his back pocket and tossing a twenty on the table. He stood. "Tell Amka to keep the change."

Ophelia cleared her throat. "I know that Hank was in pain and dying from pancreatic cancer."

All three men stilled. As one, their focus centered on her, and it took every ounce of her self-control not to shift on the seat. "Anybody who shot him might've considered it a mercy killing." She met each of their gazes in turn, trying not to squirm. "Brock has an alibi. Do either of you two have one?" It was the most direct she'd been able to be with them. She finally understood their refusal to help in the investigation.

"You can speak with our lawyer after I find one." Damian stood and left money as well, his expression unreadable. "Christian? I'll walk you out."

Ophelia's jaw firmed as frustration simmered beneath her skin. She didn't have enough to take either man into custody. Not yet, anyway. So they did not have to speak with her. "Also, I heard you're quite the good Samaritan, allowing Wyatt and Sylvie Yankovich to take the supply plane to Anchorage. That's a new development, no?"

His grin was perfectly charming in that Osprey-badass way that seemed almost rehearsed. "The kid nearly lost his feet, and the plane was already headed to Anchorage for the next couple of weeks, so why not?"

Neither Brock nor Christian revealed their thoughts, their poker faces ironclad.

Ophelia tilted her head, narrowing her eyes. "Are you sure you didn't want Wyatt talking to me about monsters in the mountains that take out eyes?"

Damian's amusement deepened, darkening his eyes even more. "I'm sure." He knocked Brock lightly on the shoulder and gave Ophelia a polite nod. "Brock? Let's meet up later today. We need to talk."

With that, he followed Christian out into the already dwindling daylight, their boots thudding against the wooden floor.

A rush of cold air swept inside, chilling Ophelia to the bone as the door swung shut behind them. She shivered, irritation flaring as she wrapped her hands around the warm bowl of chowder. "He has a new policy just allowing folks to jump on his plane? I don't think so." She'd already contacted the FBI in Honolulu, since Wyatt and Sylvie had hopped on a plane. They'd be taken into custody upon landing.

Brock shrugged, though tension rippled across his broad shoulders. "The guy almost froze to death. Heading somewhere warm for a little while makes sense to me." He took another spoonful of soup as if the matter was settled.

He could be such a pain. She stared at him, wondering if he cared how much his calm demeanor riled her up. "I don't think your brothers like me." She dug back into the chowder, trying to clear her mind. She needed to catch Ace while he was drunk—it wasn't exactly by the book, but it might get the job done. Maybe he'd confess, or at least give her a lead. He'd been sleeping with Tammy, after all. Maybe she'd discovered he killed Hank. Would he then kill her?

"They like you."

Ophelia looked at Brock, her gaze steady. "I think your brother Damian has narcissistic qualities."

Brock's lips quirked as he finished his beer. "Most good leaders do." His phone buzzed, and he tugged it free of his back pocket, his features tightening as he glanced at the screen. He sighed and stood, muscles rippling beneath his flannel as he moved. "Another damn cat in a tree. We need to elect a sheriff." He dropped cash next to his bowl, more than enough to cover his meal and tip. "I'm sorry to ditch you."

Sure, he was. She forced a smile. "No worries. I want to work from here for a while today." She planned to create a detailed murder board on her laptop, connecting everyone involved in the two cases—three, if she considered the dead man in the EVE jacket whose body had mysteriously vanished. "Have a nice day, Brock."

He hesitated, a rare softness flickering across his features. "We also need to talk."

Her heart thudded once. "What about?"

His eyes darkened, and for a brief moment, he looked like everything strong, wild, and untouchable in the world. Not literally untouchable, but definitely figuratively. "Us."

He didn't mince words, didn't play games.

"I know," she murmured, even though she had no idea what she'd say when that conversation finally happened. Just being near him sent her mind spinning when she needed to focus on her job.

Brock tugged his coat off the chair and shrugged into it. "Later, then."

He moved past her, the heat of his body brushing close as he left. She didn't turn to watch him go—but it took everything she had.

Finally, she could take a deep breath. Something about the Osprey brothers stole all the available oxygen in a room. It wasn't just their size, either—it was the intensity they carried, like they'd been born ready for battle. Shoving her now-empty bowl to the side, she pulled out her laptop and went to work, letting the hum of the bar around her fade into the background. The murder board she created on-screen filled up quickly with faces, dates, and speculative connections that tangled together like a web. There wasn't enough to arrest Ace. She needed answers, and fast.

"Can I get you another soda?" Amka asked.

"Sure." Ophelia looked up.

Amka shifted her feet. "Also, I've decided not to attend the interview with you later this afternoon."

Surprise filtered through Ophelia. "Is that a fact?"

"Yes." Amka met her gaze directly. "Apparently I'm under no obligation to do so. So either arrest me or forget about it."

Interesting. "Did you kill Tammy because she and your fiancé were having an affair?"

"Of course not." Amka rolled her eyes. "Seriously." The woman seemed truthful.

On to the next investigation, then. "Monica Luna told me she saw you opening the tavern late the morning she and Brock found Hank's body." Ophelia watched Amka carefully, not seeing a bit of surprise. So Amka knew about the one night stand...and morning.

Amka looked around the tavern and then leaned in, lowering her voice. "Sometimes I open late. It happens. Please don't tell anybody about Monica and Brock. They partied here the night before and left together, and I'm sure both regret it. Monica loves David. She's my friend and I don't want her hurt."

That made sense. And Ophelia truly believed one of the Osprey brothers had mercy killed Hank, so Amka wasn't a suspect there. "All right." She'd gotten the questions answered she wanted. "Please reconsider coming in for a formal and recorded interview."

"Nope." Amka turned and returned to work.

Dinnertime came, and Ophelia ordered a burger, savoring the smoky char of the meat as she kept working. The fire crackled nearby, and she resisted the urge to stretch out like a lazy cat basking in the warmth. Too many connections and secrets existed in a small town. Gossip twisted into half-truths, and old grudges lived side by side with whispered warnings. Someone here knew what had happened to Tammy Randsom—and Hank Osprey. She just had to find a source willing to talk.

By seven, the bar started to really hop. Locals crowded in, laughter mingling with the occasional clink of beer mugs and the thump of boots on the hardwood floor. She packed up her belongings, sliding her laptop into its protective case. Spending the day by the fire had been productive—and oddly comforting—but now it was time to go.

She made her way to the counter to pay a rushing-around

Amka. The bartender flashed a quick smile as she rang up the order. "Everything okay?"

Ophelia nodded, sliding over a generous tip. "Thanks, Amka."

"No problem. Stay warm out there." Amka apparently didn't hold on to grudges.

The moment Ophelia stepped outside, the icy air rammed right through her jacket like a physical blow. She ducked her head and tucked her chin into her scarf, carefully navigating the slick sidewalk. The streetlights cast long, silver streaks across the snow-covered street, providing just enough glow to combat the winter darkness.

When she reached her Jeep, she stopped dead. What the heck? She leaned down, the frigid air burning her lungs as she inspected her tires. Both on the driver's side had been slashed to shreds. Heart pounding, she stepped around the front of the vehicle to check the passenger side. Same story. All four tires —destroyed.

Her head dropped, and a wave of frustration settled in her chest. Now what? The freezing cold didn't invite her to walk all the way to Flossy's cabin, especially with the wind cutting through her clothes like knives. And it wasn't like they had Triple A in Knife's Edge. The local garage wouldn't open until tomorrow morning, and she couldn't bring herself to ask Flossy to bundle up and head out into the night for a rescue.

She mulled over her options, her breath clouding the air in front of her. Only one choice made sense. She wanted Brock. Man, she was tired of being alone. Soon she'd have to arrest one of his brothers, and no matter what he said, that would end them. Could she spend one more night with him? Just to hold on to for the future? She pulled out her phone and made a call, hoping they both had service right now.

"Osprey," Brock's deep voice answered on the first ring.

Relief flooded through her, warming her more than the fire had. "Hi. It's Ophelia. I need help."

CHAPTER THIRTY-FIVE

As he drove into town and pulled up next to Sam's Tavern, fury slid through Brock's body faster than one of Amka's specially-made glacier shots with homemade moonshine. He opened his door to jump out of his truck, leaving the engine running. "What the hell are you doing just standing in the dark?" It took him a second, but he caught sight of his spare weapon in Ophelia's hand. "At least you show some sense." Although the surrounding buildings were shrouded in darkness, and even a subpar sniper on a rooftop could've easily caught her unawares.

She snorted. "Do you have a melee of snipers here in Knife's Edge?"

He'd said that out loud? Crouching, he took in the slashed tires. Sharp blade, strong strokes. Somebody was coming for her, and he had to figure out who before they actually struck. His anger spiraled even hotter. "We'll have the garage tow you tomorrow." He stood, noting the snow in her dark hair. Man, she had a lot of hair. His hands clenched with the need to tunnel through the thick strands and hold her in place. Any place. "Get in the truck."

She didn't need a kinder invitation because she dodged into the street and jumped into his passenger seat, shoving the gun into her pocket and holding her gloved hands out to the heater. Her laptop bag hit the winter mat with a soft thunk.

He sat and shut his door, the smell of strawberries instantly assailing him. Not the soft scent of those in the grocery store. No. The full-on, sweet, and succulent smell of wild fruit. The sensation added to the already boiling temper at the top of his spine. The pressure threatened to explode and spiral outward, ready to decimate anyone in his path.

"You're in a mood," she observed mildly.

He kept perfect control as he pressed on the gas pedal. A mood? Yeah. He was in a fucking mood. The entire world frustrated the hell out of him. Ace kept drinking himself into oblivion, Damian appeared embroiled in something possibly dangerous at EVE, and Christian had already lost his patience with everybody. In addition, Brock didn't know who'd killed Hank, and burying his head in the snow no longer worked because the woman he was falling hard for would discover the truth. He had to get there first.

Worse yet, the woman wouldn't let him provide cover. He needed to shield her from the shitstorm coming. Yeah, she worked as a trained FBI agent, which impressed him. Even so, she didn't know the wilderness, and she sure as shit didn't know Knife's Edge. Dangers lurked everywhere, even for somebody who knew how to handle a gun. "You coming to my place?"

"Yes."

Something in him eased. Finally.

Her phone rang, and she jumped, glancing at the face. "That's odd. It's late in DC." She answered. "Hello, sir." Her entire body stiffened. "No, but—" Seconds ticked by as she listened. "Who called you? I don't understand. What in the world is going on?"

Brock's gut turned over. *Consider it taken care of, then.* Casual words from Damian that hadn't meant much in the moment.

Ophelia pulled the phone away from her ear and just stared at it. It seemed, the caller had disconnected. "I can't believe it."

His eyebrows shot up. Anger vibrated from her, hitting him hard. "What?"

She swiveled, her sapphire eyes glittering in the darkness. "I have three days to wrap up the investigation into Hank's death, and then I'm apparently on leave. Possibly permanently."

Brock kept his hands loose on the wheel. Just what kind of power did Damian have in DC, anyway? "Why?"

"No reason. Just that the FBI has decided to turn the Knife's Edge cases over to the locals—to the sheriff, whomever that might end up being. What did you do?" She swept out her hands. "That's impossible. My boss\had a friendship with Hank way back when, which is the main reason I'm here. So, somebody *above* him yanked me off."

Brock frowned. "Even so, why is he going to put you on leave?"

She pushed her wild hair away from her face in quick and angry motions. "I fell into a bit of trouble from dating a coworker who sucked, and this was my last chance for redemption." She eyed him. "Tell me you didn't make this happen."

"I didn't. No pull in DC, baby." Not exactly true. He wasn't even sure Damian had done so, but he'd find out. He felt for her as he drove and parked outside his cabin bypassing the shop, cutting the engine. "I'll help you solve Tammy's disappearance. Maybe that'll get your job back." Although her switching to a different job would help him out tremendously.

He believed in duty and honor. He'd fought and nearly died for his country and all the good freedom represented. But above all, he believed in family. At any cost. "Have you ever thought about a different line of work?"

She punched him in the arm. Full-on and with a closed fist. It wasn't a love tap.

He instantly retaliated, grasping her biceps and dragging her across his seat and out into the snow. A quick duck, and she was over his shoulder, heading into the cabin. "Hitting isn't nice, Olly." He planted one hard smack on her curvy ass to prove his point.

Her response was a perfectly placed punch to his ribs.

He chuckled and slapped her again, putting some effort into it this time. The sound she made was half fury and half chuckle.

"You're ridiculous," she said as he kicked open his cabin door and strode inside to drop her onto the sofa. Her hair flew in every direction, and her cheeks flooded with a lovely pink color. "If you want to go hand-to-hand, let's do it, Osprey."

Now, that was an offer he'd never refuse. "All right." He yanked both boots off her and returned to the door to shut and lock it, kicking out of his footwear. They both needed to burn off steam and if this was the way she wanted to do it, he was all in. He returned to her, dropping his coat onto the floor. "But we're playing my way, sweetheart."

Her breath came in pants, and her eyes sparkled. Oh, she wanted this as much as he did. Wanted to forget everything but just the two of them. Even for only one night. "What does that mean?"

"First one to get the other naked wins. We'll figure everything else out after that." Including them. Despite everything happening around them—and there seemed to be a lot—he grew tired of resisting her pull. Tired of fighting his needs. Tired of being without the scent of strawberries around him at all times. "Deal?"

She bunched her legs as if to attack, anticipation lighting her stunning face. "Deal."

He lunged.

MAN, she wanted this. Ophelia kicked out, nailing Brock in the gut and stopping him cold. The impact would've knocked most men to their knees, but not the badass ex-SEAL turned sheriff. His smile widened.

Unease filtered through her, along with a sense of playfulness. Of challenge. So, she rolled to the side, hoping to angle over the edge of the sofa.

He was quicker, grasping her jacket and yanking it over her head.

She took advantage of his hands being full of her leather jacket and leaped over the arm of the sofa, landed, then somersaulted to her feet before turning and dropping into a fighting stance. "Thanks for the assist. I wrestle better without the jacket in the way."

"Anytime," he murmured, tossing the coat over his head and stalking toward her.

She couldn't breathe. Just looking at him took her breath away. He was all man, and at the moment, all intent. Broad chest, glittering eyes, powerful hands. "You should give up now," she suggested, keeping her focus on his feet.

"Don't know how," he admitted, his gaze on her feet. "I don't like being kicked."

She feinted to the side. "Most mules don't."

He cocked his head. "Did you just call me a donkey?"

"Jackass," she agreed, having more fun than she'd had in months. For the moment, she forgot about her job, the cases, and her unsteady life. There was just here and now and the sexy Brock Osprey while she still had him. "Surely, you've been called that before."

"I surely have." He ducked and moved for her.

She jumped out of the way in time, spinning and kicking him in the thigh. Her landing graceful, she struck out with the second kick to take him down, but he moved faster than she'd imagined.

He grabbed her ankle with one hand and lifted, wrapping his free arm around her waist and taking her to the floor. His arm and knees took the brunt of the impact, keeping her safe. Rough hands grasped her shirt and ripped it down the middle. He nipped her neck, then rolled off her, coming to his feet. "Pretty bra."

Damn it. She shrugged out of the useless shirt and stood, slightly out of breath. So far, she wasn't winning. It was time to play dirty. Her shoulders went down, and she shook out her hands as if injured. He paused. Then she struck, tackling him at the thighs. His arms windmilled as he went back, landing on his butt with his torso going down.

She rapidly unbuckled his belt and stood, pulling it free.

There was absolutely no doubt in her mind that he allowed her to take the leather from him. Even so, she cracked it in the air, coming precariously close to his right ear.

He sat, and one of his eyebrows rose. "You'd do well to remember that I hit back, sweetheart. I have no problem turning you over my knee, so watch it with the belt. It's a threat you can't back up."

His words were a low rumble that licked across her skin, flaring nerves to life. Her butt more than likely still held the imprint from his hand, and the warmth there hadn't abated. Her entire body fired up. For him. "Is that a threat?"

He levered to his knees, still looking powerful. Those eyes glittered a surreal green. "Damn straight."

Her butt actually clenched. It wasn't like she would smack him with the belt. "Whatever." She threw the belt across the room.

"Good choice." Then, he waited.

She paused. "Stand up."

"No." His reach was longer than hers by far, so she bounced away.

"Don't take it easy on me." She didn't want to win by default.

His grin was too sexual for any woman to stay sane. "I won't. Trust me."

She swallowed as her body performed a long, shivering roll. Darn it. He saw that. "Fine." In one fluid motion, she grabbed a sofa pillow and pummeled his head with it while reaching for the bottom of his shirt.

His chuckle was calm as he yanked the pillow, tossed it, and dropped her onto his lap. A flick of his wrist released the front clasp of her bra. "There we go," he murmured, his gaze on her breasts.

She took advantage of his distraction and reached for the hem of his shirt.

In some unfathomable movement, he lifted her, spun her, and somehow dragged her jeans right off before landing her back right where she'd started. She let out a startled yip and then dissolved into laughter, perched on him in only her panties and socks. "How did you do that?"

"I was inspired." His fingers curled around her nape and drew her closer. "I'm done playin'." He kissed her, hunger in the movement. His hold tightened, and he went deeper, his free hand sweeping down her body in a show of possession.

She broke the kiss only to have him lick along her jawline and sink his teeth into her earlobe. She yelped, even as he soothed the small sting. Her entire body tingled like she'd been wrestling for hours instead of minutes, and she shook her head to retain control. Any control. "I'm not done playing." Was that her voice? Breathy and deeper than usual?

He blinked.

She shoved him back with both hands, straddling him and pulling his shirt over his head. Ha. She got it. His broad chest was now bare to her.

"All right." He slid one arm beneath both of her bent legs, lifted her, and flipped her over. It took her a second to realize her elbows were on the floor and her body over his lap.

"Hey," she said, trying not to laugh again, even though she was so turned on she couldn't see straight.

"You said you weren't done playing." He gave her the gentle reminder in his gravelly voice right before his hand descended on her ass. "I like your pretty pink thong." To emphasize his point, he smacked her two more times.

Her body jerked, and heat tore through her from his hand. "This isn't playing," she gasped, needing more.

"It is for me." He spanked her three times in succession. "You done playing yet?"

There was no way she could get free. "Yep. Totally done with the playtime," she ground out.

"Good." With way too much ease, he flipped her right back around to sit and took her mouth.

Hard.

CHAPTER THIRTY-SIX

Brock forced himself to slow down, even as he tightened his hold. The scent of strawberries surrounded them, sliding beneath his skin to caress each nerve, throwing his heart into the thundering range. He enjoyed playing with her, the challenge of it, and the memory of his prints on her sexy ass would stay with him for a long time.

He liked his marks on her.

His cock hardened to a steel rod in his jeans, demanding relief. Raw need and lust pounded through his body, just for her. He'd known he was falling desperately for the stunning agent, but he'd thought they couldn't work unless he figured out who had helped Hank die.

He didn't know, but had faced the reality earlier that he had to find out so he could help whichever brother needed it.

Ophelia moaned against his mouth, and he caressed her breasts, spending time with each nipple and giving her a small pinch. Her gasp sounded sweet, and he turned his attention to the other nipple, knowing just how much of a bite to give her.

His girl liked a little bit of pain with her pleasure. They were absolutely on the same page there. He stroked her inner thigh, smiling when she arched her sweet body toward his hand. Leaving it tantalizingly close, he sucked her bottom lip into his mouth and then leaned back to look into her sapphire-colored eyes. "We're doing this, Ophelia."

She blinked, nearly naked on his lap, and then grinned. Lust glimmered in her eyes and tightened her delicate jaw. "Yeah. I got that." She smoothed her hand down his bare chest and hummed in appreciation.

"No." He tangled his fingers in her hair, fisting the silky mass. "You and me. No more games, and no more playing around. We're giving us a shot." Controlling her head, he kissed her again, sweeping his tongue inside her mouth and tasting strawberries. He didn't care how he sounded. She'd given him this, and she'd given herself. He wouldn't lose her now. No matter what. "Understand?"

Her hands halted, and she flattened them on his chest. Confusion mixed with need in her expression. "Brock, there's too much between us. You're not telling me the truth."

He jerked slightly, tugging back her head and enjoying her quick intake of breath. "You and I are separate from all the bullshit in our lives." The woman had a right to make her own decisions, especially one this absolute. Even so, he didn't have it in him to play fair, so he left his fist in her hair and his fingers on her trembling thigh. "This is your decision."

"What?" She blinked and dropped her gaze back to his mouth.

He tightened his hold until she couldn't move her head and watched as her eyes widened in surprise and then need. "If you want, I'll take you back to Flossy's right now." He'd have to keep watch to make sure she stayed safe. "But if you stay, you're all in. No more hiding behind a cold case, no matter what we find out. No more trying to stay emotionally absent. You decide to remain with me tonight? You're staying and seeing us through."

She nibbled on her bottom lip, looking both scared and hopeful. "Brock, that's crazy."

"Maybe," he allowed. "But it's absolute. I give you my word that I don't know who shot Hank, killed Tammy, or destroyed that EVE victim who disappeared. Regardless, all of that stays separate from us. From you and me. No matter what we find out, we're in this together. I don't do the dating game—or any other games. This is it. I feel it, you feel it, and you're no coward. In or out, Olly?"

She took in a deep breath and exhaled, so much cautious hope in her eyes that it looked like she might refuse. "I'll do my job, and if that means arresting one of your brothers, it's going to happen."

"That's fine. We'll deal with it if it happens. But we're solid regardless." He'd have to find a good lawyer.

"I don't see how, but I'll give it a chance. Okay." She steeled her shoulders, even though he still controlled her head. "All in, then."

His body settled, and his mind cleared. "Good choice." Then he kissed her again, giving her all of him. Somehow, kissing her felt like a new experience. No question remained—she was the one for him. Liquid flames spread through his veins, gliding like century-old wine throughout his entire body. Need pounded harsh and wild in his groin. Nerves fired down his spine, up his legs, and right to his balls with a fiery demand. He finally gave her what she wanted, sliding the pads of his fingers across her sex and dipping into her panties.

She moaned into his mouth, and he scraped his thumb across her clit, setting her off. The climax took her hard and fast, and the second she relaxed, he pressed two fingers inside her, prolonging the waves consuming her body.

Even then, he didn't release her sweet mouth. Instead, he gently bit her bottom lip, smiling as she jumped. Then he kissed the small nip. Wrapping one arm around her waist, he turned and laid her on the rug, pushing her down and kissing her neck, clavicle, and then her breasts. He looked up to see her dark hair pillowed all around her with the barely there burning embers from the fire he'd stoked that morning illuminating her like a goddess. "You're beautiful, Ophelia." And she was all his.

She watched him, her eyes soft, her body moving against his. Reaching for him, she caressed his cock. "I'm on the pill, Brock. And I'm safe."

"I just had a checkup and am safe." He couldn't wait any longer. Steadying himself on his knees, he wrapped one arm around her waist and partially lifted her, flipping her onto her hands and knees. Grabbing her hips, he started pushing inside her. She gasped and arched her back, but he was relentless, finally burying himself to the hilt.

Nothing in the entire world had ever felt so good. Her body pulsed around him, caressing him, clamping on so strongly his fingers dug into her hips. He slid out, torturing them both, and then slammed back in. She moaned his name.

At the sound, he lost control. Gripping her tightly, he pounded into her, his vision going dark. Hard and fast, he went as deep as possible, feeling her all around him. Her body started to quake, and he instantly slapped her ass. Hard. "Not until I say," he ground out.

She whimpered and somehow tightened even more around him. The woman might fucking kill him. The sound of flesh on flesh and their ragged breaths filled the night, and the smell of wild strawberries surrounded them both. His body heated, and electricity zapped down his torso to land in his balls. She threw her head back, and all that glorious hair fell down her spine.

Her body trembled again, and he could feel her quaking around him. His hand automatically landed on her butt again, and she squeaked, stilling. "Don't even think it," he warned, hammering into her even harder. The fire roared for him, and he was almost there. She felt tight, hot, and so wet he never wanted this to end.

Her body clenched around him tighter than any vise, and flames licked through him. "Now," he ordered, sending her over. She cried out, her body undulating as the climax took her. Pleasure blasted through him, and he shuddered as her sweet body constricted around his cock with a vicious heat. He emptied himself into her, letting her wring him out. Her body softened and went lax. She murmured his name.

It was absolutely everything.

While he still had the strength, he pulled out of her, lifted her around the waist to spin and toss over his shoulder, stood on shaky legs, and then walked to his bedroom. "Round one is a tie. Let's see who wins the next few."

OPHELIA FINISHED SHOWERING while Brock cooked breakfast, thankful to have a little space. The night had been both wild and incredible, but in the morning light, she felt unsettled. Perhaps a little vulnerable. Or a lot. She'd never felt like that before. He'd been thorough and controlling in a way she wouldn't have guessed she'd like.

She would've been wrong.

Slipping out of the shower, she wrung her hair out, letting the mass dry down her back. Then she borrowed one of his overlarge flannels and padded out barefoot. The smell of bacon hit her first, and her stomach grumbled, so she continued beyond the fireplace to the kitchen, stopping short at seeing both Christian and Ace sitting at the table.

Brock placed a heaping platter of scrambled eggs and bacon on the surface before moving for her. Then, in front of two of his brothers, he curled his hand around her nape, leaned down, and kissed her. It wasn't a sweet peck or even a good-morning smooch. It was full-on, hot, and possessive.

Her mind spun, and her body swayed toward his. Warmth brushed her front, and heat blasted down her entire body. How she could react to him like this after such a consuming night, she'd never understand. Then he turned her. "Olly and I are together. Period."

Ace blinked, his eyes bloodshot and his whiskers longer than the last time she'd seen him. "Congrats?"

Christian didn't blink. Didn't so much as twitch. His dual-colored eyes narrowed slightly, and his whiskers were neatly trimmed somehow. "She's a Fed."

"I'm fully aware of her job," Brock countered. "But she's mine. You'll protect her as such."

Ace nodded.

"Got it," Christian murmured, reaching for a mug of steaming coffee in front of him.

Ophelia pushed Brock's torso to extricate herself. "I don't need protection from any of you." When Brock didn't release her, she elbowed him right between the ribs, feeling vulnerable with her legs bare.

He reacted instantly, sliding his hand down her flank to wrap an iron-hard arm around her waist and jerk her flush against him. "Told you there was no going back once you committed. You agreed. This is how it is, Ophelia." His arm was rock-solid and kept her in place.

She knew about ten moves that could break the hold and take him down...probably. He was as well trained as she was, if not better, and he had combat experience. In addition, he had weight and strength on his side. "I think this is a private matter." If she were wearing heels, she'd nail his foot.

Brock shrugged, moving her with his body. "Everything is a family matter, and you're covered now, sweetheart. Like it or not." He started walking toward the table, forcing her to move with him, and pulled out a chair. "You need protein."

She sat, somewhat stunned by the entire situation. Ace handed over a plate and nudged the eggs her way. Christian just watched her over the rim of his mug. Something warm tickled her toes and ankles, and she didn't need to look down to know that Tika had flopped right on her feet. The entire scene was cozy in a way she'd never experienced. Brock took the chair next to her and started dishing up both their plates while Ace poured them coffee from a carafe in the middle of the table.

Her stomach ached. "I'm probably going to arrest one of you. You get that, right?"

They both shrugged.

"We'll deal and get a good lawyer. As I see it, you don't have evidence. Not anything concrete," Christian murmured.

Brock's gaze remained serious. "They changed your four flat tires, and the Jeep is outside by the shop. You still have my extra Glock, right?"

"Yes," she murmured. "Um, thank you for fixing my tires."

Both of Brock's brothers just shrugged.

"Too bad Damian's not here," Ace said quietly. "He needs to hear your declaration, Brock."

Declaration? For goodness' sake. Ophelia bit back a retort.

Christian cleared his throat. "I met with Damian yesterday, and I don't like his job. He's up to something, and it doesn't feel right."

Brock paused in eating eggs and looked at Christian. "I spoke with him yesterday, as you know. He didn't say much, but he's in intelligence."

Ace rolled his eyes. "Intelligence in the middle of nowhere at a so-called research facility? Even if it's some sort of former governmental and now private research program, Damian isn't just in intelligence. He's higher than that, which most people don't know. If he's there, something is off, and he's probably watching his six every second as he investigates."

"Do you think his job has something to do with the dead victim wearing the EVE jacket who somehow disappeared?" Ophelia asked.

"No." Brock scrubbed both hands down his face. "I'm takin' the sheriff's job and will start forcing him to liaise with the locals."

Christian munched on a piece of bacon. "I thought you already took the job."

Ace snorted. "Yeah, but he didn't know it. Dumbass."

Brock tossed his napkin at him.

Ophelia tried not to enjoy the feeling of being included in the testosterone-filled family, but her shoulders finally relaxed. Oh, she wouldn't stop her investigation, but for the first time, she wished she could believe that a hunter had killed Hank. He had been ill and in pain, and whoever fired the shotgun had most likely been helping him. Murder remained illegal, though. Her entire job consisted of investigating such homicides.

Hopefully, the judicial system would be kind to the killer, which could happen.

Brock gave her more bacon. "Stop thinking so hard."

She finished the delicious eggs, which had plenty of cheese sprinkled throughout. "No matter what my boss says, I'm not quitting my job, Brock. Regardless of what's happening between us."

He partially turned, his green eyes piercing. "That's fine, so long as you fully understand you're not quitting us, regardless of your job." No give showed on his dangerous face. "I gave you an out, and you didn't take it."

Her heart stuttered, and an unreal heat washed through her entire body. She barely kept from shifting on her chair.

Christian's upper lip twitched, almost forming a smile.

"When big brother makes a claim, he's kind of a Neanderthal about it."

Ace finished more coffee, his eyes sparkling. "No shit. Some people wouldn't understand that kind of thing."

Brock took a deep drink from his chipped mug, his shoulders broad and appearing relaxed. "So long as my woman understands me, I'm good. Period."

Oh, he did not. Ophelia's mouth dropped open. "You're about to get an understanding of your own, buddy."

He gently, too gently, set down his mug and then pivoted fully to face her. "Bring it on, baby. I'm ready for another round."

CHAPTER THIRTY-SEVEN

After the too cozy breakfast with the hot bodied Osprey brothers, two of whom were murder suspects, Ophelia carried the files from her three open cases to the conference room at the sheriff's station, stepping around a stack of newspapers. She had to figure out who killed Hank so she and Brock could move on with their relationship.

Could they if she arrested one of his brothers? Her stomach cramped. She sat and stretched her neck.

She owed those two brothers of Brock's for changing her tires the night before, and the feeling of being included in the family was way too tempting.

A blizzard absolutely attacked the building, and she considered turning up the heat. Flossy had called in sick with a cold, so Ophelia didn't feel right using so much of the electricity.

At the moment, Brock and his brothers had planned a family meeting at his place. Well, in a half an hour or so. Her gut told her Brock would find out who shot Hank.

But would he tell her?

She doubted it.

Going on a hunch, she'd purchased online access to the local newspaper and had spent the morning reading about town events starting in May when Tamara had disappeared through the previous December when Hank had died, just looking for any sort of lead. Taking a break from the computer, she now read through the case file for Tammy Randsom, now much thicker since her body had been found, and made a few notations of people she might want to talk to in town. She'd called and Leo had been adamant that she not speak with his kids, and she couldn't blame him too much. Perhaps Brock could get her an in with Leo so she could speak with the children about their murdered mother, and she'd be gentle.

Sighing, she pushed the file aside and turned her attention to the nearly empty file folder regarding the dead man with his eyes gouged out who'd worn the EVE logo. Not even her boss had been able to get a handle on the place.

Sighing, she returned to the computer and conducted a search specifically for Hank Osprey. The paper had featured him many times through the years, showing him in town, at events, and during many fishing derbies. He won one a couple of years previous. She looked at his strong and still healthy features. So cancer hadn't caught him yet. A knit cap was half off his head with some sort of symbol in the center. She peered closer, trying to make it out. For the briefest of seconds, she thought it formed the letters for EVE. But a closer examination proved it was some sort of smooth logo. What was that?

She couldn't make out the shape.

Ugh. How freaking frustrating. She closed the laptop, and her stomach growled. Maybe she should run down to the diner for lunch. Standing, she shrugged into her coat and strode through the office, shoving open the front door.

Snow billowed all around, white and thick. She blinked and started toward her Jeep when something hit her hard in the back of the head. She fell sideways, her vision going black. What was happening? Pain echoed through her entire skull, and she shook her head to keep conscious. Rolling onto her back, she tried to lever up onto her elbows on the freezing concrete.

A thick white boot kicked her leg.

She focused on the boot until her vision cleared and then looked up to see Monica Luna standing above her, pointing a silver weapon. "Monica?" The woman's face wavered in and out.

"Hi, Ophelia. Man, you have a hard head."

Ophelia stared up at the barrel of what appeared to be a nine-millimeter. "That's a lovely Smith & Wesson." Her stomach clenched, and blood rushed through her head, ringing in her ears. With the storm, nobody ventured out on the sidewalk or across the street.

"Thank you." Monica gestured with the weapon. "Nobody's around except Amos, who no doubt is downstairs. Come with me, and I won't have to shoot him, too."

How was this happening? "Sure." Ophelia stood and ignored the trembling in her legs, groaning as agony ripped through her head. She had a better chance of getting the gun if they were on the move. Her mind spun as she tried to keep control of herself. "This isn't making sense. Have you been shooting at me lately?"

"Yep." Monica's eyes gleamed with an odd light. "You shouldn't have come here. You don't belong." She turned and motioned again with the gun.

"I've heard that before," Ophelia murmured, trying not to throw up. The woman's hand remained steady on the weapon. "You know, you're not a very good shot."

Monica reared back. "This close to you, I don't need to be."

A true statement. Bile rose, burning Ophelia's throat. Her vision kept going black. She reached to the back of her head, feeling blood and a large lump. The door to the interior of the office remained open. Could Amos hear them? "Did you kill Hank?"

Monica snorted. "Of course not."

Why couldn't Ophelia concentrate? The world spun around her. "You hit me with the gun?"

"Yeah. Thought it'd knock you out, but I guess not. It's better if you walk to the Jeep, anyway." Monica grinned. "I still have the spare set of keys. You should've asked for them."

This was insane. The woman couldn't just kidnap Ophelia in the middle of the day from the sheriff's office. She hitched down the stairs to the sidewalk and looked both ways. The snowy sidewalks remained vacant. "This is a mistake, Monica."

"Right." Monica stepped up and pressed the barrel into Ophelia's rib cage. "I could shoot you right now, run, and nobody would even know it was me. Nobody's out in this crazy storm."

That appeared to be true. Ophelia let her body sag. Obviously she'd gotten closer than she realized with one of the cases. Which one? "Did you kill Tammy Randsom?" Had David maybe slept with Tammy? Was he one of the men she'd taken to the Tundra?

"Shut up. Let's go."

Damn it. Ophelia couldn't see clearly. "How did you get here?"

"Parked down by the river and walked through the blizzard. Nobody will see my vehicle." Monica shoved harder, and pain flashed through Ophelia's abdomen. "Start moving or I'll shoot you and then Amos."

Ophelia tried to find help through the snow, but everyone remained inside and out of the snowy day. Dizziness overwhelmed her, and she might not make it three feet. "Fine. Let's just get inside the Jeep." She started sliding across the ice.

Monica tried to grab her, loosening her hold on the gun.

Tension roared through Ophelia, and she turned, hitting down at the weapon.

The gun discharged, and the sound echoed in the silent day. A second later, agony burned hot and bright through Ophelia.

She cried out, and then she went down. Cold flashed along her hands and then her face as she impacted the ice.

Then unconsciousness took all the pain away.

IN HIS SHOP, Brock leaned over his snowmobile, tightening a bolt near the throttle assembly and adjusting the fuel line, his gloved hands precise despite the cold. He'd already replaced the spark plugs and tested the carburetor, making sure the machine could handle both the ice-packed trails and deep snowdrifts outside of town. The shop smelled faintly of grease, metal, and fresh pine from the fire burning in the corner. The wood crackled as the flames flickered and danced, casting a warm glow over the workbench cluttered with tools and parts.

The door creaked open, and cold air swept in as Christian stepped inside, stomping snow off his boots. The wolf-pup padded behind him, its fluffy coat dusted with white. It sniffed the air, spotted the fireplace, and immediately headed for the warmth, curling up in front of the hearth with a contented sigh.

"Hey," Christian said, brushing more snow from his shoulders and hair.

"Hi," Brock replied, watching as his brother's gaze followed the pup.

Christian's lips twitched in something that almost resembled a smile before his usual serious expression returned. "I couldn't get Damian to level with me yesterday. About what he's doing at EVE."

Brock's eyebrows shot up. "Seriously?"

"Yeah." Christian's tone remained calm but resolute. "I don't trust much in this life, but my instincts are usually spot on. Damian's in trouble and doesn't know it yet."

A chill crawled down Brock's spine, and it wasn't from the cold. Christian's instincts bordered on the supernatural, and

Brock trusted them more than most things. "Did you find a way in to the facility?"

Christian shook his head. "No. But I will."

Brock nodded slowly. "It might be better if you just talked to Damian again. Maybe just the two of you meet somewhere private—not in a public place like Sam's Tavern."

Christian's eyes sparked with fire. "Since when do we all talk?"

Brock exhaled through his nose. "Good point. We've all been hurt, trying to be loyal, but we haven't done ourselves much good. It's time to put everything on the table."

Christian's expression tightened, but he nodded. "Did you help Hank to die?"

"No." Brock's throat constricted. "You thought I did it?"

Christian's shoulders shifted in a half-shrug. "I figured that's why you wouldn't be sheriff. Or you knew who did it and wouldn't take the job." He brushed snow off his whiskers. "Damian?"

"No. I looked in his eyes and asked him. Wasn't him." Brock's chest ached at the memory.

Christian's jaw flexed. "Well, there's only one of us drinking himself to death. I thought Ace threw himself into a bottle because of his last mission and the plane crash he won't talk about. Guess I was wrong."

Brock's chin dropped to his chest, guilt pressing on him like a physical weight. "Guess we both were."

Christian's gaze flickered toward the wolf-pup near the fire. "We'll have a discussion topic when Ace and Damian get here in about an hour." He paused. "Your woman is smart. She'll figure it out and arrest Ace."

"There's not enough evidence."

"Will that be a problem?"

Brock wouldn't let it be one. "No." The sound of his phone

buzzing made both brothers still. He tugged it from his jacket pocket and pressed it to his ear. "Osprey."

"Hey, sheriff! It's Amos. I'm down in my apartment, and I'm pretty sure I just heard a weapon discharge upstairs." The man's voice trembled. "I don't know what to do."

Panic shot through Brock like a lightning strike. "I'll be right there."

Christian moved closer, his expression darkening. "What is it?"

"Shots fired in the sheriff's office, and Ophelia is alone there right now." Brock dropped his screwdriver and pressed Ophelia's number into his phone, his fingers nearly slipping. His pulse thundered in his ears as he waited.

She didn't answer.

He rolled his sled out the door and ignited the engine as Christian ran around the side of the building for his own, ordering the wolf pup to stay in the shop.

Brock's gut clenched. He had to get to her. Now.

CHAPTER THIRTY-EIGHT

Brock jumped off his sled before it stopped at the sheriff's station. He paused at seeing blood pooling near the doorway. Shit. His gut clenched, and he barreled inside the sheriff's office with Christian on his heels. "Ophelia," he bellowed, clearing the building room by room, his gun in hand.

Nothing. No sound, no movement, no Olly.

He reached the door to the basement and pounded on it. "Amos? Is she down there with you?"

Amos gingerly pushed open the door, his cloudy eyes wide behind his large spectacles. "Heard a gun, Brock. A gun. A loud gun."

"Okay." Brock forced himself to speak calmly. "Did you see who shot the gun?"

Amos tugged on his striped bow tie and straightened his perfectly pressed cuffs. "No. I didn't hear voices, either. Just a gunshot, and I called you." He rocked back, his gray hair feathering. "Was it Ophelia? I heard her voice earlier but then nothing. Where is she?"

"I don't know." Brock scrubbed a rough hand through his hair.

"I'm texting Ace and Damian." Christian pulled his phone from his jacket pocket.

Brock nodded, trying to concentrate. Where was Ophelia? Who had her? "All right." He had to think, damn it. "Have Ace search the river road coming in from his place, and tell Damian to search coming from EVE. You take this side of the road toward the river, and I'll take the opposite one. Talk to everyone who's out today. If you don't find people, go looking." He blinked and settled. "Ophelia's Jeep isn't here. Ask anybody if they've seen it."

"On it," Christian said, texting quickly. "She'll be okay, Brock. She's smart, and she's trained."

"There's blood on the stairs," Brock said grimly.

Amos coughed. "I'll start a phone tree to see if anybody has seen the Jeep."

"Good. Thanks." Brock nodded. "Whoever took her and the Jeep had to get here somehow. Have people look for trucks, snowmobiles, UTVs, and so on. Nobody just walked into town with this storm going on." How badly had Ophelia been hurt? She must have been the one shot, or she would've called for help.

"Let's go, Brock." Christian turned and strode out of the office.

Brock followed, and the smell of strawberries haunted him. The scent threaded throughout the entire office. Why had he let her work alone? What had he been thinking? He paused outside the door and took in the puddle of blood. Squinting through the billowing snow, he could make out droplets leading to the curb, along with scuff marks across the ice. "Somebody dragged her."

Christian dropped to his haunches to better see the blood. "Looks like." He glanced up. "I would've tossed her over my shoulder."

"Me, too." Brock looked around at the silent day and the vacant street. Only the snow looked back. "So, either she hurt the person who kidnapped her, or he lacked the strength to carry her?"

"Olly is pretty tall," Christian said. "Might've been easier just to drag her, even for someone healthy. We're taller than most."

Rage filled Brock until his fingers curled into fists. He took a deep breath, then went stone-calm. "Check out first and second streets. That leaves Main Street—I'll meet you on the river drive at the end. Keep in touch." He jumped onto his snowmobile, driving down the street and pausing at each business to see if anybody had seen or heard anything. Most places had closed down for the stormy day. Finally, he reached Sam's and hustled inside to find Amka wiping down the bar.

"Hey. You want a late lunch?" She didn't look up.

"No. I think Ophelia has been taken. Have you seen her?" He looked around the bar, but the place looked empty.

Amka straightened, her gaze sharpening. "No. Haven't seen her all day."

Damn it. "What about anybody else? Anybody been in here drinking or acting off?"

"No." She tossed the towel behind the bar. "I'll come help you look for her. I can't think of anything out of the ordinary today, except Jarod disappeared again. Probably hanging out at Lefty's still." Shaking her head, she leaned down and grabbed her coat, already moving around the bar. "Where do you want me?"

"Go to the diner and then over to the hospital and Doc's office." Brock wanted Amka safe and covered, just in case. "Call me if they know anything."

"You've got it." She hustled toward the back door. "Lock up the front, would you?" Then she headed outside.

He hurriedly locked the front door and then ran back outside to hop on his snowmobile, heading toward the river.

His phone buzzed, and he answered it, having to yell over the blasting snow. "Osprey."

"Hey, it's Damian. I'm in the helicopter and will scout from the air. If anybody has any sort of lead, let me know. I'll canvas for the Jeep and call you." His brother's voice came through along with the din of the copter's blades.

Brock's chest heated. "Thanks, D. Call me when you find that Jeep."

"Roger that." The line went dead.

His brothers had jumped into action the second he called. No matter what had happened with Hank, he never should have let them become so distant. It wouldn't do. If Ace had helped Hank to die, they'd figure it out. It's what they did. He drove toward the river road as the snow and wind pierced his jacket, freezing his skin.

Where was she?

He couldn't breathe as his mind tried to wander to what could be happening to her. No. Focus. He went cold again, letting his mind rule. He'd already figured out that he'd fallen for her, and he was going to keep her. But first, he had to find her.

Alive.

He reached the end of Main Street and turned right on the river road, headed west. Holding his breath, he scouted the forest on his right looking for any signs of a vehicle.

His phone buzzed, and he slowed the sled to glance at the screen. "Hi, Ace. Did you find anything?"

"I think so." Ace's voice came through strong. "I'm down at the cross back near the river. There's a vehicle here with footprints not quite obliterated by the snow yet. So, they're fresh within a couple of hours."

Brock flipped the sled around. "Whose rig is it?"

"I don't know yet. Give me a second as I wipe if off." Ace grunted and then paused. "Oh."

Brock waved at Christian before he could turn east on the river road. "Whose truck?"

"Crap, Brock. It's David Laurence's SUV. What the hell, man?"

"David?" How did that make any sense? Did he have something to do with Tammy's death? He didn't have any connection to Hank or the dead EVE guy. Or did he? Fuck.

Ace sighed. "He's nowhere around here, and the prints go toward Main Street. If nothing else, he might've seen who took Ophelia."

Brock's gut rolled over. "There's no reason David hid his SUV down there and walked into town, Ace. You know it, and I know it."

Ace grunted. "But why? Tammy?"

"Maybe? I don't know."

Ace coughed. "Any chance he found out about the night you and Monica spent together? Wants some crazy revenge?"

Brock opened the throttle, holding the freezing phone to his ear with one hand. "That's crazy. Maybe he killed Tammy for some reason and Ophelia figured it out."

"Maybe, maybe not. Either way, you'd better hurry, Brock. David has lived in Knife's Edge long enough to know how to hide a body in a snowstorm."

Brock's lungs seized. He had to get to her in time.

OPHELIA WOKE as Monica dragged her from the Jeep. A piercing cold burrowed through her clothing, freezing her skin. "What are you doing?" Her left arm had gone numb. What was happening?

Monica shoved her against a tree, and Ophelia fell into a foot of snow.

Her mind snapped awake. "Monica?"

"Yeah." The woman slid on the snow-covered road with the river iced over behind her. Flakes fell into her dark hair, and red bloomed across her face. "You shouldn't have gotten in that plane, Olly."

"I'm getting that." Ophelia pressed a hand to her bleeding bicep. The cold at least slowed her blood flow, but she didn't feel the wound, and that should concern her. She bit her lip to keep from passing out. "What's your plan here?"

Monica clumsily pulled her gun from her coat pocket. "I'm going to shoot you, drag your body into the woods, and let the animals have you. They're hungry this time of year." She eyed the Jeep in the middle of the road. "I like that car, but guess I'll have to drive it over one of the cliffs near the edge of town. It's too bad. They'll never find it." She cocked her head. "I guess I could leave you in it."

The woman was crazy. Ophelia pulled her legs toward her chest. Her entire body shook from the cold, and her thoughts were slowing. "Why, Monica?" There was no traffic on the road. How far out were they? The only sound around them was the wind cracking through the snow-laden trees. "Did David sleep with Tammy Randsom? Did you kill her for it?"

Monica kicked snow at her. "You are so stupid. Seriously. How can Brock look twice at you?"

Brock? Wait a minute. "This can't be about Brock. You had a one-night stand."

Monica glowered. "Brock is mine. He's been mine for years, and we were so close. I got him so drunk that night, and in the morning, I knew he was the one. Just knew it. Then we found Hank and Brock turned away from everybody. Even me."

What the heck? Seriously? "It was one night."

"A special night," Monica shrieked. "It has been almost a year, and he's healing. He's ready to love again. To love me." She shook her head. "I got back together with David for the time being, thinking Brock would eventually get jealous. It has been such a pain acting like I love the guy. All he wants to do is drive a fucking snowplow around." She gestured with the weapon. "David is nothing compared to Brock. I had the perfect plan. Until you fucking came to town."

Ophelia tilted to the side and groaned, clutching her wounded arm and sliding one boot beneath her butt. "What was your plan?"

Monica wiped spittle off her mouth. "You can draw this out as long as you want. We're way north on the river road, and it's closed. I had to open the gate to get past." She kicked a chunk of ice toward Ophelia.

Ophelia snorted. "You didn't have a plan. In fact, I think you know Brock never would've been serious about you."

Monica reared up, her eyes wild. "Not true. Brock Osprey is a protector to his very soul. I'd already hinted that David was abusive. Soon, Brock would've saved me from a bad situation. Of course, I would've killed David in self-defense first. I would've been so haunted and helpless afterward. Brock wouldn't have been able to stop himself from helping me." She smiled, her expression softening.

What a nut job. "You were going for pity?"

Monica hissed. "I shot at you twice. Why won't you die?" She kicked out again. "Of course, I had to be careful not to shoot Brock. Otherwise I would've nailed you."

Ophelia acted like she was ducking the clumps of ice and angled to the side, pulling her other foot beneath her butt. She dug her toes into the snow. "Pity doesn't last, Monica."

"No, but passion does. Our night together meant everything." Monica steadied the gun with the barrel aimed at Ophelia's head. "I'm done talking."

Ophelia bunched her legs. The woman stood only a few feet away. Snow fell from the tree and landed on her shoulders, freezing her ears. "Wait a minute. You shot at me when I rode with Brock looking for Wyatt. We hadn't started seeing each other yet. Why did you do that?"

Monica spat out snow. "Oh, I saw the way you two flirted. And you rode *on the back* of his sled. Behind him. Holding him. Don't you know what that means? It's just as serious as when a woman rides on the back of some club member's motorcycle. You had to go."

Whoa. The woman had lost touch with reality. Ophelia switched tactics. "Are you sure you're a killer? You know that kind of thing follows you to the grave, right? If you kill, that blood will be on your soul forever."

Monica faltered. "Then it's too late for me anyway."

Ophelia jerked. "Did you kill David?"

Monica frowned. "No. Of course, not. That happens later. It'll take Brock some time to get over you. I have to admit, I've never seen him act like he has with you. He was always up for a good time but he never got serious. He has never looked at anybody like he does you." She tilted her head. "That's why you have to die."

Ophelia rocked forward. "If not David, then who?" Man, her hands had gone full numb. If she could get the gun, could she get her fingers to work enough to pull the trigger? She tried to concentrate and not pass out. How much blood had she lost? She thought through the recent cases. "Did you kill Tammy for some reason?" It was a shot in the dark, but she had nothing else going for her.

Monica sniffed loudly. "Accidentally. Shouldn't count."

Ophelia couldn't feel her face. "What are you talking about?"

Monica shrugged, red infusing her face. "I heard Tammy slept with an Osprey one night, and I didn't know Brock had already left town for walkabout..."

"She slept with Ace," Ophelia snapped.

"I know. I was wrong. That's what real love does to a person." Monica shrugged. "If it helps, I left her up in the warming hut so her kids would know someday what happened to her."

Nausea rolled through Ophelia's stomach. "That does not help. You're a real bitch, Monica."

Monica glared. "You're about to be a dead bitch."

Ophelia's head swam. "Why did you take out Tammy's eyes?"

Monica wrinkled her nose. "Gross. I didn't. If a person did it, that was after I left. You sure scavengers didn't take the soft tissue?"

"No," Ophelia whispered, even her legs going numb. "Wait. What about Hank? Did you kill him?"

"Of course not." Monica snorted. "I do think a hunter accidentally shot the old guy. It happens. Brock and I found him dead together. We share that moment. It's ours. Sometimes death is just a mistake."

She obviously didn't know about Hank's illness. "You need help," Ophelia said weakly. "Let me get you help, Monica." That kind of obsession required serious intervention, and murder required jail time. "Put down the gun."

A helicopter pierced the silence above, and oncoming snowmobiles vibrated enough that more snow fell from the tree branches. Help was coming. Brock was coming.

Monica gasped and steadied her aim.

Ophelia tightened her legs and sprang off her frozen feet, lunging for the woman and hitting her center mass. They flew across the icy snow and smashed into the Jeep's tire. Pain flared through every inch of her body, but she pulled back her good arm and planted her fist in Monica's face.

The gun fired, the shot shrieking through the forest.

CHAPTER THIRTY-NINE

Brock lost his mind. He flew off his sled and ran full bore toward Ophelia. He could see and smell the blood already. Christian ran on his heels.

Snow burst in every direction as Damian landed the helicopter too close to the river, jumping out before the propellers had stopped. Ace slid his truck to a dangerous stop, nearly hitting Brock's snowmobile.

Brock noticed all the action of his family around him, but his gaze focused fully on his woman.

She rolled off Monica and came up to her feet, clutching her upper arm.

Monica lay on the ground, out cold. Blood covered her face. Monica? What the hell?

Brock reached Ophelia and pulled her close with her sweater, running his gaze over her form. "How bad?"

"Don't know," she gasped. "My arm is on fire, and I can't feel my toes."

He plucked her off the ground, holding her close to his chest while protecting her injury. "Ace? Call Doc. We're on the way."

He tucked his head over hers to protect her from the snow. "I heard another shot."

"Went wide," she gasped, her face pinched with pain.

Ace hauled Monica to her feet. The woman was regaining consciousness and swayed against him. She blinked and stared at Brock. "I love you. This is all for you."

He wanted to puke. This entire situation boiled down to a one night stand he barely remembered? "You'll have to find somebody else in prison, Monica." While she obviously had mental problems and probably needed compassion, he wanted to toss her ass into the river and say goodbye. He'd had no idea she had this bizarre obsession with him.

Ophelia lifted her head from his chest. "She killed Tammy. Got confused about you and Ace."

Ace jerked and paled. "Monica?" He yanked her around. "You murdered Tammy?"

Monica wiped blood from her broken nose off her cheeks. Olly gave her quite the punch. "I thought Tammy slept with Brock that night. Didn't know that you and Tammy had a thing together until I heard the gossip a week later. Way too late."

Christian's expletive lit the day.

Brock didn't have time for this. "Take her to the hospital for an examination and then to the jail." He turned and strode through the storm to place Ophelia into the front seat of Ace's truck, making sure the heat blasted on her. Then he jogged around and stretched inside, flipping the vehicle the other direction to head back into town.

"How did you find me?" Ophelia asked.

"Ace found David's rig, and then Damian spotted you from the air. We thought David had you. Christian and I had already started searching the river road." He had so much to say, but he didn't have a lot of words. Still, he'd almost lost her, and right now, she sat safely ensconced in his truck. "You're it for me, Ophelia."

She jolted, her hand still applying pressure to her wounded arm. "Brock."

"I know. It's quick and crazy, but most of my life has been. I learned very early on that moments are short and you have to take the good when they come. Also, you never know what's happening next. I don't have time for games or to gently ease into feelings. I have them, you have them, and I'm not waiting around to make sure."

She chuckled, but the sound held pain. "What are you saying?"

"Stay with me. Move in for good." He didn't want to push her too far or too fast. His girl seemed a little skittish sometimes. "We'll court, date, hang out…whatever you want. But there's a ring at the end of all that, as well as forever." That might've been pushing it, but he'd never again hold anything back from her and would always give her honesty.

She swallowed. Her body shook—no doubt from shock. "Brock—"

"Just think about it. Right now isn't the time for you to make a decision like that." He didn't like the pallor of her pale face, so he pressed his foot harder on the gas. The vehicle fishtailed, but he easily brought the truck under control. "Take some deep breaths, sweetheart. You're going into shock. The heat will help." He turned down the main road and drove quicker since it had been plowed. The truck skidded into a parking spot outside the small hospital. "Don't move." She'd already tried for the door.

He leaped out and moved around the truck in seconds, gently lifting her from her seat. "I've got you." He intended to keep her, but he'd probably hit her with enough for now.

Doc waited with a stretcher, looking professional in pink scrubs with her gaze steady. "How bad?"

"Upper arm shot," Brock said, laying Ophelia down and

helping roll her into an operating room that had already been set up and ready to go. He nodded at the anesthesiologist and surgical nurse. Their only ones, retired transplants from the lower forty-eight who just helped out when necessary.

Doc started cutting off Ophelia's top. "Out, Brock."

"No." He planted himself at the door.

Doc looked up, her gaze firm. "Get out. Now."

He blinked. Well, okay. Frowning at her, he turned on his heel and strode out of the operating room to find his brothers already in the waiting room.

Ace shook snow from his hair. "Monica is in the second examination room. I used a zip tie, so she's attached to the bed and can't leave. The other nurse is in there with her." He coughed. "I could stand guard but didn't want to be anywhere near her."

"She's not going anywhere," Damian said, leaning against the wall. "There's nowhere to go, anyway."

"True," Brock mused. "I'll go arrest her officially now." Guess he'd keep the sheriff job.

Christian remained near the door. "How is Olly?"

"Good. She doesn't know it yet, but she's going to be planning a wedding this coming summer." Brock grinned. Then he sobered. "After I arrest Monica, we need to head out to Leo's with the news."

Christian's eyes flared. "Agreed. What a senseless death. Poor Tammy."

"Agreed. Then we need to have a family talk." Brock kept his voice firm. "The time for secrets is over."

His brothers all nodded.

"Good." Brock looked over his shoulder at the operating room. He hadn't prayed in a long time. A very long time. But he said a silent prayer right now. Ophelia had to be all right.

She filled his entire future.

JUST AFTER SUPPER, Ophelia settled into the comfortable lounge chair in Flossy's living room. The fire roared hot and toasty, the blanket on her legs felt soft, and the painkillers worked nicely in her system.

Flossy's gnarled hands moved rapidly as she quilted. She sat on the floral chair closest to the fire. "You came out of surgery mere hours ago, Olly. You should probably be in the hospital."

"Hospitals make me edgy." Ophelia looked at the fire with its deep orange coals. "Doc says I'm fine—or will be."

Flossy's gray hair was up in curlers, and she looked adorable. "I'm sorry that crazy Monica shot you. She's Janet's niece but has never been very nice. Poor Janet and Gus. I'm so sorry about this."

Right now, the world felt so mellow that Ophelia didn't mind. "The bullet went right through my arm, and I only needed stitches. Doc didn't even have to put me out to do it, so I didn't really have surgery." Thank goodness Monica had been a crappy shot. "I'd rather be here in the warm house with you." Brock had left her with Flossy while he went out and notified Leo about Tammy's killer. David had shown up at the hospital and Brock had told him everything about his fiancée. Poor guy.

"You're so strong." Flossy smiled. "A gazelle with muscles. I'm not sure about that. I may need another animal for you."

How fun. An animal for her. Ophelia smiled. She wished Brock would hurry up and return, though. He'd been at least a couple of hours, and darkness had fallen outside. Flossy had made a dinner of warm sandwiches, and now Ophelia just wanted to sleep. But she wouldn't rest until Brock returned.

The firelight played off Flossy's papery-thin skin. "Congratulations on getting your job back."

"Thank you." The idea didn't please Ophelia as much as she'd thought it would. Once she'd reported to her boss in DC about

Tammy's murder, he'd reinstated her special assignment status. She'd called him right after Doc had stitched her up, and he still wouldn't tell her who'd gotten to him earlier. "I have several new open investigations that should arrive in my inbox this week, and I am bound and determined to identify that victim I saw by the river wearing the EVE embroidered jacket."

Flossy wrinkled her nose. "Disappearing bodies just creep me out." She kicked out her feet. "But I'm glad you have another reason to stay in town for the winter. And maybe beyond." She winked.

Heat climbed into Ophelia's face. "Maybe beyond." She looked out at the stormy night.

Flossy paused in her knitting. "Where is Monica? If Brock is out notifying everyone about her duplicity, surely she's not alone at the station."

Ophelia's arm started to tingle. "She's in a jail cell being guarded by one of the Miller kids. Brock deputized him. All he has to do is make sure she doesn't escape, and based on her fiancé's reaction to the situation, she wouldn't have help, anyway." After hearing the news, David had immediately requested his engagement ring back.

Flossy snorted. "Poor David. We're second cousins, you know. He deserves so much better." She reached for her teacup on the table. "Would you like more tea?" The fragrant peppermint brew filled the air with wintery scents.

Ophelia shook her head and looked at the clock. She shifted her weight, careful to leave her bandaged arm elevated on the throw pillow. She wasn't much on girl talk, but she trusted Flossy. "Brock's getting serious about us, even though it's crazy. We just met."

"Ha. You two have tossed in an entire year of dating into one week. Just think what you've gone through." Flossy's eyes gleamed with the gossip. "I am so glad to hear that he's smart enough to want to take a chance with you. He's a sweet boy and has been alone long enough. I always knew he'd fall hard and fast. Those Osprey men are all alike."

Ophelia rubbed her eyes with her good hand. "I care about him, as well, and I'd like to take a chance. But we have issues already, and we're just getting started." But he made her laugh, and she liked his intelligence. She loved his hard body. Even his stubborn and way-too-overprotective nature appealed to a woman who'd always been alone. She sighed.

Flossy waved her hand as if ridding the air of silliness. "Issues? Come on. What issues?"

Ophelia's phone dinged, and she lifted it to her ear. "Hi."

"Hi." Brock sounded like he was far away. Too far away. "I just arrived back at the station, but am still surprised we both have cell service—must be fate. How's your arm?"

How sweet that he asked about her while freezing his butt off riding to and now from Leo's place out in the mountains. She warmed right through. "I'm fine. Flossy is taking very good care of me." She sobered. "How's Leo?"

"Not great. I'll be up to get you in about an hour. Since your shooter is now under lock and key, I'm not worried about you. Well, that much." His voice dropped to a low and intimate rumble through the phone line. "Then I'll properly baby you at home."

"At home." The words held a punch as she ended the call. She placed the phone next to her tea. "He should be here in a bit."

Flossy kept quilting. "You were telling me about issues between you and the sheriff."

Oh, yeah. "My job. His job. Hank's murder." Ophelia settled back and winced when her arm protested. The darn painkillers didn't last long enough. "I don't know if we can ever get past that." In fact, it looked like Ace might be the shooter. How would Brock feel if she arrested his brother? How in the world could they get beyond that?

"There is no way Brock Osprey shot Hank," Flossy said.

"I agree." Ophelia sipped her tea, letting the warmth heat her tingling fingers. "But I think one of his brothers did, and I'll have to arrest them."

Flossy paused, looking up through her bottle-thick glasses. "Oh. I didn't think of that."

Ophelia's heart sank. "Right? It's a horrible situation."

Flossy finished her tea and stood. "We need more tea so we can figure this out. There is a solution. I'm sure of it." She ambled to her feet and placed her squares on Ophelia's lap. "Check out the stitching. Once your arm heals, you can do that. I know you can." She bustled away and into the kitchen.

Ophelia studied the stitching. It would take her years to get that exact. She held up several squares with her good hand. Flossy had so much talent. One of the squares caught Ophelia's eye.

Her heart rate kicked into gear.

The square showed a moose. A proud, powerful, somehow stubborn-looking moose. Memories flickered through her muddled brain. Why was her body reacting? Then it hit her.

The hat Hank had been wearing during that fishing derby with the shape Ophelia hadn't been able to recognize. The hat had a moose embroidered on it. A huge moose just like this one.

Flossy used animals for people in her quilts. An owl for her deceased husband, a vulture for Monica, an eagle for Brock… and a moose for Hank?

Ophelia started to move from the chair.

Flossy returned from the kitchen with her teapot in one hand and a shotgun in the other.

"Flossy," Ophelia breathed, sinking back down. "The moose represents Hank? You wanted me to see this."

"I did. I'm tired of secrets." Flossy placed the teapot on the table. "Hank and I courted for quite a few years, but we kept our love to ourselves. Both private people, I guess. We even met at the Tundra Complex when I had boarders and he had one of the boys home." Tears filled her faded eyes behind the thick glasses. "He was in so much pain from the cancer. Yet as a religious man, he couldn't do it himself. He asked me, and I said yes."

Ophelia couldn't move. "But—"

"I killed Hank, Olly. It was me." Flossy looked down at the weapon. "With this shotgun."

CHAPTER FORTY

Brock finished filling out the paperwork for Monica's arrest, sitting at his desk in the sheriff's station.

"You're good at this," Damian drawled, kicked back in a wooden guest chair across from Brock's desk. Ace sat next to him, drinking a large mug of coffee.

"Thanks." Brock rolled his neck. They'd just finished a supper of soup from Amka, and his body felt relaxed, but he wanted to get back to Ophelia. After he led this little family meeting. The time for harboring secrets had ended.

Christian lounged against the doorframe with his wolf pup at his feet. "I came because you called. Can we have this talk later?"

"No." Brock crossed his arms. "We're a family, and we're going to handle our problems together. Now."

The outside door opened, and light footsteps sounded down the hallway.

Christian's eyebrows rose, and he slid to the side.

Ophelia walked inside with a shotgun held in the elbow of her healthy arm, the barrels pointed at the ground. She was pale, and lines extended from her eyes. With her other arm in a sling, she looked wounded.

Flossy entered after her, dressed to the nines in her pretty floral summer dress, the good one. To accommodate the winter, she wore pink tights and puffy white boots that matched her coat. "Good evening, gentlemen."

Brock stood. What in the world was happening?

Ophelia looked at the floor, and he could swear sadness filtered from her.

Flossy stood to her full five-foot height, chin up, makeup fresh on her thin face. Her curly hair had that going-to-town for the evening look. "I killed Hank."

Ophelia gave a small sound of distress.

Ace's jaw dropped, Damian turned to face her more fully, and Christian just tilted his head.

Brock took in the shotgun, and his gut ached. Hard. The reality hit him as he remembered little clues that Hank had been seeing somebody. Kind of. "You and Hank dated each other?"

"We were in love." She shrugged bony shoulders. "Our romance was private and all ours. I was the first person he told when he found out about the cancer." She paled even further, making her bright pink lipstick stand out. "We went through his illness together, and that last day, the pain became too strong for him. He only had a week or so left, and neither of us wanted him to hurt like that. I shot him and then hurried to work that morning, not knowing what else to do."

Fuck. Brock wanted to sit back down but couldn't move. "Flossy—"

"I confess." She kept her chin up. "Sometimes we met each other at the Tundra, and sometimes when the sheriff was out, well, the cells are kind of fun."

Ace made a low sound in the back of his throat.

Flossy ignored him and continued confessing. "The shotgun will match whatever the scientists found on the body." She smacked Christian on the arm—and he let her. "You boys. Not talking to each other because you couldn't face the truth. Grow up, all of you. The truth is the truth, and I've given it to you." She held out her thin arms. "Cuff me, Sheriff."

Brock might actually throw up.

The outside door opened again, and both Delores Jerky and Loretta Randsom marched into his office, wearing their Sunday best with heavy coats due to the late hour.

Flossy floundered. "Delores? What are you doing here? I called you at your quilting party to take care of my greenhouse. That's all."

Delores looked Brock right in the eye. "I killed Hank."

Loretta elbowed her to the side. "That's not true. I killed Hank because he was in so much pain and I liked him."

Obviously, the town phone and radio tree had been initiated the second Flossy called Delores. Brock sighed.

Delores elbowed Loretta right back, knocking her into Christian, who steadied her with a small smile playing on his lips. "Not true. My friends are covering for me. Everybody in town knows that Flossy keeps that shotgun by her back door to scare the squirrels, and her back door is never locked. Many of us have borrowed it through the years, and I know my prints are on it for sure."

That was all true. Even so, Brock frowned. "Ladies, I understand what you're doing—"

More footsteps, and then Amka marched in. "I shot Hank."

"Crap," Brock muttered.

Christian gently grasped her arm and pulled her away from the doorway, protecting her as more footsteps pounded down the hallway.

Gus and Janet from the diner arrived next, followed by half the town. Snowmobiles lit up the night outside, and soon people stood in every room of the station, confessing to shooting Hank. Finally, a moment of silence reigned.

"Sheriff?" yelled a timid voice from the area of the basement door.

Brock hung his head. "Yes, Amos?"

"I shot Hank."

Ace burst out laughing. Damian snorted. Christian glanced outside as if he couldn't handle being around so many people, yet he still covered Amka with his body. Nobody could breathe on the bartender without going around him.

"Everybody out," Brock ordered. "You, too, Flossy."

The elderly woman looked a little disappointed that he hadn't slapped the cuffs on her. "But I confessed, Sheriff."

"So did the rest of the town," Brock said. He had no doubt plenty of fingerprints marred that shotgun, including his. He'd borrowed it a few times. "I'm going to turn this over to the state prosecutor, and Olly has to turn it over to the federal one, but I'd bet my cabin they won't press charges and try to take this disaster to trial. Reasonable doubt is an understatement here."

A few muffled cheers echoed throughout the station.

Brock glowered. "I feel like I should give everyone a lecture about justice and all of that, but I'm too damn tired."

"Brock," Flossy admonished. "Watch your language. You're the sheriff, for goodness' sake."

Brock's mouth dropped open. The woman had confessed to murder and now lectured him?

Christian chuckled.

Brock stilled. When had his brother last laughed?

Damian finally stood. "Drinks and food are on EVE at Sam's Tavern. For the entire town." He gestured everyone out amid much louder cheers. Then he glanced over his shoulder. "Family dinner tomorrow night at your cabin. See you there."

Then the office emptied, save Brock and Ophelia.

"Come here," he murmured, taking his seat.

She crossed around the desk and faltered. Even with the sling, she looked beautiful with her dark hair in a ponytail, and her blue sweater that matched her eyes. The jeans were dark, and the boots not warm enough for the winter. He'd have to rectify that.

He helped her and set her on his lap, cradling her. "How's the arm?"

"It hurts." She snuggled into him as if she belonged there, which she did. "I didn't know what to do. With Flossy."

He rested his chin on the top of her head, his entire body settling with her in his arms. "You did your job, and I did mine. The town did the rest." He couldn't let her go. "Hank's death is no longer between us."

"I know," she murmured, her breath heating his neck. "But my other cases might cause us issues, including the Tundra Haven fire and the EVE disappearing victim. Your brother is holding something back."

"I don't care about the Tundra fire, but I understand what you're saying about EVE," Brock agreed. "I have no doubt Damian didn't gouge that guy's eyes out, so whatever it is, it's inconsequential to you and me…and family."

She softened against him at the word *family*.

He might as well lay it all on the line. "My family is everything, and I want you to be a part of that. It's messy and complicated, but you'll have a solid wall of pure stubborn steel at your back at all times." She already had that but needed to accept it. "I choose you, Ophelia. No matter what."

She placed a soft kiss beneath his jaw, sending warmth throughout his entire body. "It's crazy, and we both know it's crazy, but I choose you, too."

He leaned her back to see her eyes. "Yeah?"

Her grin looked sweet with more than a hint of sass. "Yeah. You and me, Brock Osprey. I love you."

He had no doubt those were difficult words for her to say. For her to trust anybody to that degree, especially considering the short time they'd spent together. But it had been jam-packed, and they knew each other. Truly knew each other.

Leaning down, he kissed her, going deep. Tasting strawberries and woman.

His.

Finally, he released her mouth. Their adventure had just started, and he knew there'd be a wild year coming at them, but they were together and would remain so. He'd finally found his home, and it lay with a smart city girl who'd stolen his heart. "I love you, Olly. Always will."

IF YOU LIKED Brock's story, just wait until you read Christian's romance in Thaw of Spring! Preorder now.

ALSO, *you might like the Laurel Snow thrillers. Here's quick excerpt from YOU CAN RUN...*

The dog barked louder inside the cabin.

A male voice rumbled an order and the dog subsided.

The door opened to reveal a man.

Laurel almost took a step back. Six foot four, black hair, brown eyes, solid shoulders. Large boned hands, wide chest, rugged jaw. Dark, shaggy hair that curled beneath his ears, looking both uncared for and surprisingly appealing. The brown eyes had flecks of gold around the irises, and they held a world of experience. Some good and a lot bad. He had to be in his early thirties, but if she believed in her mother's teachings, he'd be an old soul. "Captain Rivers?"

He didn't open the door but instead scrutinized her from head to toe. "Who's asking?" His voice was both unwelcoming and at such a low timbre it was soothing. Interesting.

"I'm Laurel Snow, and I need your help." Every instinct she had whispered not to flash her badge.

He immediately opened the door. "You're not dressed for the weather." His expression remained difficult to read. "You look like a Fed."

Nobody had ever said that to her. "I do?"

"Black suit, wrong shoes for the local terrain, carefully clipped and beige-colored fingernails." He cocked his head to the side. "Except the hair. You don't have the hair of a Fed."

She also didn't have an answer for that, which was unusual for her. "What do I have the hair of?" When was the last time she'd ended a sentence with a preposition? Possibly in grade school.

"Not a Fed," he said. "It's too long and probably cost you a fortune to get that color."

This was the oddest conversation she'd had in ten years. Maybe twenty. "I don't pay for color. Or a cut, usually." She hadn't had time for such indulgences in far too long. Maybe she should get a haircut from a professional hairdresser instead of from her elderly neighbor who had arthritis and cloudy vision.

"You're telling me that's your natural hair color?" He leaned in closer, bringing the scent of pine with him.

She frowned. "I'm not telling you anything. It's just hair." For Pete's sake. "It's brown."

"We both know that's not brown. It's auburn, and that combination of brown and red is unreal. Mostly." He looked down at the dog sitting patiently at his side. "Right, Aeneas?"

Laurel tilted her head to study the canine. His markings were unique: a white hourglass shape across his face, surrounded by black fur. The white fur continued down his chest and covered each paw. "Aeneas? As in Homer's *Iliad*?"

"More like Virgil's *Aeneid*," Huck returned.

A chilly wind blasted her, and she rubbed her arms. "He's beautiful."

Huck opened the door wider and gestured her inside. "Where the hell is your coat?"

"In Washington DC." She stepped inside a sparsely furnished cabin that appeared messy but fairly clean.

"Why?" He stood much taller than she, even in his sock-covered feet. His left sock had a hole in the toe. Two duffel bags, a folded tent, and muddy boots had been dropped by the other side of the door.

"This was an unexpected detour." She looked at the gear. "Are you going somewhere?"

Captain Rivers shut the door. "What can I do for you, Laurel Snow?" He crossed his arms while his dog remained patiently at his side, both of them looking like predators in a calm mood.

She faced him directly. Appealing to his need to protect would be her most strategic move. "I am with the FBI and need a guide up Snowblood Mountain. It has been years since I headed that way, and I could use help."

"Why?"

She paused. "What do you mean, why? They've found at least three dead bodies, and there are no doubt more. I'd like to observe the scene before the weather wipes out the evidence. Will you at least let me borrow an ATV?" What kind of Fish and Wildlife captain didn't want to investigate the scene of a murder himself?

"What are you talking about?" His jaw hardened.

She needed an ankle weapon and made a mental note to requisition one as soon as possible. "This morning bodies were found." She looked at the gear by the door and then at the dog. "Oh, I understand. You were training out in the wilderness." That also explained why he and the dog looked so rough. "That's why you don't know anything about the dead bodies, right, Captain Rivers?"

"Huck. My dad was Captain Rivers." He scrubbed a hand through his hair, ruffling the heavy waves even more. "You're right. I've been unplugged for three days up in the mountains training with Aeneas. No service. Just got back thirty minutes ago and was going to grab something to eat. What's this about dead bodies?"

Laurel condensed the report for him, and he was shoving his feet in the muddy boots and grabbing the heavy-looking flannel coat off the packs before she'd finished.

"Let me know where you're staying in town, and I'll call you after I've reviewed the scene." He moved toward the front door.

"No." She crossed her arms.

He paused. "Excuse me?" Apparently the captain wasn't accustomed to people disregarding his orders.

"I'm here to do a job, and it's important for me to view the scene." Although she would freeze. Hopefully his UTV contained a heater. "Either we go together, or I find a UTV myself and drive up there. I believe it would be much more efficient if we worked this in tandem." In fact, she could use his knowledge of the area. Though she'd grown up in Genesis Valley, she had left at age eleven, so it wasn't as if she truly knew her way around.

"I don't have time to babysit you on the mountain," he said, his voice a low growl that most people probably heeded.

Laurel had dealt with a few of the darkest criminal minds there were. One cranky mountain man couldn't deter her. "I don't require a babysitter. I do, however, require an authorized Fish and Wildlife officer to escort me out into the wilderness and provide background information. Are you, or are you not, that officer?"

Instead of answering, he strode to a hall closet and quickly unlocked a safe set into the wall above the top shelf. Without turning, he withdrew a badge on a chain and a black gun that looked like a Smith & Wesson M&P 2.0. She made another mental note about him. Washington's Fish and Wildlife officers were fully commissioned police officers. He strapped a tactical holster to his left thigh and around his waist, tucking the gun safely against his leg. "Lady? I don't need you with me."

"It's agent, as opposed to lady, and I don't care what you need." She kept her temper at bay because it would serve no purpose to become angry.

His low sigh was long suffering. "Fine. You can come with me, because I'll just be called out to rescue your ass if you go alone."

Her temper started to stir, apparently not caring that it would accomplish nothing to smack him on the nose. "As much as I appreciate your belief that not only do I need a knight in slightly muddy armor, but that you could also possibly be that rescuer, I promise I require only your knowledge and not any of your *no doubt* impressive mountain-man skills." Her voice was just calm enough to sound slightly haughty, and she was fine with that fact. So much for using his protective nature to get her way.

His grin was quick and a surprise, making him look much more approachable. Almost human. Then it disappeared completely. "You're cute when you get your panties in a bunch."

He did not just say "panties" to her. Was he trying to tick her off enough that she'd leave in a huff? Since he waited for a response, that had obviously been his plan of attack. So she smiled. "I'm not wearing any, Captain." Then she met his gaze, and it was his turn to be thrown off stride.

His eyes slowly darkened from light topaz to the deep stout color of a good beer. "Fair enough." With that very minor concession, he turned back to the closet and tossed her a dark blue parka. "Why aren't you dressed for the weather?"

"I was in LA," she said, slipping her arms into the thick material and zipping it up. The coat engulfed her, reaching to her knees.

He grabbed gloves and a knit hat for her, before looking down at her feet. "I don't have snow boots your size." Shaking his head, he reached into the rear of the closet on the floor and dragged out well-worn, women's leather hiking boots. "These aren't for snow, but they're better than what you're wearing." He pushed them her way.

"Thanks." She slipped out of her flats and inserted her feet in the scratched boots, even though she was just wearing thin socks. The boots were slightly too small, so she didn't ask to borrow heavier socks. They wouldn't fit. She might not be a PR person, but even she knew how to extend an olive branch so the remainder of the evening would go more smoothly. She did need his assistance, after all. "I appreciate your assistance."

He pulled leather gloves on his hands. "I'm not a helpful guy, so please remember that in the future and don't end up abandoned on my doorstep ever again. For now, I'm going to check out the crime scene, and you might as well come along. But walk where I tell you to walk and don't cause me any more problems than you already have."

Well. All right then.

ACKNOWLEDGMENTS

Thank you to everyone who played a role in bringing this Alaskan tale of survival, danger, and unexpected romance to life. If I've missed anyone, blame the sub-zero temperatures and suspiciously empty coffee thermos—it's hard to keep track when you're trying not to freeze or get eaten by whatever's lurking in the woods.

First, a heartfelt nod to Big Tone, my steady hand, partner-in-crime, and official snowstorm survival buddy. Whether we're huddling up with hot cocoa (or Fireball) after a power outage or debating plot points like it's life or death, your steadfast support keeps me grounded (and warm). You remind me that there's always a way out of the wilderness, even if it involves a snowmobile and some duct tape.

A standing ovation for Karlina, whose boundless imagination keeps me inspired, even when the plot feels like it's trapped in an ice cave. Your belief in the power of storytelling—and in me—shines brighter than the Northern Lights. Thanks for being the creative spark that keeps this fire burning.

To Gabe, for proving that managing life's chaos with calm (and coffee) is its own kind of heroism. You're the person who can thaw even the iciest moments with your humor and keep the wheels turning when things feel frozen in place. Thanks for always having my back—and for putting up with my love of snowbound disasters.

A huge shout-out to Kathleen Sweeney and the talented team at Book Brush for creating a cover that captures all the "you-might-get-stalked-by-something-in-the-woods" vibes I hoped for. Your ability to translate my chaotic ideas into something beautiful and badass is a gift I'll never take for granted.

Thanks to Caitlin Blasdell, my whip-smart literary agent and wilderness guide through the wild world of publishing. You keep me from getting lost in the blizzard of contracts, edits, and deadlines. Thanks for making this journey feel less like a survival story and more like a grand adventure (with fewer bear traps).

To Anissa Beatty, the leader of the Facebook Rebecca's Rebels street team—thank you for your creativity, dedication, and endless enthusiasm. You make every step of this process feel like a victory hike to the mountaintop (minus the frostbite). Your talent is as vast as the Alaskan wilderness—and way more reliable than the weather.

Special thanks to the Rebels—Joan Lai, Madison Fairbanks, Leanna Feazel, Gabi Brockelsby, Heather Frost, Kimberly Frost, Karen Clementi, and Asmaa Qayyum—for your Beta reads, brilliant feedback, and general awesomeness. You caught the plot holes before the characters could fall through them. You're the warming hut in the middle of my story blizzards, and I'd be lost without you.

Thanks to Writerspace for helping share this story of danger, snowy disasters, and messy romance with readers who love a bit of suspense with their snow. Your support means more than all the fleece blankets in Alaska—seriously.

To my family and friends—Gail and Jim English, Kathy and Herbie Zanetti, Debbie and Travis Smith, Stephanie and Don West, Jessica and Jonah Namson, Cathie and Bruce Bailey, and Chelli and Jason Younker—your encouragement keeps me going when the plot gets tangled and the cabin fever kicks in. You're my foundation, my joy, and the reason I can laugh through the chaos (even when there's a blizzard outside).

SERIES' LIST

I know a lot of you like the exact reading order for each series, so here you go as of the release of this book, although if you read most novels out of order, it's okay.

KNIFE'S EDGE, ALASKA SERIES

1. Dead of Winter
2. Thaw of Spring

THE ANNA ALBERTINI FILES

1. Disorderly Conduct
2. Bailed Out
3. Adverse Possession
4. Holiday Rescue novella
5. Santa's Subpoena
6. Holiday Rogue novella
7. Tessa's Trust
8. Holiday Rebel novella
9. Habeas Corpus

LAUREL SNOW SERIES

1. You Can Run
2. You Can Hide
3. You Can Die
4. You Can Kill

GRIMM BARGAINS SERIES

1. One Cursed Rose
2. One Dark Kiss

DEEP OPS SERIES

1. Hidden
2. Taken novella
3. Fallen
4. Shaken novella (in Pivot Anthology)
5. Broken
6. Driven
7. Unforgiven
8. Frostbitten

MONTANA MAVERICK SERIES

1. Against the Wall
2. Under the Covers
3. Rising Assets
4. Over the Top

Dark Protectors/Enforcers/1001 DN

1. Fated (Dark Protectors Book 1)
2. Claimed (Dark Protectors Book 2)

3. Tempted novella (Dark Protectors 2.5)
4. Hunted (Dark Protectors Book 3)
5. Consumed (Dark Protectors Book 4)
6. Provoked (Dark Protectors Book 5)
7. Twisted Novella (Dark Protectors 5.5)
8. Shadowed (Dark Protectors Book 6)
9. Tamed Novella (Dark Protectors 6.5)
10. Marked (Dark Protectors Book 7)
11. Wicked Ride (Realm Enforcers 1)
12. Wicked Edge (Realm Enforcers 2)
13. Wicked Burn (Realm Enforcers 3)
14. Talen Novella (Dark Protectors 7.5)
15. Wicked Kiss (Realm Enforcers 4)
16. Wicked Bite (Realm Enforcers 5)
17. Teased (Reese Bros. novella)
18. Tricked (Reese Bros. novella)
19. Tangled (Reese Bros. novella)
20. Vampire's Faith (Dark Protectors 8) ***A great entry point for series***
21. Demon's Mercy (Dark Protectors 9)
22. Vengeance (Rebels novella)
23. Alpha's Promise (Dark Protectors 10)
24. Hero's Haven (Dark Protectors 11)
25. Vixen (Rebels novella)
26. Guardian's Grace (Dark Protectors 12)
27. Vampire (Rebels novella)
28. Rebel's Karma (Dark Protectors 13)
29. Immortal's Honor (Dark Protector 14)
30. A Vampire's Kiss (Rebels novella)
31. Garrett's Destiny (Dark Protectors 15)
32. Warrior's Hope (Dark Protectors 16)
33. A Vampire's Mate (Rebels novella)
34. Prince of Darkness (DP 17)

STOPE PACKS (wolf shifters)

1. Wolf
2. Alpha
3. Shifter

SIN BROTHERS/BLOOD BROTHERS

1. Forgotten Sins
2. Sweet Revenge
3. Blind Faith
4. Total Surrender
5. Deadly Silence
6. Lethal Lies
7. Twisted Truths

SCORPIUS SYNDROME SERIES

Scorpius Syndrome/The Brigade Novellas

1. Scorpius Rising
2. Blaze Erupting
3. Power Surging - TBA
4. Chaos Consuming - TBA

Scorpius Syndrome Novels

1. Mercury Striking
2. Shadow Falling
3. Justice Ascending
4. Storm Gathering
5. Winter Igniting
6. Knight Awakening

ABOUT THE AUTHOR

New York Times, USA Today, Publisher's Weekly, Wall Street Journal and Amazon #1 bestselling author Rebecca Zanetti has published more than eighty novels and novellas, which have been translated into several languages, with millions of copies sold worldwide. Her books have received Publisher's Weekly, Library Journal, and Kirkus starred reviews, favorable Washington Post and New York Times Book Reviews, and have been included in Amazon best books of the year.

Rebecca has ridden in a locked Chevy trunk, has asked the unfortunate delivery guy to release her from a set of handcuffs, and has discovered the best silver mine shafts in which to bury a body…all in the name of research. Honest. Find Rebecca at: www.RebeccaZanetti.com

Made in the USA
Las Vegas, NV
16 August 2025